First Impressions

He knew by the widening eyes what she saw. Not Jon Van Castle, country rock superstar and a top pick for *People*'s sexiest men in America, but a long-haired crazy in a leather-fringed clown outfit stained with sweat.

"What do you want?" She moistened her lips. How had he missed the mouth? Rosebud, definitely rosebud.

"I, uh, want to shop."

She blinked.

"Honest," he added.

"Then, may I help you?"

"What about these?" Recognizing a title, he motioned to some books. "I want the whole series." He gathered them up and spilled them on the counter, liking it when she jumped.

"Do you want them delivered?"

"Jesu—" She gave him a hard stare. "I mean, jeepers." Jeepers? "That's a clever way to get my address."

Her mouth went slack, but she recovered fast. "Really. You might be good-looking. You might be extremely good-looking. To *some* people. But let me assure you, I have no intention of using your address for anything besides delivery."

He shuffled his feet. So, he wouldn't be asking her out. Better for everyone, anyway. "You really don't have a clue, do you?"

"I don't believe I'm the one who's clueless. What *is* your name?"

A drumroll filled his head. "Jonathan Van Castle."

Her eyes rolled halfway up. "Is that with a capital V and C?"

He deflated. . . .

SING ME HOME

Jerri Corgiat

AN ONYX BOOK

ONYX
Published by New American Library, a division of
Penguin Group (USA) Inc., 375 Hudson Street,
New York, New York 10014, U.S.A.
Penguin Books Ltd, 80 Strand,
London WC2R 0RL, England
Penguin Books Australia Ltd, 250 Camberwell Road,
Camberwell, Victoria 3124, Australia
Penguin Books Canada Ltd, 10 Alcorn Avenue,
Toronto, Ontario, Canada M4V 3B2
Penguin Books (N.Z.) Ltd, Cnr Rosedale and Airborne Roads,
Albany, Auckland 1310, New Zealand

Penguin Books Ltd, Registered Offices:
80 Strand, London WC2R 0RL, England

First published by Onyx, an imprint of New American Library,
a division of Penguin Group (USA) Inc.

First Printing, February 2004
10 9 8 7 6 5 4 3 2 1

In Loving Memory of
Bill Rundle, Mike Corgiat, Sr., and Trula Everson

ACKNOWLEDGMENTS

It took an army to see me through the writing of this book and the long haul of finding anyone who believed in it like I did—especially enough to pay me money for it. Thank you, Marcy Posner and Claire Zion, for that belief. You're both gems.

Thanks go to Denise Heying, Lisa Higgs, and Carmen Sachs, who read my earliest efforts. And to Karen Mesmer, who helped with the legalese. (It's not her fault if I got it wrong.) Sarah Buechel, Lynne Ruf, and Diana Rhodes provided terrific support, and Sarah gave me my first compliment: I made her cry.

I leaned heavily on the broad (in the best sense of the word, Bob!) shoulders of Ann Handelman, Nancy Phillips, and Pam Cyran. (Special thanks to Ann for her photography.) Libby Sternberg helped see me through lots of fits, and Karen Brichoux offered wise words and wisecracks.

Jill Meradith gets special thanks for never letting go, as does my mom, who read me *The Little Engine That Could* a gazillion times when I was young.

And to Mac, my sweetest guy, thanks for your belief in me. You're the best there ever was, punkin. And for my husband dear . . . this writer is at a loss for words. We both know this wouldn't have happened if I hadn't ridden on your faith far more than my own. I love you.

Chapter 1

Off in the distance, the steep hills of the Missouri Ozarks were shrouded in blue, arcing to meet a sea foam sky, dipping into timbered hollows and fresh-water lakes—all of it way too close for Jonathan Van Castle's comfort.

From under the brim of his Stetson, Jon stared out of the tinted bus window at the rolling pastureland that marked the start of the hill-and-lake country in the southern half of the Show-Me State. His fingers, long and tipped with calluses from his guitar strings, drummed on his thigh. He'd grown up in that back-woods, and every turn of the wheels brought him closer to Monaco. And his ex-wife. Ex-wives had a way of spoiling even the prettiest scenery, and his was a regular vandal.

Unearthed from mothballs eight weeks ago, the Van Castle Country Tour bus took the leading country rock singer in America and his band around the curve on the two-lane highway. The bus slowed as it entered Cordelia, the last burg of any size before the lakes. The town slumbered in bucolic glory under the haze of late July.

Inside the custom-built bus, his companions were quiet. Beside him on the opposite end of a leather sofa, bass player Zeke Townley put his long legs up and locked them at the ankles. Idly, he flipped through the pages of *GQ*. In a set of swivel chairs nearby, several security guys played cards with the band's stylist Sidney. Today Sidney's hair was green, his pants purple. Snores issued from behind a curtain at the rear of the bus where Van Castle's drummer Three-Ring slept.

Several dozen of his crew and his business manager, Peter Price, had gone ahead to Lake Kesibwi, another fifty miles down the road. They were likely already lined up on deck chairs at the Royal Sun Resort, knocking back beers.

Jon squirmed, and Zeke nudged him with the toe of a black boot that matched the bass guitarist's hair, beard, and eyes. "Ants in your pants?"

"No, just the pants. Damn uncomfortable."

Zeke eyed the fringed leather pants with the air of a man whose perfectly creased white trousers would never dare ride up.

Jon grimaced. "Got up late, and these were on the floor." They'd left Kansas City at nine, not an early wake-up call—unless you were coming off two gigs at Sandstone, and umpteen others at similar burgs.

Zeke nodded and looked out the window.

The driver took Cordelia's outlying area of tract housing and fast food joints at an even gait. As they passed a school yard, some kids paused in their play, wrapped grubby fingers around a chain-link fence, and gaped. No wonder. Rendered in Outlaw Purple Metallic, a pair of outsized guitars plastered the sides of the bus.

"Look familiar?" Zeke asked.

"Haven't been through here in eighteen years." A scared teenager on a Greyhound bound for the big time. Zeke knew all that. They'd been together ever since Jon had stepped off that bus and into a bar in Nashville.

"And what changes time has wrought." Zeke's voice was laconic. Zeke's middle name was laconic.

"Take away the cars, plant a few hitching posts, and it'd look like it did a hundred years ago."

The highway narrowed into a shaded street lined with gingerbreaded Victorians and airplane bungalows, all fronted with broad porches. Jon noted the padded swings, the hanging pots of fuchsia and ferns, the freshly swept walks. His mother had liked fuchsia. "I always wanted a house like one of those."

"Let's see. A manse on twenty acres outside Nashville versus Ma Kettle's abode in the middle of the back of beyond. Tough decision."

Jon's lips curved, but he didn't comment. A home, a mansion didn't make.

"I'll raise you two." Sidney threw two quarters on the table. "And I'll see you."

The change hit wood. The bodyguard Roy, rock-hard and squat in a seat near the driver, groaned. Sidney swept up the pot.

Following the highway sign, the driver curved onto Main, one of four streets framing a church in the middle of the town square. Looked like God and state must have battled for supremacy, and God had won. The lawn around the church was sun-crisped, but ribbons of red geraniums cabled the walkways twisting between maples and sycamores. Surrounding the church were rows of two-story brick buildings, each with lower level shops and upper level windows with white trim, shades half-pulled like lids drooping over sleepy eyes. Leftover from Fourth of July, patriotic bunting drifted from concrete cornices.

The bus slowed to a judicious crawl. A getup like this spelled money to small-town sheriffs with their eyes on the municipal coffers. Around here, money was scarce. Jon knew.

Up-in-the-Hair Beauty Salon slid by, its windows full of flounced pink curtains and steam, followed by Peg O' My Heart Cafe. The meat loaf was on special.

A few doors down was O'Neill's Emporium. Out front an old geezer swept the sidewalk. As the bus passed, the guy propped forearms on his broom handle and watched. Merry-Go-Read Bookstore stood next to the Emporium. Except for the old guy, the square was empty. According to the driver, this month was one of the hottest Missouri had ever seen.

They neared the green-and-white-striped awning of a parlor on the corner. Zeke's eyes were amused. "Sin-Sational Ice Cream? The mind boggles."

"About as clever as those last lyrics you came up with." Jon snorted. " 'Maiden fine in my mind'? Gimme a break."

Zeke lazily kicked Jon's thigh. "Let's see. And what did you come up with? Oh, that's right, I remember. Nothing."

The corner of Jon's mouth hitched, although inwardly he sighed. As the trip to Monaco had neared, words had dried up.

The bus braked at a stop sign.

Jon leaned toward the driver. "Stop at the park." Zeke raised narrow eyebrows, and Jon shrugged. "I need a walk."

"What you need is a spine. She won't eat you."

He wondered. "Just give me a few minutes to get the wool out of my head."

When Jon got off the bus—alone, despite bodyguard Roy's protests—Sidney gave his hair a pointed look. "Tuck it under, or you'll be sorry."

Jon rolled his eyes at the stylist, and wondered why he kept Sidney around, except for the obvious entertainment value. Sidney cheated at cards and his garb wasn't a country fashion statement. A moment later he felt penitent. Shit. It wasn't Sidney.

Still, he left his trademark blond-and-brown-ribboned hair pulled back, not up and under.

*   *   *

Minutes later, he found himself fervently wishing he'd listened to Sidney, but mostly missing Roy.

He hadn't tucked his hair up, he hadn't stayed in the park. He'd picked Maple Woods Drive at random. Now his boots scuffed along, not with the pace of a leisurely stroll, but with the stiff-legged gait of a man wanting to run and trying to hide it.

Sweat rolled from under his hat, but he didn't dare take it off. He'd already caught a startled look from a young woman with apricot hair. She'd been lounging on the porch swing of a rambling bungalow about a block behind him.

He pulled the brim on his Stetson low, and glanced behind. Sure enough, she'd followed. She was about a half block back, her hair looking like it had exploded from her head like shook-up Shasta orange soda. She was just this side of skinny. And he'd bet she was fast. He picked up his pace, hoping to put more distance between them before she realized she'd seen what she'd seen.

"Jooonathan Vaaan Castle!"

Too late.

She shrieked, then shrieked again.

Shit. It was like the blaring of bugles. Her screech pierced the rattle of air conditioners, stilled the birds, almost tore a crack in the earth. Screen doors banged open. Faces peered out.

She started running, still hollering. He started running, still sweating. And pretty soon a whole gaggle of women had fallen in with her.

He darted into an alley, crashed over a picket fence, hugged the side of a house, caught his breath, moved on, and pretty much lost himself in the lanes and alleys between the park and the square.

Just in time, he glimpsed a green-and-white-striped awning. Sides heaving, he burst onto Main, saw nothing, saw nobody, and bounded across the street toward the church. Running low, darting between trees, he flew up the sweep of steps at the church entrance. The doors were ornately carved, heavy oak—and locked.

Swearing under his breath, he twisted, just in time to see the redhead and her rabble-rousing crowd— well, really only a half dozen women, but even two was one more than he could handle in this condition— explode from the ice cream parlor. They must have gone in through the rear.

The apricot head started to swivel his way. With what he thought was admirably fast thinking, he dove over the railing and into a clump of shrubs. Hat askew and flat on his back, he lay perfectly still, mostly because he wasn't sure he could move. Thirty-five was way too old for this crap.

The voices faded and he raised his head. The square was empty. No sign of anyone, not even the geezer.

Jon stood up, swiped his fingers through his hair, and plopped the Stetson back on his head. He didn't know which way they'd gone, and he didn't know if he could outrun them again.

As his heart slowed, his brain kicked back into gear. All he needed to do was call the bus and tell the driver to pick him up. . . . He pawed at his pants, then dropped his hands and groaned.

He'd left his damn cell phone back on the bus.

He needed a phone. He studied his options, which weren't many. Both the Emporium and Merry-Go-Read had SORRY, WE'RE CLOSED placards leaning in the windows. In small-town fashion, the proprietors had closed for the noon hour. He shuddered at the idea of entering the beauty shop, which left the ice cream parlor and Peg's diner, both undoubtedly stuffed for lunch.

He was about to check out another street, when the door to Peg's arced open.

A tall, slender girl with short lemon curls, and a not-so-short lemon dress, stepped from the cafe. Her gaze focused dead ahead, she neared Merry-Go-Read, and pulled out a key.

While her attention was on the lock, he took a step toward her. A branch snagged his boot. He lurched forward, crashed out of the shrubs, windmilled across the green, and caught himself just short of a dive onto Main.

Her head snapped sideways, and she froze.

No girl, a woman. In her late twenties, or early thirties. As their eyes met, the line of a new lyric darted into his brain; it always happened at the damnedest times. *China blue eyes . . . Such a surprise.* He steeled himself for a shriek of recognition. Instead, she bent her head to the lock, her movements now frantic.

A distant voice sounded from Maple Woods Drive. "Back this way!"

Shit. He bounded across the street, straight at the blonde.

She glanced up, then fumbled some more at the knob. The door swung open.

The redhead burst into view, head turned away as she shouted over her shoulder. Without missing a beat, he charged into the blonde's back, shoved her inside, and slammed the door. Chimes jangled.

The blonde skidded into the bookstore and barely kept her feet. Skirt swirling, she spun around to face him. They stared at each other. She was a looker. No trendsetter, but a looker. The dress was old-fashioned, sleeveless, but even buttoned up to the neck, it didn't hide her willowy figure. A silhouette of long legs was spoiled only by a pair of flat brown shoes. Her curls were caught back by a ribbon, not gunked up by mousse. Nothing lined her eyes . . . *china blue eyes . . .* except a fringe of dark lashes and an arc of dark brows. Emotion, not powder, colored her cheekbones. The lack of window dressing was nice.

He realized by the widening eyes what she saw. Not Jon Van Castle, a top pick for *People*'s Sexiest Men in America, but a long-haired crazy in a clown outfit stained with sweat.

Looking like she faced a mad dog, she backed up and kept going until her hips bumped the counter at the rear.

"What do you want?" Her voice was hoarse, but her chin came up.

He held a finger up, and turned away to peek past the edge of faded curtains. The redhead-led crowd milled about in confusion. He locked the door.

Behind him, a dial tone buzzed. Quiet as a sigh, she'd moved behind the counter and picked up a phone.

He closed the space between them, his boots gunshots on the pocked wood floor. "Don't." He made the word more plea than threat. "I only want to use the phone."

Some of the color returned to her face, but a vein pulsed in her long neck. Carefully, he placed a hand over her hand holding the receiver, and let a smile renowned for making women swoon spread over his face. He squeezed her fingers. "Please."

She moistened her lips. How had he missed the mouth? Rosebud, definitely rosebud. And with those sweet lips parted, she looked . . . well, not to be immodest, she looked kind of swoony herself. Familiar as it was, that look was something coming from her.

He looked down at the hand he held. A band wrapped her ring finger. He loosed his grip. *That* was territory he never wandered into.

"And the locked door?" she asked.

"A . . . phobia."

She paused, keeping her eyes on his, and wordlessly handed him the receiver. He held on to his smile, still waiting for recognition, shocked surprise, but she only folded her hands on the counter and waited. Feeling unreasonably irritated, he dropped the smile and reached to punch a number. Then stopped. All he knew were his speed-dial numbers. One for Peter Price. Two for Zeke. And three for Roy. Helluva lot of good that'd do him now. He slammed down the phone.

The woman paled again. God, she probably thought he was a robber—or worse. "I, uh, changed my mind." He thought fast before she screamed and bedlam ensued. Last thing he needed was his face splashed all over the *National Tattler*—again. "I decided to shop."

She blinked.

"Honest," he added, thinking he might touch her hands, to reassure her, that's all. When he moved, though, she drew back, slowly, like she didn't want to spook him. Sweet Jesus, there was something about her.

"Then, may I help you?" Her voice hardly wobbled, and her chin stayed up. He admired her for that.

He tipped his hat back, tried an I'll-charm-you grin. "Sorry about shoving you. I stumbled."

"Mmm." Her baby blues said she didn't buy it. "So, what are you shopping for?"

What was he shopping for? He glanced around, and noticed for the first time the quantities of children's books and videos spread out on tall shelves like notes on a staff. Everything was as neat as three-quarter time, except for one corner that was piled with cartons. Runners as faded as the curtains ran between shelves; a kid-sized table squatted in front of the bow window. The walls were blotched with stains. The odor of mildew underlay the smell of her perfume, and the light from the window was harsh against the miserly glow of several globes—one cracked—that hung from the stamped-tin ceiling. He'd guess the place wasn't a gold mine.

He pushed himself up. "Kids' books. I'm looking for kids' books." Wouldn't hurt to show up with presents for Melanie and Michael before he hauled them out of the only home they knew. "For my daughter."

"How old is she?" She hadn't moved, but her voice was stronger, maybe because this was familiar ground.

"Ten, maybe eleven."

There was silence, and he read her mind. He warmed. It wasn't his fault he couldn't remember Melanie's age. His ex-wife Belinda defined "visitation rights" narrowly. If he couldn't come to them—and he usually couldn't—he couldn't see them. Period. She named every excuse from school schedules to fear of flying (which he thought was her own invention) whenever he suggested they visit Nashville. But this time he had her over a barrel—and she knew he was ready to crack a whip.

"Does she read a lot?"

"I think so."

Another silence. He felt stupid. "What about these?" Recognizing a title, he motioned to some books. *Little House on the Prairie* was a damn fine TV show, even in reruns, no matter what Zeke said.

"Which ones has she read?"

The question held the tone of a challenge. He shot a look over his shoulder, but except for an odd light in her eye, her face was smooth. Still, he bristled. Everybody judged him. What did *she* know?

"Well?"

It *was* a challenge. Something had moved her beyond alarm.

He straightened to his full height, which was a good six feet, but, he belatedly realized, only a couple of inches taller than she was. She didn't look intimidated, only disapproving.

"I want the whole series." He gathered them up and spilled them on the counter, liking it when she jumped. Moving over the runners, he grabbed a couple of Disney CDs, a few videos, and some picture books. "And these."

"X-Men aren't very popular with girls, and these picture books are too young for an eleven-year-old."

Then she added, disdain no longer hidden, "Or even a ten-year-old."

"I have a son, too. He's younger. Five. Definitely five. I'll take these, too."

She sniffed. If he meant his extravagance to impress her (and he suspected he did), his ploy hadn't worked.

A thought struck him. He'd forgotten his fan club. He paused at the window, but saw nobody. He pressed up closer to see down the street. A wrinkled face, pocked with liver spots and grizzle, popped from the side and peered back. He got an impression of sharp bones and bib overalls before the face disappeared.

He fell back. "Who in the *hell* is that?"

"Paddy O'Neill. He owns the Emporium and takes pride in knowing everything that goes on in this town. You're a stranger. A rather odd-looking stranger. I'm sure news of you is now winding its way down to Peg O' My Heart. Will that be all?"

He blinked at the sudden flood of words. The appearance of the town's rumormonger had obviously dispelled the rest of her nervousness. It had increased his. "Huh?"

"I said, is that *all*?"

"That's it." He needed to get out of here, but he returned to the counter and leaned against it. He watched her hands as they ruthlessly sorted his merchandise. They tapered long and narrow, proportioned, strong but feminine. Musician's hands. His eyes traveled from her hands, adorned by a cheap watch and that blasted wedding band, up to her face. He tried to make amends. "So, do you have kids, too?"

She snapped up like an overtight guitar string. "No."

Under a glare as hard as sapphires, he held up his hands. "Sorry." He fumbled for a change of topic. "You and your husband own the shop?"

"He's dead. That will be $243.60." She held out a hand.

About to suggest rudeness wouldn't help sales, he changed his mind when he saw her hand shook. "I'm sorry. Really." And he was, for upsetting her, but not, he realized, because her husband was gone.

He dove a hand in his pocket, but emerged with only a few melting M&M's. "Uh—"

She snatched a container from under the counter, yanked out a towelette, and thrust it at him.

Dare he ask her out? He hadn't had a real date in years; he hadn't wanted to risk one. Wiping his fingers, he considered. He doubted she was the type to play "come see my guitar," or visit a man she didn't know in the confines of his resort cabana. Or, he gave a sigh, go out with the madman who'd almost knocked her on her butt.

But those eyes . . . He smiled, thinking chatty might do it. "Ah, that smell reminds me of the last time I saw Michael. He was three, still in diapers." He wadded the towel and when she didn't take it, stuffed it in his pocket. His hand still came up empty. He felt his face flame around his smile. No cell phone. No wallet.

"I don't have the first Wilder book." Another pause. "You haven't seen your children in two years?"

"Don't judge me. What book?" Maybe he didn't want to ask her out, after all.

"You asked for the whole series. *Big Woods* is out of stock, although I can order it if you'll pay in advance. And I'm not judging you. I don't even know you."

"In my experience, that's not a requirement." If the news of his two-year absence had thrilled her, the next piece of information he had for her would drive her wild with excitement. "I have a problem."

Picking up a pen, she nodded emphatically, but said, "It's not a problem. We deliver to the Sedalia and lake areas, both Ozarks and Kesibwi. I can have it there within a few days."

"Clever."

She laid the pen down, and explained in the same voice she would use with a village dunce. "You see, in order to deliver the book, we have to know *where* to deliver the book."

"Jesu—" She gave him a hard stare. "I mean, jee-pers." Jeepers? "I know that. I meant, that's a clever way to get my address."

Her mouth went slack, but she recovered fast. "Really. You might be good-looking. You might be extremely good-looking. To *some* people. But let me assure you, I have no intention of using your address for anything besides delivery."

He shuffled his feet. So, he wouldn't be asking her out. Better for everyone, anyway. "You really don't have a clue, do you?"

"I don't believe I'm the one who's clueless. And if you don't wish to give me your address, that's fine."

Once more, she picked up the pen and waited. Great, now she thought he was a paranoid, *arrogant* madman.

"What the hell. I'll be at the Royal Sun Resort for the next six, seven weeks."

"And your name?"

A drumroll filled his head. "Jonathan Van Castle."

Her eyes rolled halfway up. "Is that with a capital V and C?"

He deflated. "Yes. Deliver it to the front desk. They'll get it to me."

"$243.60?"

"I still have a problem."

"Which problem are we discussing?"

"I seem to have left my wallet in—" He backed toward a door he assumed led to a storeroom with a delivery door, and motioned at the pile of books. "Just pack it all up. I'll be right back."

He turned, headed through the back room before she could protest, and found the delivery door. Just as he'd thought, it led to an alley.

"We do have a front door. The one you came in."
She'd paused in the doorway, arms crossed.

He peered up and down the alley, then looked at
her over his shoulder. "My phobias."

"Oh, yes. Your phobias."

The thermostat in his face ratcheted up another
notch. He turned and almost banged the nose *Country
Dreaming* called "regal" into the jamb. Muttering a
curse, he slipped out.

Dodging through the warren of alleys at full tilt, he
wondered if he'd gone nuts. What difference did it
make if he returned? From the tone of her voice to
the slant of her eyebrows, it was obvious she thought
he was a jerk. A few bucks wouldn't change anything,
and it wouldn't matter even if it did.

He reached a copse of trees that bordered the back
of the park. The bus slumbered in a clearing, and
hadn't gone undetected. He spotted an orange head
among a few women leaping to try to see through the
tinted windows, but most milled yards away around
the park entrance. Roy stood at the closed bus doors,
thick arms crossed. Only his eyes moved, sweeping the
park and finally lighting on Jon. His chin, the edge of
an anvil, moved up a notch in acknowledgment.

Taking a deep breath, Jon sprinted. He was on them
in seconds. Before the women could squeak, Roy had
shoved him into the bus, and muscled in after him.
The driver slammed the doors.

Roy flopped into the first available seat and mopped
at his head with his bandanna. Jon patted thanks on
his shoulder.

Zeke turned a page of his magazine. "Having an
adventure, my man?"

Jon leaned down to give the driver directions, then
shoved Zeke's feet off of the couch and took their
place. Zeke gave him a look of mock annoyance, and
straightened the crease in his trousers.

"Just a slight detour," Jon said.

The driver shifted into gear. Zeke's eyebrows shifted higher. "She must really be something."

"She? I just found something I want—"

"I'll bet."

Jon frowned. "And I forgot my wallet."

"Mmm."

The driver eased up to Merry-Go-Read. The bus halted with a hydraulic wheeze. The bookstore lady couldn't help but notice.

Jon stood up, signaling Roy. The other security guards also stood, abandoning their cards, and got out. Sure she was watching, Jon bypassed his usual leap from the bus, gathered his dignity, ignored Zeke's eyebrows, and promenaded between his sentries the eight feet to her door.

Inside, everything was still in its place, including the bookstore lady. She stood behind the counter, her hands folded, and if she'd noticed his triumphant return, she didn't betray it by even a blink. "$243.60?"

Wilting, he approached. "I know. You told me." With one final flourish, he handed over a Platinum Visa with Jonathan Van Castle emblazoned across the front.

Now she would recognize him. She would finally put two and two together. He pasted a modest look alongside a grin, and waited for her hand to fly over her fluttering heart. But she only slid the card through the machine, and waited for it to belch out a receipt.

His grin faded. He reached for the card, but she pulled it back, and slid the receipt in front of him. "Please sign."

Hell. He grabbed a pen, scrawled his John Henry, and when he was done, she by-God picked it up and compared it to the card. Satisfied—and she'd better be—she offered him the card and receipt. He snatched them from her.

"Thank you. Have a nice day." Polite words, no smile.

He'd have a nice day all right, no thanks to her. He grumbled his way to the door. As he reached for the handle, voices crescendoed outside.

The soft scent of honeysuckle tickled his nose. The bookstore lady had moved up behind him. "My goodness. Mari! What is she doing?"

"The redhead?"

"My little sister." Her tone was grim.

Roy held the redhead back as she and her friends tried to force their way to the bus. Apparently they thought he was in it. Jon turned to look at the bookstore lady.

For once, she was looking back. "Who are you?"

Finally. He let his slow smile surface, but didn't reply. Instead, he chucked her gently under the chin. Curiosity turned to a glare. He opened the door, and stepped into his world. Squeals rose, hands reached, but his guards held firm. As he swung into the bus, his smile lingered.

Zeke glanced up. "Get what you wanted?"

"Oh, yeah."

"A phone number? A date?"

"Nope." He tossed his sack down, settled onto the sofa, and locked his hands behind his head.

Zeke raised an eyebrow.

"I got the last word." And he hadn't had to say a thing.

The memory of a pair of startled big blues stayed with him all the way to Monaco, making him grin. Once in Monaco, though, Belinda wiped the smile right off his face.

Chapter 2

What a conceited cretin! Crumpling Mr. Van Castle's receipt in her fist, Lilac O'Malley Ryan scrubbed at her chin. As the bus pulled away—good riddance—Mari banged through the door. The patch of hot pink fabric she called a shirt was stained with sweat.

Disregarding Lil's disapproving look, Mari hoisted her narrow derriere onto the counter and grumped, legs swinging along with the earrings that almost brushed her shoulders. "I can't believe *you* met Jonathan Van Castle. *You,* who wouldn't know George Strait if he sidled up and sat on your lap."

"George who?" Lil unwrinkled the receipt, then looked at the sister ten years her junior. "If I'm supposed to be impressed, I'm not. He might be good-looking in an outlandish sort of way, but he's arrogant, rude, and he doesn't even know his own daughter's age."

Plus, his smile annoyed her. His smile, and the little flip her stomach had done every time he'd used it. Still, she guessed she should be grateful. He was responsible for the biggest single sale Merry-Go-Read had made all week. Maybe all month.

Definitely all month.

She set the receipt in a prominent spot on the counter where the shop's owner, their sister-in-law Patsy Lee, would see it first thing. Still, the amount was too little and too late to save Merry-Go-Read. A chill crept over her. When Jonathan Van Castle had been here, the shop had seemed overly warm, but now it was cold.

"I'll be right back." Avoiding the sandal swinging from Mari's toe, Lil headed to the storeroom to adjust the thermostat, not that the cantankerous thing ever paid any attention. She didn't bother to flip on the lights. In the last few years, she'd gotten to know by memory the musty room where she'd methodically received and unpacked inventory. Only shipping returns to publishers was done here now.

Mari's voice followed her. "You're hopeless. Absolutely hopeless."

Lil turned the dial. Mari was right. She *was* hopeless. Hopeless and helpless. She rubbed her arms. And scared.

She turned to go back into the shop, stumbled over something on the floor, and cried out before she could stop herself. Everything was a mess since she'd started packing.

"You okay?" Mari called, with the worry Lil had learned to expect from her family.

"I'm fine."

She picked up the book she'd tripped over. *Little House in the Big Woods.* She pressed her lips together. She must have set it back here sometime this past week when she was moving books around, then forgot it.

Dammit. Double dammit. Now she'd have to run the danged thing all the way to Lake Kesibwi. Thinking of the lake, tears gathered behind her eyelids. Impatiently, she dashed them away. She'd thought she was done with crying.

"Mari, I'm going to stay back here and pack a few books I need to return."

"Are you sure you're all right?"

Lil swallowed through a tight throat. "I'm sure."

There was a pause and Lil could picture Mari worrying a lock of hair while she debated whether to check on her sister. Her family's vigilence was wearing. "Well, then, I'll pack some out here, but only if you promise me on pain of death you'll dish up every word Jonathan Van Castle uttered. Promise—or you can find another slave."

"I promise."

She'd lied to Mari. She wasn't fine, there were no books back here to pack, and everything was a mess— not just since she'd learned Merry-Go-Read would close, but since the car wreck that had taken Robbie from her three years ago.

She banged her palm on a utility shelf. Damn him for not taking care of the car. Damn him for not listening. Damn him for dying and leaving her alone.

Again Mari's voice rang out. "Did you drop something?"

Lil cleared her throat. "Just a book," she called back.

As the months had ticked by after his death, she'd slowly rebuilt an existence. But, oh, Robbie. *What should I do now?*

"Lil! Aren't you done yet? I've packed up a box, and I can't find the blasted marker for the label, and you promised me you'd tell—"

"I'm coming." Lil put her hands to her cheeks to cool them, and carried the *Little House* book into the shop.

"So. Describe him." Mari hopped back up on the counter and scrunched her freckled nose. Maybelline had never dusted that nose—Mari rejected heavy makeup and mousse, just like her sister. Although for Lil, it wasn't a cause, simply a matter of disinterest.

"I thought I did."

"Don't make me wrench it out of you." Mari twisted to turn on the radio. She tuned in a country station, cranking up the volume until Lil's molars buzzed. "Ooo. I love this song! New one by Van Cas-

tle. From their *Country Comeback* CD." She played
air fiddle, then razored her eyes at Lil. "And I don't
want editorial comments. What I want from you is a
description of every gesture, every word, every look,
every . . ."

Lil tried to tune Mari out—she could hardly hear
her anyway—put the book on a shelf, and rummaged
in a drawer, unwilling to admit she didn't want to
talk about Mr. Van Castle because she'd found his
presence unsettling.

"Come on! Tell. I hardly got a glimpse of him over
that muscle-bound bodyguard."

The image of a slow, sultry smile rose in Lil's mind.
Feeling cranky, she found a marker and handed it off
to her sister. "Ridiculously tight leather pants and
boots, melted candy in his pocket—"

"Speak up, I can't hear you." Mari bent sideways
on the counter to scrawl on a label.

Lil yanked down the volume. "I said, he was almost
poured into his pants. He had a shirt with yards of
ridiculous fringe, and some kind of cowboy belt—"

"I saw all that! What about *him*?"

"Honey skin. Straight, honey-blond hair, almost as
long as Patsy Lee's. Eyes the color of peanut brittle,
or maybe dark toffee, or . . ." Lil slapped the label
Mari handed her onto the box. "Who cares? They
changed color like a cat's. And he moved like a cat.
Sneaky. Full lower lip, ears oversized—"

Mari frowned.

"Straight nose—"

"Regal," Mari corrected, dreamy gaze directed at
the ceiling.

"White teeth. Not too much taller than me or you,
and built like a soccer player. You know—compact
muscles."

"See what I mean? He gets to you, doesn't he?"

Lil figured it would be futile to explain she'd studied

him carefully so she could identify his mug shot. She hefted the box onto the counter.

Mari reached for the radio again, but Lil gave her a look and she dropped her hand. "Well, go on. What did he say? What did he buy?"

"I thought you were supposed to be at work." A junior at Central Missouri State, Mari majored in graphic design, partied, and took a job at the paper every summer to pay school expenses.

Mari waved her hand. "The *Cordelia Daily Sun* set early today. The ad salesman—me—only brought in two ads to the *Sun*'s layout artist—me—so we both got done early. Silly old thing only poses as a newspaper anyway. I mean, is Horace Bruell visiting his mother Betty news? Or Joey Beadlesworth placing twelfth in the Tri-State Swim Meet?"

Lil looked at her watch, her last Christmas present from Robbie. That was another thing she'd almost forgotten. Joey would arrive on Lil's stoop promptly at four for the piano lesson his mother forced on him. Privately, Lil thought the lessons as much of a waste as his participation on the swim team.

"I stopped by Peg's for a donut, heard Paddy O'Neill bragging he'd spotted somebody famous. Nosy old coot. He mentioned a pair of purple guitars. Those old geezers didn't know what that meant, but I did, so I went home and kept an eye out." That explained more than anything why Mari's work day had ended early. She'd major in Country Groupie if she had half a chance. "Van Castle's headlining in Sedalia in August—although the State Fair's really beneath them. It's their last stop in the States, and after that they'll head to Canada and Europe. This will be my last chance to see them in probably *forever*. They're huge. As big as—no, bigger than!—Diamond Rio. Or at least they were before Jon split from his wife and there was a ton of ugly talk including some bull"—she glanced at Lil—"*oney* about him sleeping with some teenage tart. I, for one, never believed a word of it. I think Belinda Van Castle is a liar, even if she looks like she never farts."

"Mari!"

Mari wrinkled her nose. "Besides I think she's a porn star or stripper now. The teenage tart, I mean, not Belinda Van Castle. Although she might make a good one."

"What are you babbling about?"

"The Van Castle divorce, of course." Mari gave her an impatient look. "It was in all the papers a few years ago, but who cares anyway? Van Castle's still the absolute best, you know."

Lil didn't know. Give her Chopin.

"Not that I can get tickets to their concert. They're over forty-five bucks—and those are the cheap seats. I finally got the dough together yesterday and—wouldn't you know it?—they sold out the day before. The day before!" Mari jabbed her elbows on her knees and dropped her chin in her hands.

Lil glanced out the window. Holding a bakery bag, her former brother-in-law crossed the square toward Merry-Go-Read in long, powerful strides. She sighed. Seamus checked on her daily, and sometimes she wished he wasn't quite so solicitous. Shame followed the thought. In the weeks after Robbie's funeral, he'd performed handyman work around her house, and helped untangle her finances.

Seamus entered the store. "Afternoon, ladies." With his everpresent black hat, black jeans, and silver bolo, he reminded her of Adam Cartwright. Her dad still watched the reruns of *Bonanza*.

Still lost in self-pity, Mari only grunted. Lil frowned at her, then smiled apologetically at Seamus. "You look good today. Leg not bothering you?"

The year she'd married Robbie, Seamus had left on the rodeo circuit. When he'd retired to Cordelia on the heels of Robbie's death, he'd come back with an occasional limp. Some said the leg was the result of a battle with a steer, others said he'd just fallen when he was drunk. Lil didn't listen to the talk. He'd sobered up in rehab and that's what counted.

"Not today." He set the bag down, and pushed his hat back. "Fact is, I'm ready to do some dancing. There's a celebration at the Rooster tonight. The Tidwells' fiftieth."

Helen and Elmon Tidwell were the owners of the Cordelia Sleep Inn. Lil had called them this morning to wish them happy—and give her regrets.

"Came to see if you'd like to go. Brought you something."

He nodded at the bag, and watched while she opened it. A slice of apple pie served up by the cook at the Rooster Bar and Grill. On the heels of Robbie's death, Seamus had bought out the Rooster from his parents when they'd decided to retire to a doublewide in Orlando. Odd that a former alcoholic would own a bar, but not too odd when you thought about it. Helping out your folks was simply the way things were done in Cordelia.

"Thank you." Although she wasn't really hungry, she forked a small bite and wiped a crumb off her lip, conscious he followed every move. His eyes were the same green as Robbie's, but implacable. "You know I adore the Tidwells, but with the store closing, and Patsy Lee needing to spend time with her children since Henry . . . Well, after my piano lessons, I'm coming back here." She shied from large gatherings, weary of the sympathetic looks still thrown her way. "But maybe I can stop by later." She knew she wouldn't.

She thought anger flickered across his features. But he only nudged Mari's knee until she shifted to allow him some space to lean his long frame against the counter.

He hooked one boot over the other. "How's Patsy Lee holding up?"

To Lil's secret shame, her recently widowed sister-in-law was faring better than she was. When Henry had died, he'd not only left his three children without a father, but also debt piled higher than the St. Andrew's church steeple. A bad heart, the doctor had said. Thinking about it, Lil almost snorted. A bad heart? It was just like her brother to bow out when the going got rough. She flushed. Hadn't she done almost the same thing herself? Henry had just been . . . Henry.

Seamus's gaze sharpened, and she busied herself neatening things on the counter. "Patsy Lee is doing pretty well, considering. She's thinking about working at PicNic." PicNic was the poultry processing plant outside of town. "And with interviewing, her job at the bank, the children—well, she couldn't handle all that, and closing the store, too. So I said I would." Even though she wasn't sure she could handle it either. With every box she packed, she felt she stored the last remnants of Henry's dreams, pie-in-the-sky though they'd been. "And maybe we'll get enough out of the closing sale to help tide Patsy Lee over until—"

She broke off. Until what? A miracle happened? Whatever pittance Patsy Lee salvaged from the store wouldn't last long, and her sister-in-law still faced a staggering debt to the bank—two mortgages on her home and a loan on this place.

"Have you decided what you're going to do?"

"I haven't thought about it much," she lied.

She'd scanned the want ads, but knew she didn't have many marketable skills. She wished she could trade her three part-time semesters in business school—taken more to fill the hours when she wasn't working while Robbie went to classes at CMSU—for one solid course in computer software. Finding a job that offered benefits and enough money to pay her own mortgage, not to mention one that didn't involve hacking chicken at PicNic, kept her awake nights. But she didn't want to worry Seamus.

"I still have some money from the insurance to tide me over while I look for a job, thanks to your advice." She stacked some labels into a neat square, then laid her hand on the ridged muscles of his forearm. "I'm still grateful for all your help."

He looked at her hand, pale gold against his darker skin. When his eyes met hers, their warmth unsettled her. She dropped her hand.

His mouth crooked in a wry smile and he pushed off the counter. "I won't bite, Lil."

Mari suddenly came to life. "Hey, Seamus—I've seen some lowlifes at the Rooster. Know any scalpers? I need tickets to the Van Castle show, and I'd be willing to pay . . . I guess I'd pay sixty buckaroos if I could get a good seat. Who needs to buy an art history book? I'll just borrow someone's. Whaddaya say? Know anyone?"

Still flustered at the strange glow in Seamus's eyes, Lil was relieved Mari had shifted his attention. Her eyes slid to the copy of *Little House in the Big Woods* on the shelf behind the counter. Why not? Somebody had to go. The memory of a crooked smile wafted through her mind. She didn't want to, that was certain. "You wouldn't want to help me with a delivery, would you?"

Mari frowned. "Quiet. Seamus is thinking." Lil wasn't the only one of the O'Malley sisters that treated Seamus like Dear Abby.

"That book"—Lil pointed—"goes to Jonathan Van Castle."

"If I worked some overtime next week, I could maybe even spring for—" Mari swiveled to stare at her. *"What?"*

Seamus's mouth quirked.

"That book was promised to Jonathan Van Castle. Want to deliver it?"

"That book? To Jonathan Van Castle? Of course I will. Right now! Where?"

"I'll tell you *after* you help pack all these books. Deal?"

Mari jumped off the counter. "When do I start?"

"Tomorrow."

Mari's face fell. "I have to wait *that* long?"

Chapter 3

To Jon, it seemed a lifetime ago, and not just earlier that day, that he'd had his fun with the bookstore lady. To Zeke's amusement, he'd diddled with the lyrics of his new creation during the forty-mile drive to Monaco. It wasn't just a ruse to escape his thoughts of what waited for him there—he just couldn't shake that blue-eyed gaze.

Of course, after they'd reached Monaco and picked up his kids, he'd had to put the song aside. In an atmosphere made uneasy by Jon's forced jocularity and their wide-eyed wariness, they'd traveled another ten miles to Lake Kesibwi, a wide swath of water that sparkled through the valleys of the Ozark hills, just south of the larger Lake of the Ozarks. Their journey ended at the Royal Sun Resort, a complex built on a private, gated finger of land jutting out into the most populated part of the lake, Shawnee Bay. None of them could wait to escape the confines of the bus.

That was eight tense hours ago. In one of the resort's massive two-story cabanas that hugged the hillside, Jon paused on the upper landing. Hearing nothing from the bedrooms where his children slept— he hoped—he padded down the stairs to the living room.

Over his head, beams matching the oak logs that formed the walls crisscrossed the vaulted ceiling, track lights tucked against their sides. Straight ahead was a wall of windows. By day, the vista would encompass a chunk of the lake. Now somebody had pulled drapes across the lower half, leaving only a gap where sliding doors led to a broad deck. A native stone fireplace dominated the room, its grate a silent black hole.

The clock squatting on the mahogany mantelpiece bonged once. Roy and the nanny he'd hired had already turned in. His drummer Three-Ring, manager Peter Price, secretary Lydia, and the rest of his road crew had crashed in similar cabanas. Cabanas. Right. More like villas.

A maple leather sofa and two bulky chairs divided by a coffee table sat on a plush rug in front of the fireplace. His feet riding an ottoman, Zeke lounged in one chair under a pool of lamplight, reading.

Jon flopped on the sofa. The cushions heaved a sigh. "The next few months will be a real laugh riot if *that* was any indication."

Zeke turned a page. "Things'll get better, my man. The kids just aren't used to you."

Jon debated between peanut M&M's and a Tootsie Roll Pop, finally choosing the latter from his stash on the table. Sugar was a new habit he'd picked up since he'd quit smoking. He lay his head back, willing the tension to drain from his muscles. It didn't work. Biting off the candy, he pitched the stick toward the table and yawned, a huge, jaw-cracking yawn.

When the stick hit the bottom of his foot, Zeke looked up. "Hell, man, go to bed."

"Can't sleep." What was he going to do about his kids?

Melanie wasn't a problem—which *was* a problem since she'd hardly opened her mouth all evening and just sat there staring at him like a scared rabbit— but Michael . . .

Jon had practically peeled him off the ceiling to get him into bed. He'd sung every ditty he knew to calm him, including the alphabet song, but the kid didn't know his ABCs. He could, though, recite verbatim the refrain of every TV commercial ever made. Michael was completely manic, and no match for Tina-the-Nanny. She'd come from a reputable agency, but the wispy blonde was young, longer on legs than sense, overawed by his celebrity, and not much of a match for Michael. He gave a long sigh.

Zeke's brows snapped together, and he leveled his eyes at Jon. "Okay, out with it."

"Out with what?"

"Whatever has you sounding like a bellows. Is it Belinda?"

When Jon had arrived in Monaco, he'd had the pleasure of reliving any number of scenes they'd enacted during their marriage. Fortunately, though, before the blowout, they'd hustled Mel and Michael out to the bus in a Jeep Roy had rented in Cordelia.

Equally fortunately, no media had arrived on the scene. Peter Price had thrown them off the scent with rumors of a trip back to Nashville during this semihiatus between the last two U.S. venues on Van Castle's Country Comeback Tour. The reporters would figure it out, they always did. But for the moment, he and the kids could live without looking over their shoulders.

"Let's just say it wasn't a reunion made in heaven." Unless heaven included artillery ranging from cigarette packs that had bounced harmlessly off his chest to a heavy butter crock that had put a dent in her mother's floor, but, fortunately, not his head.

"Ah, so our Miss Belinda hasn't changed, has she?"

"Hardly. Still looks like the Flying Nun, talks like a longshoreman, and has one messed-up head. I don't know how long she's been using this time."

"But you're sure she's back at it?"

"Yeah." He dipped into thought. Zeke let him. It was one of the nice things about Zeke. He never pressed.

Sometime back in grade school, when Monaco still

had a cinema, Jon had scrounged up a few bucks to go to a Saturday matinee featuring Sally Field. *Smokey and the Bandit,* maybe. That was where he'd met Belinda. She'd sat a couple of rows behind him and pelted him with popcorn; he'd yanked her hair afterward, and she'd punched him. He should have known then a relationship would never work.

It hadn't. Three years ago, after they'd split, she'd parked the kids with her mother Dodo in Dodo's neat, but sparse, frame house, and whirled off around the world, headlining tabloids with a succession of boyfriends at the Cannes Festival, Aspen, and the casinos at Monte Carlo. From Nashville, where he immersed himself in rebuilding the career she'd almost wrecked, he followed her antics, wondering why none of her admiring press guessed how close she lived to the edge. They loved her. The cameras ate up that innocent face—and the reporters ate up whatever garbage she fed them.

He was concerned about his kids, sure. But, scrambling to keep his band from going under, he let her convince him again she'd stayed clean, and he buried his qualms under the thought that Mel and Michael were safe with Dodo, who after all had once been his own surrogate mother.

Before he felt compelled to act, the publicity stopped. Probably because the money was gone— every last red penny of the fifty percent he'd handed her without a fight as a sop to his conscience. Debts and creditors followed. He knew because no way would Belinda return to Monaco unless she had to. The media had followed, but not for long. There wasn't much to film at Dodo's, nor would Belinda have wanted them there.

He cleared his throat. "Yeah," he repeated, "I'm sure she's using again. Coke probably, since she always claims she and the kids can't get by on the insane amount of child support I send her every month."

The money went to dealers. He knew it, but couldn't prove it. To dealers, and to the toe rings, high-heeled sandals, inch-wide gold bangles, and white leather shorts that had molded her ass when he'd seen her earlier today. A late-model red Camaro, front headlight smashed, had been parked in Dodo's driveway. When he'd asked about the car, she'd said it was a repo, gotten cheap. He didn't believe her.

He drummed on his knees for a minute. He sent Belinda money, gave in to her demands every time, and still remorse ate up his insides.

Zeke guessed his thoughts. "It isn't your fault, my man. She always liked things fast. Fast food, fast cars, fast living. What happened at Dodo's?"

"She screamed and swore and threw things, but she finally went with that guy from Serenity Gardens." His hands stilled. He wondered about the drug rehab's choice of a counselor. The guy—Neil—was youngish, soft-bodied with a pasty complexion, weak chin, and didn't look like any contest for Belinda. "It was already a done deal, but you know Belinda, she put on a show. Our lawyers worked out things. If she goes to rehab for sixty days, then stays clean another six months, I'll foot the bill and her attorney fees." Plus some extra, under the table. The extra was more than the bill for the rest. Belinda always charged a high price. "We filed, citing exhaustion or something on her part, and the judge granted me temporary sole custody for the duration. Thank God for Judge Dougherty. He did what he could to keep it all low profile."

He, Belinda, and the judge went way back. As Dodo's long-time neighbor, the judge had taken an interest in them since they were kids. Lucky for Jon. Judge Dougherty had given him probation instead of clapping him in juvee, where he'd undoubtedly belonged at the time. The judge should probably bow out where they were concerned, but, if they could agree on nothing else, he and Belinda agreed on one thing. They trusted the judge, and would rather wash their linen in front of him than anyone else.

"How's she going to prove she stays clean?"

Jon scooped up some M&M's. "Pee in a cup. She's thrilled."

"But she'll do it?"

"Better than jail; cops could have thrown her in there for DUI." They'd hushed up more than one offense in the past. "Plus custody reverts to joint after eight months. She doesn't want the kids, though, as much as she wants the money that goes with them."

Dodo had phoned just over a month ago to tell him that Belinda and the kids had been in a car wreck. Once she'd assured him the kids were fine, Belinda's mother had fallen silent, probably at war with herself over love for her grandchildren and the natural desire to protect her daughter. He'd finally gotten the whole story. Belinda had zoned out at sixty miles an hour on the winding highway that led to her mother's, drove over the middle line, narrowly avoided making mincemeat of an oncoming car, and ended up in a ditch. The cops knew she was high, but couldn't prove it. Thank God, the kids were strapped into the tiny backseat. Nobody was hurt.

He'd seethed with frustration. There were so many demands on his time. But this involved his *kids*. Since he'd already planned to take them during the tour's pause at Lake Kesibwi, it was a simple matter to give in to Dodo's apologetic pleas to take them for Belinda's eight-month "sentence," although he'd wondered why Dodo was so uncharacteristically insistent. She usually asked nothing of him, already flustered at the amount of money he showered on her, even though he'd assured her it was no more than he'd do for his own mother. If he still had her.

When he'd seen Dodo, though, he'd quit wondering. "Dodo's not looking too good. She's aged a lot."

Jon tipped more candy into his mouth. Thinking of Dodo, the stuff had all the flavor of sawdust. "I'm worried about her. I gave her money to go visit her sister. She said she'd be back, but I don't know if she will. And I don't know what I'm going to do with the kids if she doesn't come back—or can't care for them."

Weary lines had dug furrows around Dodo's mouth, and more gray than brown washed her hair. She'd watched Belinda with the alertness of a stray cat wary of a swift kick. The last few years had taken their toll. He didn't know how much more he could ask of her.

As a kid he had been smitten with Belinda, but he'd loved her mother without reservation. A widow, she'd always had time, a hot meal, and refuge for the scroungy kid Belinda dragged into the house. Since a rebellious Belinda rebuffed her mother at every turn, Dodo turned to him, lavishing him with maternal affection, and he'd soaked it up. After his first successes, he'd assumed Dodo's mortgage and footed her household bills, knowing he could never really pay her back. Belinda had called him "Mama's boy." She had never liked it when he'd paid attention (or money) to anything, or anyone, else.

Not only had Dodo changed, his kids had changed. His reunion with them had been strained beyond the situation. Ten-year-old Melanie, the baby-round face he remembered now thinned into prettiness, stared warily at him from beneath too-long brown bangs, and Michael, all thin limbs and round almond eyes glittering from under a mop of bowl-cut dark hair, didn't stand still long enough for a hug. Their clothes looked like they came from the Swap 'n Shop. He hadn't expected hearts and flowers after a two-year absence, but Mel's apathy and Michael's manic behavior sounded an alarm. Just what in the hell was going on?

Zeke said mildly, "Keep the kids. I'll help out—we'd do okay."

"I thought of that, but it just doesn't play. I'm willing to fight for them. Even Peter's for it—he thinks me as a family man would be a great hook for Van Castle's image after the battering it's taken."

But he didn't live a life fit for a child. In just over a month, Van Castle would leave for Canada, then Europe. Peter had scheduled charity events, a TV special in London, store appearances, radio shows. It would be a zoo. Even afterward, their schedule was packed.

"It's bad enough I have to shunt them off to Nashville when we leave for Canada, but permanently pushing them onto someone like that nanny, or worse, boarding schools, isn't any solution. Hell, my life didn't do Belinda any favors. Think she would have hoed the same crooked row if she'd had a nine-to-five husband? Eight months of me will be plenty enough for the kids. Longer-term, I could really mess them up. Truth is, they're better off with Belinda—a sober Belinda—than with me. As long as they have Dodo."

Zeke zeroed in on his rhetorical question. "Actually, I do think Belinda would have gone the same route no matter who she'd hooked up with, my man, but we've been over that ground before and you don't listen."

Because it wasn't true. Belinda had once been free-spirited and wild. Now she was grasping and bitter. Life had changed her. *He* had changed her.

Jon shifted. "Doesn't matter. Think about it. We can't keep them."

"Not to mention a fight for custody would mean dragging the band through the muck again." Zeke's voice was dry.

Jon fell silent.

During his divorce from Belinda, she'd squawked half-truths and outrageous lies for every tabloid reporter who'd listen—and most did. Knowing she lashed out from hurt, and feeling each blow deserved, he'd weathered the punishment in silence, even though some of the lies got pretty bizarre, and even though Peter had badgered him to tell his side of the story. Unwilling to drag Belinda down further, unable to pit his children between their parents, he'd refused. His silence almost cost him his rights to his children— and his career. Fortunately, Belinda had realized she was killing her golden goose, and she'd finally shut up. But not before a lot of damage was done.

For the last two years, he, Zeke, Three-Ring, and Peter had worked to mop up his image. He'd submitted to boring publicity dates with up-and-coming country queens whose trilling remarks about his good character were planted in the idol mags, bowed to "serious" interviews with journalists ranging from *Country Dreaming* to *Time,* held court on late-night talk shows, and shelled out a lot of money to charitable causes, including, most notably and ironically, one to do with child exploitation.

He popped a few more M&M's. "You know the publicity a custody battle'd bring is the last thing we need right now. The press and public still love Belinda and she would play them for all they're worth. We can't take another hit like the last one—not this soon. Besides, the kids don't need me. What they need is a different mother."

Zeke smiled wryly. "Kind of hard to pick those off the shelf, my man—especially since you haven't even been on more than a promotional date in three years. Perhaps you should try your hand with 'China Blue Eyes.' God knows you have a jones on over that song."

Not just over the song. He'd never forget how those blue eyes had blinked at him in total lack of recognition. Thinking about it now, he realized he'd felt a strange relief. Before the muse struck him again, Jon stood up. "I don't have time for dating. I'm going to crash." No, he didn't have the time, but he sure did have some kind of inclination where that bookstore lady was concerned.

Chapter 4

On Tuesday afternoon, the day after she'd met Jonathan Van Castle, Lil was still peeved he'd had the nerve to appear in a dream she'd had last night. Standing up from the carton she was packing, she stretched against the noodle of pain in her back. She looked around Merry-Go-Read with mingled sadness and satisfaction. Only a few more hours of work, and the store would be ready for the final sale that would close its doors.

She and Mari had worked all day, and in the last hour, Mari had finally stopped trying to tease more information from her on the whereabouts of Jonathan Van Castle.

Now her sister emerged from the back room, flipping the tab on a soda she'd retrieved from the minifridge. She took a gulp, burped, then set the can on the counter. "So, you gonna go?"

Pretending ignorance, Lil leaned over and scooped a pile of books into the open carton. "Go where? Ouch." Her ring had caught on the lid. Sucking on her knuckle, Lil pulled it off, along with her watch, and walked them to the counter.

"To the lake, that's where." Mari slapped a label on a box. "Don't try to change the subject. Mom's gathering the clan for a big powwow over What To Do About Patsy Lee, and you know it. And while she's not saying so, I'm sure she plans to settle your future, too. Besides, the family always goes now. Or at least a few of us still do, even if some members of our family have chickened out the last three years."

Lil stilled, and Mari backpedaled. "Sorry, 'chickened out' wasn't the right phrase. I know you don't want to go because of Robbie, but, dammit, Lil—I mean, darn it—it's been three years. And Patsy Lee is going even though she *just* lost Henry. Besides, when you don't go, it's a bore because Hock and Stan just babble on about how much better their place is on Shawnee Bay—where they're staying this time, thank God—and what merger made their stock split umpteen ways to Sunday."

She grinned at Lil, as though encouraging her to join in on trashing their oldest sister and her husband Stan, a pastime they'd sometimes shared, but Lil only said, "Don't call Alcea 'Hock.' She doesn't like it." The rebuke was automatic. At the ripe age of five, Mari had discovered Alcea was the formal name for the hollyhock flower, and she'd gleefully christened the sister eleven years her senior.

"Do you know where Alcea is, by the way?" Lil asked. "She said she'd give me a ride home—the Escort's in the shop again. I'm tired. We can finish this in the morning."

"I forgot. Hock called because she can't make it. Actually she called Mom, but Mom and Pop are helping out at church camp this week, so Mom called me. Alcea said she couldn't reach you—like she tried—and then, naturally, left Mom figuring out how to get you home. Hock's such a jerk. She had to pick up precious Kathleen from a fifth grade something, then deliver one of her oh-so-famous cakes to her Rich-People-Pretend-to-Help-the-Poor Meeting, and—hey, Patsy Lee told me Stan's banging his secretary."

"Hush. Ho—I mean, Alcea—is not a jerk and Patsy Lee didn't say any such thing. You shouldn't spread rumors about your brother-in-law."

Mari looked smug. "Maybe she didn't say it in exactly those words, but she told me Stan's always got 'business meetings' with that bimbo behind closed doors, and she comes out with her eyeballs rattled. And Patsy Lee would know, wouldn't she? Since her desk is right next to Stan's office." Stan was the bank president; Patsy Lee was his assistant's assistant. "Wonder if Hock knows about his latest."

"Whatever problems Stan and Alcea have, they're none of our business. Alcea tries, Mari. She's just not very self-confident, that's all. She's . . ." Lil stopped, tired of Mari's gossip, and weary of trying to defend her oldest sister when she didn't understand herself why Alcea had married, let alone stayed with, the philandering Stan.

"Poop. You used to be more fun." Mari abandoned the box she was packing. "Anyway, instead of walking over, I brought my trusty steed to do the queen's bidding, and rescue the damsel in distress." Mari lived with their folks around the corner on Maple Woods Drive, while Lil lived nearer the town's outskirts.

Mari motioned to the street where her battered VW slumped by the curb, looking anything but trustworthy. "Couldn't have you walking home. You'd melt into a mere puddle on Main Street, then we'd have to hold a wake, and I'd have to eat more of Helen Tidwell's tuna casserole surprise, which positively makes me barf."

Lil frowned.

Mari managed to look contrite. "I'm sorry. I didn't mean—oh, forget it." She grabbed the soda and took another swig. "So, are you going?"

Lil blinked. Mari changed subjects faster than a remote changed channels.

"To the lake, dummy! You've got to go. This year will be worse than usual. With Henry gone, everyone'll mope around."

As Mari continued arguing, Lil moved to the window and pushed aside the faded curtains. Across the street, St. Andrew's huddled as though looking for shade.

She and Robbie had played at the lake as children, frolicked on tire tubes in the water, and roasted marshmallows in the barbecue ring Pop had built out back. As newlyweds, fumbling and giggling, they'd made love for the first time on the sleeping porch while stars blinked across a black velvet sky. They'd returned there for vacation each of the seven summers they were married.

She didn't want to go back there, not to discuss Patsy Lee's future, not to discuss her own, not even for old time's sake. Especially not for that. "I'm sorry, Mari, but—"

"Come on. When we aren't powwowing, Mom'll piddle with her flowers while Pop reads. Hock and Stan will brag. And all Patsy Lee will talk about is the new baby."

Lil's hand dropped. "What do you mean?" she said slowly. "What new baby?"

Mari looked like she'd rather be anyplace else. "Mom didn't tell you? Dammit—I mean, darn it—she said she was going to tell you!"

"What new baby, Mari?" Lil whispered.

"Patsy Lee is pregnant."

Lil sat down hard. Gnawing on the inside of her cheek to keep the tears from spilling, she bent her head and stared at her hands.

"Oh, Lil. I thought you knew! She's four months along and said it must have happened right before . . . right before Henry died." Mari rushed over and knelt next to her. "Please don't look like that. Say something."

Lil didn't reply, just continued to stare at her hands. She noted her ring finger narrowed just before the knuckle, right where her wedding band normally rested. Now she understood how Patsy Lee stayed so strong.

Mari stood up, hands on hips. "Don't you do this!"

Lil looked up. "Do what?"

Mari stamped her foot, her expression equal parts sadness, entreaty—and anger. "I can't stand to see you like this anymore!"

Lil smiled weakly and dropped her gaze to the old dress she'd thrown on this morning. Like the one she'd worn yesterday, she'd found it in a box her mother had put out for a church rummage sale. "I didn't think I looked that bad."

"Although they could certainly use some work, you know I'm not talking about your clothes!" Mari paced, dragging her hand through her hair until it stood up in kinked horns. "You go through your days like some kind of damn robot. Up at dawn, tend your garden, work at this nothing job, home to teach piano to airheads like Joey Beadlesworth who thinks Mozart is the name of a car, for God's sake. You're not living, you're only existing. You're half the person you used to be. You used to joke, used to laugh, and now you hardly ever smile. I mean, dammit, Lil, it's like you died, too. Ever since Robbie . . ." She ignored Lil's cringe and plunged on. "Ever since Robbie died, ever since you lost *your* baby, you've been—"

Lil blanched. "Mari—" It was rare for anyone to talk to her about Robbie, and a tacit agreement had grown to never mention the unborn child she'd lost the same day he died.

"No! I won't stop. You listen. Everybody's pussyfooted around you, like they're afraid you'll break. It's been three years, Lil. Three! And you've been gone. Oh, you nod your head and talk, but you're not really there. You're closed off somewhere inside and we can't find you. *I* can't find you. And Lil, I need you! We all need you. Especially now that Henry's gone."

Mari paused at the counter, then whirled around. "But if you're too selfish you can't understand what you're doing to us, then go ahead and think about yourself. But really *think*. Patsy Lee told me you're both planning to work at PicNic. I can understand why she would. She's got no education and three kids, almost four now. But you? Why? You're only thirty! You could do anything. You could go back to school and finish your degree, or switch majors to music, or move somewhere and start all over. Maybe you'd even meet someone and fall in love, and—you could still have kids. Oh, I know you can't have your own, but you could always adopt instead of forever pretending Patsy Lee's or Hock's are yours."

Lil's eyes burned. "That's not fair—"

"So what? Life isn't fair for anybody, so what makes you special? You can mope around, or you can do something about it. *Think* of the possibilities, Lil! I can tell you I'm not wasting *my* life. As soon as I graduate, I'm outta here." Mari's pace slowed. She rested her elbows on the counter, bottom poked into the air. Her eyes turned dreamy. "I'll rent an apartment—maybe even in Chicago—anywhere besides this burg. I'll be a sought-after graphic artist and I'll go to art shows and concerts and I'll travel. Eventually I'll marry some marvelous, sophisticated guy with a pile of money and—oh, Lil, don't you see? There's a whole, big, beautiful world out there!" Mari swept her arms across the counter. Invoices scattered, along with Lil's watch and ring.

Horrified, Lil watched the ring ping against the register, rattle across the wooden floor, and disappear into the shadows under a bookshelf.

"God, Lil—I'm sorry." Mari scuttled around the counter and dropped to all fours. "I would never hurt you in a million years." She swept the floor under the shelf. "You know I love you. You know I'd never—"

"Stop! I'll do it."

Chewing her thumb, Mari sat back. Lil knelt and frantically patted the floor until her fingers wrapped around the ring. Breathing a sigh of relief, she slid it back on her finger, then looked at Mari. Mari's nose had pinked and her eyes swam.

"Oh, Mari. Come here." Mari fell into her arms, and Lil hugged her close. Behind Mari's back, Lil stared at her ring. "I'm not trying to shut you out. It's just . . . I loved him so much." With every ounce of her being, every fiber in her soul, just as he had her. "And I still miss him. Every day." She tried to straighten the wobble in her voice. "I miss his touch, his glance, his strength, and especially his optimism."

Mari's arms tightened. "I remember he always called you Calamity Lil."

Lil's laugh caught in her throat. "You remember that coverlet for our bed?"

"The one made from Grandma O'Malley's rose-bud sheets?"

"Yes. He said it wasn't like me, to make a bed of roses when I was always on the lookout for thorns." Under that coverlet, she'd curl into his body. His arm would draw her close until his breath teased her ear, and she'd let his warmth wash away her anxieties. "That last day—"

"Lil, you don't have to—"

"I need to," Lil said, realizing she did. She'd stored it up for too long. "I told him the car wasn't safe, not until the brakes were fixed. But he . . . he just picked me up and swung me around, and told me not to worry." She'd pushed at the dark shock of hair that tumbled across his forehead, and had let him silence her with a kiss. "Every day I've asked myself what if I'd insisted?" But she hadn't. She'd rarely insisted on anything.

"It wasn't your fault." Mari was vehement.

"I know that, but it took a long time to feel it." For weeks after the funeral, she'd barricaded herself in their little house. She'd wrapped herself in his letterman sweater and curled on the sofa they'd bought at the Tidwells' garage sale. It seemed so strange that his things had survived without him.

Mari moved restlessly. "Why didn't you tell us you felt guilty? Maybe I—or Mom, or one of us—could have helped you work through it."

"I— It's hard to explain. It's like I wanted to examine every memory." From sharing a sandbox to sharing a home. "I needed quiet. It's like I couldn't *remember* without quiet."

"And we put a stop to that, didn't we?" Mari said dryly. "Nothing gets in the way of the O'Malley clan—especially Mom—when we put our minds to it."

Lil smiled. Her family was not known for restraint, and "interference forever" should be their motto. She'd managed to hold them at bay for some weeks, preferring Seamus's quiet support and the help he gave her only when she asked him. But eventually, they'd stormed her citadel. She had to get up. She had to go out. They had it all figured out. She'd work for her brother Henry. She'd return to teaching piano.

"That's all right. It was time to move on." Even though she hadn't wanted to. And even though she'd only moved a few paces. Her gaze wandered around Merry-Go-Read. Time to move on. Sighing, she drew back and studied Mari's tear-stained face. "Okay, I'll go. If Patsy Lee can do it, so can I."

Chapter 5

On Friday morning, Jon sat elbows-to-knees on the leather sofa in the cabana, looking out through the wall of windows. Drapes flung wide, a torrent of sunshine flooded the room. In a corner near the windows, Zeke noodled on a set of electronic keyboards, completely absorbed. Zeke was working on a bridge for "China Blue Eyes." They'd hammered out the melody yesterday.

Jon twisted to look over his shoulder. Behind him, Melanie showed equal concentration, curled onto a padded settee nestled next to the staircase, eyes fixed on a book. He sighed. Melanie had rarely moved from that bench. After four days, she now managed more than two-word sentences, and sometimes he even got the sense she'd like to confide in him, but nobody could call her a chatterbox.

He took a sip of his coffee, and the brew dropped into a sour stomach. Until he'd arrived at the Royal Sun, he'd rarely seen ten in the morning. After just a few days of early risings, the novelty had worn thin. As far as he was concerned, mornings were for sleeping, and breakfast was a noon gig.

At the mind-numbing hour of six, whoops and thumps had jarred him awake—again. Groaning, he'd staggered out to the landing. Through bleary eyes, he'd watched Michael karate-kick his way down the stairs, on each step booting a pajama-clad leg into the air, then landing hard on his heel with a yell that'd turn Jackie Chan green. Seeing Jon, he'd grinned hugely. "Sorry, Charlie."

Full of murmured excuses, Tina-the-Nanny had scurried past Jon and pulled a bellowing Michael off to the kitchen. He'd fumbled his way back to bed, but had abandoned sleep when the yowls from the kitchen told him Tina-the-Nanny hadn't defeated Michael-the-Ninja.

He dropped the cup on the coffee table, its surface marred with the rings of the five that had gone before it.

Michael had ricocheted around the cabana like a pinball until Tina had blessedly taken him off to the pool. He hoped Michael didn't drown her. He loved that kid, but using "handful" to describe him was the understatement of the year.

He ignored his stomach's grinching, again focusing his attention on the scored papers littering the table. *China blue eyes. Such a surprise. I looked up and you were by my* . . . side? Gag. What else rhymed with "eyes" that hadn't been overused and overdone? Wise . . . Lies . . . *Agonize* . . .

Leaning back, he choked back a yawn and once more stared out of the windows. They opened onto a shady deck offering views from the wooded hilltop to the lake shimmering beyond. A cherry-and-yellow-striped parasail soared by, tugged by a speedboat slicing the surface below. The sky was a beckoning blue.

Most of his people, from crew to musicians, were catching needed rest and cocktails by the private pool that lay a short trek down the hill. Some had opted to play golf while others had rented water sports equipment.

The lodging, the food, the drink, the amenities would all fall on his tab, but he didn't mind. Everyone needed the break before they launched back into rehearsals for the Missouri State Fair. They worked hard. If they didn't, they wouldn't be part of the Van Castle conglomerate.

Peter Price had checked in this morning, wren-brown hair parted and slicked back along a razor-sharp line, his usual suit replaced with an Izod shirt and sharply creased Dockers. Peter was a Hah-vahd graduate and the most uptight twenty-five-year-old Jon had ever met. But a helluva manager.

Jon had an agent in Nashville, producers there and on both coasts, a road manager, a stage manager, and a staff that ranged from his fan club coordinator to a stable he employed in his own music publishing company. Peter Price ran the show with Jon's secretary, Lydia—under Jon's strict direction. Mismanagement had screwed too many musicians and he'd be damned if that would happen to him.

His ubiquitous cell phone clipped to his belt, Peter had waved away an offer of coffee, stood in the doorway and assured Jon the overseas fall concert series continued to gel, reported the CD they'd recorded in May needed overdubbing but the label told him it would be ready for Jon's approval in August, and, oh, the studio's graphic artist had just faxed samples of the cover art, so could Jon take a look?

All information Jon already knew, but Peter wasn't happy unless he'd triple-checked every detail. After Jon chose the artwork and Peter realized there was no further business in the offing, he'd looked so hang-dog that Jon had suggested he check into renting a few houseboats for the next day. Pale eyes brightening at the prospect of haggling over fees, Peter had scurried away on his mission after reminding him *People* magazine would be there at eleven tomorrow for a photo shoot of him and the kids.

People magazine . . . Guilt pricked him. He hadn't planned to use the kids to polish his image, but Pe-

ter'd yapped on and on about the great publicity, and
Jon had surrendered to shut him up. Now if only he
could gag Peter on the subject of marriage.

His business manager was certain a wedding with
one of those ambitious, model-perfect "dates" would
cement his popularity. He'd joked with Zeke about it.
Privately, though, Jon didn't think giving the kids a
new mom was a bad idea, although the "who" was a
definite question mark.

Good thing he'd convinced himself that after she'd
gotten some rest, Dodo would once more return.
Some men weren't meant to be married.

He yawned again, reached for a fistful of candy,
then changed his mind and shoved the bowl out of
reach. Sidney would yammer if he had to let out those
sequined tights that passed for pants before the next
concert. As it was, he got a daily lecture to lose the
pounds he'd put on since he'd given up his smokes.
Good God, he'd only gone up one size; it wasn't like
his butt had spread like butter on a griddle.

"I think the harmony needs a minor key," Zeke
spoke up, frowning at the keyboard. "It'd add more
pathos. Driving guitar, then bleed into . . . I dunno.
Fiddles?" Zeke flipped some switches and strings
whined. He stroked his beard. "What do you think,
my man?"

Jon rubbed his eyes and wished for eight hours of
dead-to-the-world. He tossed his scribbling aside and
stood. "I *can't* think any longer. And if I can't come
up with anything better than this, we won't need to
worry at all. Let's shelve it. I'm ready to catch a few
Zs by the pool."

He rounded the couch to Melanie, hesitated when
she didn't seem to notice him, then finally reached out
to stroke her hair. It slid like silk through his fingers.
"Whaddaya say, Mel? The pool sound cool?"

He'd treaded softly with the kids. Michael had
warmed after a few rides on his shoulders, but Mel

was something else. Without looking up, she mumbled something.

"What're you reading today, baby?" He knelt beside her. Tipping up the thick tome, he frowned. "One of my Tom Clancy books? I don't think those are rated PG."

"I already finished the books you bought for me." Her voice was higher than usual.

His frown deepened, not at her resistence, but at her reaction. She'd hunched her shoulders defensively, but at the same time, the look she cast him was reluctantly determined. "Every one of them?"

"I still have the Laura Ingalls Wilder books to read, but, you see, I want to read them in order and I don't have the first one." To his surprise, fear darkened her eyes, but she resolutely continued. "Reading the others first might spoil it, so I—"

At that moment, Michael ran in, Tina behind him and scrambling to keep up. Wet from the pool, Michael slid across the tile and almost took a header into an end table.

"Watch it, Michael!" Still puzzling over Melanie's reaction, he let his voice come out sharper than he'd intended.

Michael's round eyes filled with tears.

Immediately contrite, Jon rose. "Hey, bud, I'm—"

Before he could get the apology out, a small hand grabbed his arm with surprising strength. "Leave him alone!" Mel's voice was fierce.

Zeke's eyebrows went up.

Confused, Jon looked back at her. "I just want to apologize, Mel."

Her face went red. "Oh." She released her grip.

She sat there unmoving while Jon wiped Michael's eyes, then handed him off to Tina. Tina led Michael to the kitchen. When he returned to the settee, Mel wouldn't look at him.

"I wouldn't hurt him. You know that, don't you?" he asked.

"I guess so," she mumbled.

Jon was at a loss over what to say next. He fingered the edge of the Tom Clancy book. "If you don't want to read those other books now, we can get you new ones."

Some of the tension left her body. "It's not that I don't like what you bought. I know you spent a lot and I'm not trying to be an in-grade—"

"You mean 'ingrate,' Mel?"

Melanie's chin sunk into her chest. "Sometimes . . . sometimes Mommy says that when I ask for something new."

Jon's gaze fell on her thin pink T-shirt with its frayed hem. From what he'd seen, Mel had very little that was "new." He frowned. He'd tell Tina to take her shopping.

Mel reacted to the frown, and her words rushed out. "But I'm not an in-ingrate. It's just that the books go in order. Not that I don't like them or anything."

"Hush, baby." He brushed her bangs back. "Are you scared I'm mad?"

She studied him, and her eyes grew less wary. "I guess not." Then she added, "But you don't have to buy me anything else. I know there's not always the money to get everything I want. I understand, I really do, even though Mommy says I'm selfish."

His hand paused. "And what else does your mom say?"

"That—that I'm stupid." She hesitated before continuing. "I get bad grades and then she has to go talk to the teacher."

Zeke was now openly watching them.

"*You* get bad grades?" Jon's confusion increased. He'd tried his best to wipe his memory clean of the last years of his marriage, but he knew that during her first few years in school, Mel had surpassed her classmates and the school had placed her in—what were they called? Enhanced classes? Honor classes?

Shame struck him; he hadn't asked to see even one of her report cards in the last two years.

"Not *all* the time." She turned earnest eyes on him. "I'm really good at spelling and math and reading. But sometimes I need supplies for projects, and sometimes we can't afford it, and it's embarrassing to ask the teacher to get them for me, and . . . well, sometimes I don't turn them in. Please don't be mad at me."

He'd thought the changes he saw in his kids were part of a normal adjustment. After all, they hardly knew him. But he'd fooled himself. Memories of his own old man nudged him, and the hair rose on the nape of his neck.

"Melanie, is your mom, uh, mean to you?"

"Sometimes. She yells a lot." Her voice was so small he strained to hear. "But mostly she's not there, she has lots of dates and stuff. But I don't mind being alone. I'm a big girl. I can take care of Michael."

Jon's jaw clenched. Mel was *ten*. Too young to be left alone with her brother on that isolated patch in the Ozark hills. "But where's Gramma when your Mom's not home?"

Her gaze flew up, then back at her lap. "Don't be mad at Gramma. She's usually there, but sometimes she says 'Everything is just too much.' " Melanie had a talent for mimicry, and she'd nailed Dodo's tired voice. "Then she walks up the road to the judge's and asks him to drive her into church. Sometimes she goes to Bingo Nights."

"Tell me more about life at Gramma's."

The encouragement was like unleashing a flood. Her recitation made gooseflesh bump on his arms and turned his thoughts black. From what Melanie said, Belinda usually stopped short of physical abuse—mostly because Dodo was there or the kids were adept at hiding from her. But at any petty infraction—spilled milk, for God's sake—it seemed his ex-wife doled out punishments that ranged from withholding dinner to taking away their nightlights and scaring them with tales of monsters. According to Mel, Belinda was out all hours, Dodo went to bed early, and the kids were largely left with the TV for company—when Belinda hadn't taken away those privileges, too. When Dodo wasn't around, they didn't escape the occasional vicious backhand. One had apparently sent Michael crashing into a wall. Jon's mind fogged with rage. He glanced at Zeke's grim face.

"One time . . ." Mel stopped.

Jon's teeth had locked so tight he could hardly speak. He took a calming breath. "One time what, baby?"

"One night when Gramma went to bingo, Mommy locked us outside."

Zeke muffled a curse, and Jon shot him a look, afraid he'd spook Mel even more.

She looked up at him, her dark bangs tangling in wet lashes. "I'm not a baby. I know there aren't monsters, not real ones, but Michael doesn't." She hesitated. "There aren't monsters, are there, Daddy? I didn't see any, but maybe that's because Gramma came home and we weren't out there all night. It was cold, though. Icy."

Bright red anger blurred his vision. He pulled Mel close and she started to cry in earnest, her body curled against him. "No, there aren't monsters, but . . ." Sweet Jesus, he didn't know how to deal with this. "Some people can act like monsters, even mommies and daddies."

Like it had happened yesterday, he felt the crack of a belt across his back. His mother clung to his old man's arm, mewing, until he cuffed her across the mouth and she slammed to the floor. Only five years old, he'd had no power against his old man's towering rages.

This was surreal. It couldn't be happening, not to

his kids. He clasped Mel tighter. "Sometimes people get mad and do things they know are wrong. But, baby, I won't let you be scared again. Ever."

To hell with his agreement, to hell with joint custody, to flaming hell with Belinda! He might have driven the sweetness right out of her, but he wouldn't, couldn't, take responsibility for this. She could beat on him all she wanted and he'd take it, but he'd be damned if he'd stand around drowning in self-recrimination while she dished it out to his kids. And damn Dodo! Why hadn't she told him? His tumbling thoughts stopped short. Because either she didn't know, or Belinda had threatened her. Or, more likely, she thought he'd chalk it all up to the whining of an old lady, throw more money at them, and let things take care of themselves. It wasn't Dodo's fault. She'd done the best she could, and she *had* called him this last time. And, by God, it would *be* the last time.

He didn't care what it took, how many lawyers, how much dough, how much time—there was no way in this bloody lifetime his ex-wife would ever get her hands on the kids again. He'd call his attorneys, Judge Dougherty, and whoever the hell else could help him—and screw the tabloids.

No. His thoughts grew coldly clear. Not screw them, *use* them. He'd show Belinda. He'd take a page from her book and fight dirty this time. He'd drag her through the muck, just like she had him, until she was bankrupted by legal fees, her character shredded, her life destroyed . . .

Mel made a little mew of protest. "Daddy . . ."

He relaxed his grip. "Sorry, baby."

She shifted, then burrowed back against him, sighing as he stroked her hair. His dark thoughts skittered back under their rocks. He couldn't shove all the blame on Belinda. It wasn't her fault he'd ignored her when they were married, and it wasn't her fault he'd ignored the kids since they'd split. Destroying her wouldn't serve any purpose. The fallout would only hurt the kids . . . and the band. There had to be a better way.

A tattoo of drumbeats sounded against the glass doors. Zeke straightened like somebody had slapped him. Mel started.

Out on the deck, a tall drink of a woman bounced from one foot to the other like she'd better find a bathroom—soon. She looked like a ditchdigger. Mud clung to her knees, her puce blouse had come untucked from her jean shorts, dirt was smeared across her face, and her apricot hair radiated around her face in shock waves. Oh, God. The redhead.

She cupped a hand and leaned against the window to peer inside. Spotting him, her face lit up. She lofted something, her generous mouth forming words he couldn't hear. When he just stared, her smile turned to a scowl. She clobbered the door again.

Fans. His lifeblood, his nemesis, and this one was a crazy. Zeke recovered first and grabbed the drapery pull, shutting out the sight. The banging continued.

He edged Mel behind him on the sofa. "Roy!" he bellowed.

Swiping a forearm across his mouth, Roy barreled in from the kitchen. Planting himself flat-footed in front of the door, he slid it open a few inches and growled at the intruder.

"But I have a delivery for Mr. Van Castle!" The woman's voice, clear as cold water, penetrated the drapes.

Roy's voice rumbled, but she interrupted him. "Look, Shorty, I have been through absolutely *enough*. First it was the dunderheads at the front desk—thank God, I know the concierge—then I had to wade through a stream where I *completely* ruined my shoes. I have so many chigger bites, I'll be up every night for the next week scratching like a dog. I won't—absolutely will *not*—have you stand there telling me Mr. Van Castle is busy."

Both hands now gripped the draperies and yanked them apart, allowing determined blue eyes to peer at Jon over Roy's head. His gaze moved to the thing she waved at him. A book . . . The bookstore lady's sister. He sighed. "It's okay, Roy—let her in."

Roy stepped aside and the woman stumbled across the threshold. She righted herself and patted the top of Roy's bald head. "Thank you, little man."

Roy scowled. Dismissing him, she swiped at her dirt, then strode toward Jon. "Hello, Mr. Van Castle. I'm Mari O'Malley and I have a delivery for you."

Bemused, he stood up.

"Oh, good!" Mel clapped her hands. "Daddy—look what she brought."

Mari stooped and laid the book in Mel's hands. "So *this* is who ordered it. I didn't think some old geezer like your pop would want to read it, and I'd hoped it would end up with a pretty little girl like you." She pulled a scrap of paper and a pen from her pocket, and offered them to Mel. "Well, madam, I'm glad we have *that* matter straightened out. Now, would you please sign here?"

Mel giggled again, a fluttery, joyful noise, and her dark eyes sparkled. "I'm so glad you came. I've been wanting to read these books for ages and, you see, Daddy's books are kind of boring, so—" The end of Melanie's tongue poked out as she wrote her name on the receipt, a receipt he'd bet Mari O'Malley had hoped he'd sign.

He watched them and an idea bloomed. If she checked out and wanted to, why not? Tina-the-Nanny hadn't proved any great shakes at handling the kids and he hadn't seen Mel this alive since she'd got here. He smiled.

"So, I got here just in time. Good thing." Mari fingered the edge of Tom Clancy. "I saved you from having to read even one more page about—what?— submarines? Barf."

Mel grinned up at her and handed back the receipt. Mari riffled her hair, then turned blue eyes to Jon. *China blue eyes.* "It *is* a good thing, isn't it?"

He realized his gut no longer ached. "Sorry—I seem to have forgotten my manners. Something to drink, Miss O'Malley?"

Across the room, Zeke eyed him and stroked his beard.

Chapter 6

On the opposite end of the ribbon of water that wound through the hills forming Lake Kesibwi, Lil rummaged through the attic of her family's cabin amid the detritus left by four generations of her family. Nearby, her mother Zinnia prodded with a broom at some blankets just out of reach on top of a wardrobe. It was hot under the rafters, the air stale and misted by dust motes. The only light came from one overhead bulb and what could filter through a gauze of spiderwebs on the windows at either end.

Lil dipped into a cedar chest. "I wonder what's taking Mari so long?"

"Don't you worry, honeybunch." A quilt collapsed over Zinnia's curly salt-and-pepper hair. Her glasses had skewed sideways, and she plucked them off and stuck them in the breast pocket of her overall shorts. Her torso had plumped with age, but she still liked to show off the legs she'd bestowed on her taller daughters. "You know how our Mari is."

Lil wasn't worried about Mari. She was wondering if Mr. Van Castle had withstood the assault Mari had likely launched, despite strict instructions to just drop the book off.

Lil straightened with an armful of sheets. Her gaze fell on the flowered linens that had covered her bridal bed. Resolutely, she averted her gaze. "How many beds do we need?"

"Seven. These'll have to be aired out. We'll need four twins—Mari can bunk with Patsy Lee's three on the sleeping porch. And we'll do up three doubles. One for Pop and me, one for you, and one for Patsy Lee and Hen—" Her mother's easy humor crumpled. "Oh, Lil, sometimes I can't hardly breathe, I hurt so much."

Lil stepped toward her, but her mother sniffed and waved her away with a plump hand. "We're not going to mope. I won't have it. It'll be fun having all of you here once we get this business settled, and Henry'd want it that way. Now, let's get this done. Alcea and Stan'll be here any minute. They're bringing Patsy Lee and my grandbabies. Although I guess I shouldn't call them that anymore."

Zinnia's "grandbabies" spanned Alcea's ten-year-old Kathleen to Patsy Lee's three, Daisy, Hank and Rose, spaced two years apart. Rose, at five, was the youngest.

Lil hesitated. "From what Mari tells me, it won't be too long before you have a real grandbaby to hold."

Zinnia looked guilty. "Ah, Lil. I'm sorry I didn't tell you before. I just couldn't find the right time, what with all the worry we've had since Henry passed, God love him. I know how you must feel, honeybunch."

Lil picked up a blanket and shook it, sending up another cloud of dust. "The idea took a little getting used to." She didn't tell her mother she'd cried into her pillow the night Mari had told her. "But I'm happy for Patsy Lee, I really am. I just wish she didn't have so many money worries."

"We'll figure it out—that's what we're all here for."

Tires crunched on the drive. Moving to the window, Lil rubbed a hole in the grime. Beneath her in a clearing circled by woods, Pop puttered with the vining pink geraniums that spilled from pots on either side of the kitchen door. He held a battered watering can in his hand, and a fishing hat was perched on his head.

He straightened and waved. From under a canopy of trees, a minivan jostled along the red clay drive between sweeps of black-eyed Susans and daylilies Zinnia had planted eons ago.

Zinnia joined her. "There's our Alcea now."

Lil was surprised. Stan despised minivans. When Alcea had nagged for one to transport their daughter Kathleen, her friends, and all Alcea's committee supplies, he'd brought home a Lexus instead, then found excuses to drive it more than her.

Alcea, Patsy Lee, and the four children piled from the car. Stan wasn't with them. Alcea and Kathleen disappeared through the door. Patsy Lee and her brood swamped Pop with bear hugs. "What happened to their Lexus?"

"Well . . ." Zinnia's mouth twitched. "Alcea sank it in the fish pond a couple weeks back. She says she lost control, which I don't doubt a bit, one night when Stan was, uh, working late." Lil stared at her mother, who stared back. Zinnia added, "Alcea's teachers always said she was a creative problem solver."

Lil laughed. "I wish I could have seen Stan when she told him that car was full of pond muck."

"Lord love a duck, it must've been a sight. I don't think Stan'll be 'working late' for a while." Zinnia shook her head, eyes turning somber. "Not for a while. Poor Alcea."

"Yoo-hoo!" Alcea's voice rang out, and she appeared above the last riser, her usual proud expression in place on a face blessed by heaven, her gold hair twisted into a smooth knot. Two years older than Lil, she'd always been considered the most beautiful of the three O'Malley sisters with her molten brown eyes and patrician features. Kathleen, tall, slim, and blond, a twin of her mother at age ten, crowded behind her.

"Kathleen! You're pushing me, sweetheart."

"Sorry, Mother," Kathleen said, and took a step back.

"Well, come on." Alcea beckoned her forward with a manicured nail. "Can't you see your grandmother and aunt need our help?"

Irritation had become a part of Alcea's nature since her marriage. Lil exchanged a look with Zinnia, then helped her pile linens into Alcea and Kathleen's arms. Picking up her own bundle, she followed her mother and sister to the stairs.

"Patsy Lee is getting the children settled. That Daisy! If Kathleen talked to me like that, she'd be grounded for weeks. I brought you some salmon salad. It's in the refrigerator. I practically had to sneak it by Stan, he loves it so much. He says—" Alcea shouldered a fine sheen of sweat off her cheek. "Oh, who cares what he says? Lord, it's hot up here, Mother. I don't know why you and Pop don't install central air."

"Oh, we're not up here much, honeybunch. The unit downstairs suits us fine."

Behind them, Lil shook her head. After years of being Mrs. Stanley Addams III, Alcea had forgotten not everyone had her buckets of money.

They reached the kitchen. The one room had once comprised the entire original native stone cabin. Over the years, different O'Malleys had added rooms up and down and sideways until the structure now resembled a stack of books with log bookends on either side, all resting on a shelf that gave way to the wooded slope that led to the cove.

On the lake side off of the kitchen, the O'Malley men had built an odd-angled deck with a room below, screened in and lined with bunk beds. Lil's great-grandfather had added bedrooms and an attic on top of the original cabin. Her grandpop had contributed the plumbing and wiring. One bookend housed a low room heated by a wood-burning stove where they gathered to read, talk, and play Scrabble on rainy Memorial Day weekends. The other bookend contributed another two bedrooms and bath. Pop had built that end with Henry's help when Lil was in middle school.

The entire ramshackle result was furnished with castoffs, garage sale finds, and needlework from every O'Malley woman, including a half-hearted wall hanging Mari had stitched for Girl Scouts. Only sheer determination to get more badges than anyone else had seen her through. Patchwork pillows, curtains in primary colors, floral slipcovers, and table doilies were scattered throughout. Nothing matched, everything went together.

Just as in her parents' home on Maple Woods Drive, the heart of the place was the kitchen. When the deck was added, so were broad windows on the lake side, open to the dogwoods and redbuds that flowered in the spring, and now washing the room with light filtered by the trees that grew up through the deck.

The women crossed the hardwood floor, dumped their loads on a linoleum table pocked by long use, and started sorting sheets and blankets. The window air-conditioner rattled reliably, keeping the room tolerable. Trays of oatmeal raisin cookies Zinnia had baked that morning rested on the counter. The scent of cinnamon lingered.

"Stan said he can get you a deal on central air, Mother. Brisco's owes him a favor."

"Yes, Father said—" Kathleen piped up, snatching a cookie while her mother wasn't looking. Zinnia winked at her.

"Please, Kathleen, don't repeat me." Alcea frowned, but there wasn't any force behind her words. She plucked at a blanket. "Um, in case you're all wondering . . . Stan couldn't come. He wanted to, he really did, but he's just so busy at the bank."

Lil's hands stilled. Despite everything, she'd held out hope that Stan would agree to help Patsy Lee, but she should have known better.

Zinnia's face mirrored Lil's thoughts, but she said nothing. She piled sheets near the doorway that led to the bedrooms, plucked a straw hat off a hook, and plopped it on her head. Its faded pink ribbon fell between her eyes. "Well. We're all here then. I'll go get Pop and we can get started. We won't wait for Mari. No telling where that addlebrained child is, and I don't think she'd be a lot of help anyway. I'd wanted her to be here, though, and I'll tell her just that when I see her. Kathleen, honeybunch, you go on down to the sleeping porch with your cousins while we adults talk. Take some of those cookies and you and Daisy keep Hank and Rose busy with a game of Chinese checkers."

Minutes later, they were all seated around the table, except for Zinnia. After pointing them to their places, she busied herself pouring a pitcher of sun tea.

Pop had relaxed his tall bulk into a chair at the head. He sported a rumpled short-sleeved plaid shirt that in no way matched his equally rumpled green shorts, and he still wore his favorite hat, a few lures poked through its sides. In the past few months, new lines had etched around his mouth, but the fan of laughter at the corners of his eyes still dominated. His broad, callused hands, equally proficient at casting a line or changing a diaper, played with an unlit pipe as he waited for Zinnia. Stomach burbling with nerves, Lil still smiled. He might be at the head of the table, but he knew who ran the show. He looked around, caught her eye, and winked.

Zinnia's seat was reserved to his left, then Alcea, who'd served up a plate of cookies and placed a napkin just so in front of each person. The cookies were going untouched. Lil sat across from Zinnia's chair. Patsy Lee was lowering herself into the seat on her right. Lil knew the seating arrangement wasn't chance. She and Patsy Lee were in the "hot seats." Zinnia always liked to face the current targets of her maternal concern.

She clasped her hands, trying to hold back anxiety, and wondered how many of these confabs they'd had over the years. She also wondered exactly what Zinnia might propose at this one. Both she and Patsy Lee could use some ideas that ranged beyond PicNic, but curiosity warred with a sudden perverse streak that didn't want to do what anyone told her to do, whether it was good for her or not.

Patsy Lee sighed as her weight shifted off her feet. She leaned sideways to slip off her sandals and her length of brown hair almost brushed the floor, a gentle sweep, just like her voice. "It feels so nice to sit down."

Lil gave her a nervous smile. Resembling a bird with her wings of hair and round brown eyes, Patsy Lee had a plump robin's body, and she favored loose India print cotton dresses in the summer. It would be a while before her pregnancy really showed.

At Merry-Go-Read's closing sale yesterday, Lil had told Patsy Lee with all the sincerity she could muster how pleased she was about the baby. Patsy Lee had accepted her congratulations, her soft eyes glowing with gratitude at Lil's reaction. Lil was determined not to let any envy show.

Zinnia plunked the pitcher in the middle of the table, and took her seat. "Everybody ready?" Without waiting for an answer, she continued. "Henry, rest his soul, was a dear, dear boy, but I'm first to say he wasn't one for thinking any too far ahead. He's left Patsy Lee in a pickle. Two mortgages on their old farmhouse, a store up to its tutu in debt, three babies, another on the way, and no life insurance. Lil's also out of a job. Well, we've had problems before, and survived 'em, so let's see what we can work out of this mess. Your Pop and I have some ideas, but we'll see what you all are thinking first."

Everyone looked at the table.

Lil felt a flash of anger at her brother, followed by a wave of guilt. Even in her numbed state, when she'd first entered Merry-Go-Read as an employee, she knew the store was in trouble. Knew, but didn't much care. Henry had never had a head for business, or, for that matter, work. He'd stumbled through every job Cordelia had to offer, from flipping burgers to a stint at PicNic, where he'd met Patsy Lee.

After PicNic, marriage to Patsy Lee, and the births of their first two children, Henry got a job at Stan's bank. Henry couldn't balance a till to save his life. Stan had finally edged him out, lending Henry the money for the store and finding a clerical spot at the bank for Patsy Lee. She imagined Stan would have paid about any price to have Henry out of his hair.

Henry loved the store, the customers, the children, and even sweeping the front walk in tandem with Paddy O'Neill, but he still couldn't balance a till. Dipping into it had been his forte. If she was honest, though, she couldn't blame only Henry for Merry-Go-Read's demise, and the pot of trouble he'd left for Patsy Lee. Lil had seen what was happening, and had done nothing to stop it. She'd known he paid her an inflated wage, much more than her job was worth, but she'd never protested.

Sure, she suggested they offer gift-wrapping to pick up sales, and they did; delivery service, and they did. But when Henry balked at her ideas for a storytelling hour on Saturdays (saying it would interfere with fishing), and a monthly newsletter to their customers (because he'd rather spend evenings tinkering on his old Chevy), she stopped making suggestions. And she'd been relieved. Because even the idea of doing half those things had left her exhausted.

Face flushed, Patsy Lee finally spoke first. "Because we liquidated the inventory at the store and put the building up for sale, Stan's lowered the loan payment."

Alcea looked down at the table, and Lil wondered if Stan would do more.

Zinnia didn't just wonder. "So will your husband do anything more?"

Alcea glanced up, face pink, but chin high. "He said—he said to tell you he's had some business reversals lately and our portfolio isn't doing as well as he'd hoped and—and we have a lot of expenses, so . . ." Her composure cracked. "I did what I could, Mother, I really did. But he doesn't listen to me. He—" She broke off and pressed her lips together.

Zinnia's face softened. "I know you're having a rough time of it, honeybunch." Lil knew she wasn't talking finances. Alcea looked away.

"Really, Alcea, it's okay. What's happened isn't Stan's fault and I know he's doing what he can." Patsy Lee reached across the table and squeezed Alcea's hand. Lil moved restlessly. Sometimes Patsy Lee was too much like Melanie in *Gone With the Wind*. "When the building sells, I'll be able to pay off the bank loan and part of the second mortgage. In the meantime, well, I've—I've—" She faltered, then steeled her shoulders. Her next words came in a rush. "I've applied for the night shift at PicNic. I think I can get on since I worked there before, and I'm changing my hours to part-time at the bank. With food stamps, that'll be enough to get by." She looked from Pop to Zinnia and back. "That is, if you're willing to keep the children overnight during the week?"

"No." Zinnia slapped a hand on the table. The pitcher jumped, Lil and Alcea jumped, and Patsy Lee's mouth dropped open. Pop tried to hide a smile. "Real estate moves about as fast as a tortoise in Cordelia, so, much as you might want to, you won't be selling that building anytime soon. I'd have you move

in with us—heaven knows we've got plenty of room
in that old house—but your farmhouse wouldn't sell
none faster either—a big old rambling money pit,
that's what I told Henry when he bought the thing.
And there's still a matter of those two mortgages.
Whatever you'd get wouldn't cover both. Besides,
we'd be short a room with the baby, since Lil will be
using her old one."

Now Lil's mouth dropped open. She would?

"Then I—" Patsy Lee started.

"Then you'll just listen to me for a moment longer,
because there's no way I'm letting my grandbabies'
mama work her fingers to the bone. Not good for you,
and not good for the baby. And on food stamps? Not
while I draw breath. Lord love you, honeybunch, your
sweet spirit would wither away under the burden of it
all. No, no, there's a better way." Her fierce expression
wavered. She reached over and clasped her husband's
hand. "Pop and I—we've talked. I've decided—we've
decided—to sell this place."

Pop squeezed Zinnia's hand. They suddenly
looked old.

Patsy Lee, Lil, and Alcea all sat stunned. Sell the
Lake Kesibwi cabin? All three found their voices at
once and there was a chorus of objections, Patsy Lee's
the firmest.

When the noise died, Zinnia said, "It'll fetch a
whopping amount of money, and you three know it.
It's the only way, and, really, we won't miss it all that
much—why, we're hardly ever here anymore." What
she meant was their family was rarely there anymore.
Pop and Mother spent most of their weekends here.
They'd planned to retire here, too, once their grandbabies had grown up. The bravado in Zinnia's voice
didn't reach her eyes. She blinked rapidly behind
her glasses.

Lil tried to think of an alternative, but couldn't.

Nobody else appeared to have anything else to offer

either. Zinnia looked at each of them, then sighed. "No more long faces. We're blessed to have this place to sell, after all's said and done. Like I always say, when God hands you a lemon, you make lemonade."

The O'Malleys should have drowned in the stuff by now.

"Now, that's settled. As for Lil—"

Lil cleared her throat. "I'm not moving in with you. I—I appreciate your offer, but I'll think of something else."

Zinnia snorted. "Like PicNic? It seems everybody's stuck on that place all of a sudden. Honeybunch, I understand how you feel about that house of yours, but it's not worth hanging on to if it means doing that backbreaking labor. There *is* a market for small places not far from town. We'll put it up for sale, you'll move in with us, and continue giving piano lessons. This darned arthritis keeps me from sewing much anymore, but people still ask. I'm turning down paying business right and left. You can do that, too."

With a gigantic effort, Lil kept her face impassive. The picture her mother painted was tempting. She could move back into her room, let the days slide by, and not worry about anything beyond where to place the next stitch. But she couldn't do it. Not if it meant giving up her yellow house. "I—"

Mari banged through the door. Lil breathed a sigh of relief at the interruption.

"Where have you been?" Zinnia demanded.

Mari didn't seem to hear. She floated to the table, straddled a chair, and smiled dopily at nobody in particular.

"I take it you met Jonathan Van Castle?" Lil asked.

"Met him? I spent the day with him. With him, and Zeke Townley, and Three-Ring, and Jon's children . . ."

Zinnia stared at her. "Aren't we pleased you've had a humdinger of a good time while we've been trying to figure out how best to care for Patsy Lee and your sister."

"That's nice," Mari said.

Zinnia frowned. "Don't give me any lip. While you were out with your friends we've decided we have to sell this cabin. What do you have to say to that?"

"That's nice." Mari wore the same enraptured look Moses must have had when God handed him the tablets.

"Nice? You think that's—"

"I'm going to marry him." Mari swept the frozen table at large with a dazzling, ear-to-ear smile. Even Pop's mouth dropped open. "He proposed, and I said yes."

Chapter 7

Zinnia thunked the plate down. "You're going to what?"

"Marry Jonathan Van Castle."

"That boy you used to chase home in third grade? Why, he's—"

Pop cleared his throat. "Dear, I believe that was John Vandahlenberg."

"It was." Alcea's mask had slipped. She stared at her sister with an emotion akin to awe. "Jonathan Van Castle's a country singer."

An equally round-eyed Patsy Lee interjected, "Not a singer. A star. A superstar!"

Lil did an inner eye roll and said, "And somebody she just met six hours ago."

"And you think you're going to marry him? Why if that isn't the craziest . . . Marigold O'Malley, you've done some pretty foolish things in your life, but—" Zinnia sputtered.

"This is absolute nonsense," Alcea said. "I've read all about him in the *National Tattler* and—"

Five surprised pairs of eyes looked at her. All she displayed on her coffee table was *House Beautiful*. Alcea flushed. "It, uh, has some good recipes. Anyway, if the *National Tattler* can be believed, Mr. Van Castle is hardly a paragon of virtue. There was a huge scandal when he divorced his wife. Apparently he'd hooked her on drugs, then kept her dependent on him, so she wouldn't reveal what went on in their home."

"And what was that?" Patsy Lee breathed.

"Orgies. He had orgies. Three-ways, five-ways, every which ways." Alcea lowered her voice. "Some say he was involved once with a teenager. Can you believe it?"

Lil could. She already knew he was a deadbeat dad.

"That's not true. None of it's true!" Mari burst out. "I asked him, and he told me. That teenager was some groupie that hung around his ex-wife. He didn't even *know* her. He said that's only what *she* said, his ex-wife. What really happened was his ex got hooked on cocaine and their marriage was rocky and he didn't want to hurt her or his children anymore so he—"

"It doesn't matter what went on." Zinnia glared at her youngest. "This whole notion is just plain silly. You aren't marrying the man. Lord love a duck, you just met him, so of course you aren't." She peered closer. "You haven't been drinking, have you?"

"No, I haven't been drinking! And you can't tell me what to do. I'm twenty-one and I can do whatever I want to."

The argument raged for the next hour, a good six-oh on the Richter scale of O'Malley disputes. Her parents, sister, and Patsy Lee reasoned and railed until they were as winded as Paddy O'Neill after swapping scandal at Peg O' My Heart Cafe, but they didn't budge Mari. Only Lil sat silent. Part of her admired her little sister for taking a stand. The rest of her knew badgering Mari would only make her more stubborn.

Mari stood up. "There's nothing you can say that's going to make me change my mind. You can't live my life," she said to Zinnia, the same argument she'd been using since she was two. "And, you—" She sneered at her oldest sister. "You're just jealous because I'll have more money than you do."

"That's a lie!" Alcea stood up, too.

"Now, now—" Pop made a placating gesture with his hands.

Mari ignored him. "Only Lil understands, don't you, Lil?"

Lil opened her mouth, intending to tell her little sister that while she might understand, she certainly didn't condone her plans, but Mari continued before she could reply. "The *limo* is picking me up in a half an hour. If you'll excuse me, I have a date and I need to get ready." Nose in the air, Mari flounced to the doorway that led to the sleeping porch. "And tomorrow, Jon's *yacht* will pick me up for a day trip out on the lake."

"Good." Zinnia talked to her back. "Because I have a few things I want to say to Mr. Jonathan Van Castle."

Mari stopped in midstomp and twirled around. "Oh, no, you don't! I'm not going to have a swarm of goddamned—I mean, gosh-darned, sorry, Mother— spoilsport busybodies ruining my life. If any of you so much as says 'boo' to Jon, I'll—I'll leave tomorrow and you'll never see me again." She pivoted and ran down the stairs.

Zinnia looked around. "Well, if this isn't just a kick in the head."

Alcea had sunk back in her chair. Now she looked across the table at Lil. "You have to do something."

Lil stared at her. "Me?"

"Yes, you. You're the one who sent her off knowing she's gaga over him. And you're the only one of us who's met him before. So you're the one who has to talk to him."

"That's ridiculous. I only saw him in the store for a few minutes. It isn't as though we established a relationship."

Alcea and Lil bickered for the next fifteen minutes, and would have continued for another fifteen, if Pop hadn't raised a hand. "Alcea has a point."

"What?" Lil frowned at him.

"You're the only one who's met him, and you're the only one of us Mari isn't mad at. You need to go with her and find out what's really going on here."

"I agree," Zinnia inserted. "Something's not right. Why would a man like that just up and propose to our Mari?"

"Besides," Alcea said. "You're the only one Mari listens to."

"I can't see why he'd tell me," Lil said, although Alcea did have a point. Lil was the only one of the family Mari might heed, emphasis on the *might*.

Thinking of Jonathan Van Castle's heart-tugging smile, Lil wondered for an instant if she'd behave any differently if she were in Mari's shoes. Of course, she would. And, once a little time had passed, Mari would abandon whatever scheme Jonathan Van Castle had up his sleeve. Her sister might be impulsive and flighty, but she wasn't stupid.

She stood to clear the pitcher and cookie platter. "It doesn't matter what *we* decide. She won't take me with her. Mari has already said if any one of us—"

"So it's decided," Zinnia said. "You'll go."

"I didn't say I'd—"

"Shhh." Patsy Lee touched her arm. "She's coming!"

Lil sighed. She put the platter on the counter and heard Mari enter the room behind her.

Zinnia started in, her voice half sugar, half steel. "If you're so set on this, then—"

Lil turned, intending to set things straight, but instead her mouth just fell open.

Gone were Mari's T-shirt and sandals. What was left was a vision of young womanhood. Mari had donned an ebony over-the-hip satin blouse that emphasized her breasts, slim fitness, and porcelain skin, and a short—a very short—skirt. Dark hose outlined her shapely legs; one ankle was wrapped with a deli-

cate chain, and the legs ended in a pair of take-me-
I'm-yours spiked black high heels. Everything matched.
Her head was still topped by her usual riot of peach
curls, but she'd smoothed the sides up and back—with
gel?—securing them with silver-filigreed combs. From
her ears dangled the set of long sterling earrings her
parents had given her for graduation. And, worst of
all, Lil spotted black eyeliner, a coat of mascara, and
a dusting of powder that dulled Mari's freckles.

Lil's eyes narrowed. While she didn't think even
Mari had hoped for the offer she'd received, it was
obvious her little sister had planned ahead for a possible tryst. She looked beautiful and sophisticated and
stunning . . . and vulnerable and achingly young.
Alarm bells buzzed in Lil's brain. She *was* twenty-one.
But *only* twenty-one. Jonathan Van Castle would eat
her for lunch.

Mari frowned at her. "What?"

"Uh, nothing."

Zinnia met her youngest daughter's gaze. "Now, as
I was saying. I don't want this cockamamic plan of
yours to cause a big to-do. If you're so set on this
outlandish idea, why, we'll just have to meet him."

Her mother wasn't the type who put much stock in
how famous or rich a person was. She prided herself
as a fierce judge of character, and her children had
long grown resigned to her scrutiny of anyone who
crossed their paths.

Still, Mari opened her mouth, but Zinnia stopped
her with a raised hand. "I know the whole bunch of
us at once can be a lot to take in, so I can understand
why you don't want us swarming all over him tomorrow. Now Lil . . . Lil's already met him, so why don't
you just take her along—and maybe Daisy, if Patsy
Lee says its okay. Didn't you say he's got a daughter
about Daisy's age?"

Lil wondered why Daisy, then decided it was just
Zinnia's way of conducting covert operations. Extin-

guish any scent of possible suspicion Mari might cast on her request.

Mari's face lit up at her mother's reasonable tone. "Cool! I'll ask, but I'm sure he'll think it's okay, he's so nice. Lil, you're just going to love him."

That night, up in her bedroom, as crickets chirruped through the window she'd opened in a vain attempt to catch a breeze, Lil carefully rehearsed the speech she'd use on Mr. Van Castle. She had to revise it several times, feeling the words "cad" and "libertine" and "perverted" wouldn't bend him to her cause.

As she reached to turn off the light, she paused and stroked a finger over the photograph of Robbie she kept at her bedside. "Wish me luck," she whispered.

He smiled back.

Chapter 8

The Gibson houseboat glided into the cove where Mari O'Malley's family had their cabin. Jon stood at the bow and shaded his eyes. The cove was mirror-smooth under a sky still streaked with rose-petal dawn. Unlike the waters surrounding the Royal Sun, this side of the lake was quiet with long expanses of wooded shoreline. The high-powered crafts towing early-morning skiers across Shawnee Bay lay far behind, replaced by flat-bottomed boats with trolling motors. More than one fisherman had frowned at the rumble of the three-hundred-horsepower engines.

At the shoreline, Mari waved him in with a pinwheel of arms. She danced from one bare foot to the other, wearing nothing more than three scraps of turquoise that passed for a swimsuit. She looked like a nymph.

And last night she'd come on like a siren. He frowned. Evidence this wouldn't work. After dropping her off last night, he'd fallen into bed, exhausted by his efforts to fend her off. This morning he'd woken to regret yesterday's work. It hadn't taken Zeke's harangue—"Have you lost your friggin' mind, my man?" was the paramount theme—to convince him he'd made a mistake. And now he had to undo it. But first he'd let her enjoy the day. Payment for her time, so to speak. A story she could tell her grandkids.

Captain Sam, the fellow that came with the rental,

piloted the craft alongside a weathered two-hole dock. Mari leaped down a ramp from the shore. The dock held a battered bass boat, and a 1960-something Mark Twain runabout with tattered vinyl cushions. Captain Sam scrambled down from the helm to tie up. Jon tossed the end of another line to Mari.

She caught it and flashed him a smile. "I thought you'd never get here!"

He jumped down beside her. The dock pitched beneath his weight. "Good morning."

Mari almost quivered with excitement. He averted his eyes from the flesh jouncing above the half moons of her top.

"You bet it is!" She pushed her head his direction, and he realized her intention. He averted his face so her kiss landed on his cheek.

She didn't seem to notice. "Where is everyone?"

"Tina and the kids are down below changing into swimsuits."

She waved a hand. "I meant your band!"

"In the kitchen." Captain Sam frowned. "I mean, galley. Fixing Bloody Marys." Three-Ring, Zeke, Peter, and Lydia were shaking the day's party into gear. Fleetingly, he wished he'd left the kids behind, but he hadn't realized until they were underway how much booze Three-Ring had hauled on board—along with a keg of beer and a couple of babes who packed more jiggle than IQ.

Mari's gaze scoured the houseboat. "Awesome!" He didn't know if she meant the boat or the Bloody Marys or the band.

Captain Sam assumed she meant the boat. He tugged on his yacht cap. "One thousand square feet, ma'am. Three decks including the sun deck aft, plus the helm."

She shoved the rope into Jon's hands. "Here—you tie up. I'm just dying to explore this thing. Lil and Daisy should be along any minute." In a flash of turquoise fanny, she disappeared through the gate the captain opened along the side.

"Two bedrooms, two heads, a fully-equipped galley . . ." Obviously smitten by her enthusiasm, Captain Sam followed her.

Jon looped the line over a cleat and pulled it taut, hoping the weight of the craft didn't yank the rotting wood right off the barrels. What a mess. The dock was a mouthful of planks that looked like so many loose teeth. Gentle currents tugged at the boat, but to his relief, nothing splintered.

Last night Mari had related the hullabaloo he'd sparked in her family, and told him her sister and niece were intended today as some kind of emissaries. Still too filled with anger to think things through yesterday, he hadn't spared her family a thought, but now he shifted uncomfortably. His proposal probably hadn't surprised the bookstore lady. Lil. He liked the way her name rolled on his tongue.

Spikes of gold-tipped flowers waved amid lavender spires and lacy white things all the way from the water's edge up and along a path canopied by sycamores and oaks. Halfway up, a skinny boy, maybe seven or so, rocked in a glider. Even from here, Jon could tell the boy was watching him. And the boy wasn't alone. Through the leaves, he glimpsed a bulky house and angled deck. Flashes of color told him people were leaning over the railing.

Just then, a girl in a yellow-and-white-striped shirt, a towel unfurling behind her, whirled onto the dock. She stopped and stared at him, sides heaving. He smiled and she gave him an infectious grin back.

About Melanie's age, the youngster was a miniature clone of the bookstore lady—the same curly blond mop, the same long legs, and the same hypnotic blue eyes, which he'd decided must be a strong current in the O'Malley gene pool. Right now, hers were as round as the lifesavers strung along the houseboat.

They glittered with excitement and a load of lime eyeliner and eyeshadow. She looked like a tropical fish.

"Daisy, right?"

"Jonathan Van Castle, right?" Taking the sass out
of her reply, her grin grew broader, full of teeth she'd
yet to grow into. "Wow! Just wait until I tell the kids
at school." She pumped the hand he gave her with
enthusiasm, then pointed at the boat. "Can I—?"

He flexed his hand to make sure it still worked, and
nodded. "Your Aunt Mari is already on board."

"Wow!" Disdaining the gateway, she hopped the
boat's railing and scurried to the helm, where he
glimpsed Mari trying out the captain's chair. Captain
Sam hovered nearby.

Still conscious of eyes on him, he turned—and
sucked in a breath.

Standing above him in the drift of watercolor flowers, the bookstore lady—sweet Jesus, a real angel—
stared down. The sun struck her like a spotlight, turning her hair into spun silk and her skin into satin. His
gaze traveled up legs Tina Turner would kill for, lingered on soft, feminine curves covered by a modest
white swimsuit more alluring than Mari's bikini, and
settled on that heart-shaped face, its plump lower lip
nipped between her teeth. She knocked the wind right
out of his lungs.

Realizing he was gaping like a hooked fish, he
snapped his mouth shut. He thought of Sidney and his
constant harangue about his ears—although he didn't
think they were that big—and loosened the band on
his ponytail, letting his hair fall in waves past his
shoulders. He sucked in his stomach. Considering the
candy he devoured, it was still pretty flat.

He looked back at Lil and told himself to breathe.
She was flawless, made perfect by the slant of the
light, by the floral bounty that curtsied before her. . . .
He gave his head a shake. Good God. Too little sleep
and too much coffee. Disgusted, he yanked the band

out of his pocket and wrenched his hair back into its tail.

Her canvas shoes skirting the worst of the rotten planks, she approached him. The uncertainty he'd seen in her face had disappeared. Her eyes bored in on his like a pair of lasers, and the angelic illusion shattered. The bookstore lady was back, her face pruned into a frown and that luscious lower lip pulled thin. When he took her hand to help her onto the boat, she nodded up at Captain Sam, and called, "Good morning." To him, she said nothing. No need. Her eyes said it all. If looks could kill, he'd be a goner.

Jon followed her straight back—any straighter and she'd pop a vertebrae—to the open deck aft. Three-Ring, Peter, and his secretary held drinks bristling with celery sticks.

Lil's frown didn't lift, not even for Zeke, who took her hand and bowed slightly. "Ma'am." The coffee mug he held did get a look of approval.

Peter wiped his hand on blue creased shorts, and offered it to Lil with a "Nice to meet you." Jon frowned. There was no sign of the cell phone, Peter's hair was mussed, and there was a pink smudge on his mouth. Lydia murmured a greeting, and Jon saw Lil's gaze drop to Lydia's mouth. His secretary looked no-nonsense with her dark bob, navy swimsuit, and matching straw hat, but her lipstick was smeared.

Sweeping off a water-stained Stetson that tamped down muddy-blond hair, Three-Ring loped up to Lil and pumped her hand. The shorts riding low on hips as narrow as his bare chest threatened to slip. "Hey, what's happenin'?" The three earrings on his ear glinted. Lil looked bemused.

During the introductions, Three-Ring's two "dates" hadn't stirred from their lounge chairs. Displaying more curves than the road between here and Cordelia, they greeted Lil with a toss of blond tresses. One slanted her eyes at Jon, although he'd never laid eyes on her before this morning. Lil's face pinched. He flushed, bugged that he cared what she thought.

"Lil! You have to see this." Mari hurtled up the four steps from the main cabin, grabbed Lil, and hurtled back, nearly bowling down Daisy, who'd followed her up.

Daisy looked at him questioningly. Winking, he took her hand, and they followed Mari and Lil below. Wrapped with windows, the main cabin held a galley and a living room lined with padded benches, some easy chairs, and a table. Mari bubbled with excitement, arms flying as she pointed every which way. "This must cost an arm and a leg!" She swept by Mel. His daughter curled like a cat on one of the benches. She sucked a strand of her hair, her everpresent book in hand.

"Hi, sweetums," Mari said. "Whatcha reading?" Mel gave Mari a shy smile, and opened her mouth. But before she said anything, Mari was off again, running her hand over the keyboards Zeke had set up. "Isn't this unbelievable, Lil?"

Hair curtaining her face, Mel dipped back to her book, but not before he saw her disappointment. He frowned. If he'd needed more proof Mari was a poor choice, he'd just received it.

Abandoning the instrument, Mari traipsed down some steps to the lowest deck. "And down here—" Her voice got lost in the thrum of the engines as they revved to pull away.

"—are some bedrooms and bathrooms. Heads, they call them." Jon finished for her.

"Very impressive," Lil murmured in a tone that said she wasn't impressed at all. Her gaze softened as she looked at his daughter. She settled next to Mel. "May I see?"

Mel glanced at her. Apparently reassured the lady with the gentle voice didn't plan to disappear, she turned the book so Lil could see the cover. A thumb hooked into the bottom of her swimsuit, Daisy stayed by Jon's side.

"*Little Women,*" Lil read. "One of my very special favorites—I especially like Beth."

"Me, too. But it's so, so sad when she dies. I cried," Mel confided. "Did you?"

"Of course. Do you remember when I read it to you, Daisy, and we cried buckets and buckets?" She held out a hand and Daisy sidled over to them. "This is my niece, Daisy O'Malley. Daisy, this is—"

"Melanie. Everybody calls me Mel mostly."

Daisy wrinkled her freckled nose. "Mel Mostly?"

Mel's walnut eyes lit with laughter. "No, silly. I meant, most people call me Mel."

"Oh. Do you really read big books like that?"

Mel nodded.

"Cool! I can't. I mean, I've never tried. I play baseball, though. And soccer. Do you? Maybe when I'm ten, I'll read more. That'll be soon. My birthday's August sixteen. How old are you?"

"Ten."

"No way! I'm yards taller than you. My dad just died."

"Oh. That's awful." Mel paused for a beat. "My parents are divorced."

"That's awful, too." Daisy perched on the other side of Mel, and glanced back at Jon. "But it must be awesome having a famous dad."

Mel shrugged. "Do you always wear that stuff on your eyes?"

"Sure."

"Daisy . . ." Lil interrupted.

"Okay, okay." Daisy gave a long-suffering sigh. "Mom only lets me wear it on weekends. You should try it. With your brown eyes, I think Morning Sky would be the best color for . . ."

Under their combined attention, Mel's shyness faded like the last chords of a dirge. He gave Lil a grateful look, but she missed it because her eyes never left the kids' faces.

"Hey-yaa!" Michael flew from the top step on the sun deck and landed in a wide stance in the doorway, ready to one-two any enemies that might crawl out from under the cushions. Tina-the-Nanny fluttered behind him.

He ruffled Michael's bowl-cut brown hair. "This Kung Fu Kid is my son, Michael. And this is Tina, their nanny." Michael punched a foot in the air, narrowly missing Tina's knee. "Watch it, bud, somebody's going to get hurt."

"Hurt," Michael affirmed, then warbled the stuck-on-me Band-Aid jingle.

"He may watch a little too much TV," Jon murmured.

Lil nodded at Tina, then turned to Michael. "Let me guess. Are you Tum-Tum or Colt, or maybe Rocky? Tum-Tum, I'd bet, because his real name is Michael."

Michael's arms dropped to his sides and he, along with Jon, goggled at Lil with deep almond eyes. "*You* saw *Three Ninjas?*" Michael breathed.

"Only about four dozen times. I have a nephew, you see."

"Nef-U? Is that like a Tee-Vee?"

For the first time he saw Lil smile. A slow smile of pure delight, beginning with a tug on one corner of her mouth and spreading across her face until a single dimple appeared. His heart squeezed.

"No." She gave him a gentle poke in the tummy. "He's a little boy—like you."

Michael clambered up beside her. "How old is he?" he demanded. "Do you like Jackie Chan?"

"Hank is *real* old. He's seven. And, yes, I like Jackie Chan."

"Me, too." Michael nodded, expression serious.

"Hank's a *big* boy." He held up four fingers. "I'm five. But I'll be six soon. On August—August—"

"Seventeen," Mel supplied.

"Really?" Lil's eyes went wide in exagerrated amazement. "Why Hank's sister, Daisy—this is Daisy—has her birthday only one day before yours."

"Way to go!" Daisy gave him a high five and Michael grinned.

Mari bounced back into the room. "I'm going up to the whatchacallit—the place where you drive this big sucker. Do you think that guy would let me drive?" She darted up the steps and, reluctantly, Jon followed. It was a kick listening to the kids; he wished he could be as easy with them as Lil. When he glanced back, all four of them were bent over Mel's book while Lil read aloud. She paused and met his gaze.

Hers turned to frost. "I'd like to speak to you later," she said. "Privately."

Oh, he'd like to get private with her, too.

By one o'clock, the party rocked on the aft deck. The babes' squeals and giggles punctuated the sizzle of guitars on the stereo. The keg was half gone.

Up by the helm, Jon slouched in a canvas chair shaded by a canopy. A hot breeze lifted his hair. Zeke sat in a chair beside him, ankle crossed over his knee, a loafer dangling from his toes. Every so often, they'd trade some chat with Captain Sam. Jon faced rear to keep an eye on the party. He told Sam he'd yell if somebody fell in the drink, but privately thought he'd enjoy seeing them all swept off in the boat's wake.

He'd retreated to Sam's lair when the party nonsense had made his head ache, and found Zeke already there. He'd like to go below and join the kids, except that pair of cold blue eyes spooked him.

He swished the melting ice cubes in his tumbler of tea, plucked a Tootsie Roll Pop from his pocket and shoved it in his mouth, then looked across the sun deck where an acre of skin baked.

As the keg had gone down, the temperature had gone up, but they all seemed oblivious to the heat, even Peter, who'd long ago shed his last hang-up. Pink blotches bloomed on his shoulders. Her hat askew, Lydia (normally prim as Amy Vanderbilt) sat on his lap, keeping up a stream of giggles punctuated by an occasional very unladylike snort. Maybe he was working them too hard.

The two brown-bodied blondes had lost any semblance of modesty, straddling the lounges with no thought about thong swimsuits. Their hair color wasn't natural.

Weaving unsteadily, Three-Ring untangled himself from a chair between the blondes and made his way toward the steps down to the cabin. He looked up and gave them a sloppy grin. "Refill, anyone?"

Jon shook his head, then cocked an eyebrow at the blondes. Even for Three-Ring, they were a tad crude.

Three-Ring's teeth flashed. "One of them reads Kerouac," he said as though that explained everything. He ducked his head and disappeared through the doorway.

"Kerouac?" Jon asked Zeke.

"Amazing they read at all, isn't it?"

That's not what he'd meant. He didn't know Three-Ring read Kerouac. Although he'd known the drummer since his early days in Nashville, every time he thought he had a handle on him, the man threw him a curve.

The three permanent members of Van Castle melded harmonies on stage, but with women, each flew solo. Zeke had been true-blue for six years to a lawyer in Nashville. Three-Ring was between women. Three-Ring was always between women. As for himself . . .

He'd made a bad husband, but he'd always been faithful. He didn't know if that was due to morals, or a lack of time. None of the women Peter had lined him up with had tempted him into a fling, and a more serious relationship was out.

Monkhood didn't suit him. Neither did mindless screwing. However, given the surge in his pants this morning as he'd watched Lil posed above him, maybe it was time he . . .

A sudden thunk against the side of the boat raised Zeke's eyebrows and had Jon on his feet, peering over the side. Mari teetered along the gangway. Spotting him, she saluted him with her cup, sloshing half its contents into the drink.

"Kids're A. O. Kay. Just checked on 'em," she called. She stumbled and thudded into the side of the boat, then bounced toward the water.

Zeke blinked. "Thank God for railings. Still think she'd make a good mommy?"

"Quit rubbing it in. You were right, okay?"

"As usual."

"The idea isn't a bad one. It was the choice that was wrong."

Zeke's loafer stopped wiggling. "You don't mean you're going to—"

"Look—" Jon glanced at Sam, but the captain was intent on his driving. He lowered himself back into the chair, lowered his voice, too. "Any judge in the country is going to take a look at my life, and Belinda's, and decide it's a toss-up where the kids should land. You know they favor the mother. I can holler abuse, which I will—but I don't know if what she's done qualifies. Besides, what can I offer? Money, yeah, but a home I'm never in? And Dodo's worn out. Who would run it?"

"Take Belinda on and she'll trot out all those old lies. Especially one."

"You mean Gabby Groupie or whoever the hell she was? No, she won't. She knows she'd kill the fatted calf."

"I believe the stage name is now Glory Galore. Charming. But I think you're wrong about our Miss Belinda."

"Look, Belinda's going to stay clean for the next eight months. You can bet on it with this much dough at stake. Custody will revert to joint, and she'll haul the kids back to Monaco before I can blink. I find them a mom now, while I have sole custody, there's more of a chance they land in my ballpark. I'll only ask a couple of years from the lady. After that, she can walk away one rich woman."

"You're messing with someone's life, Jon."

"Won't be the first time, will it?"

Zeke sighed, but didn't respond. Jon stifled his conscience. He'd make a business arrangement, pure and simple. Nobody's affections involved, he wouldn't be able to break any hearts. "Think of the band, then. Belinda's going to wage a battle in the media. She won't drag out lies, because she saw what almost happened last time, but she will do the whole I'm-Gidget-He's-Lucifer act. Belinda was the press's darling the last time, and you can bet she'll prime her image again. I can play the same game. With a June Cleaver at my side, I'll smell like a rose. We'll be a shoo-in at the CMA Awards this fall. Even Judge Dougherty likes a winner. Plus, Peter'll wet his pants." He looked down at the group. "If he hasn't already."

Peter wore a goofy grin as he watched Mari toddle onto the deck. Jon didn't know how many beers she'd guzzled—he'd stopped counting at six.

He grimaced, and, guessing his thoughts, Zeke murmured, "Brings back some memories, hmm?"

"Nothing I care to recall."

He'd been a teen rebel when he'd cut and run from Monaco without a glance back, not even at Belinda.

By that time, she'd latched on to some kid with a cherry '67 Mustang, and it was aloha, Jon. In Nashville, he'd cowritten ditties with Zeke, played backup for two-bit bands in smoke-filled honky-tonks, waited for his break, and partied. Hearty.

Then one morning he woke up in some dump beside someone he didn't recognize, and realized he was following the Brumley tradition. He was drunk, getting mean, and, if he didn't watch out, he'd soon to be on the dole, just like his old man. Not him, he'd decided. Not Jonathan Van Castle. Except for the occasional cold one, he'd renounced booze right there and then, and thrown himself into his ambitions. But he'd still had a live and let live attitude about anyone else's choices, until Belinda had crossed the line.

The boat bobbed over a wake. Mari tripped and landed in Three-Ring's lap. Her guffaws clamored over the music. Disgusted, he turned his gaze to the shore sliding by.

Nope, she wouldn't win Mom of the Year.

During the morning, it was Lil who had corralled Michael and sweet-talked him into a game of Go Fish with herself and the girls. When they anchored to swim, it was Lil who had buckled the kids into life jackets and kept a tight leash on Michael. At lunchtime, it had been Lil again. After the kids yowled at the iced shrimp Tina set in front of them, Lil had rummaged through the galley and emerged to applause with peanut butter and jelly.

If only Mari was more like her sister.

She fascinated him, this bookstore lady, with her perfect posture, her distant manner, her come-kiss-me lips that clamped together in a tight-assed line, at least while he was around. *China blue eyes . . . Such a surprise . . . Face full of secrets, tell me no lies?* Argh.

Face full of secrets was right. Earlier he'd sought Mari out under the pretext of wanting to know her better, but really curious about Lil. They'd sat on the bow, forearms on the railing, legs dangling over the froth of water sliding under the boat. The liquor had made Mari obligingly loose-lipped.

"How'd her husband die?"

"Car accident. Poor Lil. Almost killed her, too. They'd been together since they were kids. Played dodge ball and kick-the-can in our backyard. Y'ever play it?"

He ignored the question. Except for Belinda, he'd never had playmates. They were too scared of his old man. "They marry young?"

"Right outta high school. Then they went to college, or rather, *Robbie* did. Oh, she took some classes, but she wasn't all that interested. Mostly waited tables and taught piano, which is a damn shame." Mari swung her head in maudlin sorrow.

"Lots of women put their husbands through school or the other way 'round."

"But she's so *smart*; she could've done anything she wanted. But all she wanted was wifedom and babies and a life in Cordelia, the dummy. So, he brought her back and bought her a house and painted it yellow, not a yucky yellow, a nice pale, pretty yellow, and not because it needed it, but just because it was Lil's favorite color. The way she acted, you would have thought he'd bought her the moon. They were always all over each other. It was kinda sweet—when it didn't 'bout made you want to puke."

Jon wondered what it would be like to love like that.

With the lightning recovery powers of the very drunk, Mari zipped from despair to perky. She drained her beer, and flashed him a smile. "Oh, well. Tha's life. I'm going below for another—want one?" She'd stumbled off, and he'd sighed. His idea *was* insane. At least the one featuring Mari O'Malley.

Glancing at her now, he rolled the lollipop into his other cheek and checked his watch. He'd give them two more hours—if Mari didn't pass out first—then he'd smother this party with the proverbial wet blanket, and haul them all home.

Pitching the stick into an empty sack, he tipped the edge of his tea tumbler at Zeke and Sam. "I'm going below. Want more?"

Zeke shook his head, but Sam handed over his cup and Jon loped down to the cabin. He'd ring Mari tomorrow, after she'd sobered up, and tell her the deal was off. He'd ask Lydia to find her some kind of gift to soften the blow.

He twisted the latch on the cabin door, stepped inside, and halted.

Alone, Lil played the keyboards. Chopin. Her scent, the honeysuckle he remembered at the bookstore, floated through the cabin. Those beautiful hands wandered the keys, long fingers with nails unpainted, trimmed short, and smoothed to follow the pink curves of her cuticles. The music washed over him.

She glanced up and stopped.

Moving into the cabin, he waved a hand. "Keep going."

After a moment's hesitation, she obeyed.

Tea forgotten, he crossed to a bench. Through the window, he caught sight of Michael's bare feet planted on the fiberglass, one leg kicked skyward. Jon smiled, then turned his back and settled against the cushions, hooking an ankle over his knee.

Outside, Michael yelled, "Cowabunga!" Inside, Lil's gaze stayed on her hands. A few curls wisped over a knit brow, and her lashes cast a shadow on flushed cheeks. He toyed with his ponytail and listened with a critical ear. He'd give her major points for technique, but while the chords resonated with melancholy, soothing and lovely, the whole effect was too uptight. She'd be better if she'd loosen up.

She sounded the last note, dropped her hands, and pinned that unbelievable blue gaze on him. For a moment their eyes linked in appreciation of the old master. He felt a stirring at the back of his mind, gentle and soothing, curling like tender shoots out of the ashes of his damaged boyhood. Impatiently, he yanked them out before they took root. This woman was far too . . . good . . . to survive what he'd do to her. If she'd even let him close enough to do it.

With a tug, he dropped the ponytail, and cast for thoughts in his shaken brain. "Lil. Is that short for something? Lilith, maybe? Lila?"

"It's short for Lilac."

Childhood images of dappled spring mornings full of promise and the delicate aroma of dainty lavender flowers wafted through his head like the perfume she wore. But, in those days, spring never stuck around for long and those promises were dashed against reality. He linked his hands behind his head and leaned back, his eyes still bound with hers. "Pretty. It suits you, but I don't think I've ever heard of anyone named Lilac."

"It could have been worse. It might have been Spiderwort." A hint of that gut-clenching smile appeared, and her eyes shone as clear as a cloudless day. A guy could bask in those eyes forever.

"Spiderwort?"

Then she did smile, that heartbreaking, heart-stopping, slow smile, and the tendrils started wending their way up again. "It's a custom of sorts. All the women in the family are named after flowers—except Kathleen, my oldest sister's daughter. That sister is Alcea—that's the formal name for the hollyhock flower. You've met Daisy. My mother is Zinnia—and I have another niece named Rose. She's Daisy's sister."

"And Mari?"

"Short for Marigold."

He reached for a bowl of M&M's on the coffee table, and tried to distract himself from the feelings she stirred in him. The name thing was a little too cute, but still it touched a chord of regret in him for what never was. "Nice tradition. I have no idea where my own first name comes from. The last name I got from a phone book on my way to Nashville." Two reasons: Jonathan Brumley would have looked stupid on the marquee at the Grand Ole Opry, and he didn't want to share the same name as his old man.

As for his own two kids, no tradition or family ties there. Belinda had slapped the names on their birth certificates before he'd ever seen them. Munching, he considered Lil again. "Alcea, Lilac, and Marigold."

The smile fled, like the sun had scampered behind a cloud. "And speaking of Marigold, we need to talk. I don't know what you think you're doing, but . . ."

He didn't hear her. He'd zoned out on her eyes, marveling at how they changed from the transparent shimmer of a crystalline lake to the coldness of its depths, all in seconds.

"My family and I have discussed this. In fact, we've discussed little else since yesterday. And we're asking you—" White spots appeared on the knuckles of her clasped hands. "*Begging* you—to call off this—this arrangement. Mari is too immature to know what she's doing. 'Restraint' isn't a word in her vocabulary. You've seen how she's handled one day of this craziness. What do you think a couple years of it would do to her? For God's sake, we read all about your exploits. My older sister looked you up on the Internet. Is that what you do for sport?"

Still hooked on those eyes, he repeated, "For sport?"

"Marry young women, feed them drugs, and watch while they ruin themselves? Or is it just the *teenaged* ones you prefer?"

That hit a nerve and his reverie snapped. He sat up, leaned forward, reached for the candy, then changed his mind and cracked his knuckles. "You shouldn't believe everything you read."

"You've seen how Mari's acted today. She can't handle your lifestyle." She made "lifestyle" sound like a dirty word.

He felt his face grow hard and hot. He started to tell her he'd come to the same conclusion, but stopped as her eyes shot wide open. She bolted for the stairway, nearly knocking over the keyboard. He gaped as she hurtled through the door and left it hanging.

Stung and bewildered, he stood up. Through the door, he heard yelling topside. The throb of the engines and the music went dead. He turned and peered out. The lake, placid, calm . . . then a flash of legs, Lil's legs, past the window. He heard a splash.

"*There!* He went down right there!" Captain Sam roared.

Jon leaped up the stairs, his heart crowding his throat. Bursting from the cabin, he rushed port where everyone stood along the railing staring at the water. Only Three-Ring's grip on Mari's arm kept her body upright. From the bow of the boat came the babble of girls' voices, high with excitement, and Tina's shrill "Hush!"

From the helm, Sam twirled a life preserver in a loop, then zinged it over the lake. It arced in the still, humid air and plopped in the water, fifteen yards from the boat, where it bobbed, undisturbed. Without missing a beat, Sam grabbed a float and leaped after it.

Jumping on one bare foot, ripping a loafer from the other, Zeke grasped Jon's shoulder to steady himself. His face was white under his tan. "Michael." He uttered the one word, grabbed a ski belt, and dove over the side.

Mind numb, Jon stared after Zeke. Except where Zeke and Sam churned water, the lake lay still and silent, a flat silver disc in the high sun. He shivered. *Michael!*

Near the life preserver, a head broke the water. Not the gleaming brown head he'd hoped to see, a blond one. Lil. She gulped in air, then dove again with a flash of white rear and a powerful kick. The sight broke his paralysis.

Tearing off his sandals, he grabbed another preserver, and launched himself over the railing. Adrenaline roared in his ears. Each heartbeat held a thousand nightmares. He pumped past Zeke. Lil broke the surface again. This time, this time, thank God, two heads appeared.

Michael's head lolled and Lil struggled to keep his face up, going under herself. With a powerful sweep, he thrust his life preserver toward her. She snagged an arm over, keeping Michael afloat, and sucked in air. He reached them at the same time Sam did and they heaved Michael's body over Sam's float. His thin limbs drifted like a starfish's.

Without pausing, Sam turned him on his side, releasing a trickle of water from Michael's mouth, then flipped him back, and began mouth-to-mouth. Zeke swam to Lil's side, where he shoved half his ski belt under her free arm, then clung to the other half.

Jon continued to tread water, steadying himself with one hand on the life preserver, the other smoothing the hair back from Michael's forehead. His eyes caressed his son's face, seeing, as if for the first time, the generous black lashes that spiked from his closed eyes, the blue veins under his translucent cheeks. They poufed in and out as Sam breathed life into his lungs.

As Sam caught his breath, Jon studied Michael's mouth, the mobile mouth that stretched in a yell or an uproarious laugh, that now, as in sleep, fell into the pouty lines of childhood. Sam pinched Michael's upturned nose and renewed his efforts. Michael's thin chest rose and fell, each rib a stair step to the sweet cleft of his navel. He marveled at the perfection of his son. His son.

Michael had to live.

He gripped the tube tight, closed his eyes, and

willed Michael to breathe. Willed life back into his son.

He opened his eyes and met Lil's gaze. Her face was pale, her lower lip trembled, and he lost himself in the depths of her eyes, naked eyes, washed violet with emotion. Eyes that held heartrending pain and fathomless understanding, eyes that shared his anguish, his hope, his torment, his love for his son.

He blinked, and when he looked again, her eyes were again pale blue—and shuttered. And he wondered if he'd only imagined that communion of souls.

A sudden splutter, and Michael coughed. Sam tipped him on his side. Michael threw up in the lake and moaned. His eyelids fluttered. "Daddy?"

Joy mushroomed in Jon's chest and burst out in a sob. He flung an arm over Michael's shoulders and held tight, not bothering to hide his tears. Zeke let out a whoop and sent a thumbs-up toward the houseboat. The group along the railing erupted in cheers, sweeter music to his ears than any roaring crowd he'd ever heard.

Chapter 9

The day following Michael's near drowning, Lil worked in the early morning quiet of her mother's garden along the cabin's graveled drive, a circle path hollowed out through the dense woods. Birds chirped around Pop's feeders, and honeybees droned over black-eyed Susans. Relentlessly, she clipped dead leaves and pulled up bindweed, moving toward the road until the oaks completely hid the cabin. Except for Mother and Pop, the rest of the household slept. Her parents had gone into the nearby village for groceries. Mother had planned a family picnic for tomorrow. Lil grimaced.

Shoving the clippers into the gardening belt at her waist, she straightened and swiped her forearm across her face. She wore only her swimsuit, terry-cloth shorts, and canvas gloves, but already the curls at the back of her neck were damp. She still felt chilled whenever she thought of yesterday.

Shivering in a towel, she'd watched along with the others as Jon had tenderly laid Michael on a bunk in one of the bedrooms. After sitting with Michael until he fell asleep, he'd turned to Sam to make arrangements to get them all back to shore.

Three-Ring, sobered as he hadn't been all day, had clapped an arm around Jon's slumped shoulders and murmured to him in a low voice, comforting him.

Now, as then, Lil felt a flash of anger. She bent,

yanked up a dandelion, and flung it toward the woods. The man didn't need comfort, he needed a new brain.

At the time, she'd turned away without speaking her mind, only to encounter Zeke's level gaze. From the way his eyes had penetrated hers, she knew he'd guessed her thoughts. She'd started to follow Daisy and Melanie to the upper deck, but had stopped when he'd touched her arm.

Of all the adults on board this ship of fools, Zeke had seemed the most sane. He'd watched the day's antics with those alert but tolerant black eyes, and she'd appreciated his easy camaraderie with the children. More than once, he'd offered a distraction to keep the three entertained—and away from the drunks on the sun deck. It hadn't escaped her notice that he and Jon (and Sam) were the only ones not knocking back drinks like popcorn. In fact, until Michael went overboard, she'd softened considerably toward Jon Van Castle. He hadn't exhibited any of the wild tendencies she'd read about, and she'd decided most of it was gossip. His children obviously adored him, which said something. As the day had passed, her hopes that Jonathan Van Castle would see reason had risen.

Glancing at Michael, Zeke had kept his voice low. "That was quite a piece of heroism back there. You saved Michael's life." He paused. "Don't be too hard on him. He does care. A lot."

She tried to keep her voice as reasonable as Zeke. "He's all concern for his children now. Now when it's almost too late. If I hadn't seen Michael fall off . . ." She shivered. Stupid man. Stupid, stupid man. "A simple life jacket could have saved us all a lot of grief. He should have insisted the children wear them. He should have—"

She stopped, remembering the devastation on Jon's face as they'd treaded water while Sam breathed life into Michael. For an instant, his agony had been tangible, a black and bruised tornadic emotion that had whorled between them and sucked her into a maelstrom of reliving her own past anguish.

Shoulders slumping, she faced facts. *She* should have insisted on life jackets when he hadn't. She blamed him because it hurt less than blaming herself. Blaming him was easier than facing the eruption of emotions Michael's near-drowning had brought her.

"He should have," Zeke agreed. "But he doesn't make mistakes because he doesn't love them. He makes mistakes because he's not used to being a father."

She couldn't resist. "And whose fault is that?"

Zeke leaned against the jamb, and regarded her a moment. She dropped her gaze, knowing she'd sounded shrewish.

"His, partly. His ex-wife's, mostly. Ask him and he'd say it was all his fault, although I personally don't think a man should be blamed for growing up without an example to follow. His old man was a total loss in the fatherhood department."

Strangely, she'd wanted to ask Zeke more about Jon Van Castle, but at that point, Michael had made a mewling sound. "Something to think about anyway," Zeke had said, his voice mild as he'd turned toward Michael.

Nearing the exit to the road, Lil yanked up another weed. At the opposite end of the drive, she heard wheels crunch on gravel, and the slam of a door. Her parents were home. Half-hidden in the brush, she didn't turn around to wave a greeting. She wasn't pleased with them either. While she was sorry about Michael, she'd been happy the near-disaster had called a halt to the day's "fun," even though (maybe especially because) she hadn't finished talking to Jon about Mari. But now they'd roped her into trying again tomorrow when Mari would trot Jon out at the family picnic. The affair was her mother's idea, a ploy to give Lil another opportunity. A still-tipsy Mari had embraced the idea wholeheartedly and had arranged things last night with Jon's business manager, who'd been none too sober himself.

Lil snorted, pulled out her clippers, and slashed at a patch of dead iris leaves. The man had someone to do everything for him. She wondered if he hired an assistant to wipe his—

A hand tapped her hip. She bolted straight up, dropping the clippers, and her head bashed into something hard. She heard a gasp of pain and whipped around to see Jon Van Castle tearing up and rubbing his nose.

Surprised, she took a step back, stumbled, and would have fallen if he hadn't reached out to grab her shoulders. "Hey, steady there."

For a moment they stood one step apart, his head only inches from hers. The flecks in his eyes shimmered in the sunlight. His hair, as light as Robbie's had been dark, fell straight and thick like a gold curtain. Her breathing grew shallow. Afraid to look into those eyes for reasons she couldn't explain, she stared instead at the tanned V bared by the button-down shirt he wore tail-out over shorts, sleeves ripped off at the shoulders. Staring at the hard muscles of his chest didn't help her catch her breath.

His sheer physical magnetism was overpowering. When she'd first seen him lashing the boat to the dock yesterday, she'd been mesmerized by the hard ridges of his back aglow with the sheen of sweat. His muscles had bunched as he'd tugged on the mooring line, and her tongue had stuck to the roof of her mouth. Well, why wouldn't it? He hadn't become a superstar because he looked like a toad.

Suddenly restless, she met his gaze. His eyes were soft, serious. His hands still lay on her shoulders, fingers long and warm against her bare skin. Her muscles shivered, then relaxed. Only Robbie's touch had ever been so . . . well, loverlike, but this was different. This was— Warmth blossomed in her belly. She realized she was leaning into his hands.

Annoyed at herself, she stepped out of his reach. "You scared me."

His eyes flashed, then grew still. But he only bent and picked up the clippers. Handing them to her, he said quietly, "I'm sorry. Is there somewhere we can talk?"

Without a word, she turned and led him to a crumbling concrete bench a few yards away in a copse of dogwoods. She settled on one end and put the clippers on the seat right next to her. His mouth twitched, and he settled further away. The bench was chill under her legs, and she wished something would cool the heat in her face. She turned toward him, but carefully kept her eyes away from his eyes, the V of his shirt, and the smooth muscles of his bare thighs.

He motioned toward the cabin. "Roy drove me over. I wanted to talk to Mari—"

"She's still asleep. When she wakes, she'll be hungover." Her voice held accusation, even though she knew that wasn't his fault.

He acted like he hadn't heard. "—and to you. I'm at a loss over how to thank you."

"No thanks are necessary."

"Yes. They are. If it wasn't for you, Michael would've drowned. Every time I think—"

At the intensity in his voice, she glanced at him. He'd gone pale.

"Then, don't," she said, looking away. Michael's face as he lay sprawled on the float rose in her mind, blue-tinged, too quiet. Unconsciously, she reached to toy with the clippers, turning them over and over in a dull thunk-thunk against the concrete. "Don't think." Don't think about it, don't dwell on it, go about your daily routine, and don't let the images in.

His hand covered hers, stilling her movements. Her

body stilled, too, as though waiting. She drew in a sharp breath. She didn't need this feeling again, didn't want it, especially from some egomaniacal, perverted country superstar who didn't even have the foresight to slap a life jacket on a rollicking five-year-old ninja.

"I want to do something for you," he said. She looked at him again. In this deeper shade, his eyes were darker, more feral. "Something special. Is there anything you want? Anything you need? I can—"

Without warning, anger rose like a fist in her throat. She snatched her hand away. "Who do you think you are?"

He drew back as though she'd hit him. She'd like to. She gripped the edge of the bench instead. "Have a lonely daughter? Buy a few books. Need to entertain them? How about a few hundred acres at a resort. Almost lose a son? No problem, buy the gal who saved him a present and ease your conscience. What did you promise Sam? The moon? Good God. Kids need a mother? Buy one of those, too."

She jerked to her feet, faced him, amazed at the depth of her rage. "When I first set eyes on your children yesterday, my heart cried, do you hear me? If ever there was a case of 'poor little rich kids,' it's them. It's obvious your daughter is neglected. She's starved for affection, from anyone, even a stranger. And your son acts up because it gets him attention. Being yelled at is better than being ignored. Yesterday, his bid for attention, and your neglect, almost cost him his life. Can't you see they need *you*? Not a nanny, not a bunch of hangers-on, not a floating palace. *You*."

Jon had risen more slowly, and watched her openmouthed. Now his fists clenched, his eyes narrowed. "For someone with no kids, you're quite the ace all of a sudden."

"A day on your boat made me an expert!" She realized she was yelling. She hadn't yelled since she didn't know when. She hadn't felt so alive, so aware, so *mad*, in ages—and it felt good. Really good. "It's no wonder you almost had a disaster. You stick them on that boat with no life jackets and only some simp of a woman to watch them while you and your buddies carouse with your bimbos—"

"I wasn't *carousing* with any—"

"—the music turned up so high you couldn't hear yourself scream. You all get drunk, you get my sister drunk—"

"I wasn't drunk. And I didn't pour beer down your sister's throat."

"—and then you expect to buy a clean conscience with a present for *me*? I'll tell you what you can do for me. You can retract that vile proposal you made to Mari. And then you can go to hell!"

They both fell silent. Jon studied her and she eyed him. Tiger eyes, dangerous and unreadable. She crossed her arms. He was as tense as stone.

Suddenly his body loosened. He slipped a thumb into his pocket and laughed. "I probably will rot in hell. But not yet. Tell you what I'll do for you. I asked your sister to marry me for a reason—a good one— and I'm not ready to drop the whole idea." She shifted with frustration and he held up a hand. "Hear me out. I'll tell her I've changed my mind, on one condition."

"What?"

"That you marry me instead."

For a moment, she just stared at him. Then she thumped her hands onto her hips. "Of all the—I just can't believe you'd—" she sputtered, unable to complete a thought.

Amusement gleamed in his eyes, amusement and determination. He put a finger to her chin and tilted her head up. She couldn't read what was in his eyes, but his expression was odd. No longer angry, but not compassionate, just . . . odd.

He smiled. "I'll go chat with Roy. Take a few minutes to make up your mind." He dropped his hand, and strolled—strolled!—toward the cabin.

"I don't need a few minutes! The answer is—" He kept going and didn't look back.

She whirled around, picked up the clippers, and hurled them at a tree. Then she stalked in circles around the bench. "Of all the—" She imagined his face. She imagined punching his face. "You—you arrogant, conceited idiot. You manipulative, conniving *rat,* if you think that for one minute, I'd even consider marrying anyone remotely like you, you must be completely out of your mind. You can just take your indecent proposal and put it—put it where the sun doesn't shine, you hear me? Because I'd never, ever—"

Maybe she would.

Aghast, she halted midstride, anger fading into amazement, then thoughtfulness. She sank onto the bench and propped her chin on her hand, feeling more clearheaded than she'd felt since Henry's death—since *Robbie's* death.

After a few minutes, she heard Jon returning. She straightened, sitting with her ankles crossed and hands clasped to hide their tremble.

A few yards away, he met her cool stare head on, but his eyes no longer looked dangerous. Instead she detected uncertainty and a hint of . . . shame? He halted in front of her. "Look. Things got a little heated and I said some things that—"

"I'll consider your proposal."

"What?"

Her pulse hammered. "I said, I'd consider your proposal."

Tiger eyes wary, Jon crossed his arms. "Why?"

"I have my reasons. If I decide to do this, I'll let you know them."

That charming grin appeared. "I bet you will."

"But I'll only consider it if you agree to tell Mari your engagement is off."

Jon's eyes veiled, although the smile remained. "I'd be letting one bird go without having another in hand."

"That's the risk you'd have to take."

He continued to stare at her, assessing. "No dice. I want your promise first."

"I—" She couldn't do it. With his gaze on her like that, she couldn't tell him a bald-faced lie. He'd see right through her. "I'll give you my answer tomorrow."

She'd practice tonight, practice looking honest as she promised to marry him, knowing all the while that once he broke off with Mari, she'd pitch his proposal back in his face.

If she wanted to.

She almost gasped at the thought. *Of course* she wanted to. She'd take great satisfaction in doing it, too.

Chapter 10

The sunset bathed the lake in ripples of molten gold. A few cicadas whirred to life in evensong. In the cabin up slope from Lil, country music rolled from speakers placed in a screened window. *Van Castle's Greatest Hits,* no doubt. The party that had started in the afternoon with the family picnic shouldered on. Mari's laugh rang out from the cabin's deck, just visible through the trees.

Lil trod a path through a stand of bent oaks and emerged on a promontory ten feet above the water. She settled herself on a log, and her denim skirt, chosen mostly because it was less worn than her other clothes, brushed the tops of her canvas shoes. She hugged her knees, stared out over the cove, and waited for Jon. Surely he had noticed her nod, signaling him to join her on the promontory. She was ready to give him her answer. Then he'd tell Mari their engagement was off, Lil would laugh in his face, and they could all go back to the way things had been before he'd burst into their lives.

Somehow, the thought was dispiriting. Or maybe she just had a bad case of nerves. She'd never tried a whopper like this, and had felt nerve-wracked the whole day by the thought of it. Somebody switched off the radio and more cicadas lifted their voices. A breeze puffed curls into her eyes, and she pressed her fingers briefly to her temples. Her head hurt.

As the water lapped the shoreline, the tension eased a little in her shoulders, and her face relaxed, shedding the polite smile she'd carried all day. She breathed in the summer evening. She loved this place. The whole family loved it.

And, an inner voice whispered, saving it was within her grasp. The muscles in her neck tightened again. But at what cost?

The party welcoming Jonathan Van Castle into the O'Malley family had seemed . . . normal. Everyone appeared to have forgotten their objections. Just like Robbie, Jon had a winning personality, and he'd conquered them one by one. Now and then, he'd caught her eye with a raised eyebrow, asking her silently when he'd have her answer.

He'd won Patsy Lee's approval when he played catch with Daisy and talked fishing with Hank. He'd loosened the tension in Alcea's face when he engaged her in conversation about Kathleen's schooling. He had even unearthed common ground with Pop, who'd quit smoking himself the year before, and recommended Jon chew on an empty pipe like he did. "No calories, you see, son, unlike those suckers you're using."

Lil's heart had clutched. Her father had, of course, called Henry "son," and later Robbie had earned the title. Pop still didn't use it with Alcea's husband Stan. His easy acceptance of Jon disturbed her. If she couldn't call a halt to this nonsense soon, more people than Mari were going to get hurt.

Jon didn't need to make any efforts with Stan. Alcea's husband normally stood aloof from the O'Malley clan, uninterested in anyone who wasn't impressed by the gold chains looping his beefy neck or the cigarette boat he'd thundered to a stop alongside the dock. Today, though, Stan had almost usurped her father's place as head of the family. He'd clapped Jon on the back, making him stagger, and declared him a more than suitable candidate for his "sweet sister-in-law's hand." Behind his back, Mari had stuck out her tongue.

Even Patsy Lee's shy Rose had fallen for Jon's easy good humor. When Lil had last seen the five-year-old today, Jon had been bouncing her on one knee. Rose's straight blond hair had flown around her face, and her brown eyes had sparkled with glee.

Lil hadn't heard Rose laugh since Henry had passed, but today the sound had been sweet music. Even better, the teddy bear the child had given up at three, but had taken to carrying again since her father's death, lay abandoned on the edge of the deck.

Jon had established a quick, teasing relationship with Zinnia. God, even her mother was acting like today wasn't some kind of charade. She'd bustled from kitchen to table with bowls of creamy cole slaw, vats of potato salad, crocks of baked beans, and layers of Alcea's chocolate raspberry cake. She headed off words between Alcea and Stan before they dissolved into bickering, whipped out a chef's apron and fastened it on Zeke, who gamely helped Pop with the barbecue, poked marshmallows on sticks for her grandchildren, ". . . including the beautiful Miss Melanie and handsome Mr. Michael. Such a big boy. Why, I can't hardly believe he's only five years old."

And she'd completely ignored the fact her youngest daughter was getting increasingly tipsy on wine coolers, flirting with every male in sight, including Jon's stylist Sidney (an obvious ill choice) and his business manager Peter (who already had Jon's secretary Lydia possessively clinging to his arm), while loose-limbed Three-Ring drummed on his knees with a pair of sticks and watched Mari with a glint in his eyes.

Three-Ring had already hit on Lil. It hadn't offended her; the scruffy drummer was one of those men who flirted with abandon, and only shrugged and grinned like a naughty child when he met a rebuff.

Harmless really—unless he was given encouragement, which her sister seemed to have in ready supply. So far, though, Three-Ring had kept his distance from Mari, impeded perhaps by the few words she'd seen Jon whisper in his ear. Three-Ring reminded Lil of some of the good ol' boys who frequented Seamus's Rooster Bar and Grill, more interested in the game than the conquest.

The only person who'd seemed unimpressed was Seamus. Zinnia considered Robbie's brother as much a member of the family as any of them, so she'd included him today.

Usually a comfort, today Seamus's gaze held hostility. Sometimes Lil had watched him watching Jon, who watched her with golden eyes turning grave and appraising, while she tried to ignore them both. Her mother had followed these unspoken exchanges, eyes flicking to Jon, then to Lil, then to Jon again. Her face would grow thoughtful. Between Zinnia's thoughtful expressions and mother-of-the-bride playacting, Lil didn't know what had gotten into her.

Or Seamus. After each of these staring matches, Seamus's attentions to her would grow more marked, Jon's movements more restless, and Lil more uneasy.

Zeke hadn't been a comfort either. Earlier today, one corner of his mouth had lifted and he'd whispered, "You could do a lot worse." Had he meant, worse than . . . Jon? He must have. He must know about the proposal Jon thought she'd accept. Somehow, his wry sympathy with Jon's outlandish proposition made the arrangement seem more defensible. It would be a comfort having him around if she . . .

Lil rubbed her temples. Could she really be contemplating accepting? Think what that would do to her sister.

Mari's chortle sounded over the creaking of the dock, and Lil looked up. On the deck, Three-Ring reached out and playfully pulled Mari down onto his lap.

But think what Jon's *life* would do to her sister. Let loose from the confines of family and lack of money that kept her in check, Mari wouldn't resist any excess. If Lil refused Jon after he'd broken his engagement with Mari, would he simply crook his finger in Mari's direction again? And would Mari be incensed enough with him to turn her back? Or would she throw pride away and marry him anyway?

Lil thought she knew.

Behind her, something rustled in the underbrush. Heart thudding, she twisted toward the sound. But it wasn't Jon, it was Melanie.

Pulse slowing, Lil smiled. "Get tired of the party?"

"It was nice. And the food was really good."

Melanie wore faded yellow shorts streaked with barbecue sauce, matching similar smudges at the corners of her mouth. Lil patted the log and Melanie joined her. Daisy would have sprawled. Melanie tucked up and rested her chin on her knees.

She glanced at Lil with a shy smile. "I like your family. Especially Daisy and your mom. She's a great grandma. And I like Patsy Lee and Hank and little Rose and your funny cabin and . . . it's *all* wonderful." Her gaze fixed on the horizon. The sun had dipped behind the hillside, bruising the sky purple and pink. She stirred, then whispered, almost to herself, "I don't want to ever go home. Not *ever*."

Startled, Lil looked at her. When she was Melanie's age, the only place she'd wanted to be was home. Home meant Pop's bear hugs, and Zinnia's quick affection, and homemade oatmeal raisin cookies. It meant squabbles with her sisters and brother that melted into laughter, songs around the piano, and kids—Seamus, Robbie, even Stan—playing hide-and-seek and catching fireflies in mayonnaise jars in the big backyard scented with her mother's flowers. She couldn't imagine a better life.

"You don't miss your home, not even a little?"

Melanie shook her head.

"Not your friends?"

"I don't have any. We live outside town, you see, and nobody ever comes out there. It's boring sometimes. It's lonely."

"But surely your mother or grandmother are willing to bring out playmates?"

"My grandmother doesn't drive anymore. And my mom . . ." Her voice trailed off. "But it doesn't matter. Nobody at school likes me."

"Whyever not? You're a very likable person, you know."

Melanie gave her another small smile, but it quickly faded. "They think I'm weird. They think I lie when I tell them my dad is Jonathan Van Castle because I wear hand-me-downs. And they call my mom . . . names."

Lil hesitated, then asked, "What kind of names?"

Melanie dipped her head and her hair fell around her face. "Things like tramp and slut, some other words I'm not supposed to say." Through her hair, the tips of Melanie's ears turned a dull red.

"That must bother you a lot."

"It used to." She shrugged. "But now I'm used to it."

"Well . . ." Lil couldn't think of what to say. Heart aching for the waif beside her, her anger stirred. Her eyes fastened on Melanie's old shorts. "Surely your daddy can afford some new clothes for you?"

Melanie looked up, her expression earnest. "Oh, he sends us lots and lots of money. Every month. I've seen the checks and they always have three zeros, sometimes four. But Mom says it's never enough and I just have to learn to do without."

Lil's anger gathered, but she did her best to keep it out of her face. Impulsively, she put her arm around Melanie's shoulders and gave her a quick hug. "I'm sure while you're staying with your daddy, he'll get you every single thing you want." Including a new mother?

"I know he will. He already said Tina's supposed to take me shopping. He called it a 'spree,' and said I *can* get anything I want. Anything! Can you imagine?" Melanie's face glowed. "And best of all, Michael doesn't have to go with us. Uncle Zeke said he'd watch him since Daddy says Tina's no match for him." She looked up at Lil. "I love Michael, but . . . do you think Michael has DDTs?"

Lil laughed. "I think you mean ADD, and no, I don't. He just has a lot of energy, is all. They thought Daisy had that, too, when she was little, but she didn't, and she's grown up fine. So will he. And so will you."

Melanie smiled. Lil's heart did a little flip, and she looked away. Melanie had her father's smile, and it transformed her narrow face into a thing of beauty.

Melanie slipped her hand into Lil's. It was warm, smooth. "I'm glad he doesn't have ADD. Mom says he does. She says if he doesn't calm down she'll put him in an insti-, insti-, a place for crazy people. He's a pain sometimes, but I'm glad that won't happen."

What kind of monster was this girl's mother? "No, it certainly *won't* happen." Jon wouldn't allow it. But could he prevent his ex-wife from doing something equally nuts if he didn't have complete custody?

Melanie squeezed back. "You know what?" she asked, voice shy.

"What?"

"I like you."

Lil smiled. "I like you, too." Idly she rubbed her thumb across the top of Melanie's hand.

For a minute they were silent. Then Melanie spoke again. "I wish my daddy was marrying you instead of Mari."

Lil started, realizing that for a brief moment, she'd been wishing exactly the same thing.

Chapter 11

"Mel? Hey, Mel!" Jon rounded the path and stopped at the edge of the clearing behind them. "There you are. Daisy's looking for you, baby."

Melanie leaped up, her happiness at being wanted so transparent, Lil's throat burned. She flashed a good-bye grin at Lil, then hurried into the deepening shadows of the woods. Lil's eyes followed Jon's daughter along the path until the girl's shorts had faded to a faint lemon glow. Her gaze flicked to Jon. He was still watching Melanie, hands shoved in his pockets, a thoughtful look on his face.

He turned, and their eyes met. "Are you ready to talk?"

Heart moving into her throat, she shrugged and looked away. He approached on cat's feet, then eased into the place Melanie had vacated, his thigh brushing hers. The gold hairs on his legs glinted in the dusk-light. She frowned. She was thinking about his leg hair? She eased away until they no longer touched.

His gaze was on the view, but he smiled slightly. "Sure is pretty out here. Mari said your parents have decided to sell, and why. Sound reasons, but I can see why they'd be so unhappy about having to let it go."

She didn't think Mari should be discussing the family's business. "Mm."

The discouragement seemed to work. He shifted topics. "Must be great to just be able to kick back in a place like this. Shawnee Bay's no contest. It's got boat engines going day and night, mega-homes carving up in the hillsides. What's kept this side so unspoiled?"

She glanced at him. He actually seemed interested. "The locals didn't want the same thing happening on this end, so they made it hard to develop new homes or businesses here. The only way to get a place is to buy out somebody else." Even with an inch of space between them, she could still feel the heat of his thigh through her skirt. She fell silent, wondering when he'd bring up the proposal, wondering if she was ready.

"And your family is great, too. Especially your mom. I would have given up my guitar to have your mom, and that's saying a lot. That guitar was the only thing I loved as a kid."

This family seemed to be full of problem mothers. "Didn't you love your mother?"

"Yeah, I loved her. She gave me the guitar—stole from the grocery money to save up for it. But she died when I was six."

She thawed a little. "I'm sorry. Your father—did he die, too?"

"Not until long after he'd smashed that guitar up." He gave a humorless laugh. "I patched it back together with tape and kept it hid over at Dodo's—Dodo is my ex-wife's mother. It never sounded quite the same, though. No, the old man didn't go to his great reward until a few years back. He lasted too long in my opinion. But at least he waited to croak until I'd proved him wrong, not that he ever admitted it."

She frowned. She couldn't imagine feeling that way about Pop. "Proved him wrong?"

"He said I was worthless. Worthless little assbite." Jon's voice was bitter. "His pet name for me. He lived to see my name in lights. It was the only reason I was glad he did."

She felt another tug of sympathy, and Zeke's comment on the boat now made sense.

"You know," she said quietly, "your dad was wrong. No child is worthless."

His eyes met hers. Before she could react, he gave her hand a squeeze and released it as fast as he'd grabbed it. Flushing, he looked away. "Your cabin's old, but it looks like your family's kept it up. I wouldn't think you'd have much problem selling." He paused, glanced at her again. "Under certain conditions, maybe I'd buy it."

Arms tightening around her knees, Lil stayed silent.

"Of course"—he twisted to stare up over his shoulder—"some folks might object to that deck. Looks kind of funny with those trees poking through it."

She stiffened. "My husband built that deck. My husband Robbie, Pop, and my brother Henry." She remembered the summer they'd worked on it, Robbie's back glistening with sweat and the beginnings of sunburn, the incessant pounding of nails, the camaraderie of the three men—and Zinnia wringing her hands over her oaks and dogwoods and threatening to never serve them another piece of her apple pie if they damaged so much as an inch of bark. The night they'd finished the deck, the family had held a celebration. Her mother triumphantly lit the lanterns the men had nailed on the deck's mismatched corners, and proclaimed it a huge success. Later, Lil had rubbed aloe vera on Robbie's back, and then . . . "And they built it that way on purpose. To preserve those trees. My mother loves those trees."

"And in your family, how people feel is more important than things, right?"

"Every family should be that way."

"Still, I'd think a new owner with the money it'd take to buy this place would make a lot of changes. Probably tear that deck out and put up something different."

"They wouldn't. They couldn't! It'd be like . . ." Lil stopped. A new owner could do what he wanted.

"It'd be like ripping out a piece of your heart." Jon finished for her. He turned his head and she felt his gaze on the side of her face. "You loved him a lot, didn't you?"

"Robbie? He was my life," she said simply.

Jon's hand brushed hers; she wasn't sure this time if it was intentional or not. "Lil?"

"Hmm?"

"I wouldn't rip the deck out."

They both stared out over the lake. The moon had pushed up behind a hill into the deepening violet of the sky, laying shimmering crescents across the water.

She thought over Jon's question about love and decided it was odd. Of course she'd loved Robbie a lot. Didn't everyone love the person they married? Why else would anyone take those vows? Then she almost snorted at her own naiveté. Of course there were other reasons. Look at what she herself was considering. She started. When had she decided to take his offer seriously?

Around them, more cicadas joined the evening chorus until their rhapsody drowned the lake's gentle waves. Something shuffled nearby in the earth floor debris, probably a raccoon or possum trundling off in a nocturnal search for food. With the setting sun, the humidity had lifted and the night, though still damp, was turning chill. Wearing only a thin cotton eyelet blouse, she shivered. Noticing, Jon shifted until his warmth lay along her side from shoulder to ankle. She appreciated the heat, but her chill deepened. Still, she didn't move.

"Didn't you love your wife when you married her?"

"I thought I did." He hooked his hair behind one ear.

She liked his ears; they kept him from being too perfect. She sighed. First his leg hair, and now his ears.

"But maybe I was more in love with the idea of marriage, of a family, you know? She followed me from Monaco down to Nashville. I took off when I was eighteen and she dropped out of school and just followed me a year later. I didn't know she was coming. Before I'd left she'd latched onto some other guy. I was lonely, and— Anyway, she got pregnant. And I married her. And then I hit it big. She, uh, didn't handle success well."

"I would think your success would have thrilled her. No more money worries."

"Yeah, you'd think." His shoulder shrugged up, a gentle rub against her arm. "But, as you already pointed out, there are some things more important than money. And I didn't give her any of them. Not my time, not my attention. I was too busy making sure the band's first hit single wasn't a one-shot deal."

"So your marriage died of neglect?"

He hesitated. "Yeah, neglect."

Lil thought about the gossip she'd read. She'd reread those articles yesterday, not really understanding what she was looking for or why. Still, no matter what the papers reported, she hadn't seen any depravity, and he didn't seem the type. Not that she'd know the type. Still, she doubted he had a yen for teenage girls and orgies.

Up the hill, the stereo started up again. The soft country music harmonized with the night.

"That's why I've never gotten hitched again, or even serious about anyone. I've seen what my life can do to a woman, and I don't want to hurt anyone."

Lil's hackles, lulled by his story, went back up. "Unless it's my sister. Or me."

"That's different. She doesn't love me. I don't love her." He didn't mention her. She guessed it was a moot point. "Besides, just say the word and I'll call the whole thing off. Have you thought about my proposal any more?"

Up the hill, on the deck, Mari's excited giggle could be heard over the music.

Lil's chill deepened. Would he really marry her sister if she didn't say yes herself? She closed her eyes. Behind her eyelids, a collage of images jostled for position. Mari's face, flushed, overexcited. The odd angles of the cabin deck around the trees. Patsy Lee's strained and shadowed eyes. The shabby facade of PicNic Poultry. Melanie's smile . . .

"I'll do it." Lil barely breathed the words. She was astounded at herself. She wasn't lying. She'd really do it.

"What?" Jon twisted abruptly. She opened her eyes and his gaze, now deep brown shot with flickering gold light, pinned full on her face.

"I said, I'll do it."

"You mean it? You're sure?"

She nodded, afraid if she opened her mouth again, she'd bite back the words. Her heart pounded until she thought it would jump out of her chest and into the lake. In the moonlight, Jon's eyes deepened to almost black as his pupils expanded. In them, she thought she saw an odd excitement, relief, pain, and . . . something softer, something promising. The moment passed and his eyes resumed their normal tawny color. She'd only imagined that strange look of mingled fear and hope. It was just the intensity of the occasion, born out of her own tumble of emotions.

"I'm sure. But I have a few conditions."

He gave a half smile. "Of course you do."

"First, it's a marriage in name only. Mari told me why you want to get married so I'll pretend for your ex-wife, and the reporters, and whoever else I have to pretend to, but between the two of us, it's strictly a business agreement."

She darted a look at him, but he just nodded. "Go on."

"Second, just like with Mari, I walk away in two years, and you won't try to stop me."

"Three years. And I'll make you one rich woman."

Her eyes whipped to his. "I don't want your money! At least, not like that."

The amused look returned and she wanted to slap it off. "Then how do you want it?"

She tried to pick out the right words. "I'll accept your support—a salary—during the time that we're—we're—"

"Married? How big of you."

"Don't interrupt me. I'll accept your money during that time, but what I really want is for you to buy this place. Buy it, and then at the end of the two—" He straightened, frowning. "Okay—*three* years, you deed it back to them."

"So how much are we talking here?"

She named a figure she suspected was way over market value.

Jon whistled. "That's a shitload, but I could manage it. From what I've seen of your tribe, though, your family won't like it. There's something medieval about it, selling off the daughter for land, that kind of thing."

"No more medieval than buying a mother, which is what you intended to do with Mari. Besides, I have another condition."

"I figured."

"You're right. My family won't like it a bit, if they know the truth. They'll object as strongly as they did with Mari. None of my family are to know we have an agreement. As far as they're concerned, I fell head over heels in love with you and vice versa. And the last condition—" In the gathering gloom, she was pretty sure Jon rolled his eyes. "I'll become attached to your children. In fact, I already am. More important, they'll become attached to me. At the end of three years, we'll need some kind of visitation agreement."

Jon's teasing stopped. "I don't want to hurt them."

"From what Mari has told me, you're trying to protect them—and your record sales."

She felt his body tense along hers. "I'm not—"

"I don't give a fig about your image or your sales, but I will help you protect those children."

"Let's get something straight. I'm doing this for my kids. The image spin won't hurt things any, but it's a bonus and keeping a clean public image'll help my case. It'll also keep what the band's built back up from crashing around our ears, and, yeah, that's important to me. Damn important. I've spent most of my life creating Van Castle. But it's not the main reason."

"At least you don't think it's the main reason." She held up a hand when he opened his mouth. "It doesn't matter what your reasons are. Still I'm curious. Why marry a perfect stranger?"

"Because perfect strangers can't be hurt." As soon as the words left his mouth, he fell quiet like he wanted to take them back. He sighed and leaned forward, elbows to knees. "Look, I don't know what kind of picture you have of my life, but I can tell you it's not the norm. I'm guarded twenty-four/seven, my schedule is crazed, the only guys I hang with are other musicians. I don't hunker down long enough in one place to join a block party, or barbecue, or whatever the hell else it is that people do in the burbs. I have houses, but no home. People come in and out of my life all the time, but they don't hang around long enough for me to decide if I like them. Or can trust them. It's not the kind of life most women can live with."

Well, the way he lived wouldn't matter to her. Unlike Mari, she wouldn't be after his heart, his bed, or his money. At least not much of his money. She'd be a nanny with a ring on her finger. A few years of indentured servitude to his children beat hacking poultry at PicNic. She could help her family, and she'd fallen . . . for his children. "Melanie and Michael's best interests will always be my first priority. You have my word. Now, the sixth condition—" Jon groaned. "I want all of it in writing. Detailed. All spelled out."

"A prenup that will go down in legal history. Well . . ." Jon looked out over the lake, lost in thought, then turned back to her. "Peter will get off just thinking about how to pull this over. He's been wanting me to play Ozzie and Harriet ever since I split from Belinda. He'll drool over you. If he can cross all the Ts and dot all the Is, and I'm sure he can, then, Lil, we've got a deal." Was it her imagination or was his face closer? "I'll have the papers ready to sign tomorrow. Is tomorrow okay for you?"

She was not imagining things, his face was closer. Before she could react, though, his lips had settled on hers. There was no pressure, and he didn't touch her anywhere else. His lips were soft, quiet, and she sat stone still like a startled rabbit, eyes wide open. His eyes were open, too—merged into one big eye at this distance, and she felt sucked into their vortex. She breathed in his breath, felt the slight whisker growth above his upper lip, and then his hand lightly curled around her upper arm, warm, so warm, against her chilled skin. Inside, a quivering started that suddenly had her trembling with fear. Another animal rustled through the underbrush, the cicadas sang, and all else was quiet.

He dropped his hand and drew back. "Just wanted to seal the bargain."

"I—" She stopped, found herself unable to form a coherent sentence.

He smiled, but he looked as shaken as she felt. "I know you said no intimacy, but we need to give at least the appearance of love at first sight."

Lil took a deep breath. What had she gotten herself into? "When should we tell Mari?"

"I had planned to tell her earlier today, but I

haven't had the chance, too many people around, so I'll—" He bit off the words.

She narrowed her eyes. "You were going to tell her even if I'd said no?"

He hesitated, then smiled wide and cocky. "Caught me. Look, I'm not an idiot. I could see she wouldn't be able to handle motherhood, or my life, for that matter."

"You tricked me! I thought you—"

"Does it really change anything? I need a mom for my kids, you need money for the old homestead. We're both getting what we want. Mari has nothing to do with it."

Lil fumed and tried to sort out his logic. She gave up. She'd made a commitment, and he was right. Her mission was to preserve her family's heritage, save Patsy Lee, and help him save his children. Protecting Mari was an added bonus, even if Mari didn't think she needed protecting. "I think we should tell Mari toni—"

"You don't need to tell Mari one damned thing!" Behind them, an unsteady Mari crashed through the underbrush and into the clearing. Seamus followed, grabbed Mari's arm to keep her from falling. She shook him off and glared at Jon and Lil, hands clamped on her hips.

Lil felt Jon stiffen. His plan to gain custody depended on total secrecy, and Mari had never been one to keep secrets unless it was in her own best interests. Lil wondered how much they'd overheard.

She stood up. "Mari, Seamus—I—we—"

"I saw the whole thing!" Mari's face contorted in anger. "Do you think you're invisible from up there on the deck?"

Lil was relieved. Mari had seen the whole thing, but she hadn't heard anything. "Mari, we couldn't help it."

Tears spouted from Mari's eyes. "The whole fucking family was watching you. Watching you in the moonlight, talking, leaning on each other, kissing each other, and—how could you do this, Lil? How could you? It was supposed to be me! *Me!* You've made a complete fool out of me, you've ruined my life, and I'll never forgive you, never!"

"Mari—" Lil moved forward, reached out, but her hand only brushed the back of Mari's blouse as she turned and ran back through the trees.

Seamus stared straight through her. "What are you doing, Lil?"

"I, uh—" She retreated to Jon's side, giving herself a moment to recover her wits. It was time to pretend. She hesitated, then laid a hand alongside Jon's cheek. Under a light stubble, his skin was smooth, taut. Her fingers trembled. Except for her father, Henry, and Robbie, she'd never felt another man's face. Jon's eyes grew amused. He tilted his head to capture her hand between his shoulder and chin, then twisted to lay a kiss on her palm. It took an effort, but she didn't flinch. She looked back at Seamus. "I . . ." Looking at the concrete set of his jaw, she couldn't continue.

Jon raised his head and gave Seamus an artless smile, but when he spoke steel underlay his words. "We've fallen in love," he said firmly.

Without another word, Seamus turned on his heel and marched up the hill. For a few long moments, Jon and Lil stood rooted in place. Lil didn't know where to look—certainly not at Jon.

"Shit," Jon muttered.

That about covered everything she was feeling. Lil started up the path. She hesitated near the top and waited for Jon. In the face of Mari's rage, he was better than no ally at all. Taking a look at her face, he grasped her hand and they mounted the steps together.

On the deck, Mari sobbed in Seamus's arms. Zinnia fluttered around the pair, and Sidney fluttered around Zinnia. Three-Ring watched them with undisguised fascination. Muttering to himself, Pop slipped into the cabin, but Lil noticed he stayed just inside where he could watch and hear. Looking wild-eyed, Stan muttered, "I think I left the stereo on in the boat," then almost killed himself with a quick vault down the steps. Peter and Lydia huddled in whispers. Patsy Lee tore her eyes away from an apparent fascination with the nighttime sky. "Um, I'll go start the dishes." She glided inside.

Lil's stomach churned. "Where are all the children?"

"Fortunately, playing flashlight tag out front." Alcea watched Mari, lips pursed in distaste. "What *is* this all about?"

A lounge chair creaked. Lil glanced over her shoulder. Zeke had settled back, hands behind his head, looking for all the world like he expected high entertainment. She frowned, and he winked. Instead of angering her, somehow the wink settled her stomach.

"I'll tell you what this is all about!" Mari pushed away from Seamus. Tears ran in funnels down her cheeks. "How dare you, Lil? How dare you decide what's right for me? Don't give me all this shit about love at first sight. I may have been drunk yesterday, but not that drunk. You despise him."

Lil winced, and Jon squeezed her hand. She waited for the rest. There was no appeasing Mari until the rampage subsided. Zinnia tossed an alarmed look at her youngest, but when her gaze turned on Jon and Lil, it was full of speculation.

"I trusted you, I've always trusted you, and I can't believe—just can't believe—you'd betray me like this." Mari balled her fists into her hair. "You've ruined my life. I hope you and Jonathan Van Castle rot in hell. You can just go fuck yourself. I mean it! Just f—"

Zinnia gasped. Expression neutral, Seamus grabbed

Mari and gave her a sharp shake. Face crumpling, she collapsed on him again.

Over her shoulder, Seamus pinned Lil with a gaze as hard as malachite. "You are out of your mind. This man isn't worth the trouble it would take to squash a bug. He's evil."

Jon's mouth dropped open. "I beg your pardon."

Seamus ignored him. He stared at Lil, his face so full of accusation, she had to struggle not to blurt out the truth.

"He's not," she finally uttered, but without any heat. Jon stared at her, but she ignored him. She thought she understood Seamus's reaction, and she didn't blame him. She knew it must wound him to see someone taking Robbie's place and his.

Seamus's mouth tightened. He gave Jon a look of pure venom, then wrapped an arm around Mari and led her inside. Feeling bereft, Lil let him go. She'd explain later. She owed him that, and he was so close-mouthed, she could trust him with the truth.

Jon turned to the rest and made some garbled explanation that she couldn't remember later. In the face of her family's dead silence, Jon's party made awkward farewells. All except Zeke, who seemed as unperturbed as ever.

When Jon said good-bye to her, he took her face in his hands. His fingers nestled under her curls, and his thumbs stroked her cheeks. The intimacy widened her eyes, until she remembered they were supposed to be in love and everyone was watching. She made herself relax, but her heart pounded. One corner of Jon's mouth quirked, then he lightly kissed her lips. Butterfly wings, and her heart soared after them.

She yanked the miscreant organ back to earth. "Don't do that." She kept her voice low.

His grin spread, but concern shaded his eyes. "Courage," he whispered, and with that, he was gone.

Chapter 12

The next day, Lil again joined Jon on the houseboat, resigned to play her part and do right by his children. Jon had called earlier to propose another lake excursion so they could tell his children of their impending marriage. She was no less exhausted this morning than she had been last night, but even another party was better than facing her family.

As before, Jon met her at the dock, this time giving her a low whistle. She blushed, adjusting the straps of a pale blue sun dress she'd borrowed from Alcea. She relinquished the beach bag she held into his outstretched hand, and climbed onto the boat.

"How are you holding up?" He glanced toward the cabin as they made their way aft. "Was it bad?"

"Bad enough. But Mother put a stop to it." Lil paused, wishing she knew exactly what her mother was thinking. Surprisingly, Zinnia seemed to accept everything Lil had told them. In fact, even Pop's resistance to her engagement had faded once Zinnia had pulled him aside for a "chat." They'd returned united to support her.

Jon smiled. "Your mother's a good egg. What about Mari?"

"She left last night to go back to Cordelia with Seamus." Her stomach clenched. She'd never seen Mari so unforgiving.

They'd reached the sun deck. It was empty.

"She'll get over it." Jon turned to set down her bag. When he straightened, he caught her looking at his tanned hard belly below his torn-off tank top. He winked.

She blushed and looked away. "Where is everyone?"

"Just us today. Us, the kids, and Captain Sam."

Above them Sam gave her a salute. She called a good morning, then followed Jon below to the cabin.

Inside, Melanie sat curled with a book. She wore an orange headband that pulled her bangs back and matched a terry-cloth cover-up that was stiff with newness. Orange flip-flops decorated with purple rubber flowers sat on the floor beside her. She confided Tina had gone shopping for her yesterday while everyone else was at the picnic, but she would still get her spree in the coming week.

With a cape tied around his shoulders, and his bowl-cut hair flying, Michael zinged from corner to corner with a Power Ranger doll. He was stuffed into a life jacket. Spotting Lil, he ran up to her. "Good! You're here, and now I can have my present."

Puzzled, Lil looked at Jon, but he only smiled. "In a minute, bud."

She settled next to Melanie while Jon chased his son around the room, finally plopping on the opposite bench with Michael in his lap.

When Michael had stopped wiggling, Jon tweaked his nose. "I have a story to tell."

Michael stuck his lip out. "You said we'd get a present."

"I said a treat. The story's part of the treat."

"Hmph. I want a different treat."

"Shhh. Just listen, buddy. I promise you'll like it."

Michael looked skeptical, but subsided.

"Once upon a time, there was a boy, a singer, who'd

never found his lady fair, but one bright, beautiful day, a day made for dreams coming true, an angel in a white bathing suit appeared—"

Michael giggled. "Angels don't wear bathing suits!"

Eyes lighting, Melanie hooked a glance at Lil.

Jon went on in this vein, elaborating on their meeting, spinning fantasy out of air. He got so caught up in his own words, Lil was certain he'd start crooning any minute. ". . . and so the boy and his own special blue-eyed angel decided to get ma—"

Melanie wriggled around to face Lil. "You're going to marry my daddy!" She threw her arms around Lil and hugged her so tight, Lil lost her breath.

Michael frowned. "But what happened to the boy and the angel? And where's the treat?"

Jon sighed and ruffled his hair. "I see I may have made things more complicated than I needed to." He poked a thumb to his chest. "I'm the boy."

Eyebrows puckered in concentration, Michael nodded.

"And that"—Jon pointed at Lil—"is the angel. She's also 'the treat.' "

Michael's brown eyes popped. "You mean *you're in love*?" he breathed.

Jon gave Lil a wry glance. "Yessir, we are."

"Yippee! She'll make the best mom ever. She knows important stuff like the names of the Karate Kids, and she likes peanut butter and she reads and everything!" He scrambled out of Jon's grasp and threw himself at Lil and Melanie, landing on them with a grunt.

Even as she laughed and returned their hugs, Lil wondered at Melanie and Michael's easy acceptance. They'd spent only one day in her company, and a few hours at the family picnic. Were they that starved for love? The fact that Jon had bounced between prospective brides like a Ping-Pong ball didn't seem to bother them at all. Was this the kind of behavior they expected from him? She put her concerns aside for later thought.

After that, the morning was spent gliding along the shoreline. Jon and Lil sat cross-legged with the children on the sun deck, playing with Michael's X-Men, then followed Melanie's lead and affixed decals into a sticker book. When the sun grew hot, Lil changed into her swimsuit and Sam anchored the houseboat so they could swim. At lunchtime, Jon hauled out a tray filled with peanut butter sandwiches, pickles, chips, and root beer. "No shrimp salad." He grinned at her. After dining al fresco, they tossed swim rafts overboard and floated like the puffball clouds in the sky.

Lil watched Jon through half-closed eyes. Without his entourage, he was different. More relaxed, his smile more ready. He splashed with Melanie, then tossed Michael from a raft and swam after him, never letting the boy drift too far out of his reach. He wasn't a bad father. A little too indulgent sometimes, a little inattentive at others, but she could see he tried. Zeke might be right . . . he did care. A lot.

Gradually she relaxed. With the children acting as buffers, Jon proved an easy companion. She learned he had a weakness for M&M's, both peanut and plain, and hated lime Jell-O

"Yuck," he said.

"Yuck," Michael affirmed.

His idol was Willie Nelson; his rival, Diamond Rio, and the band had been nominated Entertainers of the Year for this year's Country Music Awards. They faced stiff competition in the form of Alan Jackson. "He's good, I'll give you that." Jon grinned. "But we're better."

To her surprise, he was also widely read. "Nothing else to do on the bus, except play cards with Sidney, and he cheats."

Their talk ranged widely. They avoided discussion of recent events, and simply got to know each other. She learned he could be sensitive. When talk turned to Robbie, she grew quiet, and he changed the subject.

When she asked about his family, he easily talked about the children's grandmother, Dodo, short for Dorothy, and the ties he felt with Zeke and Three-Ring. But he steered away from any conversation concerning his childhood. Nor did he bring up Belinda.

She remained curious about Jon's ex-wife, but was hesitant to ask him any questions. Nobody mentioned Belinda, at least around her. Not even the children, unless she prodded a little. It was as if the woman didn't exist. She couldn't help but wonder. After all, if it weren't for Belinda, she wouldn't be getting married.

Chapter 13

One week and three days later, on the first Saturday of August, Lil stood beside Jon amid a torrent of lace and yellow satin ribbons. The scent of roses from her mother's garden spiced the air. Early evening sunlight drenched the beamed hollow of the Royal Sun banquet hall, packed with bodies politely perspiring under their formal dress.

The preceding ten days had been a whirlwind of press parties, preparations, dress fittings, publicity photos, and legal papers. She'd spent more time with the children than she had with Jon. As the wedding approached, he'd been forever huddled with Peter or Sidney or his publicist. When they had seen each other, it was always part of the "show."

In front of a crowd peopled with both famous faces and the familiar ones from her hometown, she faced a judge and promised to have and to hold for the rest of her life. She felt vaguely faint. Reporters and photographers packed the rear of the hall. Videos whirred and cameras clicked, filming the event for posterity.

Peter, Jon, and his publicist had carefully orchestrated the media. She'd objected to the attention at first, especially when her natural reserve had proved no defense with reporters. The more reticent she was, the more questions they hurled at her. Over time and with Peter's coaching, she grew more adept with her public appearances, and even started to enjoy some of the fuss, except for a few rough days when someone uncovered her past and trotted out the details of Robbie's death. But she tried to take even that in stride for the children's sake. Jon had explained that "going over the top on the Ozzie and Harriet thing" would later benefit his custody case. She deferred to his judgment, but wondered if he wasn't more concerned with his daily sales report than with Melanie and Michael.

She was grateful to the media for a different reason. If she had to play the adored and adoring fiancée, it was easier in front of cameras and reporters. They gave the whole affair the air of a performance. She could ignore the amusement that crossed Jon's face when she forced a dewy-eyed gaze, and she could discount the blip in her heart when he caught her hand, or pressed a kiss on her cheek. The press made it easy to ignore the pain when she thought of her first wedding. Her *real* wedding.

She was learning to handle the attention, and she could handle the gaze of the cameras. But standing here at the altar with Jon, she wanted to flee from her family's eyes. They bored holes in her back.

She shifted in her pastel yellow shoes. When the matching tulle of her dress brushed Jon's pants, he cleared his throat and reached up to straighten his tie, already held solidly in place by a diamond pin. His attire was Western formal, honey leather and silk, coordinated with her dress. She moved the dress out of his way. The glass beads festooning her from the top of her veil to the tip of her long train sparkled. Brushing back a strand of hair, Jon smiled his thanks. Sidney had wanted to weave a leather band through his hair, but Jon had put his foot down.

Sidney had flown into raptures and sank in despair at the news of a wedding, ecstatic at dressing the bride and groom, but moaning at so little time. He'd wanted to drape her in "a heavenly blue that will match your eyes," but to her private delight, Jon had insisted on yellow. She hadn't known they shared a fondness for the color.

Sidney's disappointment over the blue dress was sharp, but Peter placated him with the suggestion he revamp her wardrobe. She hated to admit it, but that task had been fun, even though Sidney's haute couture leanings conflicted with her more pedestrian tastes. Learning of the dispute, Jon had again intervened, and she'd filled a closet with casual attire in the pastels she preferred. Working as hard as Sidney, the troops of decorators and florists and caterers and musicians had also performed miraculous feats in just over a week. Amazing what money could do.

Amazing what money had brought her to. She shivered, and her bouquet of pale yellow and white sweetheart roses trembled.

Jon dipped his head, his eyes warm. "Over soon, Lil," he whispered.

She tried to concentrate on Judge Dougherty's words, but couldn't shake all those eyes on her back. Mari's gaze, though, was the worst—skewering her right between her shoulder blades. Somehow Zinnia had managed to drag her to the wedding. As Lil had walked down the aisle, thunder had darkened Mari's brow.

Judge Dougherty raised his voice. She heard Jon's vows in one detached corner of her mind and automatically held out her hand for the diamond-encrusted band he slipped on her finger. The cameras purred and clicked. Overhead the massive chandeliers glittered.

Beside her, Melanie stirred, and Lil glanced down. Coiffed and costumed by Sidney, Melanie's hair glistened in ringlets. Her dress was an inverted buttercup from waist to ankle. Last night, she'd stayed with Lil at the cabin and Lil had brushed that hair one hundred strokes, delighting in its silky fineness. Melanie

had tried on her dress almost as many times, giddy
over her role as maid of honor. They'd spent the evening talking girl talk, Melanie chattering as though
she'd never been tongue-tied. Lil hadn't expected to
sleep a wink, but with Melanie's warmth spooned in
front of her, she'd fallen into a dreamless sleep.

At her glance, Melanie looked up. Her sweet smile
was an arrow straight to the heart, and elation mixed
with horror almost jolted Lil out of her shoes. In a
few minutes, she'd have the right to have some claim
to this girl. To these two beautiful, trusting children.
What business did she have messing with this child's
life? Or Michael's? Lil smiled back, hoping her expression didn't look as sick as she suddenly felt.

"I now pronounce you man and wife," Judge
Dougherty intoned.

Relieved the end of the ceremony neared, and aching to get out of the stilts she wore, Lil tilted her head
up for the obligatory kiss.

And forgot the cameras, forgot the audience, forgot
her family, as Jon's lips settled on hers. Unlike the
chaste pecks and light kisses she'd almost grown used
to, this time he put in some effort. There was pressure,
and pliancy, and movement. This time his tongue ran
a teasing race over her top lip. A river of sensation
swamped her. Warmth curled inside her belly like a
living thing, sending tentacles down her arms, her legs,
and curling her toes. She responded, her lips parting,
breath quickening. Flesh rose on her back. Shocked, her
eyes flashed open and she swam in the honey depths
of his.

Then he pulled away, looped her hand over his arm,
and turned her to face the hall. Spontaneous applause
broke out. Dazed, she blinked into the cameras, then
shuddered. Wrapping her train around her arm along
with the remnants of her dignity, she held her head
high and walked down the aisle.

*   *   *

It was after eleven, and still the reception rambled on. Lil had smiled until her face had almost splintered. The chandeliers glittered with cold, diamond light, hurting her eyes. The drums of Fruit Stand, the band that opened on tour for Van Castle, kept time with the throb in her head. Her shoes were vises, the train of her gown a menace, and, after sampling crab puffs and sherried chicken and marinated mushrooms, plus the towering mansion of a wedding cake, her dress pinched like a corset.

Across the room, her groom was busy working the crowd. She took the opportunity to escape. Hoisting her train, she slipped past the security people at the ballroom's open double doors, slid around a potted palm, and settled on a bench behind a pillar in the lobby. Nobody followed. Peter had arranged a photo op after the wedding, and the paparazzi had abandoned their cameras to mingle with the crowd and belt back crystal flutes of Dom Perignon.

Sighing, she eased off her shoes. Really, despite the famous faces sprinkling the crowd and the outsized luxury of it all, it wasn't that different from any other wedding she'd ever attended. Crowded dance floor, overheated faces, overwrought children, and too much food.

The banquet table reserved for her family was visible through the doorway, empty except for her niece Kathleen, Patsy Lee's Rose, and a number of abandoned drinks. Frosting smearing her mouth, Rose watched the dancers, ducking her head when anyone approached, self-conscious in her party dress and new shoes. Kathleen, hair done in a gold knot like Alcea's, was equally enthralled with the star-studded company. Distracted, they didn't see the marauding band that crept up behind them. Sporting a lime-green frock and smudges of purple on her eyelids, Daisy, trailed by her brother Hank, Melanie, and Michael, reconnoitered the table, then filched the cherries and olives from the cocktails. Kathleen shrieked, sounding a lot like Alcea, and they scampered off in a fit of giggles.

Watching their antics, Lil smiled, but her chin wobbled.

Dancers twirled past the doorway. Her mother, in a swirl of deep mauve that matched the high color in her cheeks, twinkled up at Pop, dashingly military in a blue suit, as he led her past the door. Alcea and her partner, an old friend from high school, stumbled by next. Alcea looked beautiful, blond hair pulled back on the nape of a patrician neck, red chiffon twirling around her ankles. But she wore a pained expression. Maybe because the friend did more dancing on her feet than on his own—or maybe because Stan was off in a corner, his beefy body crowded up against his secretary. The owners of the Cordelia Sleep Inn, Elmon and Helen Tidwell, floated behind them. Helen's sweet smile turned to a grimace when the piano-challenged Joey Beadlesworth bumped up against her, racing past with a mouthful of cherries, Daisy on his heels.

Tears gathered in her throat and Lil looked away. She'd canceled her piano lessons last week. She'd canceled her entire life last week. What had she done? Her marriage to Jon could take her to all corners of the world. She'd seen the schedule for the continuing tour to Canada and Europe. They'd be traveling from September until Christmas. The idea horrified her. Unlike Mari, she felt no need to traipse to foreign parts—she didn't even like spending the night in Kansas City.

She took a deep breath, fighting hysteria. She had to remember she had good reasons—excellent ones, really—for entering into this agreement. It was only three years. Even Robbie would understand if she could tell him.

She looked back at the ballroom. To her surprise, Seamus's lean figure appeared in the doorway. Lil had added him to the invitation list Lydia had put together, but she hadn't expected to see him.

Heart lifting, she stood and beckoned him. Seamus hesitated, then came to join her. Snowy cuffs glowed beneath a suit coat as jet black as his hair. She hadn't seen him dressed like that since . . . Robbie's funeral. Her heart fell as she noted his stony face and the green flash from his eyes. She wasn't forgiven yet.

Trying to keep her smile steady, Lil seated herself and patted the bench. Seamus crossed his arms and leaned against the pillar. "What is it, Lil?"

Her smile gave up. "I need to talk to you. I need to explain." Clasping her hands, she slowly outlined the bargain she'd struck with Jonathan Van Castle, all of its details and all of her reasons.

Unmoving through her recital, Seamus watched her without expression. When she finished, she exhaled slowly, feeling lighter than she had since she'd met Jon. But Seamus remained silent. She glanced up. He'd never looked at her with so much ice in his eyes.

"Congratulations. Sounds to me like you've sold yourself for a chunk of land."

Lil sucked in her breath. From the corner of her eye, she glimpsed Mari flicker past the ballroom doors. "That's not fair. I saw an opportunity to help my family, and help myself, and I took it. If I hadn't, we'd be dancing at Mari's wedding right now, and you *know* Mari. She couldn't have kept her head straight in this—this—"

"Bacchanalian romp?"

She gave a shaky laugh. "It is, rather, isn't it?"

He didn't smile.

"Please don't be upset. You've been such a good friend since Robbie . . ." She blinked. A tear dropped on her hands, and the diamonds on her finger winked at her.

"Shit." Seamus pushed off the pillar, and sat, covering her hands with one of his. That odd light she'd noticed in his eyes that day at the bookstore had returned. "Dammit, Lil. Do you know what you've done? What you've let yourself in for? The guy's no good. Worse than no good."

"If you're talking about all those articles in the papers after he got divorced, he told Mari they aren't true."

"You don't know the half of it. If I'd known you had gotten mixed up with him, I would have—"

"Where's my bride?" Jon parted the fronds of the palm and she snatched her hand away from Seamus. Jon smiled at her. "Gotcha. No fair playing hide-and-seek and leaving me to fend off the masses by myself."

His grin evaporated when he noted her companion. He looked from Seamus's set expression to her tear-stained face. "I owe *Country Dreaming* some exclusive shots, so . . ." He bent forward, gripped her hand, and, with more force than necessary, yanked her to her feet. She scrambled to stick her feet in her shoes. "Later, uh, Seamus, wasn't it?" He turned his back and pulled Lil after him.

"That wasn't very nice." She panted, struggling to match his long stride and not trip over her train. He didn't have any reason to be angry. She jerked the train aside before someone trod on it. "Seamus is a good friend. I know he wasn't very nice at the cabin, but he was just upset because—well, you see, he's helped me out many times, and for you to act like some prima donna superstar is—"

Jon twirled her in front of him, nearly throwing her off her shoes. A muscle in his jaw pulsed. "Dammit, Lil—" he started. When interested faces swiveled toward them, he plastered on a smile and lowered his voice. "The man's mooning over you, you're sitting there with a wet face—"

"Seamus doesn't moon!"

Jon kept smiling, but hissed through his teeth, "Speak up. The folks in Omaha can't hear you."

She lowered her voice to match his. "He didn't

moon over me. He's a friend, and no matter what you think, that doesn't give you any right to treat him like that."

"Let me tell you a thing or two about rights. Use your head. If that'd been a news hound who'd snuck up on you two instead of me, your picture—with him—would be plastered all over tomorrow's rags."

"They're already past deadline." She'd learned a few things.

Turning red, he tugged her through the crowd, as though if he didn't move, he'd blow. "Plastered all over the *next day's* papers. They're everywhere, Lil, with their telephoto lenses, and don't forget those papers you put your John Henry on. One whiff of a scandal, one little stink that our marriage isn't all we're working to make the media believe it is, and my ex will be hollering foul from the courtroom rafters."

"And you'd lose that award you want, wouldn't you?"

"*And* I'll lose Mel and Michael and our deal will be off. Then I'll slap you with a lawsuit for breach of contract."

She'd been about to tell him she didn't care about the photographers, that marrying him didn't mean she wouldn't see her friends anymore, and that he couldn't tell her what to do, but at these last words, she stopped dead, yanking him to a halt. "You wouldn't dare!"

He leaned down next to her, his eyes lit with golden fire. "Try me."

Before she could reply, he swept her into his arms and twirled her off around the dance floor. He held her in an iron grasp, and while she could sense he still pulsed with anger, he smiled at the well wishes thrown their way. So alarmingly conscious of every inch of him, by the time the dance had ended, she had totally forgotten what she'd intended to say.

Chapter 14

In the small hours of the morning, after they'd bid good-bye to the last of the guests at the reception and Roy had driven them back to the cabana, they were alone. Tina-the-Nanny had maneuvered, with a flash of intelligence Jon hadn't figured she possessed, to bunk elsewhere with the children on their daddy's wedding night.

In the cabana, candlelight flickered on the walls from holders scattered around the great room, and a bowl of gardenias graced the coffee table. The drapes on the windows were wide open, revealing a half-moon that cast a shimmer across the obsidian mirror of the lake. Despite the damp heat of the summer night, even a fire flickered in the fireplace.

Someone had set the scene for seduction. Probably Zeke. Ha ha, Zeke, very funny. Jon flipped on the lights, blew out the candles, and bent down to turn off the gas jet.

Along with Peter, Jon had told Zeke, Three-Ring, Roy, and Lydia his little secret, figuring that in the insular life they led, he couldn't keep it from them anyway. He'd also need them to keep up the pretense that his hasty marriage had resulted from a lightning bolt from heaven. Leaks to the press didn't worry him. They'd always watched each other's backs. Plus they knew the futures of his kids—and the band—hinged on secrecy.

His secretary was too professional to show surprise, and his bodyguard had accepted the news with his usual silence. Three-Ring had only uttered a mild, "Cool," then turned back to *Zen and the Art of Motorcycle Maintenance*. Surprisingly, Zeke hadn't harangued him, but only smiled.

He'd debated whether to tell Tina-the-Nanny, and decided against it. She wouldn't figure it out even if he waved the papers he and Lil had signed under her nose. He also doubted Mel or Michael would see through the fake marriage. After all, what did they have to compare it to?

Behind him, Lil lowered herself to the sofa and slid off her shoes. Once they lay near her feet, though, she didn't relax, but sat bolt upright. She'd been silent ever since they'd left the reception and he'd put it down to tiredness, or anger over the argument they'd had about her *friend*. But now, from the way her eyes fastened on his every movement, he wondered if she was scared of him. Not that the idea of ravishing her didn't tempt him. She did things to his insides he'd never felt before. Funny, warm, molten things.

But despite her stiff-upper-lip manner, during their brief engagement he'd already learned she was too fragile by half to withstand a real involvement with him.

More than once, he'd considered calling the whole thing off. He almost had after he'd found her collapsed in tears after a press conference where some jerk had asked her about her husband's death. But when he'd broached the idea, she'd tilted that chin up, dried her eyes, and insisted they go forward. He'd thought of his kids and reluctantly agreed.

Up until now, her life had been insulated by the customs and traditions of a small town. He was determined to see her through their arrangement unscathed.

Her eyeballs looked like they were about to pop

out of their sockets when he crossed to the draperies and yanked the cord, pulling them tight across the windows. The moonlight playing on the water blinked out.

"What are you doing?" Her curly hair, bare feet, and flouncy dress reminded him of a little kid worn out after a birthday party.

He smiled dryly. "You mean, before or after I force-feed you drugs?"

If possible, her eyes grew rounder.

"Would you relax? You know all that muck you read in the papers wasn't true. I'm not going to attack you, I'm not going to corrupt you. Telephoto lenses, remember? Pretend every window has eyes."

"Oh." Did he detect a small note of disappointment? She cleared her throat. "I mean, oh, I remember you told me I had to be careful about what I did from now on."

He moved over to the sofa, and if possible, she sat up straighter. Hell with that. He took a seat on one of the chairs and stretched his legs out. "Like Peter said, we feed the beasts, then we hope they'll leave us alone, until we're ready to give them more. From now on you live life in a fishbowl." He grinned. "Life-saver Lil."

She flushed. "That's a ridiculous name." His publicist had milked her rescue of Michael for all it was worth. "I feel like Dudley Do-Right in skirts."

"Better than Weeping Beauty."

That was the moniker the media had laid on her after she'd lashed out, tears in her eyes, at the moronic reporter that had asked her about Robbie. The press had lapped all that up. They loved her. An innocent small town girl, an impoverished beauty with a sad past. Together, the two of them were media magnets.

"Everything's working out great. Peter said you've got just the right touch." He clasped his hands behind his head, feeling satisfied, then he noticed she'd fallen silent. She'd looked away, and her chin quavered. "Hey, I'm sorry. I shouldn't have brought up that Weeping Beauty thing."

The chin clenched. "I'm okay."

Now they both fell silent. There was none of the easy camaraderie he'd felt with her on the houseboat, and he realized that although they'd rarely been apart since their engagement, this was the first time they'd been alone. As the quiet stretched between them, he shifted uneasily and launched a new topic. "You never did tell me how you brought your family around."

"All those bouquets you sent didn't hurt. Nor did this." Lil stretched her hand out and looked at the rock he'd put on her finger, then she touched a thin chain around her neck. He frowned. He suspected her old wedding band hung on that chain. A ghost of a smile crossed her face. "But it wasn't you, or me. It was Mother."

Jon raised his eyebrows.

Lil gave a slight shrug. "At first they all suspected what was up, even though I did my best to convince them it was"—coloring, she darted her eyes toward him, then away—"true love. Patsy Lee told me not to do it for her, and Alcea warned me against marrying for money. Pop, the sweetie, was just confused. Mari—"

"I know."

"Yes. But Mother—" He noticed when she was puzzled, a cute tiny line would appear between her eyebrows. "She listened to the whole fantastic tale, then she just hugged me and said . . ." Her color heightened.

"What did she say?"

She picked at the beads on her dress. "That she knew what was up from the way we looked at each other, so it didn't surprise her a bit. After that, everyone else just followed her lead."

He liked Zinnia.

"Except Mari of course. I've seen Mari angry before, but never like this. She won't talk to me at all." Catching her lower lip in her teeth, she looked away.

He watched her a moment. For the last week plus some, she'd been a real trouper. Although she'd be well paid for her part, this hadn't been easy. He'd seen enough to know how close she was with her family, and her sister's reaction must be cutting her to ribbons. He got to his feet, and moved toward the sofa.

She grabbed her shoes and stood up. "I'm going to bed. I'm exhausted." Those child-wide eyes narrowed. "By the way, where is bed? I didn't agree to sharing a bedroom."

"And I didn't ask you to," he retorted. He'd only intended to comfort her, for God's sake. Feeling foolish, he dug his hands in his pockets. "Roy put your things in Tina's old room. She's bunking with Mel. You're upstairs at the end of the hall."

"And where are you? I mean, in case I need to explain to the children why . . ."

"Why Mommy and Daddy don't sleep in the same bed? Just tell 'em I snore. They'll believe you. I do. With gusto."

Lil turned toward the stairs that led to the second floor. She was in such a hurry to get away from him, she apparently forgot about her unwieldy gown. She was five paces underway when the train snagged under the legs of the coffee table and sofa, pulling her up short.

"Darn it all!" Kneeling, she wrestled with the train, but the stuff snarled around her hands. She gave up and rose, back straight.

He couldn't help the twitch that tugged on his mouth. She looked so regally helpless, her long legs twisted in netting, her chin tilted up like a queen, and her eyes flashing cool fire. Underneath that rosebud mouth, he figured her teeth were clenched. He pulled a stick of gum out, took his time unwrapping it, then pushed it in his mouth and watched her.

"Instead of standing there with that goofy grin, do you think you could *possibly* lend me a hand?"

He wiped off his smirk, but couldn't look her in the eye, sure he'd bust out laughing. He lifted the table and the sofa off the train while she stood in frigid silence, then knelt by her feet and tried to unleash the netting that hobbled her. Her struggles had tugged the stuff into a mess and he was afraid he'd rip it. He sat back on his heels and looked up.

She stared down her nose, graceful brows raised, and he couldn't resist a sly smile. "You'll have to take it off."

Her eyes widened and peach bloomed on her cheeks. "If you think I'm—"

"Not the whole dress, dummy. The train."

With a grunt of impatience at her skittishness, he rose and grasped her waist, just above the swell of her hips, not bothering to hide that he enjoyed the soft feel of her under his hands. He purposely leered, snapping his gum, and enjoyed watching those blues shift from royal frost to pale alarm. "You can't—"

He winked. "I'm not."

She made an exasperated sound and he swiveled her around. Modest in front, the gown dipped alarmingly in back and her nakedness faced him, a field of sun-kissed, satin skin that hollowed between her shoulder blades and over the pearl strand of her spine.

The air in the room hummed, suddenly as charged as a preconcert arena.

His jaw stilled. He swallowed hard and made himself concentrate on the tiny buttons that hooked around the seam of the dress from her shoulders to the swell of her bottom. His fingers skimmed the smooth flesh, his breath fluffed the sprinkle of curls that lay on her neck, and her floral scent made it hard to think. She shivered.

"Cold?" he murmured.

He wasn't cold, he was hot. Wild and hot.

His hands trembled with the urge to yank her around and crush that full mouth under his. He remembered the feel of her under his lips after the judge had pronounced them man and wife, the yielding of her body, the tremulous sigh. His resolve to leave her alone began a slow slide to oblivion.

He unhooked the last button and the train dropped. His hands lingered, as if they had a will of their own. With a nearly inaudible groan, he bent his head, his hair drifting against her back. He aimed for that tender spot where her shoulder slid up to her neck.

As though guessing his intentions, she sucked in a breath and went rigid. If he gave her a push she'd keel over like a domino, face down, knees locked. Reconsidering, but not yet ready to yield, he pulled back. When he did, she twitched once, enough to make him drop his hands. Without a glance behind her, she went toward the stairs. Her steps, normally light, were wooden. "Thank you. Good night."

He thought her voice caught on the words, but she didn't turn around. He was left standing in the middle of the room like a clown, tongue hanging out, arms dangling loose at his sides. No less than he deserved.

Muttering a curse, he kicked the train aside, grabbed his Fender, and sprawled on the sofa. He had no right to toy with her. He had a genetic predisposition to shatter the heart of anyone who loved him. He wouldn't let himself fall for her and, with her prissy attitude, she wouldn't find him any great shakes even if he did.

He closed his eyes, gave his knuckles a long crack, then fingered his guitar pick. *China blue eyes. Such a surprise. Gentled and soothed under my hands, your face a disguise . . .* Yuck.

Upstairs, Lil locked her door, then leaned against it. Her blurred gaze traveled the sterile confines she would have to call home for . . . she didn't know for how long.

Brushing at her eyes, she peeled off her dress and hung it from the closet door, running her hands down the folds. The glass beads twinkled, and her tears spilled onto her cheeks.

In the attached bathroom, someone had laid out her toiletries. Yesterday, she'd gone home to pack up her luggage for delivery to the resort, taken a long look at the contract she and Jon had signed before stuffing it out of sight in a kitchen drawer, and walked slowly through the rooms of her little yellow house, clutching her cat Petunia and wondering when she'd see them both again.

Thinking of Petunia, her eyes filled again. She missed her purring comfort and hoped Mari's ire didn't extend to her pet. Since the resort had a no pets policy, their mother had coerced her sister into caring for the cat through the rest of the summer. After that, she hoped she could have Petunia with her. Wherever she'd be.

She brushed her teeth and washed her face, careful not to look at her swollen eyes. Circling the room, she switched off all the lamps, then paused to push the curtains away from the window. Light from the half-moon spilled into the room. A lone boat skimmed across the lake, its lights like fireflies against the dark surface.

Leaving a gap in the curtains, she crawled between the covers, pulled them up to her chin, and turned her face to the soft light.

Strains from Jon's guitar and the murmur of his rich voice floated up the stairs and through the crack under her door. She couldn't understand the words and the tune wasn't familiar, but it was pretty, a haunting, mournful ballad, sung in a minor key.

A serenade for her wedding night . . .

She remembered her first wedding night, Robbie's

gentle, tentative explorations and her clumsy responses. Their limbs tangled together. Their giggles. As she drifted toward sleep, those images merged with the soft touch of Jon's hands as he'd unfastened her train, his breath warming her neck, his hair brushing her back . . . and the traitorous way her body had quickened.

Her pillow grew damp with her tears until she wadded it under her cheek and slept.

Chapter 15

Over the next nine days, Lil found she didn't need to fight off tears as much as she needed to stave off boredom. The Van Castle moneymaking machine had paused briefly for their wedding, but then had hummed back to life, leaving her and the children scrambling to find a place in its tempo. Steeled to defend Melanie and Michael from the excesses of their father's stardom, she'd gradually deflated. There weren't wild parties. Not a whiff of marijuana smoke, not a pill in sight. No groupies, no flunkies, no bimbos. She almost wished there were. At least it would give her something to do.

The day she'd spent on the houseboat with Jon and the children seemed part of the distant past. The man she'd glimpsed then was a mirage. He'd disappeared into a workaholic personality and a nonstop schedule. Any thought she'd had they might live with some semblance of normalcy had disappeared in the face of the gait he set—to the detriment of his children.

That was about to change. On the second Tuesday following her wedding, filled with determination, Lil tiptoed down the stairs in her bathrobe, and moved to the windows overlooking Shawnee Bay. She tugged open the drapes. Night still pressed against Kesibwi, but a faint light in the east hailed dawn. A fishing boat puttered through the haze lifting off the lake. Jon should be home soon.

Van Castle was gearing up for the state fair concert in Sedalia less than two weeks from now. The late-August concert was the last event in the United States leg of their tour. Over the last week, more of Jon's "people" had filtered into the Royal Sun—backup singers, stage crew, road musicians, dancers, all a blur of unfamiliar faces. Roy had explained them all to her. Heaven knows, Jon hadn't been around to do so.

So this morning, she had decided they were going to talk about that—and a few other things.

Behind her, she heard a rustling in the kitchen. A few moments later, she turned to see Roy with two coffee mugs in hand, brows raised at seeing her up before him. Every morning she joined Jon's bodyguard on the deck, where he'd have a steaming mug of coffee, creamed and sugared just how she liked it, waiting for her on a table next to a canvas-backed chair that matched his own. They'd been meeting at first light ever since the morning after the wedding, when they'd surprised each other by colliding on the deck. Now the ritual of sharing the dawn had already become habit. She'd learned that, along with sunrises, they shared an enjoyment of classical music and cozy mysteries. While Roy was intensely loyal to Jon, he longed to settle in one place. The burly, bald bodyguard had a poetic soul.

They exchanged murmured good mornings, but when he opened the door to the deck for her, she shook her head. "You watch without me this morning. I need to catch Jon before he goes upstairs."

Roy's bushy eyebrows rose higher, but he said nothing and moved outdoors, sliding the door shut behind him. She set her coffee mug on the table.

As soon as the sun met the horizon, Jon would arrive, probably with Zeke. Jon would immediately stumble up the stairs, following a mumbled hello, but Zeke often joined her and Roy with a cup of tea.

He'd entertain them with a humorous rundown of the night's rehearsals before heading off to the cabana he'd rented after the wedding.

As though Zeke's departure was his cue, Michael would appear. And she'd face another expanse of hours trying to keep him entertained, while she simultaneously labored to entice Melanie out of her books.

They couldn't go on this way forever. She couldn't go on this way. Pacing, she tugged the sash on her robe tight, and paused to switch on a CD, volume turned low. Vivaldi soothed her.

She appreciated Roy's easy companionship, Zeke's dry humor, and the children's company, but it wasn't enough. Jon had packed Tina back to wherever she came from, and the O'Malleys had returned to their lives in Cordelia. At least six times in the past nine days, she'd called her mother. But Zinnia was busy and couldn't indulge in the kind of conversations Lil longed for. Instead, she received only a hurried account of her family's news. Waiting for her baby's birth in early January, Patsy Lee still clerked at the bank. Surprisingly, the building housing Merry-Go-Read had sold, so that was one less debt. Alcea had flung herself into organizing the fall PTA events, and Mari was preparing to return to school. She'd call her mother more often, except the conversations left her battling a hollow feeling of homesickness.

She rarely saw Jon. Mostly she felt he never gave her and the children a thought, but sometimes she suspected he was intentionally avoiding her. He sidestepped attempts at conversation, and if she happened to brush up against him, he jumped like a rabbit. But most of the time, unless playacting was called for, he acted like she wasn't there.

She heard the front door click open, then closed. In a moment, Jon rounded the fireplace, alone. Zeke must have gone directly to his own bed. Head down, Jon didn't notice her.

"We need to talk." She took a few quick steps and intercepted him near the stairs.

Jon's head shot up. Tired lines webbed around his eyes. He looked longingly at the staircase, but stopped. "Something wrong?"

"Everything's wrong."

He paused, dragged a hand over the stubble on his face. "It can't wait?"

"No." The guarded expression in his eyes along with the weary bent to his shoulders almost persuaded her to just let him go to bed. But then she thought of Michael and Melanie and her resolve stiffened. Whether he liked it or not, he'd "hired" her to look after his children's best interests, and that's what she intended to do.

She locked a hand on his arm and steered him into the room, stopping in front of the fireplace. When she turned to face him, their gazes met. For a moment, a current drifted between them, then his brow tightened. He gently pulled away and scooped up a handful of M&M's from the coffee table. He didn't eat them, though, he just studied them lying in his palm. She frowned. Was her touch that distasteful?

He finally looked at her. "So, what is it?"

"The children are bored silly." She latched her arms together again. "Roy brings us books and games and movies, but Michael has the attention of a bird, and there's only so much I can do with Walt Disney and Junior Monopoly."

Jon let the candy slide from his fingers back into the bowl. "How could they be bored? There's ice skating, go-karts, a theater, a bowling alley—"

"And you don't let us go to any of them unless the crowds are thin and Roy is with us. Those two circumstances don't often come up. Of course, how would you know? You're never here to see it. Or them."

"That's not fair." His voice was quiet. "I'm knee-deep in rehearsals every night. Peter co-opted the resort's roller rink for us to use, but we have to use it at night. I'm paying a wad for the privilege, too."

"You could be home evenings if you'd use one of the public rooms during the day like normal people would."

"That's the point, Lil." He pulled out one of his ever-present Tootsie Roll Pops, but didn't look at her. "I keep telling you, we're not normal. We use the rink at night to keep the curious to a minimum. As for my rules about your activities, you've got to remember that as far as the media and my fans are concerned, Michael and Melanie aren't children, they're prey."

Apparently feeling the conversation was done, he stuck the pop in his mouth and turned toward the stairs. She hurried after him, stopping him with a touch. He flinched. When he turned around, his expression was blank. Oh, for Pete's sake, she wasn't a leper.

She tried to tamp down her irritation. "Since the wedding, I've seen only one photographer. That greasy-haired fellow with a wart on his nose. From the looks of him, he's no match for Roy, so I don't see why we need to be so cautious." She bit her tongue before she told him his fame loomed larger in his own mind than it did in reality.

"They're like roaches. If you see one, you know more are around." He crunched on the candy, pitched the stick toward the table.

Lil frowned at the stick and wrapper. With a sigh, Jon walked around the sofa. He scooped up the trash, stuck it in his pocket, and flopped down, apparently deciding the conversation would end when she wanted it to end.

Laying his head back, his eyes fluttered closed. "What about horseback riding?"

"I can't coax Roy onto one. He's scared of them."

He smiled. She perched on the chair across from

him, knotting her hands in her lap. His hair fanned over the cushions. His face was vividly handsome in repose.

"Mm. Tennis lessons?"

"We tried that. The instructor banned us after Michael fired a ball right at his crotch."

His eyes opened halfway and this time she smiled back. She had to admit, it had been funny. "The tennis coach is odious, a big-muscled blond. He flirted with me. Michael didn't like him."

"Good for Michael." Jon's eyes drifted closed again, mouth still curved. "Swimming?"

"We go every afternoon. If we're lucky, a few of the crew might be there, but since they're up all night, nobody has the energy to play with them. So Melanie sticks her nose in a book, and that leaves Michael with me. He's tired of me. He wants you."

Jon made a face. It reminded her of Michael when he'd done something wrong. "I see them at dinner, and sometimes breakfast, don't I? By the way, I like those pancakes you make. The ones shaped like bunny rabbits with raisins for eyes."

Even though she felt a silly thrill that he noticed the efforts she made, she wouldn't let him change the subject. "You see them long enough to bolt your food and ruffle their hair, that's all. We also need to talk about what happens when you leave at the end of the month. You'll be gone until Christmas and I don't want to follow you around. School will start soon. We have to consider—"

"God, I'm tired." Jon opened his eyes and stood up in one fluid movement. He stretched. "Let's talk about this tomorrow."

Exasperated, she looked up. "It is tomorrow."

He stared at her. The dawn starting to lighten the room turned his eyes to fine brandy. "You just won't let go, will you?"

"No."

For a moment, their eyes held. Then his gaze dropped, and the tips of his ears reddened. Glancing down, she realized her robe had gaped. She was wearing a filmy nightgown Alcea had given her as a wedding present. The concoction was too pretty to be left in a box, but it covered next to nothing.

She gripped her lapels. Jon looked away. There was a moment of uncomfortable silence. Shaken by the way her body had flushed under his gaze, she was tempted to let the conversation go. But she couldn't.

"It's not just the children. I'm bored, too. I'm not used to doing nothing all day. The only adult I've talked with in the last ten days is my mother—over the phone—and Roy or Zeke when you let them off their leashes."

"I'm sorry you're feeling cooped up, but you'll just have to do the best you can. I can't let you run off on your own. It wouldn't be safe. Not for you, not for the kids. You don't know what those vultures are capable of."

"Just because they raked you over the coals when you got a divorce doesn't mean—"

"That's exactly what it means." Partway to the stairs, Jon jerked around, his expression exasperated. "They lie, Lil. They take rumor and innuendo, and they lie. They almost cost me my career. Give them enough rope and they'll hang the kids, too. The partying you read about? When? I was always working. Force-feeding my wife drugs? Give me a break."

"I don't understand. I mean, lots of musicians get bad publicity." She searched her memory for what she knew about country singers. Not much. "Didn't Johnny Cash go to jail? I thought it went with the image. Why would it damage your career?"

"Outlaw singers went out in the eighties, and Johnny Cash's sins were against himself. Mine—or what they said I did—weren't. A lot of my fans are in the Bible Belt. They don't hold much with corrupting kids. That's the kind of crap Belinda accused me of."

"But nobody could possibly think you could really—" She stopped.

He looked at her. "You did."

She shied from his eyes. He hitched his hands in his pockets and stared out of the window. "Belinda wallpapered the tabloids with pictures that made her look like Mother Teresa protecting two angels. She made it sound like I'd put the monkey on her back, like I was a beast with the morals of a rabbit in heat—and that I took advantage of some teenage groupie. That shit isn't going to play anywhere, anytime, I don't care who you are. She made me look like the antichrist of American morals."

"But, still, once people really know you—"

"Things got so bad, the lies hit papers like the *Wall Street Journal*. People read it, believed it. *Parents* believed it. And they foot the bill for their kids who buy a lot of my concert tickets, my CDs. Everything I'd worked for almost went down the tubes."

"Well, obviously Belinda did it to get the public on her side, to get your children."

"And the money that went with them."

"So, if—I mean, since—it wasn't true, why didn't you defend yourself?"

His lips curved wryly at her slip. "Because it *was* my fault. I should have paid more attention to them. And she stopped all the lying once she realized she was about to shut off the spigot. I also didn't want to put Mel and Michael through any more. They'd gone through enough."

"But, leaving them with Belinda . . ."

"It wasn't just Belinda. Dodo was with them. I knew they'd be safe with her mother." He shook his head. "I *thought* they'd be safe with her mother."

Jon's stance was tired, defeated, and old. Suddenly, she felt an urge to hold him, a fierce need to protect him. It was a feeling she'd never had, not for another adult. Robbie had always been the protector in their marriage.

"It wasn't your fault," she blurted.

Jon didn't move, but the glance he flicked at her was filled with cynicism. Vivaldi and the mantel clock ticked off the seconds.

Feeling embarrassed—what did she really know about any of this?—she gathered herself. "So, can't you pay more attention to Michael and Melanie now?"

He flung up his hands. "Jesus, Lil. Give it up."

"I can't give it up. They need more of your time."

"Look, celebrity comes at a price." He turned toward the stairs.

Tight with frustration, she murmured at his retreating back, "Maybe. But the children shouldn't have to pay it."

Chapter 16

Jon knew the wiser move was continuing up the stairs, but Lil was worse than a starving dog with a meaty bone—she wouldn't let it rest. And he needed nothing *but* rest, dammit.

The approaching state fair gig, the late summer release of their new CD, and the upcoming tour of Europe kept him churning in fifty directions at once. Hell, sixty. If that wasn't enough, rehearsals hadn't been worth shit last night. He should know better than to try to slide a new song into the lineup now, but he wanted to give "China Blue Eyes" some play time. If the crowd bought the tune, he'd use it as a cut on their next CD. The piece was less country and more soft rock than what Van Castle normally gave their fans. If he knew his stuff, though, he had another first-rate crossover hit on his hands. That is, if he could finish the lyrics. They lay frustratingly, tantalizingly out of reach. Last night the road musicians and backup singers (humming what he hadn't written yet) had taken their first shot at it—and they'd missed the target completely.

He was frustrated, irritated, and he needed sleep, not a harangue from his wife.

Wife. He almost snorted. After that second day on the boat, the easy way they'd gotten along during their engagement, and the way she'd responded to him when he'd kissed her at the altar, he'd hoped . . . hell, he didn't know what he'd hoped. But he knew he didn't have the right to hope for squat. Nor should he. So he'd done his best to duck her, afraid of the feelings she torched, afraid he wouldn't keep his side of the bargain.

Yet here she was, her blond hair mussed, that ragged yellow bathrobe—the only piece of clothing she'd convinced Sidney to let her keep—giving him glimpses of things he didn't dare lay his hands on, badgering him to spend more time with her and the kids. Couldn't she see his avoidance kept her *safe*?

Looking for his notes on "China Blue Eyes" yesterday before he'd headed to rehearsals, he'd stumbled across a scene on the deck that had frozen him in his tracks.

A hose dripping from his hand, Michael had stomped barefoot through the water pooling on the planks, then unleashed the nozzle and pointed the spray straight at Mel, stretched on a deck chair and reading, as usual. She'd shrieked and rocketed up in a tangle of legs. From stage left, Lil rushed forward and grabbed the hose. Bending over, she met Michael nose to nose, presenting Jon with a long length of tanned limbs topped by a bottom clad in stretchy peach shorts. Her lips moved in a scold, although the hint of a smile played around the edges of her mouth. Lil. The name played like fine wine over his tongue. His notes forgotten, he sucked in his breath and felt his groin tighten.

Lil rubbed Michael's damp hair into spikes with a towel. Michael howled in protest and Lil laughed, a melodious sound. That fetching dimple peeked in and out. Her peach shorts and top were now soaked and clung to mind-tripping feminine curves. Her hair curled in ringlets on her flushed cheeks. She'd looked good enough to eat.

But right about now, it looked like she was ready to tear her teeth into him. While she still sat perched on the chair, she held herself unnaturally straight and her jaw was clenched. He wanted to shake her. He wanted to hold her. He wanted to do a million things to her, but most of all he wanted her to leave him alone so he could go to bed.

He closed the distance between them in a few short steps, so he didn't need to raise his voice. Last thing they needed was Michael zinging around the room chanting ad-speak.

"Dammit, Lil, I'm doing the best I can. My job, like it or not, takes a lot from me and out of me. Van Castle didn't get where they are without a helluva lot of hard work. Part of my responsibilities, as I see it, is to support these kids. And I can't do it while I'm bandying them on my knee."

That argument didn't soften her a bit. If anything, she grew taller where she sat. "They don't need more money. What they need is more of your time."

He bit the inside of his cheek in frustration, wishing he could smoke. "Look, unlike some folks, I didn't grow up cradled in the bosom of some loving family. I have only memories of a mother and an old man who said I would never be man enough for anything. He beat me six ways to Sunday every chance he got." He clamped his mouth shut. It had been more than he'd meant to say.

Her eyes lost that icy look. "Why didn't somebody stop him?"

When he didn't answer, she touched his hand. He realized both hands were shaking, and stuffed them back in his pockets. "Jon?"

"I—" He hesitated, then plunged in. If she wanted the truth unvarnished, he'd tell her. "He was a mean drunk, with a shotgun full of buckshot he used on trespassers. Even the sheriff stayed back. When I was older, Judge Dougherty tried to help; threw the old man in jail a few times. Best days of my life. Dodo tried, too. Whenever I was too scared to go home, she gave me a place to stay. I don't have a helluva lot of experience with parenthood, you know? So, I'll repeat, I'm doing the best I can."

She didn't flinch. She just reached out, pulled gently until she'd freed his hands, and then wrapped them between her warm ones, her touch featherlight. Amazed at himself, at her, his throat thickened, and he looked away. He had some friends. He had wealth. He had power and talent and crowds who chanted his name. He'd had kindness in Dodo and the judge. But he'd never bumped up against much tenderness. Until he'd met her.

"It's all over," she murmured. "You grew into a fine man despite everything that happened. You could have become cruel or bitter, but you rose above it. There aren't many people who do that." Leaving his hands lying in one palm, she reached up to touch his chin, guiding his head with her fingertips until he had to look at her. Her eyes were compassionate. "You're worthy of your children, Jon. Let me help you be their father."

Help him? Help him, how? He was afraid she wanted more from him than he had to give. And he was afraid he'd disappoint her. Frustration balled itself inside him, rose up, had him yanking back from her touch. Blinking, she let her hand drop back in her lap.

"Lil—"

Her eyes lanced up at him, then away. "Don't take them for granted, Jon."

Outside, sparrows and finches took up their morning calls. He stood before her, hands dangling at his sides. Then in one restless movement, he threw himself on the sofa.

As though swallowing her own frustration, Lil took a deep breath and rose. Rounding the table, she knelt. "Stop believing all those things your father said. You did amount to something. You're not worthless. You're a huge success and a good man. The children wouldn't love you if you weren't. They want more time with you, that's all."

"Just get over it, eh?" he said dryly.

"Well . . . yes."

He smiled, studying her until she pinked and dropped her gaze. She was so sweet, so . . . Lil. His hand hovered on the verge of curling her hair behind the cusp of one rose-tinged ear, but he wasn't sure how she'd take it. "All right. I'll try."

At that lukewarm agreement, she looked up again and clasped his knee. Underneath her hand, his flesh burned. "You could start this evening. Take them on a walk and deliver the invitations to your crew."

Heat made its way up his thigh. He didn't move, didn't breathe. Ah, Lil. How could he concentrate on—

He frowned. "What invitations?"

"For Michael's party."

"What party?"

She removed her hand, and he released his breath. "His birthday's tomorrow. They've been talking about nothing else. Haven't you noticed?"

"Uh, sure." With her looking at him like that, he'd pretend anything. A yawn caught him. He vaguely recalled Roy bundling in balloons, construction paper, and streamers, which Lil happily informed him were for crafting decorations, and there was an unskillfully iced chocolate layer cake resting on the kitchen counter. God, he wished she'd put her hand back. He'd have to ask Lydia to get Michael some kind of present. He dropped his head against the back of the sofa. "Michael's birthday. Of course."

"My mother's bringing Daisy, Hank, and Rose out around one tomorrow and—"

"Listen, can we talk about it later? I'm asleep on my feet, ass, whatever." His eyes closed, but not before he saw her shoulders slump. "Lil?"

Like a whisper, he heard her rise. "What?" Her voice seemed to come from a distance.

"Tonight." He blinked, then his eyes closed again. "I promise I'll start spending more time with the kids tonight."

In answer, she picked up his feet, swung them up on the sofa, and covered him with an afghan. He burrowed into leather heaven.

Some hours later, his eyes shot open. Thoughts and words tumbled through his mind. Confused for a moment, he listened. Nothing and nobody stirred. Lil must have taken the kids to the pool.

He swung his feet to the floor and grabbed a pad and a pen from the table. Within minutes, the lyrics that had bedeviled him ever since he'd met Lil were laid out in stark black and white on the paper beneath his hand. He read them and smiled.

Standing up, he stretched, then grabbed the pad and headed to his bedroom for a few more hours' shut-eye. When he next woke, it was to a call from his Nashville producer that left him huddled through chow time with Zeke. One of the backup fiddlers had broken a finger. They needed to find a replacement for hurried re-recording of some tracks on the CD. Since time squeezed, they scribbled a short list and he called the music men himself instead of leaving it to his producer, who'd feel he'd need to go through their agents. The high demand for good studio musicians sometimes required the personal touch. Rehearsals loomed by the time he finally snagged the guy he wanted.

It wasn't until he'd grabbed his Fender, the lyrics, and was on his way to the skating rink that he remembered his promise to Lil.

Chapter 17

At three-thirty on Wednesday, Lil seethed. He'd *promised*. Where was everyone? Where was *he*? In the airy brightness of the cabana's kitchen, she paced to the window, looked up and down the drive, then glanced at her watch for the eighth time in two minutes. He knew Michael's party started at three—everyone knew Michael's party started at three—the invitations were specific. So where were they?

She turned back toward the table where five small faces wearing party hats wavered in various shades between hope and disappointment. An orange cone perched in her curls, Zinnia watched her thoughtfully, sucking on a chocolate kiss from a bowl on the table.

Michael's birthday had dawned bright blue, bold, and hot. Through the morning, he'd been a small hurricane. She tried to shush him so he wouldn't wake Jon, still asleep behind his bedroom door. She finally gave up and took both kids to the pool again. When they returned, she'd expected to see Jon yawning over his coffee, but he'd left.

She set the children to work blowing up balloons, but after he learned his dad had left without so much as a happy birthday, Michael tended to pop, stomp, or drop-kick every other one. They hadn't made much progress by the time Zinnia arrived with Patsy Lee's children.

Daisy, dressed in pink shorts and a turquoise shirt that matched her eyelids, still bubbled with enthusiasm from her own birthday the day before. She chattered a blue streak, shared her Hibiscus Heaven lip gloss with Melanie, and tossed her new soccer ball to Michael, who hurled it straight at his cake. A surprising header from the usually dreamy Hank narrowly saved the confection. Rose kept her distance, Twinkle clutched under her arm.

After that, Zinnia had corralled the kids for a game of Duck Duck Goose, while Lil had called every cell phone number she could find in the booklet Roy had left by the phone, growing increasingly agitated when nobody answered. Phones were either off—likely Jon's edict for rehearsals—or out of service, a habitual problem in the Ozark hills.

Now she stood, hands on hips, and surveyed the ring of children. Her gaze paused on Michael. Using a fork, he methodically punched holes in the construction paper cutouts he'd made yesterday to decorate the table. When he looked up, his eyes swam.

Something inside of her snapped. So what if Jon had experienced a crummy childhood? He had no right to treat his son this way.

She forced a smile and spoke gaily. "Okay, everyone, let's get this show on the road! We're off for a day on the town."

The children scrambled to their feet and made a rush for the door, Daisy in the lead.

"We'll take your van, okay, Mother?"

"Now, Lil, didn't you tell me Jon said you're not to go anywhere without—"

"I don't care what Jon said." She grabbed her purse and slung it over her shoulder. "It's his son's birthday! You'd think he could take one measly hour out of his oh-so-important schedule to spend it with him, but no, not the busy superstar. I've tried. I arrange our schedule around him, but even when he's with us, which isn't often, he's distracted and distant. I don't even think he knows I'm—I mean, *we're*—there."

"Why, Jon didn't strike me as a man who'd—"

"Forget his son's birthday," Lil snorted.

"—ignore his new bride."

Her mother's words silenced her. In her anger, she'd forgotten she played a charade. She darted a look at her mother, wondering what she thought. Fishing for her car keys, Zinnia's nose was in her Dumpster of a handbag and Lil couldn't see her face.

Her mother surfaced with the keys, and winked. "We'll show him then, won't we?" She snatched off her orange cone and replaced it with her straw hat.

After they'd piled in the van, Lil chose the Shawnee Bay Outlet Mall, specifically the Toys 'n Stuff store, as their destination. Rolling through the green overhang of the woods to the main drag, they sang at the top of their lungs to old Beatles tapes she'd found in the glove box. As Lil joined the mismatched harmony, some of her anger dissipated in the sheer enjoyment of being free of the resort's confines.

Reaching the store, she set Michael loose to choose a present. He latched onto a lime green stuffed dinosaur twice as big as himself and three times more expensive than anything else, but she didn't care. She charged it on the card Peter had given her, along with a new game for Hank and Daisy, a doll for Rose, and a few books for Melanie. She didn't feel a twinge from her conscience.

Herding the children out of the toy store, she glimpsed the greasy-haired photographer with a wart on his nose. He'd dogged their steps at every opportunity since the wedding. She ignored him. As long as he kept a civil distance, what would a few pictures of an innocent outing matter? What had Jon said? Feed the beasts a few morsels, or something like that. In fact, Jon would probably be proud of the favorable publicity, since his career obviously was more important than anything else.

After stuffing Puff the Dragon into the van, they moved on to the Belly-Up Bumper Boats, where they butted each other until all of them were soaked and laughing. After, they tramped dripping into the Levi's outlet for dry clothes, and Lil's spirits lifted at the thought of more charges on Jon's card. Wart-nose followed, hovering in the background, thumbing through a rack of shirts, but keeping his eyes on them.

Still ignoring him, Lil retired to a changing room to try on a pair of white jeans with the sweetest pink flowers embroidered on the pockets. They were the most expensive ones she could find. As she zipped up and turned to the mirror, a lens poked through the curtains. Whirling, she snatched the camera from a startled Wart-nose. She pushed her face into his narrow one. Up close, he had large pores, thinning hair, and bad breath. She wanted to screech at him— at anybody, really—but kept her voice low. No scene would disturb Michael's day.

"If you don't keep your distance, I'm smashing this on the floor." She let the camera dangle from one finger. He nodded and gulped, Adam's apple looking like he'd swallowed a marble.

She hesitated a moment, tempted to let the camera drop to the floor anyway, but from the look of his frayed shirt and pants, shiny at the knees—not to mention the alarm on his face—she knew he didn't have the funds to replace his equipment. She couldn't do it. She shoved the camera at him so hard he banged into the wall behind him. "Get out of here."

He scampered back down the hall, and she whisked the curtains closed. Sagging against the mirror, she held her hands against her pounding chest. Maybe Jon had been right, maybe they should go home.

Michael's laughter sounded from the store, and she straightened, resolve returning. She wouldn't let his son's big day be spoiled any more than it had to.

During the next hour, Wart-nose kept to their bargain. Without incident, they visited the Old Timers Photo Shoppe, where they dressed like hillbillies and posed with straw between their teeth, then went on to Hottest Wheels Go-Karts.

While they belted into their carts—Michael and Lil in one two-seater, Rose and Zinnia in another, and the older children opting for Little Bobbins—Wart-nose folded his stovepipe legs into a racer of his own.

For the first two loops, he clicked away from afar and Lil forgot him, enjoying Michael's squeals and the wind furrowing her hair. But on the third loop, Wart-nose darted in front of them, twisting to frame them in his lens. Lil gasped, unable to slow their cart. They banged against his back bumper, and their small two-seater swerved out of control and smashed into the wall. His cart swung around and pinned theirs. Her head whipped back against the seat, and Michael cried out. For a second, Wart-nose looked concerned, but then he yanked up his camera and snapped away.

Filled with equal parts fear and rage, Lil twirled the steering wheel and punched the accelerator, trying to find reverse. The tires whined, but the cart only rattled.

Zinnia rounded the curve. The ribbons on her hat streamed behind her. From the set of her chin, Lil knew she'd grasped their predicament. Zinnia flung an arm in front of Rose, yelled, "Hold on!" and Lil did likewise with Michael, just in case Zinnia missed her target. But she didn't. With a satisfying scrunch, Zinnia smashed the rear of Wart-nose's cart.

Photographer and cart skidded across the track. The camera flew into the air, landing on an embankment. Wart-nose scrambled out of his cart and after the camera.

Freed, Lil roared back to the starting gate, braking and waving her arms at the others to halt. Bug-eyed with excitement, Daisy and Melanie scrambled out of their carts, while Lil unstrapped Hank with shaking hands. Then Zinnia grabbed Rose's hand, Lil clutched Michael's, and they sprinted for the van. When they reached it, Lil looked over her shoulder. Wart-nose had paused at the exit, head swiveling. He spotted them and dashed toward a battered Studebaker.

Breath coming in shallow gasps, she got the kids belted and jumped into the passenger seat. Zinnia slammed the gears into reverse. A Blazer raced out of nowhere and screeched to a stop behind them. Zinnia stomped the brakes, sending everyone into their seatbelts. Rose whimpered. Frantically, Lil signaled the Blazer on, watching as the Studebaker coughed to life and lurched from its parking space. But the Blazer didn't move. Instead, its tinted windows slid down, and a flurry of cameras waved at them.

"Dammit," Lil muttered under her breath, grappling to undo her belt, and urging the children to do the same.

When they were ready, Zinnia counted, "One . . . two . . ." In a flurry, they all bailed and raced across the street to Frank's Frozen Custard, Rose's whimpers turning to tears, Daisy and Michael whooping with excitement, Melanie and Hank holding hands and running as fast as their skinny legs could carry them.

When they reached the door, almost neck and neck with Wart-nose, Lil pulled Rose and Michael in front of her and fumbled at the handle, while Zinnia sandwiched the other three between her body and Lil's. She swung her purse, a good half ton, at Wart-nose's camera. Beyond him, Lil could see the other photographers at the curb, chafing against a surge of traffic. Zinnia puffed. "Get that thing outta here."

The bag connected with his elbow. He grimaced. "Why you . . ."

Michael darted forward and kicked his shin. "Don't you touch Grandma Zinnia!"

The photographer lunged at Michael. "I'll show you

manners, my fellow," he huffed, but a swarm of children engulfed him, pulling his greasy hair, pinching and slapping.

Daisy got him a good right in the gut, just as two other photographers caught up to them. The man doubled over, and his camera clattered to the ground.

The door finally gave way and Lil pulled the children inside. Zinnia backed in, bag still swinging. Lil slammed the door. They fell back against it as the photographers yowled like alley cats and pushed from the other side. Using all her strength, Lil drove the bolt home, then turned, panting, to face the two startled clerks behind the counter. The photographers hammered on the glass outside.

Attempting to keep her voice steady, she explained their situation and asked for a phone. In her rush she'd forgotten the cell Peter had given her.

Zinnia shooed the children into a booth at the back, then pulled a sobbing Rose onto her lap. Brown eyes as big as baseballs, Hank huddled next to them. Melanie slid into the corner, her cheek turned to the torn vinyl, her hair hiding her face. Michael picked up a straw and shot at the photographers with his "gun" from over the back of the seat. Daisy danced in front of the windows, her giggles bordering on hysteria. The cameramen shot back with their lenses through the filmy glass.

One of the clerks pointed to a public phone, and the other went to bolt the back door. Hands trembling, Lil fumbled in her purse. A quarter fell and rolled under a table. She bent to retrieve it, knocking her head on the chrome edge. She blinked back tears. Michael's birthday should be a special day. Not this nightmare. Lil fed in her coins and prayed someone would be at the cabana. It was the only number she'd memorized. On the first ring, Jon barked a terse hello.

She swallowed a sob of relief. "Jon—"

"Where in the hell are you?" Fury snarled across the line.

Her anger sparked. How dare he growl at her? Maybe she'd blundered, but if it wasn't for him, they wouldn't be in this mess. "Maybe the better question is, where in the hell were you?"

There was a beat of silence. "Okay, I forgot, satisfied? Zeke reminded me when I went to meet him, but if you only knew what I've been through, trying to get this show shaped up and—"

"Spare me."

His breath came in tight rasps. He took a new tack. "When I got back here, and found only a few balloons nodding in the kitchen . . . do you know how worried I've been? I've thought kidnapping, ransom, murder, mayhem. How many times have I told you—"

"I know!" She dropped her forehead against the cool tile alongside the phone booth, anger subsiding. He was right. She should never have taken the children without Roy. In a small voice, she relayed a brief version of the day's events.

"That's great, just great."

Couldn't he offer at least a shred of sympathy? An ounce of understanding? She blinked back tears. "Please, don't scold me now. Just send Roy."

Chapter 18

On the cabana deck under a hazy morning sun, Jon dragged a canvas chair within leg reach of the edge, flopped down and crossed his ankles on the railing. The deck was shaded by oaks and positioned to catch a breeze, but give it another hour and living things would fry out here. He pulled a band from his pocket and yanked his hair back into a tail. He gazed out at the boats zipping across the ruffled green of Kesibwi, and waited for Lil.

Last evening, waiting by the window, it hadn't been until he'd spotted the limo edging its way through the canopy of trees, Roy's reassuring bulk in the driver's seat, that his pulse had returned to anywhere near normal. He'd watched as Mel had unloaded first. Her tongue between her teeth, she'd tugged on the end of something bright green and finally succeeded in freeing a monstrous stuffed animal attached to Michael at the other end. Then a slim foot had appeared and Lil had stepped out.

He'd ignored the leap in his heart when he saw she was safe—that they were safe—and stoked his fury instead. Then he had to stifle it when two bodies had hurtled through the door and wrapped themselves around his legs. Lil had hovered uncertainly in the doorway. While the kids had babbled about their day's experiences, he'd lofted Michael onto his shoulder and wrapped an arm around Melanie, feeling a faint glow of self-righteousness when he'd granted Lil only a cool stare. Tit for tat. Almost immediately, though, the glow had faded in a fit of self-blame. Only the day before he'd promised her more time, and look at him now, he'd forgotten Michael's birthday.

But it was still Michael's birthday. As the kids had chattered on, Michael in a high excited voice, Mel's more trembly, he'd inserted a word here or there and elicited an enthusiastic response for his just-thought-up plans for a poolside cookout for Michael. Zeke gathered the crew while Lil, with downcast eyes and a dutiful expression that made him want to shake her, had gathered the party goods. They'd all trekked down the hill, the party had gone off without a hitch, and then Lil had packed the kids to bed while he'd packed himself off to rehearsal.

But not before Lil had stuffed a wrapped package in his arms. "For Michael," she'd said. "He'll never know you didn't pick it out."

Damn her. Damn her stubbornness, damn her know-everything blue eyes and her clenched jaw and her gentle smile and her thoughtfulness and the soft curves of her body that swept through his dreams in the middle of the night. He gave his knuckles a good workout, and then pulled a pop from his pocket and stuck it in his mouth. He let the wrapper flutter to the wood planks and lie there.

About ten minutes ago, he'd surprised Roy and his family with a pre-noon appearance. They'd been having brunch on the deck, the kids still pajama-clad, and Lil wearing her ratty old robe. Shortly after he'd returned near dawn, he'd heard them rise, but had decided a few hours' sleep was necessary before he faced Lil. He didn't know whether to pounce on her, or beg her forgiveness.

She'd just gone in to change her clothes, apparently deciding she'd be better armored without the bathrobe for whichever tack he decided to take. She was likely formulating an attack on his broken promises, but, goddammit, this was one thing he *did* know something about, and she couldn't just—

Behind him, Lil cleared her throat.

"What in the hell did you think you were doing?" Each word was an ice chip.

She didn't respond and he twisted to see her. She stood in front of the doors in white jeans and a white top, both sprinkled with dusty pink flowers, hands clasped, head bowed, her curls a pale yellow halo. His heart softened, but when he thought of what might have happened to her—to them—it hardened again.

"I know I shouldn't have taken them without Roy, but I—"

He stabbed the lollipop stick at her. "You sure as shit shouldn't have. I've told you over and over, it's not safe for them. But no. Lil always knows what's best. Lil knows what's best for her family, for Mari, for me, for my kids, for my life."

She flashed him a look that held—what, anger? She should be glad he didn't turn her over his knee. The thought was tempting.

He unlocked an ankle and kicked at a chair only a few inches away from his. "Sit."

She sat, a demure pose, hands clasped in her lap, eyes lowered.

"Dammit, Lil, you can't just go off half-cocked and do whatever you want. Give me some credit, woman. I've lived this life for a lot of years. I know what can happen. And I've told *you* what can happen. Yesterday you risked your—risked *their* lives. There aren't any excuses." He emphasized his words by hurling the lollipop toward the lake.

Lil's head shot up and she regarded him with arctic eyes. "Excuses? You want to talk about excuses? All right, then. Let's start with why you seem to break promises faster than you can make them. And then there's the big one. How *could* you forget Michael's birthday? If you'd seen your son's face when you didn't show up for his party. . . . You didn't, but I did. I did! His heart was in pieces and you left me to sweep up the mess. So I did the best I could. I took them out because they don't have a father they can count on."

He flushed with anger, with shame—and with something else, something that escaped him, something that made heat flare in his gut and the hairs rise on the back of his neck. Lil was dynamite in her outrage. Twin spots of red stained her cheeks. Her chest rose and fell with each indignant breath. Her eyes flashed blue lightning. She was fire. She was ice.

And . . . she was right.

He stared at her, nailed by her defiant gaze, and the atmosphere shifted. Out of the embers of fury rose an emotion as illusive as smoke. He could see it in the sudden confused swirl of gray that veiled her eyes, hear it in her sharp intake of breath. It drifted between them, whispering of need and want, of desire and longing.

He leaned toward her. Her eyes widened and grew wary, but she didn't move from the hand he laid on her arm. Her skin was soft, warm silk. She shuddered once, then stilled.

His nostrils flared at her sweet scent. "Lil . . ."

Roy banged open the sliding door. Lil gave her head a slight shake and drew back. Jon looked at Roy in annoyance.

Roy shook his head. "Sorry. But I think you'd better come in here."

Inside, Jon heard a breathless voice with a shrill undernote. Belinda. His jaw clenched. "How'd she get past the front desk?"

Lil's curious gaze bounced between them. Roy shrugged, hands spread in a what-can-I-do gesture.

Jon sighed and nodded. He knew from experience that not even Roy could fend her off. Might as well get this over with—whatever *this* was.

Sighing, he got to his feet and moved indoors, Lil close behind him.

"There you are!" Belinda traipsed toward him with the effervescence of a cheerleader. Roy snuck toward the kitchen, and Jon wished he could follow.

He glanced at Lil. Her eyes had widened. No wonder. Belinda looked great. Her figure was petite, but curvy, handfuls in all the right places. A short dress revealed her well-molded legs and stretched to barely cover her tush, but its pale pink color and the tiny gold chains wrapping her waist and one ankle were demure. Matching links dangled from her earlobes. Her waterfall brown curls fell in shiny waves, her brown eyes were clear—and lit with spite when they landed on him.

Jagged shards of anger over what the kids had suffered at her hands pierced the ballooning guilt he always felt when he saw her. He studied her with the same fascination he'd give roadside kill. What was she? Demon or misunderstood soul? He tamped down his rage. He didn't want to tip his hand too soon.

His expression a mix of embarrassment and dopey lust, the guy—Neil?—from Serenity Gardens trailed behind her like an adoring beagle. Jon took one look and didn't need a score to tell him Belinda played Neil like a fiddle. "What're you doing here?"

Lil frowned at the abrasion in his voice, but Belinda only shot him a look that would wither grass. She tripped over to Lil, hand extended. "Good thing I still have friends among your guard dogs, isn't it? Else I'd never get to meet the second Mrs. Van Castle, the . . . what was it? Oh, yes. Weeping Beauty. Lifesaver Lil." Her laugh trilled. "Don't the press think they're just *so* clever? Since Jon is being rude, let me introduce myself. I'm the *first* Mrs. Van Castle." With a polite smile, Lil took her hand. "Mother of our children," Belinda continued, then added with no change in her pleasant expression, "And don't you *ever* forget it."

Lil dropped Belinda's hand. Belinda's smile widened. "So sorry to barge in, but there's a matter I need to discuss with my—sorry, I mean, *your*—husband."

She gave Lil a dismissive look, then turned her gaze to Jon. "You're looking upset. Have I disturbed you? Or is there trouble in paradise?"

"The terms of our bargain were clear, Belinda. Sixty days at the—"

"Our bargain . . ." Belinda mused, squinting at the ceiling. She tapped a long glittery pink fingernail on her chin. "Is this the one where you virtually imprison me for eight months, and then give me back my children? Is that the one we're discussing?"

She paused and drew a cigarette out of the pink clutch purse that dangled from her shoulder. Out came a silly holder. Smoking didn't quite fit her image, so she'd always been careful not to do it in public. At home, though, she'd been a chimney. She pinched the holder between her lips and Neil hurried over with a lighter. She blew out a thin stream of smoke.

Tired of the drama queen stuff, he snorted. "How'd you get out, Belinda? How'd you get here?" He lobbed a hard look at Neil. "You have it so bad you'll break the rules and risk your job?"

Neil spread his hands. "She's allowed outings, you know."

Belinda took a slow tour of the room, flicking her ashes on the floor, skimming her nails over the top of the keyboards. It was her Bette Davis performance. She paused and rolled her eyes at Neil. "Just ignore him, sweet thing. Now, where were we? Oh, yes. Discussing our agreement. I just wasn't sure if you referred to the one we *signed*—or the secret one where you take my babies away from me."

He started. How much did she know and how much was guesswork?

Belinda dropped the pose and whirled. "You know what, Jon? Screw our agreement. In fact, screw you." This was more like the Belinda he knew. "Where are my babies anyway?"

Lil winced and darted a concerned look up the stairs. He followed her gaze. Rounded eyes framed by the bars on the railing, Mel and Michael squatted side by side on the traverse.

"They're with Zeke." Nearly knocking the butt from its holder, he grabbed Belinda's elbow and steered her to the windows. Outside, the breeze whipped the water into razor-edged whitecaps.

He twisted her around. Lil slipped up the stairs, and he waited to speak until he heard the click of closing doors. "Don't get your panties in a bunch. What secret agreement?"

She yanked her arm out of his grasp. Ashes settled on his shirt. "I'm not an idiot. You can't fool me into believing this fairy-tale marriage is more than a sham. Weeping Beauty . . ." She snorted. "When I read that, I thought I'd puke. And now that I've seen her, gimme a break. Little Miss Smells-Like-a-Rose just isn't your style."

He brushed at his shirt, trying to hide his relief. Pure, grade-A guesswork.

Belinda's face mottled, but she managed to hold her temper. She tapped his arm and considered him. "So, why, I asked myself, would he saddle himself with someone like that, especially since he's vowed never to marry again? And, you know what, you don't have to be Einstein to figure it out. Pack Belinda off for eight months, play Mr. Homemaker, complete with a Barbie doll bride, and then—then, present the happy family in front of the judge and, *voilà*—" She dropped her cigarette on the slate, ground it out, then slid the holder back in her purse. "No more child support."

He crossed his arms. "Right. That's what I'm all about. Money."

"Aren't you? Ever since we were kids, money's made you high. 'Gonna make me enough to buy a palace, Belinda. Gonna make so much they'll put my name right up there with Donald Trump.' Isn't that what you said? And, God knows, you devoted every goddamn second to it. Always did and always will."

Actually, if he remembered right, he thought she'd made those comments. Belinda was good at selective memory. She clasped both hands over his arms and gazed up at him, widening those big-as-shit brown eyes and squeezing out a tear. His guilt tapped him on the shoulder, but he kept his face impassive.

"You were never home when I needed you. Never home when I was lonely, when I cried myself to sleep. Never home when the children were babies. Is it any wonder I looked around for a little love, a little attention? All I ever wanted was you, Jon. Just you. But you ran away from me. Please . . . don't take my children away from me, too."

He stirred, uncomfortable. Her words echoed Lil's. *The children need love. They need attention. They need you.*

Looking down into Belinda's soulful eyes, he almost believed her. Almost believed that if he'd given her more of himself, been capable of loving her the way he should have, they'd be one big happy family. Almost. But the memory of Mel's fear froze the slight thaw in his heart. "You're the one who's all about money."

With a nasty squeeze, she released his arm. "So what if I am? All I asked was a little compensation for all you put me through, all those lonely nights, all the—"

"Can it, Belinda." He rubbed the spot where her nails had pinched flesh. "You already got more than your share. Your little act might play for the press, but I'm not buying it."

"You can't just cut me off. I need—"

"And Judge Dougherty won't buy it either. Especially when he finds out how you've treated the kids." He hadn't meant to say anything, but he couldn't keep quiet.

Her eyes narrowed. "What kind of crap have they been feeding you? I discipline them, sure. A spank now and then, but I don't do anything they don't deserve."

"And pigs fly."

She looked unconcerned. She dipped into her purse, surfaced with a hammered silver compact, and flipped it open, smiling at her image. "And if anyone says different, my mom will back me up. Believe me, she will."

So, she *had* bullied Dodo. He itched to slap her pink mouth, but settled for clenching his fists. A poor substitute. "And your addictions? The car wreck, the busts, the trips to rehab? How's Dodo going to explain that away?"

"She won't need to." She looked up, and the eyes went round again. "Didn't anyone tell you? I'm cured. Or at least that's what my counselor will say. Won't he, Neil?" She batted her eyes at Neil and the sucker nearly drooled. Then she looked back at Jon and snapped the compact shut. "Oh, I'll do my time. Another thirty days of treatment, six months of peeing in a cup whenever I'm asked. I'll follow our *signed* agreement—a nice little legally tight document—to the letter and I'll be so clean I'll squeak when I walk. And . . ." She paused. "All the while, I'll watch you, Jon."

He snorted and she sharpened her eyes on him. "Don't believe me? Well, I had an interesting conversation today with a certain photographer. Better than a private dick, you know, they can be so resourceful.

And this one's on my payroll. Seems he's detected a certain, shall we say, lack of romance between you and your new bride. Also appears the girl-next-door put our children in danger yesterday."

He groaned. If even half of what Lil had told him about the day was true, Belinda would soon have the pictures to prove Lil had put the children in a shaky situation. Belinda wouldn't even have to pay for them. They'd be free and all over tomorrow's tabloids. He wanted to twist the sunny smile she gave him right off her face.

"Well. I've said what I came to say, so I'll see myself out. Neil?"

Neil straightened and offered his arm. Without turning, Belinda threw over her shoulder, "If you want to play dirty, I'm ready to wallow in the mud. Don't think you can screw me over. You can't."

He followed her and slammed the door shut, unfortunately just missing her ass. When he returned to the great room, Lil sat on the bottom step of the stairway. He didn't know how long she'd been there, or how much she'd heard, but from her carefully schooled expression and pink cheeks, he imagined more than enough. He raised an eyebrow at her.

"Well," she said, rising. "Well. I think I'll go see if the children want lunch. Are you going to join us?"

Chapter 19

Lunch and dinner both long past, dusk settled over the lake. The hills were a dark silhouette against sky and water, a fusion in shades of mauve. Standing at Melanie's window, Lil pulled the drapes across the view, leaned over to give her a kiss good night. Mel smiled up at her, then returned to her book. Pulling Mel's door closed, Lil tiptoed to the landing, and paused at Michael's door. From inside, she heard him humming a McDonald's ditty and smiled. Satisfied he'd fall asleep in moments, she started down the stairs, lost in her thoughts. The visit from Belinda had been disturbing.

Shortly after Belinda had left, Jon's business had intruded, and they'd had no opportunity for private conversation. Through supper—he'd made a point of joining them—she'd made light conversation, of course making no mention of his ex-wife in front of the children. She'd noticed his eyes occasionally rested on her, as though trying to assess her thoughts. Talking about his first marriage probably wasn't high on his list of fun-filled activities, but she wanted to know more. Jon thought the woman only wanted money. But, following behind Belinda as she'd uttered her parting threats, he hadn't seen her expression. Lil had seen all too clearly. For a moment, pure unadulterated hatred had flamed across that pretty face. What exactly were they up against?

It wasn't until she reached the bottom tread that she realized she wasn't alone.

Jon sat on the sofa in the great room. Unnoticed, she watched him. He was the picture of relaxation in his cutoffs and T-shirt, holding a book loosely in one hand, his sandaled feet thrown up on the table, his gold hair loose in the lamplight. Yet his expression was haunted, and for long moments, he turned no page. As she moved into view, he hesitated, then tossed the book aside and patted the cushion next to him. "Come join me."

"I thought you'd left for rehearsal."

"Zeke won't pick me up for another hour."

She didn't know whether to be glad or sorry. She did want to talk to him, but the atmosphere felt charged. Picking up his book, she perched on the sofa, rubbing a thumb back and forth across the binding. When she saw him watching her hand, she stopped.

He leaned his head back against the cushions. His pose was languid, but the fingers of one hand drummed restlessly on his thigh. They were long fingers, long hands. Slender, almost aristocratic. "About Belinda . . ."

She rushed into his pause, suddenly not wanting to know anything. "You don't need to explain. I didn't know she was so—"

"Fucked up?"

Lil fell silent. So gorgeous. So ephemeral. So . . . yes, so fucked up.

"My fault, you know. She wasn't always like that."

Lil battled between curiosity and the feeling she was getting pulled deeper into something she wasn't ready for. Curiosity won. "What *was* she like?"

"Gidget. You know, Sally Field. Only more reckless, daring. Much braver than me in lots of ways— never would have taken the stuff my old man dished out. We were playmates. Played devil-dare-me a lot, and Belinda always won."

"Robbie—" She hesitated. "We knew each other when we were children, too."

It was the first time she'd brought him up. Jon's hand stilled and his eyes moved to hers, soft caramel with gold glints. She read a question there, but he didn't ask anything. "Yeah, well, I doubt our relationship was as . . . wholesome."

She waited for more, and he sighed. His gaze moved away, wandered the room. "This won't sound pretty. We were playing 'you show me yours, I'll show you mine' at twelve. At fourteen I was copping cigarettes and beer from the filling station for her."

"Not for you?"

"Cigs, yes, beer, no. I didn't really like the stuff. Preferred messing with my guitar."

"You must have loved her, even then."

He barked a short laugh. "Ah, Lil, you are so—" Again, he glanced at her, stopped when she frowned. "Uh, romantic. No, I wasn't in love. She rewarded me with her virginity. And kept rewarding me."

"Ah." Lil was amused. Did he think adolescent sexual awakening was totally unfamiliar to her? She and Robbie had waited, but only barely.

"Anyway, I didn't make a good thief. I landed in front of Judge Dougherty more times than I can count."

"So the articles I read were true?" The confession—such a small thing, really—was made with such an air of guilt, her tension lessened. She couldn't resist a little poke. Setting the book aside, she curled her legs up and settled back. If he turned his head, their mouths would be less than a foot apart. Her eyes widened at her thoughts.

He answered her question seriously. "To a point. When we divorced, Belinda tipped the press on those stunts. They picked over my court records like vultures, made me sound like a felon."

"And the rest. Is that true, too?" Now she really was amused.

"No! I never forced drugs on her, never had orgies, wouldn't touch a minor—"

He was truly upset. She dropped the teasing tone, laid a hand on his arm. "I know."

"—especially in front of the kids and—what do you mean, you know?"

"I've been living here, remember? And while you might be obsessed with your career, selfish to a fault, and rarely think about anyone but yourself—"

His lips curved. "Gee, thanks."

"You obviously aren't running a den of iniquity."

Silence fell, but it was no longer uncomfortable. Until he turned his head. Not a foot, mere inches. His gaze dropped to her mouth. Her breathing grew shallow, and she realized she wanted him to close that short gap between their lips. She froze, denying any such thing, and he held just as still, as if afraid any movement might make her bolt.

Gathering a breath, she looked away. "You told me you married her after she followed you to Nashville, then you hit it big. Is that when she started using drugs?"

The moment passed. He hunched deeper into the cushions, and his fingers started tapping again. "She started soon after she got to Nashville. Hell, maybe she was doing it before. At first I thought it was recreational. She did some weed. That's not good either but . . ." He shrugged. "I wasn't around much. I was caught up cutting another demo, trying to land an A&R rep, composing with Zeke. The signs were there. I just didn't want to see them. After she mis—" He hesitated. For a moment, pain crossed his features, then his face went smooth. "After I, uh, hit it big, she could afford designer drugs. She got into coke, big time. Cocaine and other things."

"What other things?" The way he looked, she wasn't really sure she wanted to know.

His fingers stopped tapping. "Other men. Melanie was just a baby when I came home early from a session one night. I'd wanted to surprise her—Van Castle's first album had just gone platinum and she'd been nagging me about buying this penthouse. I'd signed the papers, and thought we'd celebrate. Champagne, even a three-foot bunny for Mel." Jon stared at the ceiling, but she knew he was seeing the past. "What a celebration. She'd started the party without me. The whole house was full of people I didn't recognize. Stunk to high heaven with weed. Melanie was screeching from her crib, but I didn't see Belinda." He frowned.

"Where was she?"

"In the bedroom. Half naked. Going down—" He broke off. "She was there with another guy. Some asshole I'd never seen." He pushed a hand through his hair. "I threw him out. Threw everybody out. Belinda just smiled. Then when I started yelling, *she* got mad. I'd never seen her that mad. She threw my Fender. Threw out a bunch of stuff about how I'd neglected her, how she was bored cooped up with the baby, how it was my fault."

"Your fault? That's ridicu—"

"Then she fell on her knees. She was pitiful, sobbing for me to forgive her. I felt so helpless, so guilty." He glanced at Lil. "Yeah, I forgave her. She was my wife. We had a baby, for God's sake. I couldn't just abandon her. She promised to get help and stay clean. I purged Van Castle of dopeheads and threatened the rest if they snorted, smoked, or swallowed anything stronger than aspirin. And Belinda . . ." He sighed. "We tried. She tried. She was in and out of rehab, and we were in and out of counseling, but it never took. Each time I thought it had, then I'd go out on the road, or have to spend late hours at the studio, and she'd slip back." He drummed his thigh again. "I just couldn't give her enough of my time. You've seen how I am."

Lil had sat silent, unmoving, through his entire tale, but now she made a sound of impatience. "Yes, I've seen how you are. And for some strange reason it hasn't reduced me to taking drugs."

He didn't reply, and she realized he didn't believe she understood. But she did understand. She understood he blamed himself for something he'd had no control over.

"Jon." She covered his hand, stilling his fingers. "Listen to me. Belinda could have fought for you, for your time. She could have fought for your marriage. Or fought for herself, for Pete's sake. She didn't want to. She wanted drugs more. It's not unreasonable you'd divorce her."

"I didn't just divorce her, Lil. At the peak of the band's success, I cut her out of my life and ran for it. And I was so relieved to be rid of her, I fooled myself into thinking she could stay clean and the children would be okay with her."

"In other words, you did the best you could at the time."

He looked at their hands. Something thrummed between them. "Lovely Lil, always seeing everything in black and white, not noticing the murky grays between." Uneasy, she slipped her hand off his. He sighed again. "Look, I wasn't stuffing drugs up her nose, but my life almost killed her, just like my old man killed—" He stopped, shook his head and continued, "I clutched at divorce, thinking if I released Belinda, I'd save her, and my kids. And myself. Probably mostly myself. It was cowardly. The best I could think of wasn't much."

"Your father—"

He shifted, ran a finger under the neckline of his T-shirt. "Sorry, I think I've had enough of true confessions for one night. Uh, the kids still awake, you think?"

She still had some questions, but he looked so tired, she let him change the subject. Considering that . . . something . . . she'd just felt, it was for the best anyway. "Probably. Melanie was reading." She smiled. "And it takes more than lights out to get Michael to sleep."

"Guess I'll go say good night before I have to head out." He twisted to look at her. "By the way, what was with that present you gave me for Michael yesterday? If I'd been you, I would have hung me out to dry."

"I let my temper get the better of me. I hurt the children and worried you. The present was an apology."

He shook his head. "You don't need to apologize. For anything. You were right. I've been an ass. From now on, I'm a better dad. When I win custody it should be because I deserve them, not because of any tricks."

She still felt skeptical, but hope blossomed anyway.

Watching her, his face grew grave. "Don't believe in me too much, Lil. I'll try, but my track record isn't anything to write home about."

She started to protest, but he interrupted. "You do owe me an apology for one thing."

She was puzzled. "What?"

"The present. Boxing gloves?"

She smiled. "I know he'll likely knock the house down around us, but I knew he'd love them." Her smile widened. "And maybe he'll lend them to you."

"To me?"

"To use on Belinda."

They stared at each other a moment, then laughed, leaning against each other's shoulders. She relaxed, simply enjoying the warmth of the moment, then stiffened when she realized that same something was growing again. Apparently noticing her tense, Jon pushed himself up. "Back in a moment."

That fleeting awareness dissipated and she could once again tell herself she'd only imagined it. She watched him head upstairs. A door clicked. She heard Michael's giggle, Jon's low voice. She'd likely have to spend another half hour calming Michael to sleep, but she didn't mind.

When Jon returned, Zeke arrived. While he waited on the outside step, Lil helped Jon collect his notes and Fender and followed him to the door. As she handed everything over, she murmured, "Jon? It's not your fault Belinda turned into the person she is. We all have choices and she made hers all on her own."

As she'd sat waiting for him to come back downstairs, she'd rehearsed this little speech, hoping it might sway him to look at things in a different light. But he didn't look convinced, he looked skeptical. Exasperated, she surprised them both by gathering him, guitar and all, into a fierce, tight hug. Before he could react, she stepped back, blushing wildly. "Now go. Go play with your friends."

Friday and through the weekend, the cabana moved to a different rhythm. When he got home after rehearsals, Jon joined her, Roy, and Zeke on the deck to watch the sunrise, then turned breakfast into an occasion, clowning in the kitchen. On Saturday, he even surprised them all with his ability to flip pancakes two feet off the stove (only three splattered on the floor instead, much to Michael's delight). He'd head to bed after, and they wouldn't see him until evening, but Lil noticed on Friday and Saturday he called a halt to business an hour earlier than was usual, and spent a good three hours with the children around dinner, even tucking them in to bed. On Sunday, he did no business at all during the day.

The atmosphere grew light, Michael's mischief grew

more benign, Melanie grew more animated. The strain between Lil and Jon dissolved, except for this odd lingering tension Lil decided to ignore. She felt it when their shoulders brushed in the kitchen, when his gaze settled on her as the day dawned, when they'd exchange a look over Michael's antics. Then came Monday, and she couldn't ignore it any longer.

Chapter 20

Monday morning following an abbreviated Sunday night rehearsal, Jon tiptoed through the cabana before Lil or Roy were up. Balancing a coffee mug in one hand, he quietly opened her bedroom door with the other. Outlined in the pearl light that glimmered at the windows, she was still asleep, turned on her side, an arm tucked under her head. He grinned. A soft snore, not at all ladylike, slipped between her lips. He approached the bed and stared down. His smile faded and he tried to ignore the urge to nibble those lips. That hug the other night . . . Her face had radiated conviction and compassion, her voice had brooked no argument as she tried to argue him out of his guilt. She was so sweet, so strong, even if she didn't fully realize it. She was . . .

Needing immediate distraction, he glanced around her room, his gaze roaming past the books lined up on a bookcase, past the clothes folded neatly on a chair, to the picture by her bedside. She was off limits—damn his scruples and damn their deal. While he was at it—damn, too, that photograph of her husband.

He sat down and the bed creaked. She stirred, but didn't wake. "C'mon, Rumplestiltskin. Places to go, people to see." Unable to resist, he scooped the curls back from her cheek. Her skin was soft, warm from sleep.

At his touch, her eyes flew open and she bolted

upright, clutching the sheet to her chin. "What are you doing here?"

Her curls were scrunched up against her head. She looked like that scruffy bear her niece Rose dragged around, but more appetizing. She tried to glare, but a yawn caught her, revealing a soft pink tongue. He thrust the mug at her before he lost control and decided to plunder that mouth. "Time to get up."

"Why?" She frowned at the mug, but he swore her nose twitched. She took it from his hands and sipped, looking warily at him over the rim. "Did you make this—or did Roy?"

"I did, of course."

Her gown had slipped and his eyes followed the curve of a bare shoulder. There was a hitch in her breathing. She shrugged the gown up, then glanced at her clock. "Of course? You're usually not home for another hour. What's going on?"

"I have a surprise. Come on, lead butt." He gave her a light slap on the side of her haunch. "Get up and get dressed in"—he stood up, rummaged in her bathroom and emerged brandishing her swimsuit and a terry-cloth cover-up—"in these." He tossed them to her and went to the door, although he very much wanted to stay. "Your coach departs in ten minutes and your loyal subjects await."

"But where are we going?"

From the doorway, he looked back at her. She was so tempting, all sleepy-eyed and rumpled. "Ten minutes," he said.

In ten minutes, he handed a puzzled Lil into the ill-sprung bucket seat of an old Jeep. Sunlight bathed the tops of the wooded hills, while the shadowed valleys lay veiled in mist. Pink and gold streaked the pale blue dome of the sky. He took the driver's seat, and they bounced out of the drive. In the back, the children he'd roused right after Lil had shed their early-morning crankies. Michael's grin stretched ear to ear.

Mel's eyes glowed. They led a string of similar Jeeps filled with the band and crew, coolers and boxes. He refused to tell his passengers where they were headed.

Through the twisted, rutted back roads, he drove feeling like a terrier unchained from a short leash. In a grind of gears, he slid up embankments to avoid crater-sized potholes, and whooped with delight when he hit one.

He flashed Lil a smile. "Having fun yet?"

Lil's mouth was clenched like she was trying to keep her teeth from rattling loose. "Oh, buckets of it."

As they tooled along, he felt her relax. The wind ruffled her hair, the lemonade sun bathed her skin. Behind her, the kids' high, excited laughter sang in his ears.

When he glanced next, their eyes met, and she suddenly smiled. "I *am* having fun." At the next bump, she threw back her head and laughed with none of her usual constraint.

He grinned. "That's my girl!"

Out on the highway, they traveled a few miles further, then he downshifted. Spraying gravel, the Jeep swerved under white wrought iron arches adorned with dancing dolphins. Surf's Up Water Park, a forty-acre complex of pools and water rides. Michael and Melanie squealed. As he jerked the Jeep to a halt, Lil's mother, Hank, Rose, Daisy, and Alcea's daughter Kathleen came running, lugging towels and beach bags.

Lil looked at Jon, her mouth an O of surprise.

He grinned at her. Slinging an elbow over the seat, he leaned into the back and ruffled Michael's hair. "This day's for you. This place is all ours for the next five hours. A belated happy birthday, buddy."

The sound of Lil's laughter zinged through him. "I think that's the first time since I laid eyes on him that I've seen him that way. Both awake—and silent."

Jon looked at his son and joined her laughter. Michael sat stunned, his chocolate eyes melted into rounds of surprise. Then he laughed, too. A wide-mouthed howl of pure joy. As he fumbled with his seatbelt, Lil hopped out to help him.

But Jon steered her away with a light hand on her back. "It's your day, too, Lil."

Hesitating, she wrapped her fingers around the arm he offered. His muscles jumped under her touch. Folding his hand over hers, he led her up a carefully tended path toward the entrance. The scent of petunias and freshly mown grass mingled with the tangy smell of chlorine. The sun and her touch were warm.

"There's an adult with each kid, so don't worry." At the top of the path, he turned her around. "See?"

Back in the lot, Zeke worked at the straps snarled around Michael. Nearby, Rose stood in a ruffled bathing suit, watching them with her hand tucked into Zinnia's. Melanie, an orange-eyelidded Daisy, and Kathleen, who for the moment had lost Alcea's perpetual regal expression, danced ahead of Three-Ring, Peter, and Lydia on the wide tree-canopied walkway. Ahead of them, his belly spilling over the waistband of his swimming trunks, Roy huffed along behind Hank, who trailed a hand dreamily over banks of violet petunias and magenta-spiked celosia. Some of the road musicians struggled up the walkway lugging baskets undoubtedly stuffed with food. Other members of the crew straggled behind them with fistfuls of balloons. Watching Lil watching them, he held his breath.

"I can see Lydia's and Peter's competent hands in this, but I know enough by now to know nothing happens around here without your supervision." Lil glanced up at him, her expression shy. "You've done well, Mr. Van Castle. Thank you."

He released his breath. He linked his fingers through hers, and tugged her forward. "I did do good, didn't I?" He cupped his mouth. "Last one to the Furious Flume is a loser!"

Everyone sprinted for the water park entrance, and when Lil would have followed, he kept a tight grip. "Let's go over to the wave pool. We need to talk about a few things, and the next couple days will be crazy." The state fair concert was only a few nights away.

She looked perplexed, but only nodded and followed him through the entrance. Just inside, he scooped up a couple of fat yellow inner tubes and they moved under an arch of mimosa and locust trees toward the Wave Pond. The Wave Pond was a monster of a pool with a concrete "beach" on one end, and heavy machinery buried in the other. At intervals, it churned the water into waves mimicking the ocean. Except for a lifeguard perched by the pool, it was deserted.

After dropping their belongings on a nearby patio table, they waded into the pool. Jon plopped the tubes on the surface, and held one for Lil to settle into. The early wake-up call must have washed the starch right out of her. Instead of a ladylike wiggle followed by her usual straight-up posture, she flopped on the tube ass-down, draped an arm on either side, and dropped her head back. Her eyes closed.

The long arch of her neck was exposed and vulnerable, her throat an inviting hollow. What would she do if he strummed a line of kisses along its arc? Slap him, no doubt.

He shifted from foot to foot. "Come on. We'll catch better waves in the deep end."

"Wouldn't want to miss a one," Lil murmured and made no effort to move.

She was a floating rag doll, except nothing was childish about the sweep of her neck to the handfuls of soft flesh mounding under her swimsuit. Ignoring the spasm in his groin, he set his teeth, and dragged her near the back wall of the pool.

After he'd hoisted himself into his own tube, he

grabbed one of the handles on hers and tried to ignore what else he'd like to grab. "We need to talk about the kids."

As he expected, her eyes popped open. They were a shattering turquoise with the water's reflection. Digging her elbows into the rubber, she pushed herself up.

"I'm sure you'd be able to make a home for the kids anywhere," he started. "But the band leaves in about a week. You didn't seem to think it's a great idea for them to go. Not that I wouldn't want them, honest. But our flight schedules are screwy, we sleep in airplane seats or in different hotel beds every night, and chow is lukewarm room service." He watched to see if she planned to reproach him.

"Sounds like lots of fun." Far from looking upset, she seemed pleased. Her toes played with the water, a gesture he'd put down to nerves, except he'd rarely seen Lil nervous.

"Used to be. I used to get psyched. I wanted to see it all, experience it all. But, as they say, the thrill is gone." This time charging himself up had been hard. He bet—no, he knew—it had something to do with her, and the aura of home she'd created for him and his kids. His gaze wandered from her toes, along her delicately arched feet, and up firm calves to a pair of sweet knees. At least he'd be leaving the agonizing temptation that grew stronger every day they were together.

A buzzer announced the beginning of a wave interval. The lifeguard stood at attention, and water churned from the bowels of the pool. As the waves gained momentum, their tubes bumped together, then apart as they plummeted over one wave and into the pit of another. They dipped, bumped, then crested, down, bump, then up. Like Mama rocking them in a big water cradle. Except Lil's posture refused to relax.

Bump. "What did you have in mind for me and the children?"

Bump. "I have digs outside of Nashville. You'd like it. The countryside is—"

Bump. "No."

In the rush of water, he didn't think he'd heard her right, although he recognized the set of her chin. "Sorry?" The waves subsided, and the lifeguard sat down.

She pushed wet curls out of her face. "I don't want to go to Nashville."

"It's not so bad. I know you're not used to cities, but Nashville isn't that big—"

"And the children don't want to go either. Michael isn't old enough to remember much about Nashville, about the last years of your marriage. But Melanie does." She paused, then looked at him in her usual straight-on fashion. "They aren't happy memories."

He looked away, staring over the woods that ringed the pool deck. A breeze surfed through the treetops and ruffled the leaves into a smatter of applause.

Of course the kids didn't have happy memories. Those last years, he and Belinda had to work at being polite. Usually they hadn't even managed that.

"You're right." He reached for her tube and pulled her alongside. "How about this. I have another home in L.A., for when we record there. A loft. But it's big enough—"

Again Lil shook her head. Feeling unusually patient, he waited to hear what she had to say, surprised at how much he'd grown to rely on her judgment about his kids. Hell, about everything. He should've known she'd already given this matter a lot of thought.

"Cordelia," she said.

Both his eyebrows went up, and she hurried on, her knuckles turning white on the tube handles. "Please, don't say no before you think about it. My house is big enough for three of us. Three bedrooms. They're on the small side and I'll have to move some things around, but that's no problem. And, there's an addition on the back where I gave my piano lessons. I can turn that into a playroom. I have a cat and they'd love a pet, you know. Out back, there's a play fort, a swing set thing that was there when we bought the house. We'd kept it for when—" Abruptly, she broke off, lips tightening.

"For when, Lil?" he asked gently.

She stared off over the treetops. When she finally replied, he could hardly hear her. "I lost my baby. I was pregnant when I got the call that Robbie was hurt in a car accident. I rushed to the hospital and when I got there . . ."

He thought of the photo he'd seen this morning. Laughing eyes and an engaging grin.

Her face mirrored pain and she hauled in a shaky breath. "You know, the doctor had such shiny shoes. Like black mirrors. Whenever I think of that day, I think of those shoes. Silly, isn't it? I remember wondering if he shined them himself or if his wife did it. I concentrated on those shoes, like if I thought about them hard enough, I wouldn't have to hear what he said. And right after he told me, I had cramps. Horrid pains ripping at my insides, and . . . there wasn't anything they could do." She looked down, blinking rapidly.

He wanted to pull her to him, absorb her grief, but the careful way she held herself told him she'd reject any offers of comfort. Instead, he gave her what he could. "I'm sorry, Lil." He spoke slowly. "You know, I—Belinda and I—lost a baby, too. Our first."

She raised her head, her expression sympathetic. "I remember you mentioned a pregnancy."

His gaze followed a mourning dove. It flitted from the ground to a low hanging branch.

He rarely acknowledged the void that yawned where that child should be. "At first I was upset Belinda got pregnant. But the more I thought about it, the more I wanted that kid, wanted to give it everything I'd never been given. So I married her. Wrote a song, too. 'Bella Linden.' " He smiled. "We were going to name the baby Linden. When the song hit the top of the charts, I thought I had it all. I'd grabbed the brass ring. Success and a family all in one swoop."

"What happened?"

His smile faded. "Miscarriage, like you. One night when she was home alone." Of course, she blamed him, never bothering to mention the drugs he now realized she took even then. Drugs or not, it didn't matter. "I screwed up. I wasn't there for her."

He'd plummeted back to earth, spent frenzied hours in the studio, on the road, while the pain settled into a dull ache that still lay heavy in his gut.

Lil touched his arm. "You know, at first I blamed myself when my baby died. I thought if I hadn't gotten so hysterical when they told me about Robbie, it wouldn't have happened. It took a while, a long while, but now I know it was nobody's fault. Sometimes things . . . just happen."

"I don't think you ever get over a loss like that. Not completely, anyway. I still wonder what my daughter would have looked like. Sounds stupid, doesn't it, since I hardly know the two I've got left. But there it is." The mourning dove settled in the shadows under the boughs. "I've had a second chance—I'm lucky. I have Mel and Michael. And you, Lil, you have that great big noisy family of yours. It's something I never had. You're lucky, too, you know."

"I guess I am."

He glanced at her. Her gaze swept the trees, lighting on the same bird he'd watched. "Did you know mourning doves select only one mate in a lifetime?" she asked. He didn't answer and her eyes moved to his. "I can't ever have any more children."

He met her gaze. "I'm willing to share Mel and Michael. For as long as you want."

She looked away. Even with the sun beating on his

shoulders, he felt chilled. He wanted to say more, say something about how from that very first day he'd seen her, she'd crept under his skin. But with the images of Belinda and the photograph of Lil's husband fresh in his mind, he could only feebly offer his kids. From Lil's reaction, even that may have been too much. He wondered how long she'd mourn her husband.

Still avoiding his eyes, she gave her shoulders a twitch. "And now," she said in a practical voice that dispelled their closeness, "we need to decide where we're all going."

He still had hold of her tube and he wanted to shake it. Shake her. Shake her out of the past, out of the tube, and right into his arms, even though he knew she deserved better.

"The children are used to small-town life. If we stay in Cordelia, they'll have friends, family. They'd go to school with my nieces and nephew, get invited to birthday parties and picnics and church socials. They'd have bikes and skates and a safe street to use them on. Anywhere else we'd go, we'd be isolated. We wouldn't know anyone."

The buzzer sounded again and once more the lifeguard stood up. Jon grabbed Lil's hand and they rode out the waves, her fingers warm and slippery in his. When the waves stopped, he opened his mouth but before he could get a word out, she was off again.

"You do see, don't you? It would be best for the children." She slipped her hand out of his and ticked off his imagined objections. He flexed his fingers; they felt amazingly empty. "Security. First of all, Cordelia's small. Oh, I know we'll be plagued by a few photographers, but they'll be bored out of their minds. And once it's known the O'Malley family doesn't appreciate their presence, the natives won't be too friendly. I give them a month. And as far as Wart-nose is concerned—"

His gaze had been fixed on that plump lower lip as she talked, but now he raised his eyes. "Who?"

"You know. The photographer Belinda hired. The Tidwells own Cordelia's only motel and they're like my grandparents. I think Helen would have a grand time making his bed with damp sheets, loosening the shower head in his bathtub, maybe clogging the toilet."

He laughed. "Why, lady, I didn't know you had it in you."

A half-smile tugging on her mouth—oh, what he'd like to do with that mouth—she raised finger number two. "There's a room with a bath over my garage. It's not very big and I'm not sure the plumbing works, but with your money it could be made into living quarters for Roy. That is, if you'll let us have him."

He smothered his fantasies and heaved a long-suffering sigh. "What else?"

"An alarm system. You could install one in the house for less than a thousand."

He stared at her and she looked sheepish. "I made some calls. Just in case."

"And have you thought about my ex? Once she's out of Serenity Gardens, she'll go back to Monaco, and the town's only forty, forty-five miles away."

"I've thought of her, too."

Of course, she had.

In as close as he thought she'd ever come to begging, she leaned over and grasped his arm. "She *is* their mother, Jon. You can't pretend she doesn't exist. And, don't you think it would look better if you showed you didn't plan to cut off the children's relations with her completely? They could have supervised visits. Roy would always be with them."

Knowing how Roy felt about Belinda, Jon thought he might dig in his heels at that assignment. But right now he couldn't care less about Roy; he was distracted by the electric pings that sizzled up his arm from her touch, then shot straight down his legs.

As she leaned toward him, the pulse of the water crushed her breasts against his tube. It took all he had not to stare. Instead his gaze shot to her face where he almost drowned in the twin pools of her eyes. His body responded, and he hunched up his legs. He crossed them one way, then the other. He couldn't take much more of this.

"What do you think?" Her grip tightened, her breath caressed, and he almost moaned.

Without doubt, one day he'd lose it if they continued to live together. Day after day, her nearness chipped away at the control he had left. A bunch of real estate between them was a good idea. Through clenched teeth, he surrendered. "Yeah, yeah. Cordelia, it is."

The lines between her eyes smoothed and she relaxed her grip, leaning back in her tube. One of her magical smiles appeared. He heaved himself toward her, ready to wipe it off with his mouth, but at that moment Michael ran up, leaving a trail of wet footprints on the concrete. Zeke followed at a trot, looking so harried he was almost unrecognizable.

"Where'd you go?" The child stopped at the edge of the pool and plunked his fists on his hips, looking exactly like Lil. "C'mon, Daddy! You've got to try the Foom."

Zeke lowered himself into a chair and shook the wet hair out of his eyes. "Yes. The 'Foom.' Quite a lot of fun, that."

Jon and Lil exchanged a look of amusement. "Be right there, bud," Jon said.

When Lil moved to get out with him, he waved her back. "This is your day off, let me handle things." It wasn't that he didn't want her with him, it was that he wanted her with him far too much. He caught up Michael's hand.

She settled back and rewarded him with a smile of pure dazzle. Flipping a lazy hand at them, she called, "Have fun."

As he walked off with Michael bouncing alongside him, Jon wondered what would have happened had the kid not appeared. He smiled down at his son. "We've gotta talk about your timing, buddy."

"I can't tell time, Daddy." Michael looked up, face bunched into a frown. "You know that."

Lil's solitude lasted all of about twenty minutes before Melanie and Daisy pounced, and dragged her off to try the "Foom," too. As the sun blazed into the sky, they flumed, shot the rapids at White Water Wonder, and rode the twists and turns of Surf 'n Slide.

She would catch glimpses of Jon, racing down a slide holding Michael in a tight grip, or pushing a laughing Melanie under a waterfall on the Lazy River. His face glowed, his flashing smile a mirror of Michael's when he'd land a well-aimed punch with his new boxing gloves on Roy's belly. Lil grinned. Roy still hadn't forgiven her for that one.

Jon was once more the person she'd glimpsed on the houseboat. As she watched the children, watched him, a flower of happiness unfurled in her belly. He'd found time for them all, time even to think of her.

Not since Robbie had anyone made her the center of his concern. From the moment he'd handed her coffee laced with just the right amount of sugar and cream, to now, when his brandy-colored eyes were lit with the joy of giving his family pleasure, she felt . . .

She would need to be careful because she felt just like a well-loved wife.

My girl. On the way here, he'd called her that. Unexpected joy had bubbled through her, followed by a disturbing tingle along her spine. It was good, more than good, they'd each go their own directions in just over a week. If she didn't mind herself, she'd turn all loopy over him, just like she'd once feared Mari would.

As the others took off for the Dunking Walk, she excused herself and escaped back to the Wave Pond, feeling the need to collect her thoughts. The lifeguard still rode his perch, and Zeke and Michael lounged poolside. Zeke sat on a chaise, reading, his aplomb recovered. She smiled. No wonder. Michael was asleep on a towel spread out in the shade. Country music played softly from a radio propped on the table near Zeke's elbow. The yellow inner tubes lay abandoned nearby.

Seeing her, Zeke saluted, then reached over and twisted the dial, stopping on Brahms. She smiled her thanks, then stooped to rummage through a cooler that overflowed with fruit, snacks, root beer—and one humongous bag of Oreo cookies.

"Having fun?" Zeke asked.

Nibbling on a cookie, she took a lounge chair. The taste of childhood filled her mouth and the sun's warmth seeped through her soggy swimsuit. "Mmm-hmm."

"He thought of everything, didn't he?"

She swallowed and smiled at Michael. His dark lashes lay on his rounded cheeks, a moist finger near his mouth. "He made Michael happy."

"I don't think that's the only person he was trying to impress."

Lil felt herself pink.

"Oh, he would have done this for Michael anyway. He felt sick over forgetting his birthday. But this much planning didn't go into the tour. We all got our marching orders, and he wasn't about to brook any argument."

She didn't know what to say.

"He's changed." Zeke leaned forward, elbows on his knees, and stared out over the pool. "I've never seen him at peace like this. His demons have stopped raging as much as they did." His head turned and his dark gaze met hers. "I don't need to look far to find the reason why."

Beside them, Michael stirred, mumbled something, then pushed himself up, blinking.

She looked away. "You must be mistaken. I didn't do—"

"You've given him hope, Lil. Hope and belief in himself. No small matter, that." Zeke looked at Michael, and heaved a sigh. "Whaddaya say, buddy? You ready for another ride on the Flume?"

Lil watched them walk off, the dapper gentlemen pulled along by the sturdy little boy. Zeke was right. Jon had changed, was changing. She was glad; the children needed their father and he was proving himself up to the task. As for her role, well, she'd only pointed out the direction. Maybe Jon felt gratitude, but that's all it was, really.

Restless, she grabbed one of the tubes and waded into the pool. Scrabbling on board, she stretched against the warm vinyl and urged her thoughts in a different direction. Cordelia. She and the children would go home to Cordelia.

She closed her eyes. She'd make a real home for them. She'd redecorate their rooms. Pink, of course, for Mel, maybe army green for Michael. She'd enroll them in the same school she'd attended. Melanie and Daisy would be classmates, and Michael and Rose would start kindergarten together. She'd have fresh-baked cookies and tall glasses of milk ready when they came home from school. She'd help them with homework. They'd go to church on Sundays followed by roast beef at her mother and Pop's. By October, they'd all be settled into a routine.

She sighed and dipped her free hand into the pool, letting the water trickle through her fingers. They'd make Halloween costumes and trick-or-treat, ending the outing with bobbing apples at her old home on Maple Woods Drive, just as she and her siblings had.

In November, when the air turned crisp and night fell early, they'd spend evenings in the playroom she'd prepare . . . maybe Michael would like Legos. She had an old desk he could use to store them. They'd read together and she'd teach them piano. When the holidays arrived, they'd decorate the house, get a tree, and she'd sew Mel a frilly red dress for the Christmas pageant at St. Andrew's. . . . Her eyes drifted closed.

"Hey, sleepyhead."

She opened her eyes, somehow not surprised to see Jon. Seated in his own tube, he floated along next to her. Feeling a bubble of warmth, she impulsively held out her hand. Jon took it and she settled back, eyes fluttering closed again. A good man lay underneath all that ambition. Where his children mattered, his heart seemed to be in the right place, at least lately. The buzzer sounded, heralding a wave interval.

As the water churned, she thought of his lost child, and unconsciously squeezed his fingers. She'd need to make sure the children and Jon kept in touch during his tour. She'd talk to him about buying a computer so they could e-mail him, and she could learn to use a scanner and digital camera. Alcea had all those things; she'd show her how. She'd send him samples of schoolwork, pictures. . . .

She suddenly realized Jon had pulled her hand onto his chest where he toyed with her fingers. Her eyes flew open. His gaze was steadfast. Caught up in her plans, she'd failed to notice the waves had subsided.

Embarrassed, she tugged at her hand, but he splayed her fingers over the smooth muscles of his chest and held them there. His heartbeat was rapid. Her insides contracted.

Without unfastening his eyes from her face, keeping her hand clutched tight against him, he slid into waist-deep water and waded to the side of her tube. Determination fired his eyes.

She tugged again, then wiggled, but the smooth vinyl ring caught around her rear. Panicked, she considered calling for help against . . . against whatever he planned to do. Her gaze skittered past his, but the apron of the pool lay deserted.

His fingers slid along her cheek and curled into her hair, their easy pressure angling her head until she had to look at him. She froze, her breath caught in her throat.

"Lil." He breathed her name, smiled. "Just this once."

He bent toward her until the curtain of his hair shut out the sky, the pool, the world, and only those molten honey-and-brown eyes filled her vision. They gleamed gently, so gently. Alarm bells clamored in her head, but a hypnotic languor crept over her. Her heart clutched and her body tensed against the sudden longing that surged through her veins.

Her eyelids fluttered closed, then shot open as the pool lapped against the sides of her tube and their noses bumped. He chuckled deep in his throat, then released the fingers he still held to his heart. His hands glided up the side of her neck and trapped her face. No other part of them touched.

For a moment he simply searched her eyes. "You know it's okay, don't you, Lil? It's been over three years."

She stared back, helpless against his gaze, unable to push him away even though some part of her brain told her she should. Slowly, one side of his mouth still crooked up in a smile, he lowered his head. His lips settled on hers. A gentling touch, a featherlight touch. No pressure. A long sigh escaped her. More than three years.

Almost against her will, her lips moved, tasting him, suddenly eager for him to taste her. He moaned. The pressure on her mouth increased until she knew he was sure he held her captive. Pulling slightly away even while she strained up, he nipped her lower lip, laid a trail of tiny kisses along the curve of her mouth, and then, when her lips parted, their surrender complete, he covered her mouth with his and devoured her.

A swirl of feeling exploded inside her stomach and radiated outward until her whole body tingled. Her flesh goosebumped despite the hot sun.

Their tongues fluttered together, then apart. He tasted of grape and chlorine and of himself. She clutched a handful of his hair, trying to catch her breath. But instead of jerking his head back as she'd intended, she pulled him closer. The kiss deepened, their tongues tangled, and she lost herself in sensation. No longer Lil O'Malley, no longer the widow of Robert Ryan, no longer aware of who or where she was.

"Aunt Lil!"

Arms and legs cartwheeling, Lil shoved Jon away. The tube tipped, and she spilled into the pool. Disoriented, she gulped a mouthful of water and batted her arms, not knowing which way was up.

A strong hand gripped her wrist, dragged her up, and set her on her feet. Sputtering, she defied the gleam of amusement in his eyes and yanked on the tube, turning her back on him before he could open his mouth. She straightened her shoulders, tried desperately to regain her dignity, and chose to ignore the fact she'd kissed him back.

Daisy stood on the shallow edge of the pool, hands on her hips. "You seen my towel?"

Dragging the tube and scolding herself, Lil plodded toward her niece.

She'd behaved like a fool. So what if he'd roused some feelings in her. They were normal, biological. After all, she hadn't been kissed like that since Robbie. Actually, even Robbie had never kissed her quite like *that*. She shied away from the thought, feeling disloyal.

She waded toward Daisy, reasserting her self-control. But her cheeks still burned with shame. "I think I saw your towel on the table. Let me check."

Conscious of Jon's gaze, she busied herself with Daisy. Then, too discomfited to return to the wave pool, she followed her niece in search of the others. For the rest of the day, she avoided Jon, but every time she risked a glance, her face flamed. He looked far more smug than he had any right to. And her heartbeat was far more erratic than his kiss should warrant.

Chapter 21

The day of the state fair concert dawned a dull gold, the air heavy with anticipation. Thunderheads boiled all day on the horizon, but as evening neared, the clouds evaporated with the humidity and left a velvet expanse of soft blue.

Jon was in Sedalia, as he had been all day and most of the past two since their trip to the water park. The day following their excursion, Jon had moved the entire Van Castle entourage from the Royal Sun to less fanciful digs at the State Fair Holiday Inn in Sedalia. He'd dictated she and the children would remain behind, deciding they'd suffer less upheaval if they delayed their move to Cordelia until workers had completed the alarm installation, garage remodel, and Internet connection at Lil's house. He hadn't consulted her about any of it, and she'd felt a mixture of irritation and pride that he hadn't needed her advice. Instead, he'd left her to handle the children's rising excitement as the concert neared.

She hadn't minded. The impending concert had made it easier to avoid him.

Since his kiss—just a lapse of vigilance on her part, and incaution on his—she'd kept a wary eye peeled for further overtures, but he hadn't made any. Of course, they were rarely together. He breakfasted with them midmorning, but didn't return until they were asleep. She'd been careful since that ill-advised kiss to keep the conversation neutral, but he hadn't seemed any more inclined than she to confront what had happened.

When she readied herself for the concert, she dismissed the real reason why she'd spent hours yesterday at Shawnee Bay, searching for a powder blue outfit that precisely matched her eyes. She also ignored the wave of melancholy that swept her every time she thought of Jon's departure next week.

As the sun dipped toward evening, Roy drove them to Sedalia. At the gates to the State Fairgrounds, Roy displayed a pass and the guard waved them through. The children gaped at the throngs of people moving between the exotic animal petting zoo, the 4-H barns, the pig races, and hundreds of other booths and exhibits. Melanie wrinkled her nose against the earthy smells drifting from the livestock corrals. A Ferris wheel flashed above. The roar and screams from the Rocket Express shook their molars. Munching on a shared bag of kettle corn, a couple in matching overalls stared after the limo, but largely they received no attention. Roy wound around to a private drive where they received laminated neck tags. He dropped them near a long row of air-conditioned trailers behind a stage erected in front of the grandstand. Right now the grandstand was deserted, but soon it would be packed.

The children scrambled out and stared. Scaffolding rose a good thirty feet into the air behind the stage, a huge network of catwalks and platforms and cables and swings. Grips wandered through the maze, slinging cable and calling orders. Amplifiers zinged and went still. A few backup dancers brushed by them, their faces masklike under a heavy layer of makeup. Lil had thought a country concert would be a vignette reminiscent of good ol' boys strumming and picking around a campfire. This was bewildering. She was relieved when Zeke approached, although he too looked unfamiliar, outfitted for the show in white tailored satin spangled with silver studs.

He smiled. "Something, isn't it?"

Lil could only nod.

"Jon's doing." Zeke turned to stare at the intricate set. "Long time ago, he grasped the showmanship rock had already mastered. It's a major reason for our crossover success." He leaned down to the children, and pointed. "See that?"

A round disk, only six feet wide, stood smack in the middle of the stage. "Everything will go dark before your daddy appears. Before it does, you find that circle and keep your eyes right there. While the stage is dark, your daddy's going to step on the disk. If you listen real hard, you'll hear some machinery start up, and it will raise him way up there." Zeke indicated the top of the set. "Then it will lower him while he starts to sing."

Melanie looked worried. Lil eyed the thing and prayed it would hold. Michael clapped. "Can I do it?"

Jostling her, a young man with a panicked expression dashed to the foot of the stage. The man waved his arms at a tattoo-riddled giant adjusting cables. She looked at Zeke.

Zeke smiled. "The choreographer. The cables are in the way. He doesn't want us tripping over them." He surveyed the scene. "Well, this is it. The last venue before we take off for distant shores. And"—he looked down at his boots and grimaced—"hopefully I'll never again have to share a stage within three miles of a four-footed mammal."

Following his gaze, Lil smiled. The boots showed signs of recent scraping, but some remnants of cow patty still remained.

Over the last weeks, she'd learned the Country Comeback tour had started at a June rodeo in Texas. As Mari had surmised, state fairs were smaller venues than Van Castle could command, but Jon had conceived the idea as a nod of appreciation to, and an attempt to recapture, the band's earliest fans who'd followed them around at the beginning of their career to state fairs, rodeos, and tractor pulls. He'd done it. Arenas had sold out, sales from the *Comeback* CD had exploded. Once more, Van Castle was on top.

Michael had been eying some electrical cable with great interest. He started to scoot off in that direction, and Zeke scooped him up. "Unless you have a sudden yen for barbecue, my man, I think we'd better find you alternate entertainment."

Michael's eyes lit up at the mention of food, and he allowed Zeke to carry him to a white box of a trailer. Zeke rapped once and opened the door.

Inside, the trailer was sparsely furnished, but laid with deep pile carpet. An easy chair, sofa, and TV ranged along one wall. Zeke took the chair, and the children scattered toward an array of snacks lined up on a table against the other wall. Jon's Fender sat on a stand. In the middle of the room, a carrot topped man Lil recognized as the crew's manager tried to engage Jon in conversation while Sidney, his mouth full of pins, tsked and fluttered, yanking at a vest of denim trimmed with glittering rhinestones. Jon wore it bare chested with nothing else on except a pair of Jockeys.

She blushed just as Jon glanced over, away, and then back again with widened eyes. Her blush deepened. Yesterday, she'd exchanged the ribbon in her hair for a new upswept hair style that allowed wisps of curls to frame her face. It wasn't exactly *Cosmopolitan,* but it was definitely less *Seventeen.* She'd also bought blue leggings with a matching tunic blouse. She hadn't felt the need to impress *him.* It had simply been time for a change, but she couldn't help feeling gratified by his reaction.

Jon gave her a half-smile, then turned his attention back to the crew manager. Sidney reached for a hanger, then eased Jon into denim trimmed with fringe and more rhinestones. It was as snug as a second skin. Lil gulped.

The door swung open and Roy stuck his head in. "Time to go."

She looked at Jon, thought of the scaffolding. It hardly seemed appropriate, but she said it anyway. "Break a leg?"

He smiled. "That'll do." He seemed remarkably calm.

She gathered the children, and followed Roy. He hadn't appeared soon enough for her peace of mind.

Twilight had deepened, and the grandstand had filled. Catcalls and murmurs drifted around them. Some of the phosphorescent lights glaring against the night winked out, leaving the arena in partial darkness. As one, the crowd paused and looked toward the stage, a hitch in their shuffling feet and rustling programs. For a heartbeat, even the vendors hawking Van Castle music, T-shirts, posters, and guitar picks fell silent. When nothing happened, the clamor resumed, this time vibrating with an undertone of expectation.

Roy led them to the base of bleachers that stacked up over the highway patrol office and press room. "Fellow'll be here soon to take us up." Roy stuck a toothpick in his mouth and lounged against a nearby wall.

Lil hugged Michael's and Melanie's shoulders, giving Michael a reassuring wink when he tipped his head back to look up at her.

Talking in high excited voices, eager to find their seats, stragglers hurried toward the stands from the draft horse sled pull over in the Coliseum. Roy watched them with hooded eyes, although in their hurry, nobody even glanced in their direction. Under her fingertips, tension quivered in the children's shoulders; they were exhilarated by their father's concert, but shy of so many strangers.

"Mrs. Van Castle? Your husband, he sent me to take you on up."

It took a moment for Lil to realize the young security guard approaching them spoke to her. Mrs. Van Castle. She wasn't used to it, and the little thrill that rippled through her was annoying. The guard switched on a flashlight, and adopted an officious tone. "Watch your step, ma'am. Parts of the grandstand's dark."

She shepherded Melanie and Michael forward. Snagging the toothpick to the other side of his mouth, Roy pushed off of the wall and shadowed them.

After their discussion at Surf's Up, Jon had told Roy he was banished to Cordelia, at least for the duration of the tour. As she'd hoped, Roy had admitted to her over one of their morning cups of coffee that he looked forward to it. "After the last few years, be like Walden Pond," he said. She loved Cordelia's lazy nature, but she hoped Roy didn't expire from boredom.

Though sorrow overlay Jon's departure—the children would miss him—she thrummed with anticipation over returning home. Back to her house, back to her gardens, by now probably parched scars in the earth, and back to Petunia. Her cat was undoubtedly peeved at being left in the care of a stranger, although Mari wasn't exactly a stranger. She sighed. Her sister hadn't been a stranger until this summer.

Lights swept the stage. Colored spots flicked on, then off, in one final check. As she and the children emerged from the bleachers, a roving white spot glanced over them. In a double take, it stopped and returned, snaring them in brilliant light.

She shaded her eyes, blinded. The crowd hushed. Then a rumble grew to a roar as recognition dawned. She was the Cordelia hometown princess who'd found her Prince Charming, the Missouri local who'd made good and now lived their fantasies.

"Lil. Lil. Lil."

The chanting began as a disorganized bleat and grew into a hammer of sound. Apparently sensing a golden opportunity, the technician kept the spot on her and dimmed the others.

Dismayed at the attention and trying to ignore the urge to bolt, she clutched the children's hands and stumbled along, eyes pinned to the back of the security guard. Aware of his sudden importance, his chest puffed out. He flourished the flashlight like he was directing traffic, and barked at those who tried to touch her. Roy moved in close.

They climbed for an eternity to the VIP box. "Lil. Lil. Lil." The noise shoved at her from every direction, catching and squeezing her chest until she could hardly breathe. Only the solid warmth of Roy's hand on her back kept her moving.

The guard waved them into the front row of the box. She edged toward her seat, glimpsing members of her family. Even her mother had gotten into the act, clapping and yelling. Nearby, Alcea and Stan flanked their daughter. Alcea looked vaguely disapproving while Kathleen attempted to copy her expression. Baring his big white teeth, Stan bellowed along with the rest.

Lydia and Peter Price sat shoulder to shoulder. Peter beamed at her like she'd arranged this sideshow for the band's benefit. He'd hate to know her thoughts. If she'd ever wondered before, she now knew she definitely didn't want the attention. Exhaling in relief, she reached the empty seats in front of her parents and started to sit.

Roy's voice in her ear stopped her. "Bow."

She looked at him, startled. She wasn't part of the act.

He nudged his glistening bald head toward the

crowd. "Bow. Curtsy. Wave. Whatever. Do something and they'll stop."

Feeling not a little bit silly, she straightened and flapped a hand before she sat down. The crowd cheered, the spot winked out, and everyone looked around for another distraction.

From behind her, her mother squeezed her shoulder. "Never thought I'd be calling one of my own a star."

"I'm not a star," Lil murmured, settling the children.

Michael's eyes gleamed like obsidian. He jounced in his seat, jostling his sister's popcorn. Looking feverish, Melanie elbowed him. Lil sighed. The children didn't need all this attention either.

"Maybe you're not, honeybunch, but, Lord, wasn't that fun?" Zinnia sat back and popped a malt ball in her mouth, her glasses white mirrors in the glare from the lights. She leaned forward again. "Did I tell you we've a buyer for the cabin? Offered us more than even *we* thought the old place was worth."

She knew Jon had finalized the papers on the purchase of the O'Malley lake property this past week, but she pretended surprise. "So soon?"

"Isn't it? Quite a stroke of luck finding a buyer that could pay that much so soon. And, whoever it was, he bought it through some representative. Didn't want his name known. Pretty strange doings all together, wouldn't you say?"

She directed a sharp look at her mother, but Zinnia leaned back and the lights played off her glasses, hiding her eyes.

"I hope you're not feeling too bad now that it's gone. I mean, it's been in the family for so long." She wished she could just hand over the deed now, but it was still in Jon's name, and would be until the conclusion of their agreement. Besides, part of the bargain was strict secrecy. She squirmed a little, thinking of how she'd spilled everything to Seamus. Well, she wouldn't repeat the mistake twice by telling her parents.

Her mother and father exchanged a half-smile. Zinnia shrugged. "What's meant to be is meant to be. We're just happy for Patsy Lee's sake. Not gonna hear anymore of that PicNic nonsense."

A shower of popcorn interrupted them. Lil glanced down the row. Cradling her growing stomach, Patsy Lee threw her a sweet smile, oblivious to Daisy, who pelted the crowd. Next to Daisy, Hank gazed in awe at the crowd while Rose, dressed in her Sunday best, peeked out from behind her mother's side.

A glow of satisfaction melted her discomfort. Patsy Lee's needs, and her parents' future, were settled. It was only a few years, and then she'd have the great satisfaction of giving them back the deed.

Curious about who else shared their box, she twisted to look. Mari sat behind her. Her eyes flashed. "Have yourself quite the fan club, don't you? Nice duds, by the way."

Zinnia rifled a look at her. "Marigold McKenzie . . ."

Mari's eyes slid away and she stared stone-dead ahead.

Lil's shoulders slumped. Once she returned to Cordelia and could see Mari more often, maybe she could mend the rip in their relationship.

The stadium went black. The crowd stilled. An eerie green glow shrouded in stage-produced mist rose from the platform and silhouetted the five members of Fruit Stand.

Around her people settled back in various shades of skepticism. Touring with Van Castle could rocket record sales and increase radio time, or it could dash a band's fantasies. So far, Jon said, response to Fruit Stand had exceeded their hopes, but an opening act had to earn the crowd's favor—they couldn't assume it like the headliners.

Fruit Stand launched into their set, a whirlwind of eccentric rhythms and glistening harmonies. The crowd simmered. A few heads nodded, some fingers tapped armrests, and soon heels jogged along with the beat. By the end of their act, Fruit Stand had warmed the crowd and bowed themselves off of the stage to a rollicking round of applause.

Again the stage blackened. She strained to hear the gears that signaled Jon's journey to the top, but heard nothing over the shuffling anticipation of the crowd. As the darkness lingered, the crowd grew edgy and the air electric. She leaned forward, muscles tense. Surely nothing had happened to him. Surely she'd hear something if a cable snapped, if a pulley broke—

A bright white spot seared the night, striking its target. Jon hovered above the stage, muscled legs planted far apart, his Fender held at the ready, head dipped so his gleaming gold hair shadowed his face. He didn't look at the crowd.

But the crowd was riveted on him. They gasped, Lil gasped, and for three heartbeats there was dead silence.

Posing as still as the night air, hand primed above the strings, Jon prolonged the moment. Tension mounted. Expectation shifted toward anxiety. Then, with a mighty downstroke, he belted one chord. It pealed into the silence.

With a mighty whoosh, the crowd exhaled, then caught their collective breath again as all four corners of the stage erupted in fireworks. From the loudspeakers, an announcer bellowed, "Va-an Ca-astle!" Jon fingered the opening measures of "Bella Linden," their signature hit. The crowd exploded.

His fingers moved like lightning over the frets, over the strings, his body hunched around his guitar, his concentration complete. He still didn't look at the crowd. He was one with the guitar. One with the music. The platform descended.

A cacophony of sound, a phantasmagoria of light, burst under his feet. The band swung into his lead. Dancers gyrated from their perches on the scaffold, and trapeze artists whirled from swings in diaphanous gowns. Behind them, massive screens glowed with starbursts of color that morphed into flickering images of Van Castle on tour, Van Castle on video. The crowd roared its approval.

The platform slid to a halt. Hands still a blur over the body of his guitar, Jon strode to the edge of the stage and paused. The lights ceased pulsing. The music stopped. The sudden silence was deafening. The wall of energy he'd conjured gathered into a fist. In one sweeping movement, he faced his audience, threw his head back, arched his body and punched the air. The energy arced from him and walloped deep in her stomach.

The crowd hooted, screamed, and pumped back. Lil stuck two fingers in her mouth and whistled, the loud piercing whistle Henry had taught her eons ago. Michael laughed up at her, and Roy shot her a look of amusement. Feeling her face heat, she dropped her hand.

As the crowd's frenzy peaked, Van Castle hurled themselves into a whirl of their classics. They pounded out dance hall thumpers and rollicking sing-alongs, voices melding in tightly stacked harmonies, then soaring in solos, backed by dancing fiddles, the grit of Zeke's bass, Jon's blazing guitar solos, and the driving tattoo from Three-Ring's drums.

Her eyes stuck to Jon. He worked one end of the stage to the other. He pranced. He strutted. He flirted. His rhinestones flashed with every stride, sweat glistened on his chest, his hair swirled in a shifting mirage of honey and amber. He rifled the neck of the Fender over the crowd, until he'd mown them all down. When the set ended, the crowd slumped with exhaustion. They belonged to him.

He stepped center stage to acknowledge the waves of applause. Her hands were damp, her knees trembling. Chopin had never affected her like this.

He gestured for silence. "Thank you." He paused for a beat. "How are you, Sedalia?"

The crowd roared back to life, and he waited until they'd subsided. "We've pumped you up, now we'll cool you down. Our next set is a series of ballads, some old, some new. This first one's new . . . 'China Blue Eyes' . . . hope you like it."

Stepping back, he signaled the musicians. Three-Ring rapped out a gentle foot-tapping beat, then the guitars riffed into a rush of sound that culminated in the soar of fiddles in flight. Jon moved forward again, and dropped the guitar to hang by its strap. A single spot locked on him; he raised his eyes and crooned a capella.

China blue eyes
Such a surprise
To find childhood reprised and
Everything that matters, in your china blue eyes.
Filling up my heart,
Filling up my mind,
Filling up my soul is
Everything I'm finding and everything I'm feeling,
Childhood unreeling
In your china blue eyes.

As the band joined him, a deep blue glow lit the stage. The crowd sighed and settled back. She closed her eyes and Jon's sweet baritone swept over her, swept through her. This time the backup singers crooned behind him. *In your china blue eyes.*

As he sang, scenes from the past weeks drifted

against her closed eyelids. His quirky half-smile when he watched Michael and Melanie frolic in the pool. The flare of relief and anger in his eyes when she'd returned with the children on Michael's birthday. The wind whipping his hair when they'd jounced in the Jeep. His sweet determination when he'd bent his head to kiss her. The way his eyes always seemed to search for hers, his hand reach for hers, almost like an old married couple. . . .

She opened her eyes. Jon's head tilted toward the VIP box. Even though she knew it was pure foolishness—he couldn't see her against the glare—she imagined he stared straight at her. Straight into her heart. A heart she'd guarded, a heart she'd armored against hurt, against pain. She sucked in air, light-headed, bewildered, aching as her heart cracked to let the sweet flow of his voice surround it, warm it, massage it to life. The song was for her. About her.

Everything that matters, in your china blue eyes.

The last note of the refrain resonated and died. There was a brief pause, and then the crowd erupted. Someone tugged her arm.

"I have to go to the bathroom," Melanie whispered. "Really bad."

She jogged herself out of her fantasies. She was mooning over Jon like some starstruck adolescent. Of course he sang to her. To her—and to every other female in the audience. He performed. That was his job. And he wouldn't have achieved such astronomical success if he couldn't, for at least one heart-stopping instant, make every woman believe he longed to be with her. Still, a voice whispered, how many of those women had been so thoroughly kissed by him?

As for the song, he'd started composing it before he'd met her, so it couldn't be about her.

But she knew it was, even though she wasn't ready to face it. It was too much to be coincidence. It had to be about her. But . . . did he mean everything the words implied, or had she just been a—what do you call it?—a muse?

Filled with confusion, she took Melanie's hand and signaled Roy. Roy heaved to his feet. The little girl danced in place. Judging from her pained expression, they'd never make the distance to Jon's private trailer so she opted for the public restrooms. With the show in full swing, there shouldn't be too many fans wandering about.

They picked their way down through the grandstand, then spilled out onto the graveled walkway that led between the grandstand and the state fair carnival. Above the horse barns and FFA building, they could see the Ferris wheel's gaudy lights. Out here in the open, the honkytonk music blended with the bass from the concert. Sounds of life swirled around them, but all she could hear was the echo of Jon's song. His song for her.

The path was deserted. They hurried past the blue-and-white striped awning of the Baptist revival tent, the red-lacquered JUMBO HOT DOGS AND FRESH-SQUEEZED LEMONADE! stand wafting with the smell of popcorn, and skirted the Budweiser beer garden. She pointed to the left. Melanie skipped ahead, then darted through a door marked "Mares."

Leaving Roy standing sentry, she followed Melanie. She scurried into a stall. Lil leaned a hip against the bank of sinks that lined a mirrored wall. One other stall was occupied.

She twisted to look in the mirror, plucking at a few curls, then looking deep into the eyes that stared back at her. Their expression was somber. Stupid to get so enraptured. It was only a song. Even if she'd been his inspiration, that didn't mean he really felt all those things. If this was all the fortitude she could show, it was fortunate Jon would leave soon. Her forehead glowed with a film of sweat. Outside, the August night was just this side of comfortable, but the bathroom still held the heat of the day.

A toilet flushed. She glanced up—and met Mari emerging from the stall.

Mari's face twisted. "So the great Lilac Van Castle is slumming, is she?" She strode to the sink and unleashed a roar of water into the basin.

Lil blinked. Taking a hesitant step, she touched Mari's shoulder. It stiffened. "Mari, we can't go on like this. Our differences are hurting Mother and Pop."

Mari didn't reply. She twisted the faucet and shook her hands, splattering water over the mirror, then stomped to the towel dispenser, her spine cast in iron.

Lil's shoulders sank, but she tried again. "Please, Mari. We're sisters. I miss you."

Mari jerked on the roll of towels, cracked off a length, then whirled around. Her eyes glinted with tears, but her face was pure fury. Her earrings trembled. "You should have thought of all that before you stabbed me in the back."

"But, Mari, we—"

"Fell in love? Don't feed me that line of bullshit. Save it for your adoring public." Mari wadded the towels. "I know about your agreement with him. I heard you telling Seamus at your wedding." She spit out the last word like it was foul. "And wouldn't the first Mrs. Van Castle love to know about that little deal?"

Lil glanced in alarm at Melanie's stall, but the door remained shut. There was no sound from inside.

Mari saw her look. "Don't worry. I'll keep your little secret. I won't tell the world how the crusading Lilac O'Malley offered herself up for sacrifice, saved the family farm, her sister-in-law, and poor, rattled baby Mari who wouldn't have been able to—" She screwed up her face. "How did you put it? Oh, yes.

'Keep her head on straight.' I believe those were your words."

"Mari, I didn't—"

Mari dashed the towels to the floor, her freckles crumpling. "It could have been me, Lil. It could have been *me*. Hock's always been the queen bee, you've been the sweet little princess, and I've been nothing. An accident in the O'Malley progeny. Jonathan Van Castle was my one-way ticket straight out of Cordelia. But no. Lil knew what was best. Lil *always* knows what's best." She swiped her eyes. "I mean, geez, give me some credit. I would've found a way to help Patsy Lee, too. And Pop. Even you. I would have!"

Despite the plaintive tone, she doubted Mari had thought further than her own bid for freedom and Jon's—she could admit it—considerable charms. But seeing Mari's misery, she knew her sister had built a romantic tragedy in her head and cast herself as the jilted and misunderstood heroine. That was Mari.

Lil felt no remorse. Mari would have expected a superstar existence, not days spent wiping noses, sharing childish confidences, playing Junior Monopoly and baking snickerdoodle cookies. And, unlike her, Mari would have misunderstood Jon's inevitable advances. She would have fallen in love, and broken her heart in the process. Lil knew she'd made the right decision, but deep regret pierced her over their fractured relationship.

She touched Mari's arm and said the only thing she could think of. "I love you."

"And you think that makes everything okay? You expect me to tell you I love you back, what a great person you are for doing what you've done? Well, I don't think you're all that noble. You didn't think about the family when you agreed to marry him. Don't kid yourself. You only thought about yourself." Without a backward glance, she slammed out of the bathroom.

Heartsick, Lil sagged against the counter. She considered Mari's words. Had she somehow warped her good intentions into her own means of escape? She thought of the pleasure she'd taken in her shopping sprees, in her growing adeptness at handling the press. Had she married Jon for more reasons than salvaging her family?

A toilet sounded and feet shuffled. Oh, God. Melanie.

The stall swung open and Melanie stood framed in the door, her thin shoulders slumped, head bowed, her bangs dipping over her eyes.

Lil rushed forward and knelt in front of her. "Oh, Melanie . . ." She slid Melanie's hair behind her ear and glimpsed tear stains. "Look at me, sweetheart."

"Lil?" Roy nudged the door open.

"We're okay," she called over her shoulder. "Be right out."

The door clicked closed. Mel's eyes remained downcast.

"Oh, honey. Oh, Mel . . ." She continued stroking the shiny brown hair, casting through her head for just the right words. But there were no right words.

Melanie looked up. Her eyes, flecked with gold just like her father's and filled with more wisdom than a child of ten should have, gazed into Lil's. "Do you love my daddy?"

She couldn't answer. She stared at Melanie, her mind numb.

Melanie sighed and reached up to toy with one of Lil's curls, her eyes fastened on her fingers. Then in a small voice Lil strained to hear, she asked, "Do you love *me*?"

The soft words sliced deep into her heart. Throat aching, she gathered Melanie tight. "Oh, yes, Melanie. I do love you."

The little girl expelled a breath and rested her head on Lil's shoulder. "I love you, too."

Lil's heart was so full it could burst. She laid kisses on the top of Melanie's burnished head and rocked her. She did love Melanie, and Michael, with a fierceness that astounded her. What had started as fondness had blossomed into a full-blown, gut-wrenching, heartaching solid core of maternal love that she knew, knew with a sudden flash of insight, would always be a part of her.

Mel stirred and pulled away. Again that steady gaze. "Are you going to leave me?"

Meeting those eyes filled with such love and trust, Lil almost broke down. She hugged Melanie again and tried not to think of the three-year agreement, salving her guilt with the knowledge she'd always be able to visit them, knowing Melanie and Michael needed stability and normalcy and love much more right now than they needed the truth. She'd find a way to tell them. But later, when they were older, less full of fear.

And because she wanted to—needed to—believe the words as much as the children did, she choked out the lie. It stumbled over the cold dread in her heart when she thought of that day in the future. "No, honey," she whispered. "I'll never leave you."

Chapter 22

The three days following the state fair concert were even busier than the three days before. While Jon huddled with Peter checking and rechecking every detail for the next phase of the world tour, Lil took the children to Cordelia overnight for doctor's appointments and enrollment in school, hoping scenes from their new life would help distract them from the melancholy of Jon's departure.

When the fourth day arrived, Van Castle left for Toronto among tearful farewells, and Lil bustled the children to Cordelia, glad for Roy's stabilizing presence. She breathed a sigh of relief that she'd gotten through the interlude without having to confront Jon.

She was still too confused about the song and the kiss, still too bewildered by her emotions, to risk any private moments, especially since she was sure just his presence would addle her thinking. His sojourn overseas would make it much easier for her to settle her feelings. Because, truth be told, she'd started to care for him. And, maybe, he cared for her, too.

Her heart pinged like a pinball at the possibility, but her mind swerved around the idea. She'd protected Mari from heading down this very path. She wouldn't endanger her own heart and coddle the notion that a country superstar and a small-town girl could chance a future together. They wanted different things.

As summer concluded with a Labor Day picnic in Cordelia Memorial Park, Van Castle moved on to Calgary and the Country Music Week at TELUS Convention Center. The children moved on to school.

Melanie proved to be a natural student, and she surprised them with a mean game of softball. Joining Daisy's fall league, in short order she ranked alongside Daisy as a top hitter. Michael, though, balked at the restrictions of kindergarten. After he drop-kicked his *I Love Numbers* book into the classroom's hamster cage, Lil suggested to his teacher that she pair him with Rose, ostensibly to help her. As she hoped, he took the responsibility to heart, his disruptions dropping to maybe one a week.

Through September as Jon jumped the Atlantic and hopscotched through Scandinavia, from Hartwell Arena in Helsinki to the Falkoner in Copenhagen, then on to the Netherlands and Belgium, Lil and the children settled into a routine. A daily priority was Daddy. Time zones and schedules caused problems with phoning, although they did manage a call every weekend. Instead, they relied heavily on e-mail.

With Melanie helping Michael, the children and Jon tapped out brief exchanges every day. Lil scanned and sent schoolwork and pictures on a regular basis, but she wrote only one lengthy missive a week. Her notes concentrated on the children. She would have e-mailed more often except she didn't want him to think that she was pining for him. He'd fallen into her rhythm, contacting her no more often than she did him, but with longer notes than the ones he sent his children.

Even with that limited contact, instead of fading in his absence, her feelings for him still made her by turns giddy or annoyed, and she was far from sorting things out.

As the leaves burst into the vibrant colors of fall, Van Castle traversed from a country music festival in

Paris, to the Hallenstadion in Zurich, and a series of concerts in Milan, Vienna, and Munich. The children and Lil collected maple leaves and pressed them between waxed paper, spent chilly Saturdays baking cookies, made Halloween decorations, and spent one Sunday at Farmer McElwain's Pumpkin Patch and Corn Stalk Maze, where Michael's howls when he got lost sent Roy crashing through the field, and left Lil doubled over in laughter. One memorable evening was spent celebrating the Country Music Awards when Van Castle took home (via satellite) the Entertainers of the Year award.

At the end of October, Jon had a ten-day hiatus before Van Castle was scheduled for performances at the American Traditional Music and Dance Festival in the Czech Republic. Because Peter had arranged a series of radio shows through the European Country Music Association, Jon couldn't come home, and they debated whether or not to send the children to him. With reluctance on both sides, they'd ultimately decided the trip would be too disruptive. Lil wasn't sure whether she was disappointed or glad.

October faded into November and Van Castle traveled to Germany. By the Sunday before Thanksgiving, Lil had lost track of whether Jon was in Hamburg or Leipzig, but she'd quit pretending she didn't know exactly how many days he'd been gone. Eighty-six, including today.

At her parents' home on Maple Woods Drive, Lil brushed some crumbled brown leaves off the swing that hung at one side of their heavy-columned front porch and sank into the faded red cushions of the porch swing. The swing creaked in reply, protesting the heaping quantities of mashed potatoes and gravy she'd consumed at Sunday dinner.

Approaching twilight deepened the shadows in the front yard. Warm earlier today, the air now held a bite that promised another night of frost. It wouldn't be long until the first snowflakes flew. She pulled her sweater over her chest.

Across from her in a lattice-backed chair, angled just so to catch the last pallid rays of the sun, Pop huddled in an eye-bumping blue and saffron flannel shirt, his nose tucked in a book. He looked up, smiled vaguely around his unlit pipe, then returned to his reading.

She returned his smile, then untucked the e-mail she'd printed off the computer. It was soft from repeated reading.

She studied the subject heading and smiled again. She wasn't the only one who'd lost track. *Frankfurt— or maybe Berlin.*

A soft snort made her look up. In a matching swing on the opposite side of the porch, Roy dozed, chin nodding. She looked at him with affection, then back at the sheet.

Lil,

   Tour's still going great. Every place we go we're mobbed and the venues are sold out. Peter tells me the comeback album is number one. Tell the kids again how much I liked the card they sent when we won the award. I saved it on my desktop so I could look at it anytime. Looks like Van Castle's made it—again. Still, I miss you all. (Here she wondered—and wondered at herself for wondering—if the "all" tacked on to the end of the sentence was an afterthought.) *Thanks for keeping me up to speed on them. Great pictures you sent of them in their Halloween gear. Mel made the perfect bookworm. Where'd you find those karate robes for Michael?*

She hadn't needed to look far. They were part of the package that came with lessons at the local Karate for Kids outlet. At least she'd channeled his kicking and punching into something positive. One of the *do-jang*'s rules was no practicing on other people, to Roy's great relief.

Tell Mel I'm proud of her report card. Don't know where she gets all those brains from. Not from me. I was a screw-up in school. Glad she likes her teacher.

At a whoop of laughter from the front yard, she looked up. Michael barreled around the trunk of a maple, Daisy and Melanie blazing on his heels. The kids had launched a game of monster tag, boys against girls, and Michael looked doomed.

She wondered what he'd think of them. They'd blossomed since August.

Michael hurdled a pile of leaves Lil and Pop had raked earlier, then whisked around the corner of the house, laughing over his shoulder. She turned back to her e-mail.

Michael's paintings are . . . interesting, I guess is the word. Think he needs a shrink?

She chuckled. She'd scanned samples of finger paintings they'd created on one rainy Sunday. With his usual enthusiasm, Michael had smeared every color of the rainbow on his paper—and on the table, the chair, and her pale yellow linoleum kitchen floor— then attacked the thing with such ferocity, he'd ended up with a river of mud. But, he'd helped her clean up, and hadn't even found an advertising jingle that fit the occasion. With some lapses, what Jon called his ad-speak had subsided, probably because he had little time for television with all his activities.

You said they visited Belinda again. I'm glad Roy goes with them and can see why you don't.

Don't worry about it, Roy'll take care of them. Hope she's not giving you any trouble. You let me know if she does.

She hadn't seen any reason to worry Jon over the taunts Belinda leveled at her when she'd call to schedule the meetings with the children. A barb sometimes found its mark, but she'd grown a thick skin. His ex-wife still didn't know Jon had no intention of returning Michael and Melanie once their agreement ended. Lil would feel sorry for her, except she remembered that look of hate.

She never saw Jon's ex-wife herself. And although Melanie was subdued and Michael more manic after seeing Belinda, Roy said she not only behaved during their visits, she was playing the model mother. Likely because she suspected what Jon was up to.

I told you Judge Dougherty sent me a heads up when Belinda got out of Serenity in September. I thought she might cause some trouble, but it looks like I worried for nothing. Guess you were right about the media, too, but old Wart-nose is still hanging around, isn't he? Only a measly snake? Helen Tidwell needs to try harder.

She leaned back on the cushions and laughed out loud, earning another vague look from her father. She'd written Jon that Helen had unleashed a harmless garden snake in Wart-nose's room at the Sleep Inn. He'd discovered it around three in the morning, curled up against him in the warmth of his bed. His resulting howls had roused the entire motel.

The other photographers had long ago grown bored with both her and Cordelia, and drifted on to other prey, but Wart-nose was tenacious. He still poked his greasy head up when they least expected it and snapped away with his camera. There was little noteworthy about his pictures. The children walking to school. The three of them buying bubble gum at the Quik Mart. Pictures better suited for *Family Circle* than for the *National Tattler*. If anything, the photos would further Jon's cause more than Belinda's.

Thinking Jon sounded lonely, she skimmed through the middle of his note, a narration of the past week, the grasping crowds, the riotous concerts, the cramped cage of hotel rooms and airplanes. Then she zeroed in on the part that intrigued her.

•

I've thought a lot about that day at the water park. Didn't get a chance to talk to you about it before I left—hell, you didn't give me a chance to talk to you about much of anything before I left. I haven't mentioned it before, but it's been on my mind more and more lately. I think it's something we should talk about when I see you.

Then there was a quick line, like he'd added it before he could think better of it.

But believe me when I say that kiss meant something to me.

That was all. Just that paragraph.

She read the words again for the umpteenth time and puzzled over what they meant, wondering why he brought it up now. *That kiss meant something to me.* Was he trying to tell her he wasn't a womanizer? That if she wanted to indulge the fantasies that had plagued her dreams since that day, he could be trusted over the course of an affair? Or . . . did he really nurture deeper feelings for her? She thought maybe that's what he did mean—hadn't Zeke said he'd tried to impress her?

She took a breath of the crisp air. All she wanted was this, it was all she'd ever wanted . . . wasn't it?

The breeze ruffled the leaves on the trees, and the calls of the children echoed from the backyard. She surveyed the sleepy aftermath of Sunday dinner and tried to ignore the kernel of discontent that had lodged inside her since summer. Certainly it was. Mari's words sounded uncomfortably in the back of her head, *Oh, Lil—there's a whole, big, beautiful world out there!*

With a sigh, she folded the paper and let it drop in her lap.

The screen door creaked. Zinnia appeared, wiping her hands on the flowers embroidered across her apron. "That's done. We'll have ice cream later." Her mother whipped off her apron and settled on the swing.

"I wish you would've let me help you, Mother."

Zinnia patted her knee. "That's okay, honeybunch. Patsy Lee and me had a nice talk while we did dishes. She wanted to talk babies and I thought you'd be—well, you know."

"Oh, Mother, you don't need to worry about that anymore. I'm not so sensitive I'm going to swoon at the mere mention of the word. Where is Patsy Lee anyway?"

Her mother watched Michael zoom into view, then dart for cover under the pile of leaves. "Taking a little snooze. Just think, soon after Christmas, I'll have another grandbaby to rock." She nodded toward the yard as Melanie appeared, jumped on the rustling pile of leaves, yelled "Gotcha!" then dashed around the corner. "Those are good kids and you've done wonders with them. Best thing that could have happened to them. *And* you. So . . . what do you have there? Love note from your hubby?"

She blushed. "Jon e-mails me and the children all the time."

"When's he coming back?"

"He's not sure. Says it could be as early as December twenty-two, but maybe not until Christmas Eve. Christmas Eve at the latest."

Zinnia dug an elbow into her side. "Not soon enough, huh?"

She creased the paper, glad in the deepening light Zinnia couldn't see her face. Her mother's frank talks on the subject of sex had embarrassed her as a teenager, and she sure didn't plan to go there with her now. "Why weren't Alcea and Stan here today?"

"Alcea said they had something doing at the country club. But Pop saw Stan's car at the Rooster when I sent him for a can of coffee. I dunno. Seems like anymore the two of them can't hardly stand to be in the same room. I worry about Kathleen, Lord love her."

"Why does Alcea stay with him? She knows he's not faithful."

"She doesn't talk to me about it, never has, not since your pop and me objected to the marriage way back. Too proud. Maybe it's because she's kinda like you in some ways."

Lil raised an eyebrow.

"She doesn't know she's strong enough to stand on her own."

Lil started to protest, indignant at the comparison, but Zinnia pushed herself up. She swiped at her husband's knee. "Hey, you old thing. Think you can take your nose out of that book long enough to take your honey for a walk?"

Pop smiled. "Think you can keep up with me?"

Zinnia snorted. "In a New York minute."

They linked hands and she dragged him to his feet. As they set off, Zinnia's head dipped onto his shoulder and their laughter floated back to Lil. Yearning tugged her heart. That's what she wanted.

From under the folds of her sweater, she pulled out a chain and fingered her wedding ring. Her first wedding ring. The real one, not the thick diamond circlet Jon had given her.

What did her mother mean, she didn't know she was strong enough to stand on her own? Wasn't that what she'd done? Idly, she compared the slender gold band with the heavy ring of diamonds on her hand. Her heart stuttered, and she slid Jon's e-mail back out and reread the last paragraph.

> *Not too much longer and I'll be joining you. We leave on the Operation Season's Greetings Tour with the USO in a few days. I doubt turkey dinner at Ramstein Air Base will taste the same as Zinnia's. We'll end up at RAF Mildenhall in England, then we're on to the Apollo in Manchester, then London. Once those are done, I'm coming home.*

Jon would be home in time for Christmas.

*　*　*

Jon was coming home. From Thanksgiving to Christmas, that thought hummed under everything she did. She and the children made the ruffled red dress for Melanie, draped their Christmas tree in strands of popcorn, made a weekend foray into Kansas City to see the Plaza Lights, and caroled their hearts out in Cordelia's square beside the mayor's tree. With each day that passed, the children grew more giddy with holiday excitement, and the knowledge their father was coming home. But nobody was more excited than Lil, nor was anyone trying to hide it like she was. By a snowy Christmas Eve day, the thought had reached a cacophony that drowned out all other thoughts.

Somehow, in Jon's absence, when her guard was down . . . somehow, over the weeks and months of e-mails and phone conversations . . . somehow, the assault he'd made on her feelings when they'd been together had triumphed. He'd sneaked past all her defenses and slid into her heart.

Chapter 23

Hands tucked in the folds of an army surplus jacket and hair shoveled under a knit hat, Jon trudged along Lil's deserted street. It was midafternoon, but the weather had brought an early twilight. Snow spit from a lead sky, and crunched under his boots.

He shifted the duffel bag slung over his shoulder. The tour had been hell. The last couple of days had been worse, a tangle of crowded airports and holiday traffic. He'd parted with the band in New York, had flown on to Kansas City, then had spent two hours suffering the chatter of his limo driver before he'd had the guy drop him at the top of Lil's street. He'd arrived without fanfare. Seemed even the paparazzi had better things to do on Christmas Eve. And he hadn't told Lil what time he'd arrive.

Solitude felt strange. He tilted his head and let snowflakes tickle his tongue. Even though he'd been alone all his life. He wanted to change that. But he didn't know how. Or even how to try.

He checked the addresses on the tract homes huddled together against the gusts of wind that swept the street. Striped awnings, decorative fences, and an assortment of mailboxes, porch lights, and storm doors didn't mask their sameness. All had single garages and a patch of front yard with a tree in the middle. Christmas trees glowed from same-sized picture windows, holiday lights crisscrossed gutters, yews, and the juniper that marked the corner of each house. Plastic Santas and snowmen hailed him with green-mittened hands. Studying the houses, melancholy settled on his shoulders. He'd had addresses, but never a home like these.

Down the street, a yellow house glimmered through the fog. His pace quickened, then slowed. Maybe Lil and the kids had made themselves one where he wouldn't fit.

Even with half a world between them and days filled with bedlam, he'd thought about them all the time. Hell, let's be straight about this, he'd thought about *her* all the time. He'd waited for her e-mails like a kid waiting for Santa Claus to drop down the chimney, and had mentally counted down the days until he could return.

Flattened by the snow, a shout of laughter sounded from the direction of the yellow house. Michael's laugh. Jon felt his face stretch in a smile, and his eyes teared. A few steps more, and he caught sight of four figures dashing around the corner into the front yard. Roy wore a red pompon hat that matched Melanie and Michael's. Jon's smile wobbled, and he halted next to a pickup parked at the curb a door away.

Powdered with snow and oxidized paint, Lil's Escort hunkered in her driveway. He'd once suggested he throw in some new wheels, but she'd set her chin. He hoped pride, not devotion, made her hang on to it, or he could be in trouble tomorrow.

Roy and Michael squatted on the far side of the car, Roy packing snowballs into a pile by the rear tire. Howling like a wild beast, Michael scooped them up faster than Roy could make them. He pelted them over the hood.

A turquoise scarf tangled around her neck, Lil dodged Michael's artillery. Mel, coattails at full sail, ducked in and out from behind a maple where there was another mound of snowballs. Mel's laughter rang out. "Take that . . . and that . . . and that!" Concentrating on their battle, they hadn't noticed him.

His grin grew stronger when his son scored a hit on Lil's coated rear end.

"Oh, no, you don't!" Lil and Mel advanced. Roy scrambled to grab more snow. Michael hollered. The girls backed the defenseless guys against the side of the house next door. "Uncle. Say uncle!" Mel insisted, threatening her brother with a faceful of snow.

Roy flung up his hands, and a disgruntled Michael plopped onto his seat in a drift. Arms raised boxer-style, Mel and Lil sashayed across the front yard and hooted their victory. "We are the champions, we are the champions . . ." Lil's navy cap tumbled from her head, her curls caught in the wind, and the fringe of the scarf fluttered an invitation around her swaying hips. He couldn't resist. All his good intentions to keep Lil at arm's length crumbled in a surge of yearning to grab a little bit of belonging.

With a roar, he dropped the duffel and launched himself from the side of the truck.

Four shocked faces turned toward him. Mel and Michael squealed. They surged forward, and he scooped them up, dropping to his knees, kissing two pairs of sweet lips, losing himself in their down-filled hugs. Roy and Lil looked on, smiling. Then he straightened, caught Lil's gaze, and was moving again. Her eyes widened, but her smile didn't fade. Before she could swerve, he was on her. With a *woof,* they went down. He rolled to catch the brunt of the fall, pulling her on top. The children danced around them.

Looking down into his face, she laughed. "Why, merry Christmas, Mr. Van Castle."

He felt her muscles bunch to shove herself off, so he tightened his grip and kissed the tip of her rosy nose, refusing to let her escape. He'd save that full lower lip for later. "I'm glad I could make it, Mrs. Van Castle."

She bloomed in confusion, then two bundles of energy walloped them. He hugged them all, let his head fall back in the snow, and laughed, feeling lighter than he could ever remember. He'd just been welcomed home.

Roy retrieved Jon's duffel and they all tramped to the back of the house. Lil disarmed the alarm, and the children shed their boots and coats on the screened porch without being asked. Roy dropped his pompon hat on top of the pile. When Jon raised his eyebrows, Roy raised his back. "She made it for me."

Lil held the back door open, and they stepped into a rec room neatly furnished with pine, an upright piano, and a Lego table. The children ran into the narrow kitchen to the left and snatched a few cookies off a trestle table lined by stools. Taking his duffel from Roy, he followed, conscious Lil hadn't looked him in the eyes since their tumble in the snow. The kitchen was spotless and a splash of sunshine yellow. A crock of philodendrons sat on the table. She pinched off a dead leaf and dropped it in the trash. Her hand was trembling. Inwardly, he smiled.

Michael snatched another cookie. "Those are for the pageant tonight," Lil admonished without any heat. She glanced at him. "I hope you won't mind. Melanie is Mary, and Michael's a shepherd."

"Yeah, Daddy. A shepherd, with a stick and everything."

"I can't wait to see it."

Scattering crumbs, Michael grabbed his arm and pulled him through an L-shaped room, dining room in the short end, living room in the long. Jon got a glimpse of cream walls, Christmas lights glancing off polished blond wood, and a tree groaning under the weight of ornaments, popcorn, and inexpertly pasted red and green paper chains. Michael tugged him down the hall. Mel danced along behind them. Lil followed.

Ahead, a calico cat pranced out of the way and disappeared through a doorway.

"That's Petunia. She's ours, too. Lil said so." Michael pulled hard. "Come see my room. You're staying with me. Lil said so."

Jon veered into the first opening off the hall, a room lined in pink. Michael frowned. "Not there, Daddy. You don't want to stay in some old girl's room."

The bedroom was feminine and neat. Books lined wood shelves over a desk. Stuffed animals lounged on a bedspread scattered with rosebuds, and a matching border lined the ceiling. His eyes roamed the pictures arranged on the bureau. Some of him, one of the band, a couple of Lil and Michael, and a portrait of Daisy. Even one of Belinda. Mel wouldn't have put that there. Watching him, Lil murmured, "She *is* their mother."

Losing patience, Michael yanked him further down the hall and through the second door. Jon grinned. This room was a total mess. Bunk beds draped in crumpled green quilts crowded against the far wall and cartoon wallpaper cavorted above a litter of toys and clothing. The green dragon he remembered from summer stared from a corner, and from under a large, tipped-over dump truck, the cat watched him with skeptical eyes.

Lil sighed and bent over to pick up a stuffed bear lying butt-up in a corner. "Believe it or not, this was all picked up this morning."

Frowning, Michael peered up at Jon. "Don't you like it, Daddy?"

"It's great, bud. Perfect."

Michael bounced on the lower bunk. "This bed's yours. I get the top. Lil said." The bouncing stopped and a line appeared between his chocolate-drop eyes. "Unless you want it, I guess."

"Bottom bunk will suit me fine." He dumped his duffel next to Michael. The sloppy room and lumpy bed looked better to him than all the deluxe hotels in the world.

Mel leaned against the doorframe, twirling a piece of her hair. "Why don't you sleep with Lil like other moms and dads?"

His lips quirked and he glanced at Lil. She'd frozen, her grip tight on the bear's neck. Poor thing, another minute and it'd gasp its last breath. "I dunno. Let's ask her."

Three pairs of eyes turned on Lil. She gave him a look of exasperation. "Like I told you earlier, since you haven't seen your father in such a long time, I thought you might want him all to yourself for a few nights."

His smile broadened. He hadn't told Lil how long he'd be here, but he wouldn't clear out for the coast until the end of January.

Chapter 24

St. Andrew's Church glittered with garlands, candles, and silver bells in celebration of the annual pageant. As Jon was surrounded by well-wishers, her family, and the curious, Lil greeted the Tidwells. The whole town was here, except Seamus. Puzzled, she looked around. She hadn't seen him all fall, and had hoped to mend fences tonight after the way they'd parted the last time. Spotting Paddy O'Neill, who always knew everything, or at least claimed to, she asked after Seamus. The old gossip told her he was keeping the Rooster Bar and Grill open tonight, then winked. "I think he's seeing someone. Hot little ticket."

From a pew near the front, Zinnia waved to Lil. Lil excused herself. She hoped Seamus *had* found someone special. He deserved it. Whoever it was might be the reason why she never saw him. Either that, or he was avoiding her. She couldn't blame him. Silent, steady Seamus. He must be sick of her problems.

As the lights dimmed to cue the audience, she settled in a space between Patsy Lee and Jon. As she leaned forward to address Zinnia, her thigh pushed against his, and she tried to ignore the shiver that shot through her. Since he'd arrived this afternoon, it was all she could do to keep her hands to herself. Fortunately, the children had kept him busy.

"Where's Mari? Hasn't she come in from Warrensburg?" she asked Zinnia. Her sister had spent

Thanksgiving with a school friend, the first time the O'Malleys weren't all together on a major holiday. Lil knew Mari had hurt her mother's feelings, especially since Henry's place was poignantly vacant, but Zinnia hadn't uttered a word of complaint.

Her mother's lips tightened. "Arrived today, then hightailed it down to the Rooster. Said she had to talk to Seamus."

Seamus? Deflated, Lil settled back and smoothed the skirt of the wine-colored dress she'd made for the holidays. Last year when Mari arrived home from school, Lil was the first person she ran to see. Seamus had apparently replaced her. Through the fall, she'd written and phoned Mari at college, but the e-mails weren't opened and the messages weren't returned.

She shook off her gloom and turned to Jon, still feeling shy. "How's Zeke?"

"Fine, great. He said to tell you—" Jon frowned. "How did he put it? To tell you, 'Change continues and you needn't look far for the answers.' Sounds like a damn fortune cookie. You know what he meant?"

"Uh, no. No, I don't." She fussed with the material on her skirt until he laid a hand over hers. She went still.

"You look beautiful tonight. Cold?"

An empire style, her dress's bodice was deeply cut, left her shoulders bare, and fit snugly over her breasts before draping to hit her midcalf. Certain her face matched the color of her dress, she slipped from his touch and drew a matching stole over her exposed flesh. For every pageant in the past, she'd shrugged on a pair of practical wool pants and a sweater, but this year she'd wanted to be more festive. Okay, she'd wanted to impress him. "I'm not cold," she assured him. Her flesh goose-bumped.

He smiled and draped an arm behind her, cradling her upper arm with warm fingers. The sleeve of his navy silk jacket, mildly rumpled even after he'd pressed it—a skill she'd marveled to see since Robbie hadn't even known what an iron was—tickled the sensitive skin on the back of her neck. Her flesh goose-bumped even more.

The overhead lights darkened. She forgot to be self-conscious as the pageant got underway. The children had worked so hard. She hoped Jon wouldn't let them see his amusement. She darted a worried look at him, but like all the other parents, only pride lit his eyes. He hid a grin only when the halo dipped across the shepherd's wide chocolate eyes. Relieved, she sighed happily, relaxing into his light embrace. For tonight, she'd allow herself to pretend they were a real family.

A half hour later, they neared the end of the program. An angel—one wearing neon turquoise eye shadow—had just intoned, "And, behold! A Child is born!" when Patsy Lee squirmed and gasped. Lil glanced over. Patsy Lee's eyes were screwed shut and a spreading pool of water dampened the pew between them.

On Patsy Lee's other side, Alcea hissed, "It's time."

Giving Patsy Lee's arm a reassuring squeeze, Lil leaned across Jon to tell her mother Patsy Lee's labor had begun.

Jon started. "Didn't you tell me it wouldn't be for a couple of weeks?" he whispered.

"Sometimes Mother Nature just isn't interested in our little timetables. God love us—a Christmas baby!" Zinnia didn't bother to whisper and eyes turned toward the O'Malley pew. The performance faltered to a halt.

Murmuring advice and calling out support, the congregation crowded around to help escort Patsy Lee through the church's heavy oak doors. Helen Tidwell bustled off to call the hospital, and Paddy O'Neill, in fine fuss over the doings he'd have to relate at Peg's, went to fetch Zinnia's van.

The family paused on the flagstoned threshold. Lil clutched her wool coat to her throat, grateful for the warmth of Jon's arm around her. Behind them, the children crowded in the doorway, chattering in excited voices. The snow that had fallen so lackadaisically all day now seethed against the night. The old Merry-Go-Read building was a blurry outline across the square. She felt a twinge of pain.

Jon dipped his head. "What's the matter?"

"I can just never look at that place without feeling sad for Henry. It might have really been something if he—or I—had put more into it. And tonight, well—" She gestured at Patsy Lee. Jon pulled her closer. "I wonder what the new owners will do with it."

She looked away. Down the street, the red neon of the Rooster's sign battled the gloom. Last Christmas Eve after the pageant, Seamus had comforted her as she'd cried over the holidays that stretched before her. Thinking of Robbie, she waited for the familiar sad wave to wash over her, but only a sweet nostalgia trickled through her heart. Funny. She'd dreaded Christmas since he'd been gone, yet she hadn't thought about him hardly at all today, even when he'd smiled at her from the photograph on her nightstand as she'd dressed for the evening.

With a snowy flourish, Paddy braked the van at the curb. The family started down the steps. They were salted, but the snow was falling too fast for it to do much good. She skidded in her unaccustomed high-heeled shoes and Jon gripped her elbow, smiling into her eyes and sending her stomach into somersaults.

Pop squinted into the squall, his arm wrapped around Patsy Lee. Roy propped her up on the other side. "We'll never make it to the hospital in this."

Zinnia halted at the bottom of the steps and hollered over her shoulder. "Is Doc Jacobson around?"

The crowd parted and Dr. Jacobson stepped forward, rubbing white wisps of hair that sprouted from his shiny pate. "Now, Miz O'Malley, you know I'm not a—"

"You'll do." Hurrying ahead of everyone, Zinnia bustled the wide-eyed retired podiatrist toward the van and called back orders. "Jon, Lil—fetch the children and bring them along. Alcea—don't stand there looking like a widemouthed bass. Use that phone of yours and call nine one one. Send 'em to our house. And call Mari and tell her we're on our way—she ought to be home by now."

Zinnia bundled Roy, the bewildered doctor, and a groaning Patsy Lee into the van, and jumped in after them. Pop clambered into the driver's seat and took off, fishtailing around the corner. Somehow Jon managed to cram Patsy Lee's three kids, his two, and Lil into the Escort, wrapping them every which way in seat belts, then folded himself behind the wheel. She thought it admirable he refrained from reminding her of the car she'd refused.

They followed Pop the two blocks to her parents' house, the van's taillights barely visible through the snow. They bowled into the graveled drive and halted behind Mari's Volkswagen. Roy and Pop were half-carrying Patsy Lee into the house.

Doc Jacobson slipped along behind. "But, Miz O'Malley, I don't even have my bag!"

As they pried the children out of the car, Jon grinned around the sucker he'd popped in his mouth. "Never a dull minute in the O'Malley family, is there?"

"Never."

Headlights from Alcea and Stan's car washed over them as they whisked the children into the house. In the front parlor, a single table lamp cast a muted glow. The Christmas tree was a bulky shadow in the corner.

Crumpling her angel wings behind her, Daisy flopped on the faded, claw-armed sofa and punched the television remote. Michael Landon handed a wide-eyed Melissa Gilbert a Christmas box topped with a big red ribbon. "Awesome!" Daisy said.

Melanie settled beside her, thin legs sticking out from under her red ruffles, and patted the sofa cushion in invitation, the friendship bracelet Daisy had given her flashing on her wrist. Michael shoved his halo back on his forehead and clambered up, pulling Rose with him. Rose snuggled in next to him and fastened her gaze on the TV. Hank sat cross-legged on the floor at their feet. Roy settled into Pop's recliner.

"I've seen this. It's a rerun." Daisy poked a finger at the screen. "*Little House on the Prairie Christmas Special.* Way cool."

Kathleen entered from the kitchen. She shook snow from the narrow mink collar of her bright red Christmas coat. "Stupid snow. Mother bought this just for tonight and it'll be ruined before I go to the church dance next—"

Daisy glared at her. "Take a chill pill, Kathleen."

"Humph." Kathleen perched on a foot stool.

"Yeah, take a chill pill," Michael parroted, then turned to Daisy, his nose scrunched. "But Kathleen's already cold."

Jon watched them with awe in his eyes. Lil smiled. She switched on the Christmas tree lights. The soft glow cocooned the children, turned Jon's eyes amber and his hair gold.

"They're all family. And for now—" She brushed a wet strand of hair off his forehead. "So are you."

He caught her hand in his and guided it to his lips, pressing a kiss as soft as a promise against her palm. "Family." His eyes held hers.

From the doorway behind them came a clatter of pans, and she tugged away from him, suddenly skittish. "I need to go help. Come on—every member of the family makes himself useful in a crisis."

"But I like this show." He started to sink into her mother's armchair.

She caught his arm. "Oh no, you don't."

She pulled him behind her into the heart of the O'Malley home, passing through the dining room with its dark wainscoting, bay windows, and ivory walls. Stan had settled with a bottle of wine at the table, covered in lace to hide its scars.

He raised his glass. "Gonna be a long night."

She leaned her head close to Jon. "Some people are more useful than others."

As they entered the high-ceilinged kitchen, she heard Jon suck in his breath. She smiled. This room always stunned the fainthearted.

Ladder-back chairs cushioned in a swirl of petunias ringed a massive oak table that squatted on a green and violet braided rug. Wallpaper latticed with purple trellises and violent neon pink roses hung over a lavender chair rail. A riot of Mexican pottery and baskets cascaded with magazines, books, and knitting supplies in every nook, along with a cheerful array of plants. Children's artwork plastered all the spare wall space.

Mari piled wood next to a black-bellied stove. Alcea leaned into a squat white refrigerator plastered with magnets holding everything from recipes to a year's worth of church announcements.

"Wow," Jon murmured. He turned to study the plaster rounds hanging from pink satin ribbons on the wall behind the table. "What are these?"

"Hand prints. One for each of us. All the O'Malley kids and grandkids." She pointed at two that were whiter than the rest. "Here's Michael's and Melanie's. We added them last month at Thanksgiving."

He traced the indentations in the clay, then turned to her. Softly he cupped her chin. His hand was warm, fingers strong. Her stomach quivered in response. She leaned into the caress and her eyes fluttered closed as he bent his head and let his forehead rest against hers. His breath, a hint of cherry, was a whisper against her cheeks. His lips hovered only an inch away.

Alcea thrust a box of cocoa between them. Lil glimpsed envy in her sister's eyes. "If you two can tear yourselves away from each other, we need some help around here. Here, make hot chocolate for the children. Mother's upstairs with Patsy Lee, Mari's boiling water, and I've got coffee going. Although it looks like what you need is a cold shower."

Flustered, Lil pulled away, avoiding Jon's eyes. She glanced at Mari, hoping to share a rolling-eye look like they always did when Alcea clambered up on her high horse. But Mari acted like they were all invisible. She stood stiff in front of the double casement windows over the sink, fumbling for the faucet handles through the fronds of greenery that tumbled from the sill. Water gushed into a pot. She didn't turn around.

Lil's heart sank. She hadn't seen Mari since the concert and she'd hoped Christmas warmth would thaw her sister's stubbornness.

Opening one of the glass-fronted cabinets, she pulled out a bag of marshmallows and a collection of mismatched mugs. She set them on the counter and handed the bag to Jon. "If you'll put a few in each mug, I'll get the chocolate ready."

From upstairs, there came a muffled cry. Everyone paused. When there was no further noise, the bustling resumed.

A half hour later, the baby had yet to make an appearance. All of Patsy Lee's children had come quickly, especially the last—so no one expected this labor to last long.

Alcea peered into the fridge, tsked, and pulled out a foil-wrapped roast from last Sunday's dinner. "This will do. Since we're missing potluck at St. Andrew's, we'll make sandwiches. Here, Jon."

She caught Jon shrugging out of his jacket, his brow moist from the overheated room, and he almost missed his grasp on the loaf of bread she shoved at him.

"Put some mustard and mayo on. Half of each. Make sure you get it out to the edges. Stan hates it when the condiments are all in the middle, although why we should care what Stan likes is another question. Then see if you can find some lettuce and tomatoes. Slice them thin, and don't dress the ones for the children. They won't eat it. Lil, when you're through with that, slice up this beef."

Alcea was in full bossy mode. Lil snuck a look at Jon—and he rolled his eyes at her, much like Mari used to do. She grinned and the tension eased in her back.

In the crowded kitchen, she and Mari couldn't help but rub shoulders. When they found themselves side by side at the stove, Lil couldn't stand the frigid silence any longer. She touched Mari's wrist, but Mari only looked at Lil's hand, her eyes icier than the weather. Lil tried to act like she didn't notice. "Mother said you'd gone to see Seamus this evening. I haven't talked to him for a while. How is he?"

"Fine. If you'll excuse me." Mari hefted a pot and elbowed past her to the narrow back stairs.

Alcea followed her. "I'll get clean towels from the linen closet. I remember when I had Kathleen, Dr. Stuart said . . ." Her voice trailed off.

Lil blinked back tears.

Frowning, Jon watched her. "What's with her?"

"Mari just can't accept that I . . . that we . . ." She faltered.

"Ah, Lil." He crossed the room and pulled her into his arms. Gratefully, she rested her head on his shoulder and her hands on his chest. She felt the steady beat of his heart.

He tipped her head up with a finger. Concern shaded his eyes. "What if I talk to her?"

She shook her head, then stopped. She was tired of solving all her problems on her own. Maybe it *would* help if Jon would talk to Mari.

He took her silence for permission and nodded. "Tomorrow, then."

She looked up at him, got caught by his eyes. The warm concern in their depths shifted to something molten. Her breath hitched in her throat. His hand glided to the back of her head, curled into her hair. He moved closer and she realized he planned to kiss her. All the words of caution she'd fed herself over the past months fled as her bones went liquid. She clutched his shirt, and let her head fall back, parting her lips in delicious anticipation. There was a soft sigh that could have come from either one of them. Their mouths brushed, and a long moan sounded upstairs.

Smirking, Stan swung around the kitchen doorway, a half-empty glass of wine dangling from his fingertips. "Hey, are we having a baby, or what?" he asked the room in general. He stumbled back against the wall. The wineglass slipped from his grasp, and the crystal cracked on the old wood floor. Stan giggled.

A frustrated noise escaped Jon's lips. "Your family's gonna be the death of me."

Grabbing a dishrag from the sink, he mopped up the mess while Stan watched him. After Jon dropped the remains in the trash, he took Stan's arm and steered him away from the kitchen. "Hey, man. Let's get you settled back in here and I'll grab you a cup of joe. And a sandwich. I spread the mustard all the way to the edges, just the way you like it."

Stan lurched against him. "Y'er all right, buddy, jes all right. Lemme tell you 'bout my wife. Cute li'l number, in't she? But she's always got ants in her drawers over sumpthin'. Sunk my car, my poor beautiful car. Cost me a mint, I'll tell ya. Poor pretty car. Hey! Ya know what? Passe-Lee's havin' a baby." He tried to give Jon a punch on the arm, but it glanced off. "An' it's Christmas Eve. You believe that?"

Lil sighed. Well, Jon had wanted a family and he'd landed in hers, warts and all. As the two disappeared through the doorway, Jon gave her a long level look. Her heart tripped and then raced over the mingled heat and promise in his eyes. She turned toward the stove, grabbed a whisk, and whipped at the chocolate. Is this what she wanted? Her stirring slowed. Allowing this to continue would result in a broken heart. Her broken heart. And she wasn't sure she could patch it together a second time.

An hour later, Stan's head had hit the table. His snores echoed off the dining room walls. Jon had settled between the children on the sofa, Michael on his lap, Mel's head on his shoulder. The hot chocolate had been reduced to a skein of scalded milk along the bottom of the pot. Scrubbing it, Lil stood at the kitchen sink. Sleet continued to pick at the black windowpanes. Overhead, floorboards creaked as the EMTs who'd arrived a while ago worked in tandem with her mother and sisters delivering Patsy Lee's baby. She'd peeked in on them, but the crowded bedroom and Mari's continued coolness convinced her to return to the kitchen.

A long, thin wail echoed down the stairway. She froze, then joy flared in the pit of her stomach. From the living room, she heard high voices. Feet thudded to the floor. Face alight, Jon appeared in the doorway. They shared a look of mingled relief and excitement, then she gave a silent prayer of thanks for a new life on this holiest of nights.

Chapter 25

"Come on." Lil tugged on Jon's hand. "It's okay." They tiptoed into her parents' high-ceilinged bedroom. A dimmed lamp cast a halo on the four-poster bed where Patsy Lee lay sleeping, her hair a dark tangle, her baby at her breast. She'd named the baby Lily.

The wind hurled ice pellets against the windows. A sharp stab of regret lanced Jon.

"Is something wrong?" Lil whispered.

"Uh, no." He hadn't been around for his own kids' births. He'd told himself it didn't matter. They wouldn't remember. But looking at Patsy Lee with her newborn, he realized it did matter. Maybe not to his kids, but it mattered one helluva lot to him. For the first time he thought Belinda had a damn good reason to want to hurt him. Lil was still frowning at him. "Yes," he said in whispered vehemence. "Everything's wrong."

Her frown deepened but she squeezed his hand.

He drew a deep breath. "I missed everything. Their births, those first belly laughs, first steps, lost teeth, first words. All those firsts." He'd missed birthdays, holidays, and other special occasions. He just hadn't been there. Not for Mel's spelling bees, not when Michael had learned to throw a ball, not for picnics or walks in the park or trips to the playground. He'd left it all to Belinda and Dodo, telling himself it was the best he could do. "I was a really crummy dad."

The pressure on his hand tightened. "They still love you."

He knew that. "They don't have any reason to." And unless he made some changes, one day they'd lose interest. He didn't think he could bear that. For some reason, though, instead of sinking into his usual pot of self-pity, the scene before him fired him with the ambition to do better, to *be* better.

"You're giving them the reasons. Right now." Lil looked over at Patsy Lee. Her eyes were bright with unshed tears, but serene in the kiss of the lamplight.

He realized Lil must have mixed feelings about this new baby, and wondered if she knew how strong and powerful she was. An unusual feeling stole over him. Hope. He felt hope. Maybe she could silence that grating voice in his head that murmured his old man had been right.

Turning, they tiptoed out of the room, and met Zinnia puffing up the staircase. "Well, that's that." They joined her at the landing. "Been listening to the radio. They've closed Main, the highway, just about everything coming and going. You all will have to stay here tonight. I've already shooed Roy and the kids off to bed. All the bedrooms down here are full, so the two of you'll take the attic room." She nodded her head at Jon and a sly look crossed her features. "Cold up there, but I'm sure you'll find ways to stay warm."

Amused, he saw panic bloom on Lil's face.

Zinnia patted Lil's shoulder. "Now, don't you worry none. You aren't sharin' with Alcea and Stan. There's two big beds up there, Jon. Kids used to use them for slumber parties when they were little." She addressed Lil again. "Alcea left an hour or more ago. They're going to some big 'do' at the club tomorrow morning and Alcea was all in a dither about not having the right clothes." She snorted. "Riskin' their necks to get dressed up for Christmas brunch. Serve her right if they spend the night in a snow drift. But you two—

well, you were all planning to be here in the morning anyways, so might as well get an early start."

"But—"

"Now, Lilac Elizabeth, don't go getting stubborn on me. There's a couple of new toothbrushes in the bathroom up there, shampoo, soap, brush. And I put some old robes of mine and your dad's up there, too. Slippers might be a bit big, but there it is." She slapped Jon on the back. "Welcome to the O'Malley Hotel." Then she leaned toward him, wagged a finger, and said in a stage whisper he was sure could be heard downstairs, "Now don't you go letting my daughter get cold, you hear?"

Lil stood rooted in place, gnawing on her lower lip. Zinnia gave her a devilish smile. He suddenly realized she knew the way things were, bless her meddling little heart. "Now, go on. Scoot. I'll take care of that mess in the kitchen. It's nearing eleven and, if I know my mistletoe, you'll hear the pattering of little feet around five."

Her tread hit the stairs. He looked at Lil.

She stared back at him from wide eyes, then straightened her shoulders. "Well. I guess we'll have to make the best of it. There's two beds, after all."

He couldn't help it. He grinned and wiggled his eyebrows.

With a look that mirrored her mother's, she shook a finger at him and hissed, "And don't you go letting yourself forget our agreement."

He hadn't forgotten their damn agreement, but with a heart lighter than it had ever been, he wondered if he could find a loophole or two before the night was over.

In the attic, Lil snatched one of the two pillows from the iron-steaded double bed and hurled it onto the old sleigh bed that lay in the shadows on the other side. She stalked over and punched it for good measure. The scent of lavender floated up, combating a smell of mothballs. Her mother had made up only one bed. Darned if she'd give it to Jon. He'd just have to sleep on the bare mattress of the other, but she supposed she couldn't let him freeze. Seeking anything she might use—and trying to close her ears to Jon's cheerful singing in the shower—she looked around.

The attic was lit by a single lamp. Open to the rafters, the ice hitting the shingles sounded like a hive of angry hornets battling to get in. She shivered and pulled Zinnia's faded yellow chenille robe tight. Her mother could have at least given her the sash.

She spotted a trunk. Hurrying against the time when that bathroom door would open, she pulled the cord on a light bulb and hefted the lid. Her robe gaped, revealing her plain white bra and serviceable briefs. Not the stuff of romance, thank God. After she'd showered in the tiny square of a bathroom, making sure the latch was secure because she didn't quite trust the light in Jon's eyes, she'd considered sleeping in her clothes, but abandoned the idea. Her dress couldn't withstand it, and it had taken her hours to sew.

Several quilts were folded inside the chest. She dragged them out, carried them to the second bed, and dropped them on the mattress. There. Returning to close the trunk, her eyes caught on a leather-bound book. Slowly she drew it out. Perching on the bed, she settled the heavy volume on her lap and drew a finger over gold-embossed lettering. Our Wedding. She hesitated, then folded back the cover.

Inside, a heart-shaped cutout framed a photograph of her and Robbie. Robbie stared at the camera, his eyes glowing with happiness, and Lil leaned against him, looking up with an adoring smile. They looked so young. They *were* so young.

The remembered pain of his death caught in her throat, and she touched the image. A series of vignettes unfolded in her mind. . . . Their tiny apartment in Warrensburg. Robbie walking down the shaded atrium at commencement. The funny little yellow house with its dripping bathroom faucet and uneven back steps. She'd scrubbed it until it shined, sewn curtains, packed the window boxes with cascades of coral-faced geraniums, kept its tiny kitchen full of mouth-watering scents. And dreamed of the day the bedrooms would fill with children.

She'd never forget the day she'd told him she was pregnant. She'd rushed from the doctor directly to the John Deere outlet where Robbie had just been promoted to manager. Under a brilliant blue high-summer sky, in the parking lot where he unloaded the bright green and yellow tractors, she'd shouted the news over the roar of the engines. He'd swung off one of the beasts and swept her up in his arms. They'd twirled until both were breathless. Only a few months later, he was dead. The baby was dead.

There wasn't a moment of her past that didn't hold a memory of him.

Except for the last five months. She slowly closed the cover on the heart-shaped photo.

The sounds of the shower ceased and she cast a look at the bathroom door. A pause, and then she heard the sounds of gargling.

With Robbie, she'd always known where she was going. Each step had naturally followed the last. But with Jon . . .

He had awakened long-dormant emotions in her, feelings she'd thought had deserted her. The curl of warmth in her stomach when he looked at her with that cockeyed smile, the need to smooth the crease from between his eyebrows when he worried, the ribbon of desire that twirled and tightened between them. And uncertainty. Dear God, she was so uncertain.

The gargling stopped and silence followed. Quickly, she carried the photo album back to the trunk and yanked the chain of the overhead bulb, casting most of the space into darkness. Hurrying to the sleigh bed, she sank down on the mattress, made sure her robe was closed, folded her hands, and waited.

The bathroom door creaked open. She looked up. And gaped.

Jon stood framed in the doorway, his ears peeking out between strands of freshly washed hair that dripped down the folds of Pop's robe. My, what a robe. Bright yellow with peacock purple and flaming red lightning bolts streaking across shiny rayon. A purple sash circled Jon's trim waist. His feet wore matching red velvet slippers, the size of canoes. He looked like a wizard.

A smile tugged the side of her mouth. Pop had worn that? She knew his taste was gaudy, but was this what her mother . . . her father . . . found sexy? The smile broadened and a gurgle sounded in her throat.

Jon grimaced. "Lovely, huh?"

The gurgle erupted into a laugh, then she let loose with a hoot that came straight from the belly. There was a thump under her feet. Zinnia's voice echoed from below. "Hey! Keep it down up there."

Shaking and helpless, she covered her mouth.

Jon's grin faltered as her torrent of giggles slid into sobs, then back into guffaws. Covering her face, she wept.

He covered the space between them in a few strides and sat down beside her. "Hey . . . what's all this?"

"M-Mari . . . Robbie, Lily . . . Henry." She fluttered a hand. "The holidays, m-maybe . . ." Pent-up emotion erupted, racking her body. "I've t-tried . . . I've tried so hard." To take what life had dealt her and, God help her, turn it into damned lemonade. It was what she'd been taught, all she knew how to do. But she didn't want to be strong anymore. She wanted . . . she wanted . . .

Blindly, she reached for him, tugging at the lapels

of the godawful robe and pulling him close. His arms wrapped around her. She sank her head onto his chest, clutching, hanging on for dear life. One of his strong hands furrowed through her hair and cupped the back of her head.

Safe. She felt so safe. She burrowed in against him, strained toward him.

Gently, he tugged on her hair until she looked him full in the face. His eyes were home, warmed by a flame that burned deep. "Lil," he whispered as his head dipped toward hers. "It's okay to love again, Lil."

Their lips met, tentatively at first, a taste, a nibble. Then searching, seeking, probing. Hot and consuming, their mouths melded together, and they fell back on the bed. Lil didn't hesitate, had no thoughts of stopping. A dim thought told her maybe she'd regret this tomorrow, but for right now, he was everything she needed. Everything she wanted.

She gasped as Jon's warm hands heated her cool flesh through the bathrobe, then she sought him through his, parting the robe, pressing him back against the mattress, pressing her palm flat against the smooth strength of his chest. She explored the soft burr of hair, sliding her hand lightly over his nipples, feeling the steady beat of his heart, then learning the stairstep of his ribcage, the hollow tautness of his stomach. Astonished at her audacity, she let her hand dip lower to the band of his shorts. As her fingertips slid under the elastic, he gave a sudden grunt and rose up, spilling her on her back.

"Slower, Lil. Slower," he whispered.

She didn't want slow. She wanted all of it, and all of it now. She wanted his warmth, the safety of his arms, the gentleness in his heart. She pulled him to her, shivering as his mouth danced over her neck, her face, her lips. Her hands kneaded the muscles of his back, feeling them quiver under a light film of sweat.

Impatiently, she pulled at the neck of the bathrobe until it was a puddle on the floor, then slid her hands down, his shorts down, until he was naked, his erection hard on her thigh.

With a moan, he drew back, then drew her on top. His eyes blazed. His hands, those talented, strong musician's hands, stripped her of her robe, her underwear, then played her body, stroking, caressing, dipping, following the curve of her back and over her buttocks. Everywhere he touched laid a trail of fire. She rolled sideways, opening herself, face rosy at her brashness, but unwilling to take any less than he was willing to give.

He paused, staring down at her, then trailed his fingers over the curve of her breast and down her belly. "God. So beautiful, Lil. You're so beautiful."

Words were for later. She ached, she wanted. She mewed with impatience, wrapped her fingers in his long hair and pulled his head down. She was beyond caring about anything, anything except him. His mouth found her breasts, his fingers her core. He teased, he stroked, and she shattered, her hips rising, back arching.

With a sigh, she closed her eyes and relaxed into the mattress. Her heartbeat slowed, and reason replaced rapture. Although she could feel the aroused tension in his body, Jon was still, one hand in her hair. Suddenly needing reassurance, she opened her eyes, and her gaze sought his. Was he amused? Shocked? She wouldn't wonder if he was.

But his gaze was soft and concerned. "Are you sure?"

For a fleeting moment she wondered. It felt strange to make love without mention of love, but while the words trembled on her lips, she couldn't voice them.

His eyes reflected her thoughts. "Lil, I—"

She put her fingertips to his mouth, stilling the thought before he could say it. Love implied a promise she wasn't sure she could make. To Jon, perhaps, but not to his life. Instead, she simply nodded. "I'm sure," she whispered.

And as his hands and mouth found her again, she was. Sure this was the haven she'd longed for, sure this was what she needed right now. What happened tomorrow she'd deal with tomorrow. Within moments, she gasped with an urgent need for release. "Please . . ." She heard herself beg.

His answer was a long moan and when they joined, her world flew apart and then crystallized into a single focus as she urged him upward and allowed him to take them soaring into mindless, shuddering oblivion.

The next time they made love, Jon took his time, all the time he wanted. He explored Lil's body, using his mouth, his hands, acquainting himself with every part of her, moving at his leisure from the sweet arch of her feet, to the tender, soft skin between her thighs, to the rosebud breasts, then back to find the tender center of her. Time and again, he drew her to the peak, but refused to let go, delighting at the pleasure he gave her, and giving himself a chance to recover from the absolutely mind-blowing orgasm of that first experience. He'd never felt such a rush. He'd pictured them making love before, but in his imagination, he'd been gentle, solicitous, in response to what he'd thought would be her reserve. He never suspected she'd drive him wild to match her passion.

When he entered her this time, intending long slow strokes and a leisurely stride to the top, he couldn't contain himself, and again she matched him stroke for stroke. Once more, they came fast and hard together, both crying out, more softly this time. They slumped together.

Underneath them, they heard Zinnia give a strangled yell in her sleep. Lil smiled against his shoulder. "My mother talks in her sleep."

"Correction. She talks all the time." Grinning, he laid back, an arm thrown over his head. She scooted to nestle against him, her head on his chest. He liked having her close, liked the way she felt tucked into his side. She made him feel strong, made him feel like he'd found the pieces in himself he'd been missing. "I like your mother."

"I do, too." Lil's hand brushed his chest, ran up his neck and into his hair. For a moment she was silent, playing with the sensitive spot behind his ear. Then, "What happened to yours?"

A shutter tried to descend over his mind, just like it did every time he thought of his mother. He glanced down at the top of Lil's head, and something loosened inside him. He drew in a breath, released it. "She gave up. She'd never been strong, although she tried. For me. But all the years of my old man's beatings, lying, and cheating were finally too much. One day I came home from school and . . ." His throat started to close.

He'd arrived home from school, knowing his dad had left that morning on one of the jobs he took between binges. He was excited about the B he'd gotten on a science project, bursting to tell his mother. Bs weren't that common for him, plus he thought it might cheer her up. The fighting last night had been worse than usual, and this morning she'd still been in her housedress, eye bruised, when he'd left.

When he slammed through the door, he knew immediately something was wrong. Usually she prepared a snack, and waited for him in the kitchen. Today, the kitchen was empty, no peanut butter cookies on the table, no Kool-Aid. The house was unnaturally still. He didn't call out, somehow knowing there'd be no answer. Icy dread creeping over him, he dropped his report on the table, tiptoed to his parents' bedroom. His mother had been stretched full-length on the bed, hands folded across the flowers on her housedress, eyes staring sightlessly at the ceiling.

He unconsciously tightened his grip on Lil; her hand had moved to his shoulder. She squeezed gently. "What happened?" she whispered.

"She was dead." He cleared his throat. "She'd killed herself. Taken some pills. I couldn't help her, couldn't protect her."

"Oh, Jon." Lil's head rose from his chest and she stared at him, reaching out to push the hair away from his face. It was a touch a mother would make. "You were only a *child,* just a baby yourself. You weren't supposed to protect her. That was her job. To protect you."

He wondered when his eyes had grown wet. How long had it been since he'd cried for his mother? Reaching down, he pulled Lil up and crushed her against him. Pliant, she molded herself to him, murmuring soft words, holding him tight. This time when they made love, it was slow, and just right.

Chapter 26

Midmorning Christmas Day, to the accompaniment of the children's giggles and with the rest of her family and Roy crowded behind them, Jon led Lil out onto the porch. "Close your eyes. No peeking . . ." Cold pinched her nose and snaked around her bare ankles. The purple sweatpants she'd borrowed from Zinnia were three sizes too big and four inches too short. She looked like a bag lady, but the way Jon was treating her made her feel like a queen.

She and Jon had made love most of the night, stopping only when he'd finally dozed off, exhausted from his exertions and jet lag. She hadn't slept at all. She'd lain still, staring at the rafters, a sweet ache between her thighs. She'd listened to his rackety snore. And had wondered if she'd just made the worst mistake of her life. Unable to unknot her thoughts, she'd slipped out of bed and headed downstairs.

Although night still darkened the windows, Zinnia was already up, an apron appliqued with a big fat Santa tied around her waist. Accepting a cup of coffee, Lil helped her prepare cinnamon rolls, an egg casserole, and hot chocolate. Zinnia chattered as they worked. Between comments about how surprised the children would be by the bicycles Jon had bought for each of them, and last night's excitement with Patsy Lee, she flashed Lil more than enough knowing grins to let Lil know she wasn't unaware of her escapades between the sheets last night. When Lil would have fled, Zinnia pulled her into a hug.

"Lord love you, Lilac Elizabeth," she said, stroking her hair. "You always make things so hard on yourself. He's a good man. He's got his heart in the right place, just needs a nudge here and there. You're the woman who can do that."

Before Lil could explain she knew that, but didn't really want to do it in Nashville or Los Angeles or London or wherever else Jon's career took him, a herd of children's feet pounded down the stairs, followed by Lily's tiny wail. Her mother bustled off to attend to Patsy Lee and the baby.

The activity roused Jon, who appeared in the kitchen all mussed and sleepy-eyed. At the rumpled, lovable sight of him, her heart melted, and she wordlessly followed the invitation of his open arms. She didn't know what would become of them, or what she even wanted to become of them, but for now, this was enough.

All morning, he waited on her, bringing her hot chocolate, making sure an afghan was tucked around her as they sat side by side on the old sofa and watched the children exclaim over their presents. He took every opportunity to touch her—brushing a hand over her cheek, caressing the back of her neck, dropping a kiss on her lips. And each time their eyes met, his glowed with warmth or flared with desire, and she knew he was thinking about last night. He even exclaimed with delight, much more than warranted, over the guitar strap she'd cross-stitched for him in blazing stripes of neon blue and turquoise. Now it was her turn. . . .

"Open your eyes!"

She did—and gasped. A brand-new Mercedes, painted an amazing cobalt blue and tied with a bright red swath of cloth that wrapped into a bow on top, sat in the driveway behind Mari's Volkswagen. "How. . . . When. . . ."

"They delivered it this morning." Jon leaped into the snowdrifts and dragged her behind him, uncaring of the ice that filled the old mules she wore. "Like it? I figured that heap of yours was on its last legs. The blue matches your eyes. Custom paint. Look . . ."

He yanked open the door and pushed her into the leather cocoon, then dipped his head in. "It has a V-8 engine, can hit sixty in six point three seconds, about sixteen miles to the gallon . . ."

She placed both hands on the wheel, still in a state of shock. When Stan had purchased his Lexus, she'd heard more than she'd ever wanted to know about cars. With all the buttons and gadgets and instruments arrayed on the dash, she was sure the sticker price was staggering. She'd expected a present from him, sure, but not this.

"Mind you don't get snow all over the inside," Patsy Lee called to the children from the porch, Lily cradled in her arms.

Halfway between the porch and the driveway, Mari stood still as a post.

The kids ignored Patsy Lee, shoving aside the ribbon and filling the backseat with their chatter. Zinnia, Roy, and Pop wandered around the sides, oohing with appreciation. A brand-new car was a rarity in the O'Malley family. Especially a car like this.

She rubbed the smooth leather seat, then turned to look at Jon who'd fallen silent.

"You like it, don't you?" he asked.

"I love it. But, Jon, I don't think—"

"Good, don't think. Just take it, Lil. It's a gift."

"But it's so expensive."

He laughed and shook his head, his long hair swinging. "Ever practical Lil. I can afford it. And I also expect you to let me drive it, every time I come home."

Home . . . Did that mean . . . She ran her hand over his cheek and he angled his head to kiss her palm, his eyes locked on hers. A movement over his shoulder distracted her. Mari whipped around, her natty red bathrobe swinging around her calves, and stomped back into the house.

"Oh, dear . . ."

Jon turned to follow her gaze. His voice hardened. "That's enough of that. I'll talk to her. Right now. Here—" He tossed the keys into her lap. "Take them all for a spin."

"But—"

"The roads have been plowed and there's nobody out. Just give me a few minutes. A couple trips around the square should do it."

She reached for him, but he was already heading back to the house.

Zinnia settled herself into the passenger side and patted her arm. "Leave him be, Lilac Elizabeth. He knows what he's doing. Now—" She dragged Rose onto her lap and settled Michael astride the console. "Not meeting safety standards, that's for sure, but we'll just be heading around the block." She leaned out the window. "C'mon, everybody, cram on in. Lil's going to take us for a ride."

The front parlor, littered with Christmas paper and mugs half-full of chocolate, was deserted, but from the kitchen came a clatter of pots and pans. Jon straightened his shoulders and headed toward the source of the rabble-rousing.

There was a mighty thump. "Shit!"

He paused in the doorway. Mari hopped on one foot and held the other. A cast-iron skillet big as an arena lay on the floor.

She looked up. The Christmas bobbins she'd hung on her ears swayed in agitation. "What do *you* want?"

"To talk to you." He yanked on a chair. "Sit."

"If you haven't noticed, the kitchen's a mess and I need to—"

"I said, sit."

She gave him a slit-eyed look, then hobbled over and plopped down. "Well? What do you want to talk about?"

He grabbed another chair, angling it so their knees almost touched. "We've got to talk about you and Lil. And this feud you've started."

"I'm *not* feuding. And I didn't start it. There's nothing I have to say to you about Lil."

He swore. "Your behavior, attitude, whatever you want to call it, hurts her and your family. Lil loves you. She didn't do anything to yo—"

"Lil didn't do anything?" Her voice rose and she shoved at her hair until it stood up in spikes. "As I recall, you and I had an agreement. Next thing I know, little Mother Teresa has elbowed me out of the way and taken my place. With all the best intentions, of course. Because, you know, her baby sister hasn't the sense of a turkey and can't be expected to keep her head in the presence of such a dazzling persona as you."

"She didn't elbow you out of the way—"

"What would you call it? Lil's not stupid; she knew full well that if she landed you, she'd live in the lap of luxury, have her picture in the papers, get a *Mercedes* for Christmas, for God's sake."

"Is that really what you think is important to her?"

"Money's important to everybody, Lil included. She saw her opportunity and grabbed it while I was too—too—"

"Too pie-eyed to notice?"

"That's not fair! So, I'd had a few, so what? You can't tell me you've never let your hair down before.

I know. I've read everything written about you and you used to be quite the party boy yourself. You used to—"

" 'Used to' is right. I stopped all that years ago. Even if Lil hadn't been there that day, I'd already decided our deal wouldn't fly."

She stopped sputtering and stared at him. "But why?"

"There was something about you that reminded me of Belinda."

"Thanks. *That* makes me feel better."

"Not the bad part of Belinda, the young Belinda. The Belinda I'd known before she got tangled up with me. I was afraid you couldn't handle my life. That you'd end up like her."

She studied him. "Why Lil, then? If you were being so chivalrous to protect me from my potential downfall, what made you decide Lil could handle it? I mean, from what I've seen today, the two of you aren't exactly maintaining a virginal distance."

Guilt stirred, then subsided. "Because Lil is levelheaded. Because she's sensible." He looked at Mari for a long moment. "And, because from the first minute I saw her, she knocked my socks off."

"Besides, Lil is—" Mari stopped. "You mean you love her?"

He averted his eyes. Since this morning he'd wavered between soaring elation and black despair. Yes, he loved her. Loved her with savage intensity. And last night, that love had driven him past caring she'd end up embroiled in a life she couldn't handle. Somehow during their passion, he'd kept a fingernail hold on his sanity and had swallowed the words of love that had risen to his lips, afraid she'd expect more from him than he'd be able to give—but, more than that, terrified she wouldn't say them back.

Mari slapped the table. "Great. That's just great." Her voice was flat. She stood up. "If I'd known that,

I wouldn't have—Well, it probably doesn't matter. Surely it doesn't. I mean, if I can't trust him, who can I trust?"

He wasn't unused to Mari's rapid-fire changes of subject, but this time he didn't follow. "What are you talking about?"

She flicked a look at him as if she'd just remembered he was there. "Nothing. I mean, I don't think it's anything."

The back door bounced open and the family crowded into the kitchen, the children ignoring Patsy Lee's entreaties to at least take off their shoes. Mari looked relieved at the interruption and took the opportunity to flee up the back stairs.

"Wow! That's a cool car, Daddy." Michael tugged on Rose. "Let's go pretend we're race cars. Va-room." He revved up and sped into the front parlor, dragging Rose along.

Daisy danced across the kitchen in their wake, followed by Melanie and Hank. "Awesome! The stereo system could just about bust your eardrums!"

"I know my head's still rattling." Zinnia slapped her slippers together and unleashed a cloud of snow. "You men just go on in the parlor and I'll bring you more hot chocolate."

Lil came in last, dusting snow off her sweatpants. She looked up, met his gaze, and his heart swelled with love.

She stepped in front of him, fingering the car keys. "I shouldn't accept such an expensive gift, and I'm sure I'll look ridiculous in it, but . . ." She sighed. "You can't make me give it back."

Despite all the warnings he'd given himself, he couldn't resist her. As Zinnia rattled a saucepan, he pulled her into his lap. She tucked her head under his chin.

He let his cheek glide over her curls, inhaling her scent. "I'm glad you like it."

She stirred. "It doesn't look like your talk with Mari did much good."

"Oh, I think it did." He frowned, thinking of her rambling comments. "But there was something weird about—"

As Zinnia let loose a grin and thoughtfully turned her back, her hand crept up to cup his chin. He bent his head to hers, and forgot all about Mari.

Minutes later when they surfaced for air, Zinnia was sidling out of the room with a tray, still carefully keeping them at her back. He smiled and ran a finger over Lil's lips. "Since you thanked me so nicely, I've got something else for you."

"Don't you think you've already given me enough? I mean, all I got for you was a silly guitar strap."

"It wasn't silly. It was sweet." He smoothed out the line between her eyes, then eased her off his lap to dig into the pocket of the sweatpants she'd snagged from her dad. "I kinda miss my own clothes, you know?"

She smiled. "Lime green isn't really you. We'll go home after I've helped Mother clean up the mess. But we're coming back for Christmas dinner. That is, if it's okay with you."

"I can think of a few other things I could do with my time. Think they'd settle for just Mel and Michael while we . . ." He wiggled his eyebrows at her and was enchanted at the faint blush that appeared on her cheeks. "Kidding. Of course, we'll come back. I wouldn't miss Christmas dinner at the O'Malley homestead." He unfolded the envelope he'd pulled from his pocket. "Here."

"What's this?" She took the envelope and tugged out the contents. She studied the paper. "The deed to our—I mean, your—lake property? But it's in my name." She raised her face, eyes rounded. "It belongs to me? But what about your money? The folks have already used it to—"

"Money well spent. It always belonged to you. There's more."

"More?" Hands trembling, Lil dipped back into the envelope, then unfolded a second piece of paper. "What's this?"

"The deed to the building where Merry-Go-Read used to be."

"But what—why?"

"Figured that belonged to you, too. It's a special place, you know—where we met. Couldn't let it go to just anyone."

She threw her arms around him, and he busied himself kissing that angel face.

Chapter 27

The ten days between Christmas and Jon's birthday on January fifth were the best days he could remember. They'd spent days hauling the children to the post-holiday sale at O'Neill's Emporium, sharing pizza at Sin-Sational Ice Cream, and, when the streets dried for a few days, teaching Michael to ride the bike Jon had given him for Christmas.

They took the children hiking in the Ozark hills, ice-skated on the pond in Memorial Park, and built a snow fort in Lil's parents' front yard. On New Year's Eve, they bundled up and watched the fireworks burst over Memorial Park Pond. For every activity, various members of Lil's family joined them, Zinnia always ready with a thermos, jug, or carafe of hot chocolate. He was heartily sick of the stuff, but he drank every drop she gave him.

In the evenings, they shared potluck with Lil's family, and once dined with Alcea and Stan at the country club. But usually Lil fed them at home. He liked the home evenings best. Lil would curl up on one end of the sofa, her stockinged feet tucked under his leg, and read, while he fiddled on the guitar, and Mel and Michael played Go Fish or put puzzles together in front of the TV. Sometimes they'd gather around the piano. He and Lil would play, and everyone sang in mismatched harmony.

Days were good, bone-deep good, but, ah, the

nights. Once the kids were tucked in and asleep, Lil would come to him in the double bed in her room. Her room was all her—whitewashed in the light from a street lamp, the floral scent she preferred perfuming the air. She usually wore one of her sedate night-gowns, which stayed on only as long as she was out of his reach. And once that nightgown was shed, they'd stream together in bursts of passion or eddies of tenderness.

Best of all, undoubtedly busy with their own holi-days, the media left them alone. Only Wart-nose still dogged them, but they were used to him by now. Zin-nia had pitied him shivering in a thin overcoat on the day they'd gone ice-skating and even offered him hot chocolate. Jon hadn't minded. The photographer knew to keep his distance—and that was one less cup of the stuff to account for.

The only flaw in his happiness was the dead end he'd reach whenever he broached the subject that Lil come with him at the end of the month. She avoided the topic, or refused to take him seriously. Just yester-day, he'd listened to her prattle about reopening Merry-Go-Read. Shit. He'd given her that deed as a gesture. He didn't want her to do anything that would provide yet another reason why she wouldn't leave. He supposed he shouldn't worry. She lacked the capi-tal to do renovations, or buy inventory, plus her en-thusiasm had subsided when he'd reacted with only a raised eyebrow.

On the night of his birthday, after a lusty bout of lovemaking, Jon heaved a sigh of contentment and rolled onto his side, his limbs still tangled with hers. Earlier that evening, the O'Malleys had celebrated. At the party in Zinnia's kitchen, Daisy and Mel went sev-eral rounds over a boy band poster they'd bought to-gether with their Christmas money and now couldn't decide whose room it belonged in first. Stan got shit-faced and puked up Alcea's chocolate raspberry cake all over the back steps before he headed down the road to the Rooster Bar and Grill. Baby Lily screeched through the viewing of the home video of the kids Lil had made for him, and Alcea topped the evening when she broke the news she'd decided to leave Stan. Kathleen had looked on with a white, scared face. Then they'd come home and Michael had thrown a tantrum over bedtime.

He couldn't remember a better birthday in his life.

He was beginning to believe the warm light in Lil's eyes could heal his flaws. Maybe he did deserve her love. If she did love him. Suddenly he felt cold. He tugged at the covers. "You need to get a bigger bed," he grumbled.

"A bigger one wouldn't fit," she murmured, tucking into his side, her head on the pillow next to him. He could swim in her eyes.

"It'd fit in my house in Tennessee," he said, and felt her go still.

"We've been through all this. The children are doing so well here. It just wouldn't be right to take them out of school and away from their friends."

He sighed and pulled her close, his nose brushing hers. "And you, Lil. If it weren't for the kids, would you go?" The idea of months without her tore him apart. When he left in a few weeks, he'd once again be consumed with commitments from Los Angeles to Nashville. While they'd discussed at least once-a-month weekend trips to visit each other, nothing less than all the time would be enough, and he knew it.

She didn't answer. Just stared at him with those big beautiful eyes.

"Ah, hell." He flopped onto his back and laced his hands behind his head. "I wish I didn't have to leave."

"Can't you put it off?"

"I'm doing the Super Bowl half-time show at the end of January, then everybody's lined up to start video production, camera crew, gaffers, makeup, extras. Preproduction is done. I've got to watch over the editing and dubbing, and the thing's gotta be released before we get the tour CD into stores. Videos are like previews for the main event. Then there's those Ford commercials, more recording . . ." He turned his head toward her. "I'm booked until next fall. Go with me."

Expression sad, she shook her head.

He'd known that would be her answer. Sometimes he saw her waver, but he couldn't shake her arguments about small-town girls and big-city boys. That, and the children, were the biggest reasons she'd admit. The unspoken reason, the one he suspected was the real reason, terrified him.

Framed on the bedside table, Robert "Robbie" Ryan grinned at him.

Irritated at her stubbornness and the guy's goofy smile, his pleasure in the day drained away. "Could you take that down?"

"Take what down?"

"That picture. Shove it in a drawer or something. There's something rather twisted about having your former husband staring at me while I'm making love to you."

"Oh. I'm sorry, I hadn't thought . . ." She pushed herself into a sitting position and reached for the picture. One finger traced the celluloid features and Jon wished he knew what she was thinking. "It's sad . . ."

"Of course it's sad. He was a young guy." He just couldn't dredge up more sympathy. Here she sat, buck naked with him and all teary-eyed over that guy's picture.

"I didn't mean that—or just that. It's only that when we were all young, we thought we'd be together forever. Things seemed so simple, so straightforward. And then Robbie died, and Henry, and now Stan and Alcea are separating."

"You told me this isn't the first time she's left, or he's left. So what's the big deal?"

Lil frowned. "It isn't, but maybe she means it this time."

"Yeah, well . . . he's no big prize, and some people look at change as an opportunity, not a tragedy."

She slid the photograph into a drawer. "Is something the matter?"

"Yeah, something's the matter. I'll leave in less than a week and you're staying here, stuck in your memories and refusing to think you could be happy anywhere else."

Blue lightning flamed from her eyes. "I'm not stuck in my memories. If I were, you wouldn't be here. I'm just realistic. I'd be miserable living in Nashville or Los Angeles or any other city—and I'd make you miserable, too, *if* you were around. Cordelia may not be much, but it's my home and where my family is. It's what I know. It's where I'm happy. And it's where your children are happy, too. What would we do with ourselves in some strange place when you're away? And, you know yourself, you'd be away a lot."

His anger deflated and left a hard knot of frustration. Even though she argued like she was trying to convince herself, she was right. He couldn't picture her in L.A., or even Nashville, any more than he could picture her on the moon. Maybe if he stayed with her most of the time . . . but he wouldn't. He'd tour, record, produce, practice—work. His own needs would end up on top, just like always.

"I'm sorry." He pulled her down and cuddled her into his side. "I'm just grumpy because I don't want to leave."

"Then don't."

"What?"

"Don't leave. Retire. What more could you possibly want? You have more money than Midas already, two beautiful children, and . . ." And her. She didn't say the words, but they fell between them anyway.

"I can't just stay here. People depend on me. Van

Castle is its own industry, a company. If I folded up camp, lots of people lose their jobs."

"There are other jobs."

How could he explain it to her? For someone raised like he was, enough was never enough. She took her loving family for granted. How could he explain that there was no hurt so deep as knowing your only parent had despised you? That it left a hole that had to be filled by something more concrete than people. As a kid, his dreams had replaced the family he'd never had. They'd dulled the edges of reality and given him a reason to live.

He couldn't give it up. He wanted it all—and Lil. But she wasn't ready.

Maybe she'd never be ready.

He hauled her back into his arms, with an urgent need to bury himself in her softness. But she was stiff, unyielding. "What is it?"

She rolled over so her back faced him. "I just don't feel like it. I'm just not . . . ready."

He would have laughed at the way she'd mirrored his thoughts, but he didn't find this situation remotely funny. He studied her back, the pale sweep of skin that was satin under his touch. "Not ready for love-making? Or not ready for me? For us?"

"I don't know."

With an effort, he made his tone light. "Don't know? Well, let me see if I can help you make up your mind." Tamping down his frustration, he ran a hand up her back and into the curls at the back of her head. "Ah, Lil. Maybe we don't know what to do with what we have, but what we have isn't wrong. Your Robbie wouldn't want you to live like a nun for the rest of your life, would he?"

In answer, she dipped her head and scrunched closer into her pillow, breaking contact with his hand. "There's no future in—"

He pulled his hand back. "There's no future only if you decide there's no future."

"I need more time."

"Dammit, Lil." He stared at her back, at her stubborn straight spine. "It's been over three goddamned years. And for the last half year, I've been a part of your life. I'm alive and breathing—and here. Right here! Not dead and buried under six feet of dirt."

She twisted to look at him, eyes growing huge. "Don't talk like that."

"Why not? Afraid Robert Ryan would spin in his grave at the thought you might want life to go on?" She looked at him in horror. He scrubbed at his face. "Ah, Lil. I'm sorry."

He leaned over and pinned her torso under his weight. "I care about you. Let me show you." He slid a hand down her face, along the length of her neck, and across her shoulder until his hand cupped a breast. Tenderly, he rubbed his thumb over her nipple. He felt it respond, but Lil's expression didn't change. If anything, she sank deeper into the bed.

He shoved off her, sat up. "Fine. Be that way."

She pushed herself up on her elbows, clutching the bedspread. "You say those horrible things and then you expect me to—Robbie would never have—"

As Robert Ryan's name dropped from her lips, his control snapped. He shoved back the sheets, swung his legs out. "Right. The saintly Robert Ryan would never try to drive another man out of *his* wife's head by screwing her, now would he? I'm sure he always treated you with the tenderness of an angel."

"That's enough!" Lil heaved sideways out of bed, pulling the bedspread around her.

He bolted to his feet and grabbed his clothes off the floor, knowing his words had hurt, but not caring. She'd never be his. Her precious first husband and her life here would always come between them. He yanked on his pants, then tossed a sweatshirt over his head. He gave a short laugh and ignored the tears staining her cheeks. "An angel. That's kind of funny when you think about it, since that's what he is now. Well, Lil, let's see how warm those memories keep you in bed."

He grabbed his wallet and the keys to the Mercedes. Without another word, he was out the door.

Chapter 28

An hour later, Jon sat on a hard stool in the Rooster Bar and Grill and blew across the top of a beer mug. "Ah, hell," he mumbled.

Foam splattered the bar that stretched along one end of the rustic room with its cheap wallboard paneling and painted concrete floors. He hadn't drunk more than two beers at one sitting since the early days in Nashville, and he could feel the effects of his third.

A Budweiser sign dangled over his head, red neon leaking through a blue haze of smoke. Harsh laughter and conversation buzzed at the tables behind him under the strains of some moaning country ditty on the jukebox. Stupid song.

He drained his glass in two swallows, swiped his mouth, and pushed the glass with an unsteady finger toward the empties beside him, eying that guy who'd insulted him way back when. Some friend of Lil's. Sean? Shane? Something like that. She'd cried on his shoulder at their wedding.

Some wedding. Some marriage.

The guy was on the phone, engrossed in a low conversation and knifing looks at Jon. The man's expression irritated him. For whatever reason, Sean-Shane was still nursing his hostility. Jon turned a shoulder and started to slide off his stool. He'd better figure out where he was sleeping. It sure wasn't going to be in Lil's bed, not after the way he'd talked to her.

"Here, buddy. On the house."

He turned. Sean-Shane slid another cold one across the bar. Jon frowned.

"Jonathan Van Castle, right?" The voice was affable, the eyes hard.

Jon sighed. Maybe there was no love lost, but this fellow was just another schmoe who couldn't resist rubbing shoulders with the rich and famous. Since it was good business to be polite to his public, Jon eased a hip back on the stool, resigned to playing the gracious star. "I've met you, haven't I?"

"Seamus Ryan." Seamus didn't hold out his hand and he eyed Jon like he'd hit a wrong note. "Met at your wedding. Where's Lil?"

Jon stiffened, not caring for the guy's tone. Sometimes men were just downright aggressive, as though his success threatened them. "What's it to you?"

His eyes an eerie green and steady, Seamus leaned over the bar until his face was only inches away. "Lil and I go way back, buddy. If you're in here getting sloshed, that means she's out there somewhere hurting."

Buddy? Who'd this asshole think he was, calling Jonathan Van Castle "buddy"? If the guy would step outside a minute, he'd show him his buddy. He sighed. Except the last thing he needed was a fistfight to top off the evening.

He took a swig from the mug and forced himself to relax. Seamus's eyes gleamed with sharp amusement as though he'd guessed Jon's thoughts. Didn't this guy ever blink?

"She's home." Probably crying her eyes out. He shoveled a hand through his hair. "And better off without me," he mumbled under his breath before he drained his mug.

Seamus picked up his empty and refilled it, then thunked it back down. "Maybe you've got more sense than I gave you credit for."

That last one was hitting him hard. He felt it trying

to tie up his tongue. "Wha's—*what's* that supposed to mean?" He took another swallow and grimaced. He'd regret this in the morning, but he didn't want to look like a pussy.

Seamus settled his elbows on the bar, a coffee cup in his hands. "Like you said. Lil's better off without you. The lady's never been east of the Mississippi or west of the Rockies, and not because she couldn't have, but because she didn't *want* to. She's just not a bright-lights-big-city kind of gal. Never was. Never will be. Better you figure that out now, rather than later. Before Lil's hurt any more than she already is."

Jon set the mug down carefully and narrowed his eyes at Seamus. "Jes'—*just* how close are you and Lil?"

"Close enough. She was married to my brother."

"Ah . . . the *re*-mark-able Robert Ryan."

"He was worth three of you."

"Tha's what I been told."

To his relief, Seamus relaxed. If the big guy decided to punch his lights out now, the only defense he figured he could muster up would be to heave on the guy's shiny boots. "Uh—don't want anymore, thanks." He pushed the mug toward Seamus. Pussy, he was.

But Seamus didn't appear to hear. He refilled the mug and shoved it back. With a smile that didn't reach his eyes, he launched a series of friendly questions about touring, his music, the band, all neutral subjects. Jon sipped at his beer, and answered, growing more befuddled by the moment, wondering how he could get away from here. Every time he'd drained an inch from his mug, Seamus topped it off, encouraging him to stay. After almost an hour, he decided he'd doled out as much courtesy as he could stand. And then wondered *if* he could stand. Staggering to his feet, he tugged at the car keys in his pocket. They snagged on a seam. When he yanked them free, he almost hit himself in the nose.

"Where you think you're goin', sweetie?"

Soft arms twined around him from behind and he lurched against a female. Whoa. Nice tits. He turned and almost stumbled over his ex-wife. "What're *you* doing here?"

Dressed in some kind of clingy pastel thing over tight denim jeans that left little to the imagination, Belinda didn't answer. She just winked at Seamus. Seamus smiled and busied himself with another customer.

She snatched the car keys out of his hand. "You're too far gone to drive, sweetie." She wadded the jacket she carried and set it on the bar along with her purse, then wiggled onto a stool. "You just set your cute little fanny back down and we'll share a cold one."

"Not—not on your life. Besides, aren't you s'posed to avoid thish—*this*—stuff?"

"Who's gonna tell? I'll only have one, I promise." He hesitated, and she pouted. "C'mon, just for old time's sake. I *am* the mother of your children, you know. You can at least have a beer with me."

He knew that look. In another moment, she'd launch a tantrum. He shrugged and hooked a leg back over the stool. "All right, already."

A small satisfied smile curved her lips, and she signaled Seamus. He topped off Jon's mug and filled one for Belinda, then turned away.

She took a tiny sip. "Now isn't this nice? Just a couple old friends sharing—oops."

Reaching for her purse, she'd jogged her jacket and it slipped to the floor between them. Head swimming, he bent to retrieve it. When he surfaced, she was slipping a silver vial of perfume back in her purse and tugging out the ridiculous cigarette holder and a butt. She must figure no reporters had followed him here. As she lit it and puffed a few smoke rings into the dusky air, he patted his pockets for a lollipop, but no dice.

"Let's have a toast." She raised her mug.

After a moment's hesitation, he raised his too, slopping a little onto the bar.

"To love!" she said, darting an amused smile at him. She took a deep swallow.

An hour later, Belinda still chattered at him, her words an incomprehensible babble, while the Budweiser sign faded in and out of his vision like a red fog. He had to go. To Lil. He had lots to explain and needed to make up and give her candy and flowers and all that stuff because he'd done . . . something. But when he moved to rise, his boot heel tangled in the barstool.

Belinda grasped his arm. "Whoa! Think I'll do the driving." She tossed the Mercedes keys to Seamus. "Be a doll and hold onto these, would you?" They shared another wink.

Why'd they keep winking at each other? Like a couple owls. He giggled. Belinda giggled too, and pulled him toward the door, tossing a pretty smile over her shoulder. He smiled back, feeling good, feeling goofy.

When they stepped outside, the cold hit him like a fist, popping his eyes open, although the muddle in his brain didn't clear. He allowed Belinda to shove him into her Camaro and fumbled with the seat belt. He tried to loop it in a knot, but Belinda grabbed it and punched the buckle into the slot.

She slid behind the wheel. "Monaco, here we come!"

Monaco? Wasn't there someplace else . . . Lil. He frowned. No, he couldn't go to Lil because . . . why? He couldn't think. The evening's events scrambled around in his brain while a dizzy darkness threatened, then retreated. Shivering, he pulled his jacket tight.

Belinda thrust a pint of Jim Beam at him. "This will warm you up."

He tried to focus on the bottle, then on Belinda. She gave him an encouraging grin, and feeling obliging, he unscrewed the cap and tilted the contents to his lips. She watched him a moment, then patted his knee before putting the car into gear. He settled back, feeling a glow from the liquor and her approval.

She glanced at him. "Where you planning to sleep tonight, sweetie?"

He tipped the pint again. His mind grasped an idea, and he marveled at his own brilliance since they were headed for Monaco anyway. "Dodo's!"

Dodo'd always been there for him. Nobody else had ever loved him except Dodo. He drank and hiccupped.

Belinda gave a small sigh and smiled happily. "Good idea."

Jon slapped at the snow on his rear. He'd fallen on his way up the unshoveled walk, and poor Jim Beam had flown into a snowdrift. Not like Dodo to leave the walk like that. Not Dodo. Dodo Schmodo. But Belinda'd helped him. She was being so nice, his Belinda. Bella Linden. He leaned on the doorbell. She'd laughed at him when he fell, but she'd asked him if he was okay, and now she even was waiting to see if her mother was home before she left him behind. He held his finger on the button, then played it in three-quarter time and listened to the clamor inside, nodding his head to the rhythm.

"Silly man." She elbowed him aside and inserted a key. "I live here, remember?"

His finger stilled. That's right. She did live here. He frowned. That wasn't good. Oh, well. He played the bell again and listened to the song in his head. She tried to push him inside, but he put both hands on the jamb. Wisps of thought in his bleary head told him something was wrong.

"Uh—where's Dodo? I'm lookin' for Dodo. I need Dodo." He dropped back his head and crooned at the thin clouds scudding across the moon.

"Would you shut up? Dodo's moved in with her

sister, don't you remember? You shipped me off for my lovely garden holiday, then gave Mom a fistful of cash to take off, which has left me high and dry."

He gripped his head. The shrill note in her voice just wasn't the harmony he wanted. If she could just land a G an octave lower. . . .

She shoved him again, and he stumbled over the threshold. She slammed the door shut, stripped off her jacket, and tossed her purse into a corner of the small entry.

She didn't seem nice anymore. He squinted at her. He'd leave, but it was so cold and the house was warm, she was warm . . . well, actually she looked kind of cold in that thin blouse thing, but she once was quite a warm handful, his Belinda. Bella Linden.

He sang. *"Bella Linden, Bella Linden . . . couldn't ask for more than my Bella . . ."*

Her frown faded and she switched on a light. He stopped short. The place was a mess; it was never a mess. An empty wine bottle lolled on the coffee table, an ashtray overflowed with butts. Papers and magazines and fast food containers littered the worn carpeting. When he was a kid, it had always been clean. He stood and swayed, then started singing again.

She giggled. "Our song. This is so sweet, couldn't be better."

He didn't answer. Actually, he didn't understand her, so he just raised his voice until he belted the song at the top of his lungs. When he finished, he slumped down on the bottom step and clung to the newel post. Every limb felt like a quarter ton of cement.

"That was pretty entertaining, but I think you can do better." The light at her back outlined her figure beneath the gauze of her blouse. She'd better watch out, she'd gained some weight, his Bella Linda. She was cold, too. Her nipples stood up, a pair of eyes popping against her blouse. He engaged them in a staring contest, but he blinked first.

She didn't touch him, just stood there and looked at him, hands on her hips, her brow furrowed. He endeavored to arrange his features into the same frown. She chuckled. A happy sound. He chuckled back and she smiled. He always liked her smile. Liked Lil's smile, too. Smiles were good.

"Well, c'mon then, country star. I think you need to sleep it off."

She helped him up. As she drew one of his arms over her shoulder, his hand grazed her breast. Hmm. Nice. He tweaked it experimentally, but she didn't seem to notice. He lost interest and concentrated on putting one foot ahead of the other. The floor rose and fell. He stumbled and hung onto her to avoid pitching down the steps.

She continued talking, almost to herself. "You can just sleep it off. I have to make a call. And then . . . well, we'll see."

A warning buzzed in the back of his brain, but he couldn't wrap his thoughts around it. He was suddenly so tired. His vision swam in and out of darkness. Upstairs, she led him into a room at the end of the hall. He weaved in the doorway while she flung back the covers on a queen-sized bed and plumped two pillows. Then she turned to look at him.

A sly smile quirked the corners of her lips. "What are you waiting for? Hop in."

As he continued to stare, she laughed. "What do you think I'm going to do? Rape you? Here—" She grabbed his hand, led him to the edge of the bed, and pushed him on his butt.

He fell back and his head sank into the cool hollow of the pillow. He groaned with contentment as she pulled off his boots. So tired . . . his eyes drifted closed.

"Now scoot up. Thatta boy."

She tugged at his clothing, a draft whispered across his body, then blankets enfolded his nakedness. She reached for the phone and he burrowed in deep. Hafta sleep. Sleep. He vaguely heard her murmur, and then the smooth satin of her skin slid along his before blackness claimed him.

In his dreams, Lil's sweet smile faded, replaced by a frown and flash of ice-blue eyes. He groaned and reached for her, his hand landing on a soft thigh. From somewhere, a low snap and whir sounded, hushed voices murmured, then were still.

A latch clicked softly. Had she left? He called her name, then flopped onto his back, muttering, struggling to hold onto sleep. Gentle hands moved up his thighs, skimmed over his chest, and came to rest on either side of his face. Pliant flesh pressed against his side. Pliant, *naked* flesh. His body saluted with an early-morning rise, helped along by a big wet one laid on his lips. Ah, Lil. . . .

"Wake up, sweetie," a voice purred in his ear.

Not Lil.

His eyes shot open. "Wha' the hell—?"

Hindered by the arms twined around his neck, he struggled up on one elbow, then blanched as his head shattered into a million pieces. His eyes snapped shut.

When he pried them open again, Belinda's face hovered above his. He bounded out of bed in one leap, a move made with more adrenaline than sense. Pain lanced from ear to ear. He clutched his skull, his stomach catapulted up to his throat, and he weaved side to side, confused.

Belinda sprawled belly down across the rumpled sheets. A weak winter sun poked between the draperies and highlighted the plump round curve of her naked ass. She looked up, concerned. "What's the matter, sweetie?"

Pain and nausea buckled his knees and he sank onto the bed. "What did you do to me?"

She rolled onto her back and stretched her arms to

the ceiling, wiggling her fingers. "What did *I* do to *you*? Why, sweetie, I think it was the other way around. And it was *wonderful*." She practically purred.

He stared in disbelief. "I didn't—I mean, I wouldn't have. Not if you were the last woman left on the planet." The blunt words spilled out before his brain could engage his mouth.

He immediately wished them back as the round delight in her eyes went flat. "You don't remember? Not anything?"

Slowly, in an effort to keep it on his neck, he shook his head. With alarm, he noted the ashtray on the nightstand, wondered when she'd hurl it, and if he had the reflexes left to dodge it. But while her color rose, her eyes gleamed with odd satisfaction. Instead of lunging for a weapon, she collapsed across the bed, her shoulders heaving.

"You prick!" The blankets muffled her cry. "I should've known better than to let you back into my bed. I should've known you don't care. You never have!"

Old guilt bubbled up. He'd prefer the ashtray over tears. He cursed himself. A drunken stupor was no excuse. How could he have led her to hope he still had feelings for her?

Eyes dry as toast peeked at him, then snapped shut. A single tear squeezed from under her eyelashes. He frowned, his guilt ebbed, and wariness took its place. A tiny sob escaped her, and remorse squeezed out suspicion. He hesitated, then patted her shoulder, wishing himself anywhere else, wishing he could turn back the clock. "Belinda, whatever happened, I didn't mean to hurt—"

His gut seized again, and his words turned into a groan. He stumbled to his feet and her head popped up, expression alert. He veered off to the bathroom and slammed the door—big mistake. Stomach roiling, he sank to his knees and retched up what remained of last night's dinner. Last night . . .

Trying to focus, he leaned his forehead against the mirror over the sink and twisted the faucet. Last night, he and Lil had fought, that much he remembered. She'd driven him nuts and . . . he splashed cold water on his face. Ah, hell. She hadn't done anything. His own frustrations had been in the driver's seat and he'd acted like a grade-A, first-class asshole.

Scrubbing at his face with a towel, he fumbled in the medicine cabinet looking for aspirin and mouthwash. After their argument, he'd gone to the Rooster and had a few beers. Only a few, which in the old days meant he was just getting started, and then that guy had jerked him around.

Seamus's words snaked through his brain. *She's just not a bright-lights-big-city kind of gal. Never was. Never will be.*

What did that prick know? Lil would see reason. Any day now she'd figure out she'd rather be with him than with her memories of some long-gone husband. . . . *He's worth three of you.*

Belinda had showed up and they'd had a beer, then things got murky. He vaguely remembered the drive here, but after that, it all went blank. All except the feel of flesh on flesh before he blacked out completely.

Robbie would never have . . . Lil was right. Seamus was right.

He looked at himself in the mirror. His old man stared back through sunken red eyes and stubble. He breathed in, smelling the same rot of liquor and stale perfume. He remembered the fear and astonishment in Lil's eyes as she'd clutched that bedspread to her throat . . . just like his mother had looked at his old man right before he'd raise his fist.

The enormity of his sins slammed into him and buckled his knees.

He slumped onto the edge of the tub as the realization hit him that he'd never get a chance to prove he could be different.

He'd just lost her.

He'd have to tell her.

He wouldn't drag her down like his old man had his mother, like he had Belinda. He couldn't lie and pretend this night had never happened, not to her. Maybe, just maybe, she'd believe him when he said he didn't know *how* it had happened, had never *meant* for it to happen. His chest ached. And someday the sun would set in the east. Integrity was stamped on Lil's soul, she'd never been certain of his, and there was no way she'd ever forgive—

Oh, God, she would. He cradled his head. She *would* forgive him, just like his mother had always forgiven his father. *Lil's better off without you. Better you figure that out now, rather than later. Before Lil's hurt anymore than she already is.*

His heart plummeted to his feet.

Lil's better off without you. He had to let her go. He had to *make* her go.

He slammed his fist against the porcelain and pain arced up his arm. He welcomed the punishment. He'd have to hurt her. And how it would hurt her. But one day she'd sink to her knees and thank God he had.

Lurching to his feet, he grabbed a towel and knotted it around his waist. He opened the door and Belinda looked up. Tears stained her cheeks.

He gingerly lowered himself beside her. "I don't know what to say. This—you and me—" Nausea threatened and he swallowed hard. "I made a mistake."

He braced himself for an explosion, feeling he deserved whatever she dished out, but she only touched him with a trembling hand. "Don't. Don't say that, please don't say that. I know I've done some awful things, but only because you hurt me so much, I wanted to hurt you back. But I love you, Jon, I've always loved you."

For a moment, he thought she'd drape her forearm over her eyes like a despairing heroine in a silent movie. Again, suspicion wormed into his brain, but when he searched her eyes, she looked so earnest.

She gripped his arm, her fingers ice-cold. "At least tell me you'll think about it, think about *us*. We had something once. We can have it again, all of it. Last night proved it. Give me one more chance. I'll show you how good it can be between us." Desperation blazed across her features. He'd sometimes wondered if all the threats and bitterness were a smoke screen that hid the torch she still carried for him. Now he knew.

He brushed a strand of hair from her wet cheek. What had happened between them wasn't her fault. Not entirely. But there was no going back. The way she'd treated the kids disgusted him. "I'm sorry, Belinda."

"It's *her*, isn't it? Miss Happy Homemaker."

His careful control snapped. "Leave her out of this." Belinda's face reddened and he hastily softened his voice. "After last night, I'd be lucky if she'd let me shine her shoes." He pried her fingers from his arm and reached for his jeans.

She was quiet, then her mouth crooked in an odd little smile. "You're going to tell her?"

"Does that make you happy? Yes, I'll tell her."

"Then why not me?"

He popped his head through his sweatshirt and stared at her. "Wake up, Belinda. Look where I've brought you so far." He slipped on his boots and grabbed his wallet, phone, and wedding ring off the dresser. The ring was cold in his fist. He couldn't wear it. Not today. He stuffed it into his pocket. He looked around the room; there was nothing left to do, except leave. Something he excelled at.

She sighed and plucked at the sheet. "All right," she said in a small voice. "I think I knew this was a bad idea, but I hoped . . ." She gave another mournful sigh, then angled her eyes at him. "And my babies? When do I get them back?"

He'd wrecked the kids' chances for having the mother they deserved long-term, but he wouldn't abandon them to Belinda. Lil loved them. Even after this, she wouldn't renege on their agreement. "You're not." He spoke slowly. "I'm filing for sole custody. Permanently."

"I was right! I knew you'd try to screw me." The fireworks he'd expected finally erupted, and she reached for the ashtray. "It's going to cost you, Jon!" He grabbed for the door, slipped through, and the ashtray exploded against the other side. "Did you hear me? It'll cost you big!"

Didn't it always? He sprinted for the stairway, reached the top, then paused in surprise when she didn't follow. He looked back down the hallway at the closed bedroom door. It didn't bang open, Belinda didn't hurl herself after him, there was no replay of all the fights they'd had in the past. No more screeching, no shattering glass, no sounds of wild sobbing. He shook his head to clear it. He'd never understand her.

Temples throbbing, he took the stairs two at a time, his heart aching at what he was about to do to Lil.

Chapter 29

The gray day washed fitful light through Lil's living room, leaving the corners in shadows. She hadn't bothered to switch on a lamp. Through the picture window, she saw Cordelia's lone taxi pull up in the drive. She turned away, seating herself on the sofa in the same spot where she'd sat all morning. A car door slammed, then a key scraped, a harsh sound against the Debussy tinkling from the radio. She'd expected him. He'd called Roy—not her—an hour ago from a gas station. His cell phone was out of service.

Which would be the case if he'd called from near the lake. From Monaco. Roy wouldn't tell her.

He came in, and she slowly stood, the ring of keys Seamus had delivered earlier that morning clenched in her hand. Even at this distance, she caught the bitter smell of smoke and whiskey that clung to his clothes.

"Where have you been?" She hated the waver in her voice. She should be angry, but all she felt was relief.

Jon didn't answer, just showed her his back as he shrugged out of his jacket. When he turned around, she sucked in a breath. His hair was lank. His face was slack. Worse, though, was the mix of remorse and despair in his red eyes.

"Seamus said—" She couldn't finish. Wordlessly she

held out her hand palm up, showing him the keys. "He brought the Mercedes back."

Jon slowly walked over to her. Taking the keys, he let one finger trail over the ridges they'd dug into her palm before he slid the key ring into his pocket. Then, he brushed past her and flopped onto the sofa, thrusting a hand through his hair. "Prick just couldn't wait to tell you, could he?"

Lil stood motionless, then turned. "Tell me what, Jon?"

His hand stopped. He met her eyes; his were bleak. "What did *he* tell you?"

"That you showed up at the Rooster. Then Belinda showed up at the Rooster. And, after a while, you left together."

Dragging his hand down his face, he looked away. "Ah, I—"

Suddenly, she didn't want to hear. "I told him he was jumping to conclusions. That there was some kind of emergency and you wouldn't—" She veered toward the sofa, changed her mind about sitting, and instead plumped a cushion. "The children are with Roy." Her voice sounded reedy and tight, not her own. "They're going sledding with Hank and Daisy and Rose. You see, they're staying with Mother for a few days so Patsy Lee can have some time with Lily. We thought maybe this evening we'd . . ." Trapped next to his knees between the coffee table and the sofa, she blindly straightened some magazines and pushed a bowl of M&M's in his direction. All the while, she felt his gaze. "My family's planned dinner at that steak house on the highway. All of us. Even Alcea, although I'm not sure Mari—"

"Lil, we need to talk."

His words were whispered. Her hands were cold. She gripped them together and chewed her lower lip.

He cleared his throat. "Last night—"

Quickly, she knelt, a hand on his thigh, fingertips

on his lips. "I don't blame you for feeling frustrated. I haven't been fair. I've held on to the past with one hand and you with the other. After you left last night, I put Robbie's picture away. Forever. He was a wonderful man, and I loved him, but he belongs to a different time in my life. But you—you belong right here with me now, and in the future, and—" She took a deep breath, and trailed her hand from his lips down his unshaven cheek. "I love you, Jon." Under her palm, his muscles twitched. He grabbed her wrist and pushed her hand away. She balanced on her heels, her gaze darting over his face. "I want to go to Nashville with you. I'm still not sure I'll like it, but I can try. We'll put the children in school there and see what they think before we—"

"Hell, babe. Let's give this a little more thought." She blinked. Those tiger eyes gleamed with amusement and he raised his eyebrows. "Moving a little fast there, aren't you?"

"I thought—" Hurt blossomed in her belly. Abruptly, she stood. She thought he reached for her, but he'd only moved to lock his hands behind his head. "I know you never said it, but—" She hugged herself. Her pain was alive, pulsing at her from all directions. Jon's smile didn't change, although his complexion had taken on a sickly hue. She couldn't look at him, and instead moved toward the window. "You know," she said, straining to keep her tone conversational, "for the past few nights when I've listened to you try to convince me to go with you to Tennessee, I've wondered if you weren't trying to convince yourself. You're used to a different kind of woman, someone with more glamour, more experience—" To her horror, her voice broke. She breathed deeply, then continued, "I mean, the women you dated before me are more cosmopolitan."

He cursed. "Don't you *ever* think you're not good enough for me."

His voice held such vehemence, she turned in surprise. His chin had jutted forward, but when he met her eyes, he relaxed back into the cradle of his hands and that idiot grin. He shrugged. "Because you are. Good enough, I mean."

She tried to smile. "Don't. I knew this probably wouldn't work, but I let myself believe . . . just what I was afraid Mari would believe. I guess I'm not as smart as I think."

He just stared at her, grinning like a dope. She lowered her eyes, then frowned. One of his fists clenched and unclenched on a fold of his jeans. His gaze followed hers. He stopped, once again folded his hands behind his head.

She narrowed her eyes. "But could you explain it to me? So I'll understand."

"Hell, it's been a good run, babe, and we've had some good times. You're great, really, but I guess I just need a little more variety in my life." He laughed. "Just not a one-woman man. Hey, consider yourself lucky we're ending it so soon. You're better off without me, you know. Last night wasn't an exception. More like the rule."

Why did he keep calling her babe? "Then Seamus was right about Belinda and you?"

His grin broadened. "Why, sure. Babe, last night while you were dreaming your sweet little dreams—" For a moment, the grin slipped. "I was shacked up with Belinda."

She didn't believe him. Red crept up his face. His grin was forced. She frowned, looked again at his hands. Fingers twisting, they worried at something. She focused. Their wedding ring. Abruptly, he slipped the ring into his pocket.

She continued to study him. He raised his eyebrows in a "what?" gesture.

"You're not telling me everything," she said slowly. "I know you. I know you loathe Belinda, and I know you care for me. This"—she motioned at him—"isn't you."

He leaned forward, putting his forearms on his thighs, letting his hands dangle between his knees. She could almost feel the effort he made to hold himself still. "Quit dreaming, babe. I'm not lying."

"Then tell me why."

"Dunno. Boredom, maybe. Drunk, maybe."

"I want a real reason."

"They are real reasons. Too much like my old man, maybe."

She sighed. The man was an numbskull. "Jon, I love you. I'm not Belinda, I'm not your mother. And you aren't your father. Don't do this. We had a fight. Lots of people have fights. It hurt, yes, but it's not going to kill me if we argue. Don't throw away what we have because you think I can't take whatever you dish out. I know your past, I know what you're like now, I know *you*—and I'm a big girl. I get to make my own decisions; you don't get to make them for me."

He pulled in a breath. "I. Spent. The night. With. Belinda."

Despite the false smile, she saw the honest agony in his eyes. Reason fell away and her heart clutched. Pain almost doubled her over. "You did." Bewildered, she shook her head. "You really did."

He shuddered, then relaxed. "Got that right, babe."

Of all the scenarios she'd imagined during her sleepless night, she'd never in her wildest fantasies thought he'd ever, ever turn to another woman. Especially not *that* woman. She thought she might shatter into a million pieces, but she wasn't going to let him see it. "Why, Jon? Why? Were you so *frigging* afraid you'd screw up eventually, you decided you might as well screw up now? You damn idiot!" But even as she made the accusation, she knew it rang false. He might have problems with self-worth, but he wouldn't have slept with Belinda to break them up. They'd been happy. *He'd* been happy.

For a moment, the grin dropped. She hurried on. "I'm not going to let you destroy us. No matter what you've done. Part of this is my fault."

Pain razored across his face, then the smirk was back. "Let's just call it a day, babe."

"Stop it! Just, stop it! Stop acting like some—some moronic egomaniac, quit calling me babe, and *talk* to me."

"Nah. You always talk enough for the both of us. *Babe.*"

She stared at him. She'd seen that single-minded determination before in his work. It was the reason for his success. It chilled her that the same ambition could sound the death knell of their love. Resignation engulfed her. "Then leave. Just leave."

He winced, but the grin stayed. "Well, sure. But first we need to think about the kids."

Her heart settled like a stone in the pit of her stomach. She suddenly knew, with perfect clarity, exactly what she had to do. "I can't do this anymore. Release me from the contract."

His face went white. She'd succeeded in wiping the smirk off his face, and the Jon she knew finally surfaced. She felt hope.

"Are you—are you saying you want the kids out of here?" he asked.

She nodded.

"But you know how Mel feels about you. And Michael—" His voice shook. "Hell, they both love you, more than they ever loved their own mother." He swore. "If you make them leave, it'll kill them. They'd end up back with Belinda. Don't do this. We can go on like we did at the very beginning before—before—"

"Before you decided you didn't deserve me. Tell me the truth, Jon. Tell me the truth about how you really feel, what really happened, and nothing changes." Jon's lips tightened in a stubborn line. She wanted to throttle him. If her threat hadn't reached him, what would? "Listen to me! After Robbie died, I told myself I'd had my one big shot at happiness, my one true love. When he died, I thought my turn was over and now I had to sit out the dance. Mari tried to tell me, but I didn't listen. Then, when you and the children came along, I thought maybe there was such a thing as second chances. Why not? You'd done it with the band. You were doing it with your children. It's you who taught me I could have a future, that I had choices, that I could feel, and laugh, and love. And I want to do that with you."

"Oh, God, Lil." Love glowed in his face. She'd *known* something was off here. She almost melted with relief as Jon reached for her. "Ah, Lil, you *can* do it with—"

He halted as Melanie appeared in the doorway, twisting a pair of gloves in her hands.

Jon's face shuttered. Lil almost snapped in frustration. "Melanie. Honey. I thought you were with Grandma Zinnia."

Mel advanced a couple of steps, looking uncertainly between him and Lil. "They dropped me off because my clothes got wet. She said to bring me back over after I change. Both you and Daddy are supposed to come." She looked up at Lil, tears trembling on the ends of her lashes. "Don't say we have to leave, Lil. Please don't. I promise we'll be good. And Daddy will be good, too, won't you, Daddy?" She turned to him and her voice escalated. "Promise her. Promise her *right now*, Daddy. *Please.*"

Lil looked at him, willing him to finish what he'd started to say, but he avoided her eyes and went down on one knee in front of Melanie. He hugged her stiff body. "Baby, I've done some wrong things and Lil has a right to be mad. But no matter what you heard, remember I love you with all my heart—and so does Lil. Right, Lil?"

Hope fading, Lil turned away.

Jon's voice turned desperate. "Everything'll be okay, baby. You'll see. Lil and I will talk about—"

"No!" Mel cried.

At the agony in that single word, Lil turned back, clenching her arms.

"No, no, no!" Mel pushed her fists against his shoulders and tried to shove away.

He grunted and hung on to her squirming body. "Slow down, baby, slow down."

"I won't!" She broke free, chest heaving, cheeks slick with tears. "It's just like before, just like with you and Mommy. You said all the same things then and it *wasn't* all right. You sent Michael and me away to that stuffy old house—with *her*. And she was *mean* to us. And we never saw you. And you—" Her wild-eyed gaze whipped to Lil. "You said you'd never leave me. You *said*. You *promised*."

Her ploy had almost worked with Jon, but she couldn't pursue it in front of Melanie. Of course she'd never make them go. She'd never intended to even as she'd told Jon she would. "Oh, Melanie." Lil reached for her, but Melanie backed away.

"No! I don't want you anymore. I hate you! I hate both of you!" Swinging around, she ran down the hallway and slammed her door.

Lil's gaze followed her, then she looked back at Jon.

He looked away, but said, "I'm holding you to our agreement. For their sakes."

Not knowing what else she could do, she sagged into a chair. They stayed silent through long beats of silence, then Jon rose and picked up his jacket.

As he shrugged into it, she tipped up her chin. "So, I guess we just go back to the same arrangement we had before."

She tried to be matter-of-fact. Grief etched the lines

around his eyes. She wanted to be angry, but ached to comfort him. God help her, she could forgive him Belinda. She could get over the hurt. She didn't want to give up. But his jaw was set, his expression implacable. Nothing she could say would save him from himself, or save them from him. Damn him!

"I'll stay with the children here, and you'll be on the road. Of course, you'll need to make other arrangements when you come visit. Or maybe we can send them to you in Nashville. That might be easier on all of us." She felt a sudden blaze of anger. "I'm doing this for the children. *Only* for the children."

He hung his head, but kept his eyes fixed on his fingers as he fumbled with the zipper on his jacket. In moments he'd leave. Forever. She wanted to run to him, hang on to his sleeve, beg him to stay. He finally turned his head and their eyes locked. Silently she implored him to stay, gathered all the love in her heart and poured it into her eyes.

He finished zipping. "If you'll get my things, I'll clear on out of Cordelia tomorrow. And once the custody hearing's over, we'll take it slow and easy with the kids, then see about a quiet divorce a ways down the road."

She dragged herself to her feet, and walked stiffly down the hall to collect his belongings. When she returned, she wordlessly handed him the duffel bag.

He slung it over his shoulder. "Roy can come get the Mercedes tomorrow. I'll keep in touch, babe."

The door closed, and Lil watched him back the car out of the drive. Then, pushing her shoulders erect, she went to talk to Melanie.

Chapter 30

The next day was as cold and bleak as the last. If it weren't for Melanie and Michael, Lil wouldn't have summoned the energy to leave her bed. Yesterday, she'd made a phone call to her mother. She'd asked if Mari could watch the children this afternoon, and briefly told her Jon was gone. She'd omitted the details, and had avoided Zinnia's shocked questions by claiming Melanie was summoning her. Which was a laugh. After Jon had left, Melanie had refused to talk at all.

Woodenly, Lil readied Michael for another day of sledding. She told him Daddy needed to leave for business, and he met the news with a shrug, then demanded to know if Aunt Mari would take him for ice cream.

Once Michael was dressed, she tried again to rouse Melanie. Melanie answered with a vehement "Go away!" Unable to evoke the firmness to overcome the child's resistance, Lil gave up. She shuffled down the hall and into the kitchen.

Roy was waiting, sadness wreathing his normally taciturn face. "Jon called. Asked me to meet him at the Sleep Inn, take him to the airport. He wants me to bring the kids, to say good-bye." He paused. "I won't do any of it if you tell me not to."

She gave him a half-smile. "Thank you, but, go ahead and do what he asked. Take Michael, and drop him off at Mother's after. I can't get Mel to leave her room." Her smile slipped. "Tell Jon that."

His mouth tightened. "Will do. I'll take the Escort and we'll get the cars sorted out later." He hesitated. "You'll be okay?"

She almost wept onto his broad shoulders, but only nodded. "I'll be fine."

After Michael and Roy left, she dallied for a while in the kitchen, but left her chores unfinished. She had to face Melanie, whether the child was willing or not.

She rattled Melanie's doorknob. "Let me in. It's time we talked." Her voice brooked no nonsense, but only silence met her. "Melanie!" She jiggled the knob again. "This is silly. You can't lock me out. I have a key."

Still no answer. Sighing, she fetched the tool that would pop the lock. When she returned and opened the door, an icy draft struck her from the open window.

Melanie was gone.

"Melanie!" When Roy and Michael had left, she'd forgotten to reset the alarm.

Her wild gaze swept the room and landed on a piece of notepaper. She snatched it up. Penned in Melanie's neat hand was one sentence: *I'm finding a new home!!!*

"Oh, Melanie." She scrunched the paper in her fist.

If Melanie had left right after Roy and Michael, she had a good head start. Lil ran from the room and grabbed the phone in the kitchen. She tried Roy's cell, then Jon's. Both were off. She hung up and dialed her mother. Roy had just left after dropping off Michael. After a garbled conversation with Zinnia—"Don't you worry none, honeybunch, I'll call the sheriff myself"— Lil snatched up her coat and ran out the door, not certain which direction to go.

"Melanie!" she called. The wind swallowed her voice. She traced Melanie's footprints from the child's window, but lost them in the tracks made by the snow plow. She scanned the street, hoping for a glimpse of Melanie's red pompon hat, but the road was empty— except for a battered old Studebaker nosing its way toward her. She groaned. Just what she needed.

The Studebaker crawled past the front of the house. Wart-nose's face was blurred by the condensation on the windows. When God hands you a lemon . . .

Arms waving, she ran toward him.

Looking dumbfounded, Wart-nose halted and pumped down the window.

"Will you help me?" She gripped the windowsill. He only blinked. "Melanie—Jon's daughter. She's run away and I don't have a car. Will you help me find her?"

"Run away?"

"Yes! Will you help me?"

He leaned over and unlatched the passenger door. "Hop in."

Inside the car, the heater rattled with only small effect against the cold. She shivered and wrapped her coat tight, trying not to think of the consequences of giving such a prime scoop to a reporter, photographer, whatever he was.

Wart-nose nudged the car into gear. "Where you think she's headed?"

Lil craned her neck, searching between houses. "I don't know. Maybe to my mother's. Or my sister-in-law's." God forbid Melanie would head toward the highway and take her chances on whoever came along. Surely she was smarter than that. Panic threatened to shred her reason. She shuddered, and Wart-nose glanced at her.

"Hey. She'll be okay. She's a tough little bird, that one. Smart as a whip, too." He rolled the car around a corner in the direction of the town square. "From what I've seen today, she'd likely head over to your mom's. It's where her friends are, anyway."

Of course. He'd probably trailed after Michael, and

undoubtedly knew Daisy was already there. Although she had no reason to trust him, he sounded so calm and matter-of-fact, she was suddenly glad he'd showed up.

She glanced at the camera on the floorboard, then scanned the snow-packed streets. Not many people were out. "Uh, I don't know your name."

"Walter."

Walter Wart-nose. "Well. Thank you, Walter, for picking me up."

"No problem."

For a short while, they drove in silence. Walter took the most direct route slowly, giving her a chance to search side streets, but she didn't catch sight of a single red pompon. The wind buffeted the car. She pictured Melanie doggedly slogging through the snow, slight body bent against the elements, only her coat for protection. Surely she'd taken her coat. "Oh, God. She just has to be all right."

Awkwardly he reached over and patted her hand. Surprised, she looked at him.

His thin eyebrows raised under a greasy lock of hair. "What? Think I don't have feelings?" He put his hand back on the wheel. "It's a livin', you know? Nothin' personal. Matter of fact, I have three kids at home."

She didn't answer, her mind refusing to reconcile the nosy photographer with an upright family man of three.

"Yeah," he continued. "And I can tell you, they're better off living on a shoestring than those two kids of yours are."

She shoved her hair back, gaze still darting side to side. "Why do you say that?"

"That mother of theirs . . ." He shook his head and the greasy lock swayed. "She's a real number, you know? She's paid me for stuff—like I said, gotta earn a living—but the other night, that takes the cake." The limp strand waved again.

Now he had her attention. She flushed, shamed he knew where Jon had spent the night. "Are you . . . are you going to tell?"

"Hell, no. She paid me for the pictures."

"Paid you for—"

He jabbed a finger. "There she is."

Way down the road, a bobbing red pompon flashed into view. Wart-nose—Walter—had eyes like an eagle. He gunned the engine. The Studebaker gathered itself and shot forward, grinding to a halt beside the child. Lil jumped from the car.

Melanie glanced over her shoulder. She broke into a run, but Lil's legs were longer, and she caught Melanie's hood. "Melanie!"

Trying to free herself, Melanie pulled hard, but Lil pulled harder. Suddenly, Melanie's resistance stopped. She sagged back, and Lil stumbled, dropping to her knees. She gripped Melanie's coat and pulled her in close, holding on so tight neither one of them could breathe. Melanie mewed and Lil pulled back to see her face. Tears were frozen on Mel's lashes, and her teeth chattered. "I want to stay with you, Lil," she wailed.

"You will. Oh, sweetie, you will." Lil tucked back the dark hair that had escaped from Melanie's hat. "I promised you. And I don't break promises, especially ones I make to people I love. I'm sorry I let you think I would."

Mind churning with how she could possibly keep that promise, Lil bundled Melanie into Walter's car, and he drove them home. She didn't think Jon would take the children away, at least not for the next two and a half years. But the court could, and she no longer felt confident it wouldn't. Not after Jon's activities the other night. No matter what Jon thought, Belinda would use the night's doings against him somehow, even if it hurt the Van Castle moneymaking machine. Somehow she had to make sure these children were safe. She loved them. Loved them with an intensity neither Jon nor Belinda matched. Their parents didn't deserve them. She did.

When they reached her door, she invited Walter inside.

An hour later, bundled in a blanket, Melanie dozed in front of the television. Lil closed the door on Walter, watched him back from the drive, then flew to the phone to call Jon, her mind buzzing with everything the photographer had told her. Walter didn't have many scruples, and he shoved his more questionable acts under the heading Gotta Earn a Living, but he did have some conscience where children were concerned. And, after following Melanie and Michael around for months, he'd developed an almost paternal attitude toward them.

She caught Jon at the airport, and rushed into Walter's tale before he could hang up. "Belinda paid Wart-nose to take pictures of you in her bed. She set you up!"

"Settle down, babe. I already figured that out." He laughed, a brittle sound. "You only have one part wrong. She didn't set me up. I went there willingly."

"She planned the whole thing. It wasn't just some golden opportunity. I know it. You'd know it, too, if you'd stop this stupid act and give it some thought. How much do you remember about the other night? What happened at the Rooster? Isn't it *possible* nothing happened later?"

"You're clutching at straws, babe."

Sickened, Lil fell silent. Even if he'd been drunk, he'd still know, wouldn't he? "Maybe something did happen, then. But whether it did or didn't, she'll use those photographs. She'll give them to a tabloid." She played her last ace. He had to believe Belinda would stoop to anything. "And not just those pictures, but the other ones. She told Wart-nose another photogra-

pher helped her out a long time ago, Jon. She has
other pictures. Fake ones. Making it look like you had
sex with some girl. Gloria Something." She waited for
a gasp of shock.

But no gasp came. "The infamous groupie. No
problemo."

She pulled the phone away and stared at it in disbelief. *No problemo?* She put the receiver back to her
ear. "You're not going to do anything?"

"Glory Galore is now a peep show star."

"But she wasn't then. Walter says she was only
seventeen!"

"And Belinda got her to pose for some pictures,
superimposed me into them. I've seen them." He
sounded bored. "Disgusting, but don't worry about it.
They're old news. She didn't use them then, and she
won't use them now. For Belinda, everything's insurance. She's not stupid. She knows she almost broke
me before, and she's not going to chance that. She
wants money. And I'll pony up." He paused. "Plus,
she loves me."

"Loves you?" He had to be out of his mind. That
look she'd seen on Belinda's face had been the fur-
thest thing from love. "You're wrong. It's not just
money. It's certainly not love. You've got to fight her,
you've got to—"

He broke in, the flippant tone gone. "Fight her with
what? Last time it was a lie. This time she's telling
the truth. She didn't get me drunk. She didn't shove
me in her car. She didn't push me into her bed. For
God's sake, Lil, get that through your head." He
paused. "She'll say she wants the kids, then—"

She almost dropped the phone. "And you'd let her
have them? How *could* you—"

"Hey, babe—" At the note of cocky amusement,
she wanted to reach through the line and strangle him.
"I said, she'll *say* she wants the kids. She doesn't.

She'll use everything she's got as a threat to get them, but it's the money."

Completely unconvinced Belinda would behave as Jon expected, she renewed her arguments, but all she got for her tirade was a soft click as he disconnected. She slammed down the receiver.

Stewing, she checked on Melanie. The child still slept. Grabbing a cup of coffee, Lil sat down and thought hard for a good hour. All her life she'd followed someone else's lead. She'd shuffled from her parents' home and into Robbie's arms. Then Seamus had stepped in. Now Jon wanted to save her too, even though she didn't want saving. Well, no more. She was tired of being buffeted by events like some helpless fool.

Her thoughts jelled, and she grabbed the phone. This time, it was her turn to call a meeting with her mother.

Minutes later, Zinnia had joined her at her kitchen table. Lil shoved a mug of coffee and the deeds at her mother. As Zinnia looked over the papers, betraying only a flicker of surprise, Lil launched into an explanation of her agreement with Jon, sparing nothing. In the telling, her carefully formulated reasons for marrying him sounded stupid, and she shook her head, wondering why she'd ever thought the whole thing could work.

"I convinced myself I was marrying Jon for everyone else. But, Mari was right. I married him not because of our contract, but because he made me feel more alive than I'd felt in years. And even though I couldn't admit it, even to myself, part of it *was* the money and glamour and all those things I accused Mari of wanting." Lil pushed her hands through her hair, and looked at her mother. "I married him just for myself. It's my selfishness that created this mess."

Zinnia startled her by laughing. "I know."

"What?"

"I know you married him because you loved him."

Hadn't she listened? "Mother, we weren't in love. That was just a story we invented. We didn't even like each other much then. It wasn't until later that—"

"Speak for yourself." Zinnia chuckled. "Honeybunch, maybe you weren't ready at the start to admit you had feelings for that young man, but he fell head over heels from the get-go. Now do you really think I'd have stood by and let you sacrifice yourself for all of us, if I hadn't believed you two were a match made in heaven?"

She stared at Zinnia, and Zinnia stared back. "Oh, don't look like such a gapeseed, Lilac Elizabeth. Give me some credit. After all, my careful daughter would never let herself believe she could fall in love again. She had to have a reason for a headlong rush into marriage. And, my, wasn't it something that it was only a little while later we found a buyer for our cabin? And at a price *more* than the market value? Honeybunch, your dad and me might be a couple of country bumpkins, but we're not total birdbrains."

"Why didn't you say anything?"

"Because it was such fun watching the two of you. I could see that young man was completely gaga over you, and you—why, every time he looked at you, you'd pink up like a ripening tomato." Zinnia patted her hand. "Maybe you were a little slow on the uptake, but I knew it was only a matter of time."

"Well, you were right. And look where it got me." Lil's jaw tightened. Briefly she explained Jon's departure. "But now I have to think of those children's future, and my own. I have a plan, but it will take money and these"—she prodded the deeds—"are the only thing of value I have besides this house, and the lake cabin really belongs to you."

Lil outlined what she had in mind. When she was done, Zinnia's eyes gleamed with both admiration and amusement. "Honeybunch, I say go for it."

Chapter 31

Lil did just that. Fueled by restless energy, her ambitions took root and grew. She had two goals. Independence from Jon's largess, and protecting the children. Coldly, her head considered their futures, while her heart remained torn by hope. If Jon prevailed in court, she'd be the children's adoptive mother. If he continued to spurn her and carried out his plans for divorce, she'd by God demand joint custody, and have the means to support them, with or without his money. But that motive paled beside her desire to see them safe from Belinda. And both faded in her yearning to have Jon return.

The week after her conversation with Zinnia, she lost her fluffy hair and ribbons under the scissors at Up-in-the-Hair, and emerged with a sophisticated look. She decked herself in a business suit, matching heels, and an I-Am-Woman scarlet blouse. Feeling invincible, she stormed Stan's bank armed with a business plan, the lake deed as collateral. At Alcea's threats to escalate her alimony demands, her startled brother-in-law lent her the money in record time. Lil prepared to reopen Merry-Go-Read.

Snow swirled during the last week of January, and the store's transformation began under the hands of her family and Roy. Water stains disappeared under whitewash, scuff marks under a sander. Lil worked furiously by day, keeping her pain at bay. At night, she swallowed exhaustion and hurt, and sent Jon cheerful e-mails, detailing the children's lives and her own, hoping they'd help him reconsider his decision. She also implored him to consider the threat Belinda posed.

In return, she received a note from Peter that Jon had filed his sole custody petition, along with the papers for her adoption of the children. The judge had appointed an evaluator, a Ms. Langlie, to make a confidential report to the court. She should prepare for the social worker's visit. She breathed a sigh of relief. The note confirmed Jon still planned to carry out their agreement. Peter also told her to rest easy where Belinda was concerned. Jon was "handling things." She hoped to God that meant he'd instructed his attorneys to prepare to defend him against whatever "evidence" Belinda had.

Bone-chilling cold swept through the first weeks of February. Roy and Pop replaced the cracked ceiling lamps with globe lights hooded in primary colors, and kid-sized white shelving supplanted the tall, forbidding bookcases. Lil opened accounts and placed orders. Uncharacteristically mute on the subject of Jon, but appearing determined to heal their rift, Mari showed up on weekends and covered the walls with eye-popping illustrations of book characters.

Since it appeared he was only forwarding her e-mails to Peter, her missives to Jon dwindled to lists of expenses. In return, she received checks, including travel funds for the children. As instructed by the court, Melanie and Michael flew to visit Jon every three weeks, parroting Belinda's visitation rights. Once a week, he called the children. Once a week, he sent them a box of trinkets. The handwriting and botched tape jobs strummed a bittersweet chord. He packed them himself. He didn't want to just win his case, he wanted to be a good father. She let those packages lull her anxiety concerning Belinda. He would consider all angles. He wouldn't risk the children. They received two visits from Ms. Langlie. Lil thought the visits went well.

The store's new sign arrived on Valentine's Day, a gray day accented by the vivid hearts and flowers displayed in the shop windows. The men hoisted the sign above the entrance to great fanfare from the town. Later, she caught Mother and Pop making out in the store's back room. Dragging home that night, she hustled the children to bed, then pulled out the video of last fall's CMA awards. She made it only halfway through Jon's acceptance speech before bursting into tears. Pride in tatters, she addressed an e-mail to Jon, and threw her entire heart in it, punching SEND before she could change her mind.

The next week, Zinnia sewed covers for beanbag chairs, and brought in rugs from the Swap 'n Shop. Alcea baked and froze trays of cookies, banana bread, and a half dozen of her chocolate raspberry cakes. Patsy Lee, now working for Lil part-time, unpacked inventory while Lil arranged shelves. For six days, she hurried home to check her e-mail. Anticipation shifted to growing anger when Jon remained silent. She unleashed another barrage of notes imploring him to update her on the custody case. He owed her at least reassurance.

In late February, as the skies cleared to welcome the blue-and-white bluster of March, Mari sent Lil the flyers and newspaper ads she'd created, capitalizing on the Van Castle name according to Lil's instructions. Walter took pictures of the store's facelift and sold some to newspapers. Counting on the publicity, she set up an e-mail order account.

And she finally received an impersonal missive from Jon. He simply assured her she was not to worry, Belinda was "all about money," and he had plenty he'd give her to leave the children alone. Feeling like a child who'd just received a careless pat on the head, she sat for long minutes in front of the screen, her astonished outrage growing. Money was his only defense? Hadn't he listened?

Over the next few days of early March, as the grass greened, the forsythia bloomed, and crocuses poked up their heads, hope finally died, poisoned by Jon's obstinacy and what pride she had left. She shoved the videotape in a box under the children's winter boots—and went to visit Alcea's lawyer.

"Murphy's Law" wasn't exactly an inspiring moniker, but the tongue in cheek humor went with a stern exterior and razor-sharp mind. Under the veil of lawyer-client confidentiality, Lil laid out everything, hoping he could reassure her.

Murphy led her through a morass of custody laws, then looked at her from under black brows. "Mr. Van Castle will have difficulty proving abuse without corroboration. He needs witnesses—teachers or friends or relatives that noticed something wrong. It sounds like the children were isolated, and even though you mention a grandmother, she wasn't there when these incidents took place. Abuse is a strong term. A slap or two won't do it. It doesn't sound like he's working with much."

"He doesn't think he *has* to work with much. He thinks she'll take his money and drop her objections."

"I know Langlie. She's a hard nut, but thorough—and the court will listen to her. If the children say they were mistreated, it will go in her report. The fact you're presenting a strong marriage, plus the fact the kids have lived with you since then may sway the court in Mr. Van Castle's favor." He leaned back and steepled his hands. "I emphasize 'may.' If, as you say, his ex-wife brings evidence that causes the court to question his fitness, and the social worker's report doesn't contain any proof of abuse beyond hearsay and the children's word, then the court may award them to the mother. It's a toss-up."

Lil's heart sank. "And if the court finds out the marriage is in name only?"

"Then he's hosed. What he and you are planning approaches perjury."

Lil chewed on her lip. Right now she couldn't care less about ethics. Belinda already suspected the marriage was fake. If she could prove it. . . . She had to do *something*. "What if I filed a—what did you call it? A third-party petition?—to get custody myself."

"You mean a backup plan in case the court moves against Mr. Van Castle?" He smiled thinly. "Do that, and the court will know beyond a doubt the marriage is a sham. So will the ex. The court would have to notify both natural parents you've filed, and she'd milk the deception. Unless the abuse charge sticks, it'd tip things in the ex's favor, not your husband's. If your aim is to help Mr. Van Castle, better to take your chances. You can't propose yourself as an alternative in case he doesn't win. It doesn't work that way."

"If there was any logic in all this, I should win. I'm the best parent. I'm the one they're happiest with." Lil knotted her hands in her lap. "I can't take the chance they'll end up with their mother."

"So *you* want them." He tapped a pencil on his desk. "I wouldn't recommend you go into this unless you play to win. Any half-hearted effort would likely backfire right into the mother's hands. Your chances of winning are slim, unless . . ."

"Unless what?"

"You'd have to do what your husband hasn't—sic a P.I. on the mother, find witnesses. You could do that and turn the information over to your husband, for that matter, but I don't know if luck will be with you. You said the hearing will be scheduled within the next thirty to sixty days. Time's running out and those kind of investigations take time."

"But I could try." If she could find the funds to pay for it. What she had left from her loan would only cover Murphy's fees. Still, she was the wife of a superstar. Surely her credit was good?

"And maybe you'd hit pay dirt right away," he said. "But there's more."

"What?"

"You'd have to discredit them both. If you want the court to look at you instead of the father as an alternative to the mother, then you not only have to file, you have to get both Mom and Dad out of the picture. As far as the court is concerned, third-party custody is a last, and not desirable, resort. If the ex doesn't do it first, you'd have to show evidence of some substantive reason the father is unfit. Something like that photo you mentioned of him sleeping with a minor. With the allegations of abuse against the mother, coupled with serious accusations against the father, you'd have a chance." Murphy leveled his eyes at her. "Are you willing to do that?"

Her mind whirled through possibilities. Bet on Jon, and take a chance Belinda would win? Or bet on her instincts, fight with all she had, and destroy Jon's case, his career—his life. She hesitated, asked a few more questions, then hurried home.

The next few nights were sleepless, but after several days of agonizing, her mind cleared of everything except one crystal thought. She'd promised Melanie.

On the day before the store opened, she laid out her strategy with Murphy. When Grand Opening Day dawned, he prepared her petition, and recommended a private investigator.

Now, two weeks later, the petition remained unfiled. She didn't want the court informing either Jon or Belinda. Surprise was her ally.

Chapter 32

Two weeks later, Lil pushed aside the crisp curtains framing Merry-Go-Read's bow window. Behind her, Mrs. Beadlesworth, the only customer left after the noon rush, browsed the store. Bright sunshine painted the scene outside, although the temperature hovered between cool and warm. In front of St. Andrew's, tulips jostled for room between the yellow hats of daffodils, and lilac shrubs foamed with clouds of buds. She hoped it would be as pleasant four days from now on Melanie's birthday. The day she'd see Jon for the first time in three months.

Lil's heart sped up. Jon was returning for the party Sunday. And Monday would bring the custody hearing and the decision that would affect the rest of their lives.

Swallowing the bile that rose in her throat, Lil moved toward the rear of the store. "Do you need any help, Mrs. Beadlesworth?"

"No thanks, dear."

Lil slipped behind the counter, jostling a vase of yellow roses. Exasperated, she caught them up before they spilled. She'd take them home, but that would hurt Seamus's feelings. Twice since the opening, he'd replaced the bouquet.

Since she'd started work on the store, Seamus stopped by daily, often bringing lunch from the Rooster's kitchen. Since Jon had left, he'd never once implied I-told-you-so, and his companionship was as easy as always. Occasionally, though, she felt the draft of a more powerful emotion. She hoped she was misreading signals. Because she didn't feel that way about Seamus. Because, stupid as it was, she still loved Jon. She set the roses back with a thump. Not that he'd given her roses or anything else.

She sighed, and picked up a few scattered petals. This weekend, she'd tell Jon what she planned. She hadn't wanted to give him time to stop her, but she didn't want him blindsided. Her stomach curdled. She should no longer care what he thought, but she did.

Mrs. B pushed up to the counter, dropped an armload of books, then wandered off to peruse a shelf of DVDs. Like Mrs. B, most of the customers were local, although busloads of tourists on their way to Kesibwi stopped by on the weekends. The store was a minor tourist attraction. The store was a success.

Mrs. B returned, adding a movie to her pile. "You've done a wonderful job, Lil. Joey and I are looking forward to some of those book signings you've lined up." Another bonus. With a famous name, she was attracting some stellar children's authors. The woman plucked a calendar Mari had designed off the counter. "Although Joey misses his piano lessons. How clever. May I have one?"

"Certainly. There's a map showing our delivery area, and there's also a coupon on the back for your next visit." Lil rang up the purchases and took the bills Mrs. B held out, then paused. "You know, Mrs. Beadlesworth, I think Joey might find other talents he excels at rather than piano."

Mrs. B looked puzzled. "Do you think so, dear?"

Lil nodded. "I do. He's a good—"

The entrance bells tinkled. Lil glanced up and her throat closed. Belinda stepped over the threshold. A white cloak swirled down to her ankles. A vaguely familiar pale-faced young man stepped in behind her.

"A good—?" Mrs. Beadlesworth prompted.

"Uh, soccer player." She counted bills into the woman's palm. "Have a nice day. And don't forget to sign our guest book." She kept her eyes on Belinda. Jon's ex-wife wandered between the shelves, fingering the merchandise. Her companion shifted from foot to foot just inside the door.

Mrs. B exited, and Lil placed both her hands flat on the counter. "Belinda."

She hadn't seen Belinda since that day at the resort. With admittedly sophomoric satisfaction, she noted Jon's ex-wife had gained weight. Her cloak concealed her torso, but overindulgence showed in the puffiness around her face. Lil's satisfaction was only momentary, though. The white cloak set off Belinda's dark beauty to perfection. If she dressed like that for court on Monday, the judge would think Belinda was a virginal angel.

"Well, hello, Lil." Belinda turned in her direction as though surprised, but Lil wasn't fooled by her air of innocence. "I came into town to see the doctor and thought I'd stop in. You remember Neil?"

The man from the rehab center. Lil nodded at Neil and he gave her a nervous half-smile.

"This your store? It's very quaint." Belinda ran a coral-tipped finger along a shelf. "Reminds me of you. So small town. But I'm sure the locals love it. I mean, what do they have to compare it to?"

"What do you want?"

"Want?" Belinda looked at her, rounding her eyes. "Why, nothing."

High heels tapping, Belinda continued to browse. "I suppose you've heard the latest, haven't you?" she asked, pausing at a display of children's sing-along music. She pushed a button on the front of the stand, and a ditty from *Wee Sing in Sillyville* filled the room. "Judge Dougherty has issued a gag order. Says he'll have the custody case decided in his courtroom, not in the media."

She wasn't about to discuss the hearing with Belinda. She kept her voice disinterested. "Did you receive your invitation to Melanie's birthday party?"

She hadn't wanted to invite either Jon or Belinda, but of course Melanie wanted her father there, and she'd had no choice under Judge Dougherty's visitation dictums except to ask Belinda, too. She'd stifled her misgivings with the almost certain knowledge neither would come, although that had been before she'd known the hearing would take place only one day later.

Belinda touched the button again. The music stopped. "Melanie's party?" She snorted. "I think I have better things to do with my time than spend it with your family."

Good.

Belinda gave her a look dripping with sympathy. "Don't let the judge's gag order give you false hopes."

"What are you talking about?"

Belinda shrugged. "I'll still win."

She sounded so confident. Lil kept her face calm, although her pulse beat faster. "That's not your decision."

"Despite that sniveling social worker poking her nose into every aspect of my business, I think the judge will be more interested in what I'll have to tell him." She gave Lil a sly glance. "To show him."

Lil could only hope Ms. Langlie had done her job thoroughly. Their last visit with her had been only a few days ago. Lil had tried to ferret out information that would remain confidential until the hearing. From what she could tell, Ms. Langlie took the children seriously, but it had become a matter of the children's word against Belinda's.

Still, abuse was a serious matter, and Lil would bet the scales would tip in Jon's favor. But it wasn't a bet she wanted to take. Not with those photos, real and faked, in Belinda's hands. So far, the private investigator had turned up some leads, but nothing else. As Ms. Langlie was leaving, Lil had taken a deep breath and had pressed a sealed envelope into her hand addressed to Judge Dougherty, marked confidential. Lil had asked her to include it in her report. After that, there was no turning back.

"I had something to show myself," Lil murmured without thinking.

Belinda approached the counter, eyes glinting. "What exactly did you tell Langlie?"

"The only thing Ms. Langlie is concerned about is the children's welfare and I told her—" She stopped. She didn't owe Belinda anything. "I don't want to discuss this."

"Okay, let's discuss something else. Let's discuss Jon."

"I'd like you to leave. I don't think—"

"No, you *don't* think. If you'd thought about it, you would have realized a long time ago you couldn't hang on to him."

"What's between Jon and me is none of your business."

"But I think it *is* my business. After all, I'd bet mine was the last bed he slept in, wasn't it?" Belinda's smile broke across her face like sun splashing on water. "And—guess what? I'm pregnant."

Lil felt like she'd been punched.

"Yep." Belinda pulled her cloak aside and patted her rounded stomach. Lil stared in horror, then glanced at Neil. He shifted, and his eyes wouldn't meet hers. "I wanted to make sure everything was okay before I told anyone. Then decided *you'd* be the first to know. I'm looking forward to telling Jon." She smiled. "And the judge."

Lil unstuck her tongue from the roof of her mouth. "That baby could belong to anyone." She flicked another look at Neil. He looked decidedly unhappy.

Belinda's smile didn't waver. "I didn't think you'd

be overcome with joy, but let's not indulge in too much wishful thinking, all right? Delusions aren't healthy. Well, I just wanted to let you in on my little surprise. So sorry, I can't stay to chat." She turned and signaled Neil who snapped to attention. As Belinda reached the door, she looked back over her shoulder at Lil. "We simply *must* do lunch sometime soon." She wiggled her fingers. "See you in court."

They exited in a whirl of white wool, and Lil's hands worried the hem of her jacket as she tried to make sense of the whole thing, tried to find some loophole, tried to catch her breath and decide what effect this would have on Jon's petition. A powerful one, she'd think. Her hands stilled as she realized she'd made the right decision.

Through the window, she saw Belinda and Neil step off the curb. As Belinda slithered behind the wheel of a bright red Camaro, Seamus approached, nodded at Neil, then bent down to the driver's window. Lil frowned. She didn't know they were acquainted. They exchanged some words, then the engine roared to life. The car screeched off. Thoughtful, she took refuge behind the counter and made herself sort invoices.

Seamus ambled inside. She smiled a tight greeting. Pushing his hat back, he leaned his elbows on the counter, his hands brushing hers. Avoiding his touch, she picked up the bills and tapped them into a neat pile.

He frowned briefly. "Thought I'd stop by and see if you needed anything."

She pulled a file out and slipped the invoices inside. "Disinfectant."

His eyebrows went up. "Got a problem?"

"I just want to scrub everything *she* touched." Lil put the file back, then looked at him. "I didn't know you knew Belinda Van Castle."

Seamus hesitated. "Met her in rehab a few years back."

"Ah." Lil waited to see if he'd offer more, but he didn't. It wasn't unusual for people around here to know each other, and since Serenity Gardens was the only rehabilitation center within twenty miles, his explanation made sense. It would also explain why he'd know Neil. Still, there was something disquieting about his silence.

Abruptly, he straightened. "Well, if you don't need anything, guess I'll be on my way. Stop by the Rooster later. I'll feed you and the kids a burger."

"Maybe. It will depend on how much homework Melanie has."

A muscle twitched in his jaw, and she lowered her eyes so he couldn't see her own irritation. Seamus's invitations were increasingly offered with a persistence she didn't like. After another minute's uncomfortable conversation, he took his leave. She followed him to the door and watched him through the window, still frowning.

Why hadn't Seamus ever said he knew Jon's ex-wife?

That night, Lil peeked down the hallway to make sure the lights were doused and no noises came from the children's rooms before she picked up the phone. It was after ten, but Jon would still be awake.

As the phone rang, she leaned against the kitchen stool. Tiredness seeped through her bones. The day had sapped her emotions. Listening to eighteen viewings of the new "China Blue Eyes" video Jon had sent the children hadn't helped either. When she'd finally insisted they shut it off, Michael had thrown his usual bedtime tantrum. Excited about her birthday, even the normally cooperative Melanie had dragged her feet. It had taken an hour to get them to sleep. She longed for her own bed, but first she had to tell Jon. Maybe he'd finally realize Belinda wasn't all about money.

Her stomach knotted as the phone was answered. In the background, she could hear music, voices. "Jon?"

There was a hesitation, then his voice rolled over her. "Hey, babe."

Memories nearly overwhelmed her. Would have, if he hadn't been playing the babe game again. Her shoulders slumped.

"Yeah, yeah, I'll be right back." He talked to someone else, then returned to her. "Sorry. Trying to get this video wrapped up before I head out in your direction. I'll be there Friday night. Too late to see anyone, but I'll call Roy to bring the kids over to the Sleep Inn on Saturday. How's it goin'? Everything all right with the kids?"

No mention of the Valentine's Day e-mail. She could be nothing more than the nanny. "The children are fine. They got your video. They like it." She forced her voice into routine politeness. Then, as indifferently as she'd report the weather, she let the bomb drop. "I'm sorry to bother you, but I thought you should know. Belinda is pregnant. She says the baby is yours."

There was a long silence. "Shit." His voice was barely audible. "Lil, I never meant to—" She heard a world of hurt in his voice and held her breath. Would he give them the opportunity to recover what they'd lost? But he cleared his throat and the flippancy returned. "Just one thing after another, isn't it? Hey, guess I'll be seeing you soon—and thanks. I owe you for the heads up, babe."

She stiffened. Any inclination she'd had to spill what she'd done dissolved in the acid that flooded her mouth. Whatever game he was determined to play with their lives, he could play on his own.

She didn't answer; she just let the receiver fall back in its cradle. After a few moments, she picked up the phone again. Rousing Murphy from sleep, she made sure he understood her instructions.

Chapter 33

Four days later, heart hammering, Jon rang Lil's doorbell. It was about an hour before Melanie's party, and the kids scampered around the front yard in a state of high excitement. He scanned the empty street. He'd tried to keep his travel plans secret and so far he'd succeeded. No news hounds sniffed around, not even that fellow Lil called Wart-nose. Likely that jerk and all his fellow jerks were swarming Camden County Courthouse preparing for tomorrow's hearing.

Early yesterday morning, after a Friday night redeye from L.A., he and Zeke had arrived at Cordelia's Sleep Inn too tired to wallow in memories, but it hadn't been long before they'd caught up to him. Roy had dropped the kids with him Saturday. Since then, everywhere they went, from Sin-Sational Ice Cream, where he could see a carousel horse outside Lil's bookstore, to Memorial Park, where they'd parked the bus on that long-ago day when he'd first met her, he was haunted by her. He hadn't seen her yet.

Nor did he want to.

After her phone call, he'd wrapped up the video, fell exhausted into bed, then stared at the ceiling all night. Her news about the pregnancy had rocked him, but a hurried call to his attorneys had reassured him. They'd said that short of a paternity test, the court probably wouldn't allow Belinda's pregnancy to figure in the decision of Michael and Melanie's custody.

They could worry about the baby later. They all agreed Belinda could be bought. She was dragging this affair out just to make the stakes higher. Lil would see. He'd pass Belinda a hefty check—a very hefty check—on Monday morning and that would be that.

No, he wasn't worried about the hearing. Sleep had eluded him because of all the memories that had swamped him at the sound of Lil's voice.

Since he'd left Cordelia, he'd sedated himself with work, hoping frantic activity would render him unconscious at night. Sometimes it worked; mostly it didn't. Nothing forced Lil from his head. The e-mail she'd sent in February hadn't helped. After he'd read her passionate pleas, he'd wavered, his thoughts pulled first one way, then the other, playing a tug of war with his sanity. For a time, he'd toyed with the idea maybe Lil was right, maybe nothing had happened on that night he'd spent with Belinda—but the news Lil had dropped on him scuttled that hope.

He punched the doorbell again, but nobody answered. Maybe Lil had run out on some last-minute errand.

Mel tugged his arm. "Daddy, everybody'll be here soon and I want to put on the outfit Lil made me before they get here!"

"Okay, baby." He dug in his pocket and pulled out his old key. He opened the door and music swelled from the back of the house. Lil was playing the piano. Loud.

The kids scooted around him and scattered to their rooms. He reset the alarm and took a deep breath, growing dizzy on the familiar scents. Her perfume flirted with a bowl of lilacs on the coffee table and mingled with the smell of dust wax. He crossed the room and paused in the doorway to the rec room.

Her straight back faced him. A light breeze from the door to the porch played with her curls. Her hair was shorter, still tousled on top, but cropped close at the sides and back, shaping her head and emphasizing the long arch of her neck. Sophisticated. Used to be she would have dressed in a denim jumper, but today's outfit was a stylish, smart suit.

A pang went through him. She'd changed.

Instead of the romantic composers she preferred, she played a Russian piece, a composition of large chords in a minor key, a piece of heavy drama and discordant sound. She played *adagio*. Using only her left hand, weighty chords sounded with restraint, slow, leashing the power of the music. *Piano*. Soft, then building, beckoning.

He wished he had the right to tiptoe up behind her, slide his arms around her waist, and lay a soft kiss on that smooth sweep of bare neck. Continuing his charade would take all his theatrical skill. He knew she didn't believe him, but it was a shield he could keep between them.

Her right hand joined the left. The volume and speed increased; the melody sounded above the chords, plaintive and haunting, at once tentative, then gathering strength.

Sweat built on his brow. She was more alluring than ever. *Forte*. Louder. *Fortissimo*. No holding back. It wasn't just the haircut, or the clothes, that made her a stranger. Somehow, she felt different. Her playing carried confidence and determination. Sweet Jesus, he wouldn't have thought it possible, but he loved her even more.

Her lovely hands struck the keys without hesitation until the piano rang with barely controlled violence, gasping with all it had to give. In each note he heard anguish and he was shamed at his role in her emotions. The final chord blistered. Her hands fell to her lap. Outside, a sparrow chattered.

"I've never heard you play that well."

She twisted around. Her face whitened, then flushed, eyes delft-blue saucers. "Jon."

He wanted to sweep her up, but instead he leaned against the jamb, suddenly needing something solid to prop him up. "Sorry. Didn't mean to spook you."

"Where are the children?"

"Getting ready for the party."

She looked at her watch, stood up, and made a business of stuffing sheet music into the piano bench while her cat watched her. "I lost track of time. I still have a lot to do." Avoiding his eyes, she slammed the bench shut.

When she would have pushed past him, he touched her arm and she froze. "Uh, Lil?"

Her eyes softened. Too late, he realized he'd sounded pathetic. He let his hand drop, his mind filling with past images of Lil meeting his eyes with love in her own, opening her arms. He battled to sound offhand. "Thanks. For calling me about Belinda, I mean."

When his tone changed, her mouth tightened again. She shrugged. "I thought you should know before tomorrow." The custody hearing was at ten-thirty. An uncomfortable silence gathered like a cloud between them and then she sagged against the opposite jamb. "In fact, there's a few other things you should know before tomorrow." She glanced toward the children's rooms, then finally met his eyes. "I did a lot of thinking after you left and consulted my own lawyer. I decided to—"

He couldn't stand it. He knew she wanted to tell him something about the hearing, but she stood so near, he couldn't think. All he'd need to do was reach out a few inches and he could brush the satin side of her cheek, run his hand into her hair, and pull the mouth he remembered all too well against his. The plea for understanding lurking in her eyes told him she wouldn't resist. Her feelings hadn't changed. He'd put her through all this, and still, her feelings hadn't changed.

He dug into his back pocket and pulled out a thick envelope. He'd wanted to do this gently, but if he waited, he'd succumb to the overpowering urge he had to taste her again. Steeling himself against her reaction, he handed her the envelope and reminded himself of all the reasons he'd let Lil go. Locking a grin on his face, he said, "Before this party gets started, there's a little business we need to conclude."

"Something about the depositions? The custody hearing?"

"Uh, no."

Lil gave him a perplexed look, then peeled back the flap and withdrew the contents. Jon's gut went tight as she unfolded the papers.

She looked up at him, openmouthed. "You've had divorce papers prepared?"

He held on to the grin and crossed his arms, afraid he'd reach for her. "I know we said we'd wait, but, I thought, what's the point? Figured once the hearing's over, there won't be any further need for charades. We could just move on, you know?" He didn't tell her he'd come to that decision after he'd received her Valentine's Day e-mail. Like nothing else would have, that letter convinced him neither one of them could go through another two years of this.

Her gaze continued to search his. "And the children?"

"By then I'll have custody, but you'll be the adoptive mother." He gave a nod to the papers. "You'll see some lingo in there about my visitation rights. They're generous, but the kids would stay with you." He looked around. "This is their home." He realized his voice had grown bleak and pressed his lips together.

Her gaze continued to search his. He held himself still, prepared to fend off her pleas and protests. To his surprise, she didn't clutch his arm, nor did she blink back tears. Instead, her jaw hardened and her eyes went from a springtime sky to a summer storm.

"Fine." She spit out the word. "If you are determined to believe the absolute worst about yourself, if you refuse to admit, even for one stinking moment you might be wrong about Belinda, so be it. I won't fight you. But I will fight for what's best for those children." The phone rang. Her mouth tightened. "Excuse me."

Chapter 34

An hour later, Lil slapped some fresh napkins on the dining room table and ardently wished the evening would end. Low conversation droned in the living room, punctuated by Zinnia's "honeybunches" and the children's laughter. Except for Roy, stationed in the driveway to keep an eye out for the press that had eventually followed Jon here, everyone else was watching Melanie open her gifts.

Every so often, she heard Seamus's or Jon's voice underneath the others. The looks they'd directed at each other were hostile, but they'd maintained a chilly truce. Of course, Jon had earned a cold shoulder from most of her family. Except for Zinnia, they didn't know details, but they knew the gossip and they knew he'd hurt Lil. Her father acted like he couldn't see him, Alcea was in ice queen mode, and even Patsy Lee's lips tightened when he was around. The children seemed restlessly aware of the currents beneath the polite talk, but her mother—her mother!—acted like nothing had happened at all.

Lil righted a candle on the pink-frosted cake. Once Mari arrived, they'd light the damn thing, sing happy birthday, then everyone could leave. She looked at her watch. Shouldn't be long. Mari had agreed to fill in for the layout artist at the *Sun* this weekend, and had said she'd come as soon as the paper was put to bed.

Alcea had appeared late, looking drawn and muttering curses under her breath at Stan's refusal to allow Kathleen to come, too—supposedly since this was one of his weekends with their daughter, but in reality because he'd do anything he thought might twist Alcea's nose out of joint.

Lil thunked the paper plates next to the napkins. Separation and divorce must destroy the brain cells in whatever lobe held any measure of rationality.

Jon was a case in point. He still thought Belinda would just roll over when he flashed her some green. Well, she wouldn't. And tomorrow was soon enough for him to find out exactly what Lil had done to stop her. The shock would serve him right!

She jerked up the almost-empty vegetable-and-dip platter and carried it to the kitchen. She plunked it on the counter and dip splattered her blouse. She stared down in dismay. Like a silly adolescent on a first date, she'd spent hours preparing herself for the evening.

She shrugged out of her new suit jacket, muttering. She scrubbed the offending stain, then tossed the garment on a stool. Pausing, she stared out of the open kitchen window. A shower had left the air redolent with an earthy smell. Threatening clouds were leading to an early dusk.

She looked good, but Jon didn't. The gold shirt that matched the flecks in his eyes hung from his shoulders and tapered into leather pants that looked a size too big. His face was chiseled in sharp relief. Fine lines she didn't remember cornered his mouth. Dark smudges arced under his eyes. He acted unconcerned about what would happen tomorrow, but his looks said otherwise. She felt . . . dammit. She wished she could just turn off her feelings.

As a hand reached around her from behind, she jumped. It was Zeke. Smiling, he plucked a celery stick from the vegetable plate, then lounged against the counter. "I'm glad to see you, Lil. You look good. Different."

"I *am* different," she snapped, in no mood for Zeke's oblique remarks.

He looked unperturbed. "How've you been?"

She opened the fridge, pushed Petunia's nose aside, and sent him an incredulous look. How did he think she'd been? She couldn't believe Jon hadn't told him everything. "I'm just fine." She knew she sounded petulant, but she didn't care. She dug into the vegetable bin. "Business is good. The children are thriving. And, as for the state of my heart, that's none of your business."

His eyebrows arced up. "Okay. Stupid question." He popped the last of the celery in his mouth and carefully blotted his beard with the edge of a tea towel. "If it makes you feel any better, Jon's been through hell."

"It doesn't," she lied. She hoped he'd suffered all kinds of agony, but she didn't know why he would. It seemed leaving her, *divorcing* her, wasn't any big deal. She resumed her hunt for the bag of carrots.

"He has plans to move here, did you know that?"

Hands stuck between a bag of broccoli and a head of lettuce, she froze. "Why in the world would he do that?"

"Looks good on the parenting plan he gave to the court."

She banged the bin shut. "I should have known." All fake. All of it. Their marriage, his parenting plan.

"And he wants to be near them. After your divorce."

She stared at Zeke. Would Jon really put the children ahead of his career? "Oh, for Pete's sake. He wouldn't do that. What would he do here?"

"Set up a recording studio. He's serious. He's not just talking—ah, how would you locals put it— hogswallow?"

"You must be mistaken. Start a recording studio? Here?" She snorted and thought of Joey Beadlesworth. "Cordelia's not exactly a hotbed of musical talent."

"He's an ace composer and he knows the ropes. Sessions can be done anyplace and zipped through a modem. People would flock anywhere to record with the famous Jon Van Castle. Or to record a song by him."

"He wouldn't. He cares too much about the band."

"His heart isn't in it anymore. His heart's with—" He pointed at a bag of carrots on the counter. "That what you're pursuing?"

She snatched up the bag. "His heart's with what?"

"Not what. Who. I've never seen him like this. The man loves you, Lil."

"I know that! I love him, too. Or at least, I did. Now I don't know how I feel." Her fingers tightened on the bag. "He's destroyed—is destroying—us, Zeke."

"I'd say Belinda's doing that. She always knew how to play him like a fiddle." Zeke ran a tongue along his teeth. "Have a toothpick?" She pointed to a box. "He doesn't remember sleeping with her. Says it's all a blank after he got to Dodo's house." The toothpick slipped from one side of his mouth to the other. "She's lying. Wouldn't be the first time Miss Belinda has shaved the truth."

Lil dropped the bag of carrots back on the counter and leaned a hip back, considering Zeke. "That's what I told him. Have you told Jon what you think?"

"Of course." The eyebrows rose again. "But you know him. The poor man suffers from the delusion he'll destroy any woman he touches. And now he's ready to portray himself as evil personified to protect you." Zeke sighed. "Not to mention he thinks Belinda can be bought off. She'll pull some stunt tomorrow."

"I think I've taken care of that."

Zeke smiled. "Thought you would."

"Jon won't like it."

"Who cares? Just as I told him, the man's an idiot."

Lil eyed Zeke, then relaxed against the counter as the last of her anger drained away. Her lips curved. "Yes, isn't he?"

They shared a companionable silence, then Lil straightened. "So, I not only have to take care of the hearing, I have to prove to him he's not the devil. Any ideas?"

Zeke pulled out the toothpick. "One, but you might have some objections. The gentleman—and I use the term loosely—is a friend of yours, after all."

"What are you talking about?"

"When Jon went to that bar—what's the name? Something about chickens?"

"The Rooster," she said dryly.

"Right. When he went to the Rooster, your friend, that cowboy out there, made a point of warning him off."

"Seamus warned him off?" She stiffened.

"Warned him off." Zeke nodded, the toothpick doing a lazy spin in his fingers. He watched it. "It occurs to me the timing that night was quite favorable to Miss Belinda. Very coincidental, isn't it, that she'd show up where Jon was."

"That's what I think, but how could she have known?"

"If I'm not mistaken, and I don't think I am, it seems your friend is rather smitten with you. Maybe he can shed some light on events." Zeke looked up. His expression remained languid, but his eyes were sharp and intelligent.

"Zeke, what *exactly* are you saying?"

"Am I interrupting?" Seamus materialized in the doorway and she started, knocking a few carrots to the floor.

Zeke pitched his toothpick at the wastebasket and

straightened. "We're through. Lil and I were just catching up on old times." He gave her a slow wink and ambled out.

Lil bent for the wayward carrots and busied herself washing them at the sink. Behind her, she felt Seamus approach.

"Tough evening for you, isn't it?" he murmured. One hand settled on her waist and she felt his breath on her neck.

She scrunched her shoulders and slipped from his touch. Twisting, she found him too close. She flattened her hips against the counter.

He frowned. "What is it, Lil?"

"What did you tell Jon?"

Irritation flickered in his eyes. "Tell him? I haven't said two words to the man."

"Not tonight. That other night, when he went to the Rooster. What did you say?"

"Not much. The man was three sheets to the wind. A reasonable discussion was out of his reach."

"You must have said something."

"What's this all about, Lil?"

She banged a fist on the counter and the platter jumped. "That's what I'm trying to find out. What did you say to him? What did you do?"

His eyes slipped off hers. "Might have said a few things."

"What, for God's sake?"

"Might have said the two of you don't fit. Maybe said you're better off without him."

"You told him I was better off without—"

She wanted to screech. That night, when she'd inadvertently compared Jon to Robbie, the self-worth Jon had built in the past months with her had fissured; Seamus's words would have fractured it further. Then, when Jon had awakened next to Belinda that morning, his fragile self-worth had been utterly destroyed. "And did you—did you let Belinda know Jon was at the Rooster?"

Seamus was silent. A muscle convulsed in his jaw, then was still.

She looked at the man who'd held her when she cried, bolstered her when she despaired, and, who, out of his love for her, had brought disaster and heartbreak down on her head. "Oh, Seamus."

He gripped her hands. "The truth, Lil. I told him nothing but the truth. You belong here. You belong to Cordelia. To your family. To me."

"I never thought of you that way." She pulled away. She thought of Jon, aggravating, selfish, maddening— and so very dear. "I need to tell him."

But Seamus grabbed her by the shoulders. "Hell you do. Wake up. First you carry the torch for Robert long after he's gone, now it's this jerk who's dragged you through hell and back." His eyes gleamed with an intensity she'd never seen in them before. "He's no good. I may have made a call, but he's the one who cheated on you, and now some other woman carries his brat."

She pushed off his hands. "That's only what she says."

"You'd think she'd know."

"But it doesn't mean she'd tell the truth."

"Then whose baby is it?" He halted abruptly, face suddenly going slack, then he tensed again, eyes hard on hers. "*I'm* the one who loves you. I'm the one you've always come to. Don't do this to me, Lil."

Sadness seeped through her. "I love you. But not in the way you want me to."

Face darkening, he stared at her, but she couldn't summon up any comfort to give him. She squared her shoulders. Right now she needed Jon. By God, she'd drag him off, tie him down if that's what it took, and *make* him listen to her. Before she reached the doorway, Mari rushed in. She stood there, sides heaving, eyes wide with shock.

"Mari! What is it?"

Mari threw a crumpled newspaper on the table. "I can't believe she did this!"

Lil smoothed the paper flat. It was a copy of tomorrow morning's *Cordelia Daily Sun,* still pliant and damp from the presses. Three photos splashed above the center fold. One pictured Belinda, plump with pregnancy, another was a copy of the contract Lil and Jon had signed the day before their wedding—and a third displayed Belinda's bed. Her hand resting possessively on Jon's thigh, Belinda smiled prettily at the camera. Jon lolled on thick pillows, eyes shut, a half-smile on his lips. Despite the strategically placed little black boxes, both were obviously naked.

A fist reached deep inside her and twisted. She'd imagined it, expected it even, but there was nothing like seeing it in stark black and white. She pushed down the nausea that rose in her throat and forced herself to study the lurid photo objectively. Her eyes narrowed. The casual eye might be fooled, but this was no candid photo. She knew Belinda had paid Walter to take pictures, but what Walter hadn't seen, and what seemed so obvious, was the posed artfulness. Jon's mouth was slack, only a glimmer showed under his eyelids, and his limbs were limp, albeit cleverly arranged. He looked corpselike. He looked . . . drugged. Her mind churned through the implications.

She moved on to the article. The account was mostly conjecture and rumor. Except for the verbatim language of their contract. The contract she'd left in her kitchen drawer.

She stalked to the counter, yanked open the drawer, and rifled through it. The contract wasn't there.

Controlling her rising anger, she closed the drawer and turned to face Mari. "Where did the *Sun* get a copy of our contract?"

"Don't look at me!"

Pinning her sister with a hard stare, Lil stayed silent.

"All right! I did take your copy. I didn't mean to snoop. Okay, I *did* mean to snoop. I took it when I watched Petunia last summer. That doesn't mean I did anything with it!"

Lil kept quiet and waited.

"Quit looking at me like that! I was crazed over what you'd done. At Christmas, I was still upset and when I came home, I went to talk to Seamus." Her eyes widened, and she turned to Seamus. "You took the contract and said you'd return it."

Lil swiveled to look at Seamus.

His gaze shifted from Mari to her. "That cretin doesn't deserve you and if you're too stubborn to see it, then—"

Lil crumpled the paper in her fist. "Then you planned to save me from myself."

"You're a fool, Lil."

"Better a fool than a self-serving, egotistical jerk."

"Lil!" Mari squawked. "That's not fair. Seamus was upset, too."

She whipped around to her sister. "Has Jon seen this?" She shook the paper at Mari. Mari retreated a step.

"When I came in, he saw me, asked me what was wrong, so I—"

"Where is he?"

Mari lowered her eyes. "He took one look at it and left."

Her mind raced. He'd now believe Belinda had beat him because of events he'd blame himself for setting in motion. He was going to confront her. She knew it. He'd plead with her, offer to pay her off, and when she laughed in his face, he'd . . .

She didn't know what he'd do. She shouldn't have let her anger get in her way. She should have told him about her plan, and the phone call she'd received from her investigator right after Jon had arrived.

Grabbing the phone, she dialed Jon's number.

When nobody answered, she snatched up her purse
and pushed past Seamus.

"Where are you going?"

"After him. It's time to put an end to this entire
mess."

Chapter 35

The hour drive to Monaco had taken him forty-five minutes. Jon stood just inside the circle of light thrown by the porch lamp outside Dodo's house. As though she'd been waiting for him, Belinda had stepped off the stoop when he'd yanked the car to a halt in the rutted drive. Neil hovered behind her. Around the house, the woods loomed, sounds dampened by the most recent burst of rain that had sent the Mercedes fishtailing as he'd raced along the black ribbon of highway.

"Why did you do it, Belinda?" At his tone, Neil hastily backed up a step, but Belinda just thrust out her abdomen as though her—their—unborn child could protect her. It did.

One of her hands fiddled with her stupid cigarette holder. "Ah. So you've seen tomorrow's paper. Good shot, wasn't it? And I have more." The holder flipped out of her fingers and scudded across the cracked walkway to spin at his feet. "Oops."

Reflexively, Jon bent to pick it up. As he did, a memory flashed. The Rooster and Belinda's jacket sliding to the floor. "Oops," she'd said and he'd stooped to pick it up. When he'd straightened, there'd been two beers on the bar and she'd been slipping a vial of perfume back in her purse. Perfume. He'd only assumed it was perfume. Zeke had tried to tell him the whole thing was a lie. Lil had tried. But he'd been too pigheaded to listen. Now the truth struck him right between the eyes. "You drugged me!" The words roared out of him and Neil visibly trembled.

Belinda didn't flinch. She just snatched the holder from him. "Drugged you? That's a pretty fairy tale. Try to prove it."

As fast as it reared up, his anger hit bottom.

She was right.

Squawking that she'd used some kind of date rape drug on him sounded like a desperate lie, even to him, but he'd swear it was true. All the pieces fit. And since it was true, there was no way in hell that baby was his. Blacked out, he couldn't have gotten it up. Whose baby was it? He glanced at Neil. The geek worshipped her, but Jon almost laughed at the thought Belinda had allowed that goofball in her bed. Use him, yes. Screw him, no.

"You said you have more. What?"

Belinda fit a cigarette into the holder. "Remember those pictures of little Glory?"

He snorted. "Those are fake."

"So?" Belinda lit up. "Try to prove it before the judge sees them tomorrow."

Shit, shit, shit. Lil had been right. He hadn't listened, and now he lacked the time to prove anything. And unless he had proof, who'd believe him? Belinda's pregnancy and tomorrow's paper laid waste to his argument of a solid marriage. The sleazy photos would destroy his reputation. Her attorneys would make hash of him. Nothing he could say would look like more than protesting too much—and too late.

Resisting the urge to throttle her, he shoveled both hands through his hair. "Leave me the kids, Belinda. I'll pay you a helluva lot more than the child support."

"You must think I'm pretty stupid. I'd be able to trust you only as long as it took for the ink to dry on the custody papers. Look what you did this last time."

"I mean it, Belinda. I'll pay you anything if you'll

leave the kids alone." What did she want? More to the point, how much did she want?

She studied him a moment. "You know, I really *hate* you, Jon."

He blinked. She laughed. "Isn't that a hoot? I never even liked you. You were always so *needy,* so sad-eyed and *pathetic.* Me, everyone ignored. But, you? Poor little abused boy, but, my, my, isn't he talented? Everyone stood in line to help you. Even my mother." Eyes cold, she moved forward and thrust her face in his. "Yeah, I hated you, but I could see you'd go places, and I didn't plan to get left behind. Carrying me was the least you could do, since you'd taken all my mother's time and attention."

He stared down at her. Belinda had been *jealous*?

"All the while we were married, you thought I couldn't live without you. And I hated you. After the divorce when you thought I was dying of loneliness from losing you, I hated you." She grinned, stubbed the cigarette out. "You're something else, thinking I drank and got high because of you. Hell, I did it because it was fun. F-U-N, Jon. And, God knew I needed some fun, living with you and all your moralizing, and your pathetic self-pity over your childhood, and your sad attempts to make us a family, and your saintly patience over my . . . shall we say . . . little indiscretions. But you had what I knew you'd eventually have. Money. And lots of it.

"So I bore your stupid babies, then pushed the limits until you divorced me, knowing you'd be eaten up with guilt and knowing because of that, any brats I had with you would always be my meal ticket. I was happy just to take your money. Until you tried to double-cross me with Little Mary Sunshine." Her face darkened and she leaned into him, words hissing through her teeth. "I'll be damned if I let you take those kids away. Because it'll kill you to know they're with me."

He staggered back a step, belly cramping from the words that made a mockery of all the years he'd tried to help her, all the years he'd blamed himself for what she'd become, all the years he'd thought she loved him and he just didn't have what it took to love her enough. He'd never suspected he'd been played for a fool.

A fool—a total fool—but not a villain.

Bewilderment, anger, confusion all mixed with a surreal sense of elation. He shook his head and listened. There was no mocking voice. For once, his old man was silent.

His father had been wrong. The thought made him dizzy, and his body grew surprisingly light. Lil. Lil had been right. He wasn't a flawed excuse for a human being. He was the man she believed in, but was it too late to convince Lil he knew that now?

Lil glanced in the side-view mirror of Seamus's pickup. The twin eyes of the old Studebaker glowed back. She looked sideways at Seamus. He stared straight ahead, harshly shadowed in the dashboard lights. She didn't think he realized Walter and his camera were following.

From the media's milling confusion outside her house, Jon must have eluded them just as Seamus had, with a few twists and shortcuts through a town the media didn't know. Walter, though, had an advantage— since she'd told him where they were headed.

They'd barreled through the dark in total silence for the last forty miles, the headlights throwing the spiked grasses edging the road into sharp relief. Mile markers flashed silver and disappeared. As they'd traveled southeast, the farmland surrounding Cordelia had broken into stonier ground. The highway, lined with ribbons of hard-packed red clay glistening from the rain, carved through the rocky wooded hills that butted up to Monaco.

She couldn't stand the silence any longer. Besides, she wanted answers. "You could have just lent me the truck."

He didn't look at her. "Don't be stupid. You were too upset to drive and you don't know where she lives. I do."

Seamus was the last person she'd wanted with her, but since Jon had taken her car, and Roy needed to stay with the children, she hadn't seen any options that didn't involve tortured explanations to her family. So she'd left Mari to explain, calculating by the time they unraveled Mari's tangled narration, she'd be half-way to Monaco and nobody would follow. She'd briefly toyed with the idea of relying on Walter, but decided against it. If she showed up in his car, Belinda would be immediately suspicious.

She made a conscious effort to relax and glanced at Seamus again. She was still furious with him. But she wanted answers and outright anger wasn't going to get them. "It was you, wasn't it?"

"I don't know what you're talking about."

"I think you do." He didn't answer. His profile was a pale slash against the rain-spattered window. "Don't lie to me. If I mean anything to you, don't lie. That night at the Rooster. When Jon came in. Why did you call Belinda?"

There was a long silence and she held her breath.

"He deserved it." His hand fisted on the seat between them. "He wrecked her life. He neglected her, fed her a steady diet of coke to keep her quiet about the degenerate life he led, dependent on him for her next snort. Did you think I'd just stand back and let the same thing happen to you?"

Incredulity snatched her breath. "You mean you believed all that stuff you read when they were divorced?"

"I didn't read it. She told me. In rehab. It was the year before their divorce. He'd just filed. I was there a few weeks when she showed up. Good God, Lil.

You should've seen her. Emaciated, all eyes, a broken doll. She was out of her mind. Afraid she'd lose her children, bewildered at how he treated her. We talked. We became . . . friends."

"And you believed her? Just like that?"

"What reason would she have to lie? I was nobody. Just another drunk. And she had pictures." Seamus shot a glance at her. "Smut. Your cowboy screwing a teenaged girl."

"They were lies!" Her blood heated thinking about Belinda. "She lies because she hates Jon. She lies for the hell of it. Damn you, Seamus Ryan. You've known me all my life, yet you never once asked me what I thought. Never once questioned me about Jon. Did you forget I lived with him? Or did you think I was such a mealy-mouthed, helpless little twit that I wouldn't see what was right in front of me?"

"I only wanted to help you." He reached over and laid a hand on her arm.

She jerked away. "Don't you dare tell me you were trying to help. You wanted me for yourself, so you believed what you wanted to believe. In your single-minded pursuit of wrecking my marriage, in trying to serve Jon his just deserts according to the judgment of Seamus Ryan, did it cross your mind the lives you'd destroy?"

"I wasn't trying to destroy you. I only—"

"Not me, idiot! The children!"

Seamus massaged the back of his neck. "I didn't think—"

"No, you didn't. And tomorrow, I expect you to be in court. Ready to tell the truth. And if Judge Dougherty even thinks about awarding those children to Belinda, I'll—"

A high voice sounded behind the front seat. "She can't take us back! She can't!"

Lil gasped and fumbled to undo her seat belt. As Seamus took a turn off the highway, jolting onto a gravel road, she twisted to her knees and peered in back where Melanie huddled on the narrow seat of the extended cab.

The girl's eyes were scared orbs. "Don't be mad at me, please, Lil. When Daddy left, I knew something was wrong and when I heard you tell Aunt Mari you were going with Mr. Ryan, I was scared for Daddy, so I hid and I know it was wrong, but—" Her voice broke. "We don't have to go back to *her,* do we? I want to stay with you."

"Oh, sweetie." Lil reached down, hooked her hands under Melanie's arms, and helped her scramble over the seat. In a tangle of limbs, the child fell into her lap and wrapped her arms tight around Lil's neck. "Don't you worry. Everything will be okay. You'll see."

"We're here," Seamus said.

Seamus drove past a rutted driveway where the Mercedes was parked and braked alongside a ditch that ran in front of a worn white two-story frame house.

Continuing the soothing patter of words in Melanie's ear, Lil studied the situation.

Jon, Belinda, and Neil were like figures on a stage in the circle of light off the front stoop. She heaved a sigh of relief. No press, and it didn't look like words had escalated to blows. Yet. She glanced back and saw Walter pull to a stop some yards before the driveway where he couldn't be seen. He doused his lights.

She shifted and Melanie raised her head, stiffening when she saw where they were. Lil opened the door, stepped out, then reached back to squeeze Mel's hand. The rain had cooled the air and she shivered. "It's all right, sweetie. You just stay right here and wait for us, okay? Seamus will let the truck run and you'll be nice and warm."

She looked at Seamus, and he nodded briefly before exiting the cab. Melanie bit her lip and tried to smile.

Lil returned the smile, swiped up a newspaper from

the floorboard, and shut the door. Looking back at Walter, she tipped her head briefly toward the tableau in the front yard.

She watched until the photographer had edged from his car, then pushed back her shoulders and fastened her eyes on Belinda.

Chapter 36

Over Belinda's shoulder, Jon had seen headlights wash the woods before a steel-gray pickup bypassed the drive and rolled to a stop in front of Dodo's house. Three heads were silhouetted in front, but he couldn't make out who they were. Press?

Hearing a scrunch of gravel under the thrum of the truck, he squinted beyond the drive at another vehicle. That car he did recognize. Out of Belinda's direct vision, he saw Wart-nose get out and sidle alongside the Mercedes, his movements furtive. Although he was puzzled at the man's behavior, Wart-nose's presence was enough to warn him it was time to make his exit before more media appeared.

Belinda hadn't given him what he came for. She wouldn't drop her fight. She held all the cards. He had no defense against the barrage of hate she'd leveled at him.

But, idiotically, he still felt like grinning.

Underneath the humiliating knowledge that she'd made an ass out of him, and the dread of what tomorrow's hearing would bring, the knot of guilt he'd carried had unraveled, loosened by Lil, untied by Belinda.

Belinda had glanced around as the truck halted, then fixed her attention back on him, stance defiant. "You remember what I said, Jonathan Brumley. Those brats are *mine*."

That's what she thought. He'd get them away from

her if he had to kidnap them and run off to Borneo. Relief made him giddy; he felt capable of anything. Now if he could just convince Lil. She'd balked at Nashville, but maybe Borneo was more to her taste.

He almost smiled, then Seamus ambled into the ring of light, and his mood soured. The proprietary way Seamus had treated Lil all evening hadn't escaped him. Wart-nose still hovered near his car. What was going on here?

Ignoring the photographer, he directed a hard stare at Seamus, but Belinda's glare outdid his. "This isn't a good time," she hissed.

"Wasn't my idea." Seamus looked over his shoulder and they all followed his gaze to the pickup.

A tall, slim figure marched from the far side of the truck, down into the culvert, then up the other side without pause. Her spine was iron, her curls a gold crown, and she held her head at a regal tilt. If the sight of Lil hadn't addled him, he would have smiled. No longer an angel, an avenging queen. His avenging queen, if she'd still have him.

Belinda drew a sharp breath. "What's she doing here?" Beside her, Neil quivered.

Her laser blue gaze pinned on Belinda, Lil strode right by Jon without a glance. When she was two feet in front of his ex-wife, she stopped and slapped the newspaper she held against her thigh.

Belinda started, but only smiled. "I see you like the headlines. You'll like it even more tomorrow when the judge tells me I can bring my babies home."

"Don't count on it." Lil's voice was low, hard, and even. "I may not know everything, like whose baby that is, but I know enough to convince Judge Dougherty that the night you supposedly spent sleeping with Jon is one big whopper, just like everything you've ever said about him is a pack of lies. You drugged him."

Relief rose like a tide and carried Jon off. She knew.

He didn't know how she'd figured it out, and he didn't care. It was enough that she knew.

Ready to step in should Belinda threaten Lil, Jon blinked as his ex-wife rounded on Seamus instead. "Why didn't you keep your mouth shut?"

Seamus only folded his arms. "*Did* you drug him?"

The anger slid off Belinda's face. She moved forward and gripped Seamus's arm. "I'm sorry if I sounded harsh." She searched his face. One fat tear hovered at the corner of her eye and finally slid down her cheek. It was a fine performance. "Seamus, I've told you how it was. You, of anyone, should understand what I've been through."

Unmoved, Seamus just stared back with those impenetrable eyes. Jon didn't understand the exchange, but then he could hardly hear it over the singing in his heart. Lil knew.

Belinda's face hardened and she dropped her hand. "Fine. Believe what you will, it doesn't matter." She sneered at Lil. "After tomorrow, I'll have what I want."

Lil's chin came up. "No. You won't. And I'll tell you why." Lil turned slowly and stared hard at each one of them, sparing nobody, not even him. The song in his heart faltered and fell still. Even Seamus dropped his eyes. "I have never in my life seen such a bunch of self-centered, grasping, selfish, egotistical . . ." Words seemed to fail her just as Neil made a gurgle of protest. "You, too, you timid little rabbit. I'm sure you knew what was going on and you did nothing to stop it."

She flicked a glance beyond him at Wart-nose and the photographer darted forward, raising a video camera.

Lil paused dramatically, then raised her arm and pointed at Neil. "It's your baby!"

Inwardly, Jon groaned. She didn't know Belinda as well as she thought she did.

Dumbstruck, Belinda stared, then her laughter trilled. "Him? You've got to be kidding."

Neil reddened and shuffled his feet. Lil's pose fell apart. Looking confused, she dropped her arm.

Still gurgling, Belinda glanced at Wart-nose. "Come to join the party, Walter?" She looked back at Lil. "Oh, I see. Thought maybe you could get it on tape for the judge, didn't you? The dramatic confession and all that. So sorry to disappoint. Besides, no matter what anyone's told you—" Her smile faded and her look turned scathing. "It's Jon's baby, sweetheart. Accept it."

Lil's brows collided and Jon's hopes plummeted. She still had doubts.

Seamus spoke, his words low and measured. "The baby. It's mine, isn't it?"

Belinda whipped around to face him. "Shut up!"

For an instant, they were all riveted. Feeling a trickle of pity, Jon looked at Seamus. He couldn't like the man, but he could certainly sympathize. His eyes moved to Lil's, locked on hers, and held. For a brief moment, they were the only two people in the world and hope bloomed again. Her gaze scorched him with exasperation, caressed him with love, and implored him to understand . . . something.

Then Lil rounded on Seamus, on Belinda, on Neil, and her softness hardened into magnificent rage. "Did the consequences of what you were doing occur to any of you? All of you playing your little games, running your little schemes without one ounce of honesty among you. Well, let me clue you in. You're not the center of the universe. You're not the ones who count." She was shouting now. He marveled. He'd never heard Lil shout. "Those children are what matter. And not one of you has put them first."

Silence fell, then Belinda stepped forward, clapping her hands. "My, that was a great performance, don't you all think? But, I'm afraid it means nothing, Lifesaver Lil. I'll still get what I want."

"Yes, it does mean something." Lil gave Belinda a look that would melt steel. "While all of you have been busy yanking me and the children around like puppets in your sick little dramas, I've been busy, too. Quite busy. Busy taking care of the children. Busy establishing a business that can support us. Busy preparing a parenting plan. What do you think? Sounds to me like I'd make a good mother, doesn't it?" She paused. "The attorney I hired thinks so."

Belinda's mouth gaped, then snapped shut. "So what?"

"This is what." Lil swooped up the newspaper off the ground and shook it under Belinda's nose. "The judge already knows all this. All of it."

Belinda's mouth fell open again and this time it stayed that way.

"That's right. He knows about the contract. He knows about the night Jon spent with you—a night Seamus is now willing to say you arranged. He knows how you hired Walter to take pictures. He knows because I told him."

Jon's euphoria faded and grim alarm stole over him. She'd told the judge about the contract?

She paused to let the words sink in and darted a look in his direction that again asked for understanding. With an effort, he kept his mouth shut. "I told him everything. In a confidential letter. And in the morning before court convenes, my attorney is filing my own custody request."

There was a long stunned silence.

Then Seamus's closed expression cracked open, Neil tittered, and Jon felt his own jaw drop. Confused, he stared at Lil. God, what was she doing? The court had no idea of the rift between them. Surely Lil knew, especially now, that the appearance of unity between them was the only weapon he had.

Belinda was the first to recover. "So what? You're not a natural parent. No judge is going to give you custody. And just telling him about Walter proves nothing."

"That's exactly what my lawyer told me." Lil smiled grimly. "No judge is likely to give me custody, unless I lie like you."

Jon felt weak. She loved those kids. Would she destroy him to protect them?

"But I won't lie. I won't need to." She paused. "Because what he will give me is time. Tomorrow morning, you'll pitch your lies. And I'll pitch my petition. The judge will be furious at all this last-minute chaos. He'll call for a recess to consider the matter."

Jon's head cleared. He saw exactly where Lil headed. She was brilliant. He wanted to applaud.

"Big deal." Belinda tried to sound bored, but her voice held an undernote of fear.

"Yes, a very big deal. Because when he returns, he'll talk about fairness, he'll talk about confusion, he'll talk about the need to give all parties time to respond. In short, he'll postpone the hearing."

Understanding began to dawn across Belinda's face.

"And in that time," Lil continued, "Jon will use all the resources he has to disprove every last little bit of your so-called evidence. He'll have time to take depositions from Seamus. From Walter. From your mother. And from one Glory Galore. The P.I. I hired just tracked her down in New Orleans. Along with a certain photographer who did some work for you in the past."

Belinda's face flashed white then red, but Lil was relentless. "Jon will have time to do what he should have done a long time ago. Dig up all the dirt on you." She paused. "I'd imagine that's considerable. You'll lose your children, you'll lose your free ride, and you'll likely end up in jail."

Jon felt a fizz of laughter bubble up. Sweet, soft Lilac O'Malley had bested Belinda. She'd bested them all.

Belinda's hands clenched. The cigarette holder fell unnoticed to the ground. "You bitch," she breathed. "You bitch!" Her voice rose to a shriek, Walter yanked up his camera, and Belinda launched herself at Lil.

"Lil!" A small figure exploded from the culvert and rocketed toward them. Before Jon's mind could even register it was Mel, she'd darted between the two women.

She pushed against her mother with all her slender might. "She's not the bitch. You are!"

Jon leaped, but not soon enough. Belinda shoved back and backhanded Mel to the ground. "Don't you ever talk to me like that. Don't you ever—"

"That's enough." Jon roared, yanking Belinda backward and off her feet.

Panting, Lil staggered back and pulled Mel with her. She kneeled, gathered his daughter into a quick hug, then held her out and stroked the injured cheek. "You'll be okay," she said firmly. "We'll all be okay. Come on. Let's go back to the truck."

Tears halting, Mel stared at her a moment, then nodded and slipped her hand into Lil's.

Jon fought to hold Belinda, and watched Lil half-carry Mel to the pickup. After Mel was inside, she returned.

When Lil reached Walter, she accepted the film he held out without breaking her stride, then stopped in front of Belinda. "Two can play at your game." She held up the film. "I think the judge would like to see this."

Snarling obscenities, Belinda strained toward Lil. Still hearing the crack of her hand on Mel's face, Jon felt his temper shatter. Rage reddened his vision. He flung her around to face him and shook her by the shoulders. Her head flopped back and forth. It'd be so easy. Her neck would break like a twig.

Seamus clamped down on his arm. "Think of your kids."

The crimson fog faded. Belinda twisted away. Making tsking noises, Neil reached for her. She slapped his hands away and stumbled back, her wild stare darting among them.

"You'll be sorry," she rasped. "You'll all be sorry."

Suddenly she whirled and bolted at Lil. Lil's eyes went wide, but Belinda shot past her without a glance.

As he guessed her real target, Jon's heart flew into his throat. He sprinted after her, sliding on the spongy grass. "Melanie!" His feet shot out from under him and he landed on a hip with a jarring thump. "Get out of the truck!"

Seamus and Lil stood frozen, but as Jon hit the ground, understanding penetrated. Lil flung herself toward the still-running pickup and Seamus leapt after her, but Belinda was too fast. She scrambled into the truck, fish-tailed into a U-turn that sent Seamus diving for cover, and blasted up the road in a hailstorm of gravel.

Mel's face was a white blur in the back window.

Chapter 37

Lil stared helplessly as the truck dug into rock and careened up the road. Melanie pounded on the window, her mouth stretched in shouts Lil couldn't hear. Then she disappeared completely under the dark vault of the trees.

Lil whipped around and ran for the Mercedes, hampered by her skirt. Jon already hobbled toward it, digging in his pocket for keys. Seamus flung open the doors and yelled at them to hurry. She heard the Studebaker's engine grind.

"Call nine one one," she shouted as she zipped by Neil, who'd been reduced to wringing his hands.

The car's motor roared to life and she dove for the front seat. She slammed her door while Seamus scrambled into the back. Jon skidded out of the drive. As they blasted past the Studebaker, Walter U-turned behind.

She fumbled at her seat belt, then tried Jon's phone. Nothing, no service. She threw down the cell. Gravel rattled on the undercarriage and mixed with the sound of their breathing. Condensation clouded the inside of the windows and Jon cracked his open. She did the same, and a chill wind whipped through the car.

She glanced at Jon. His hair streamed behind him and his jaw was set. She touched his thigh. "Your fall. Are you okay?"

He unclenched one fist long enough to give her

hand a squeeze. They hit a pothole and he clamped his hand back on the wheel. His profile was carved anger, but it was the fear on his features that scared her the most.

She looked ahead but saw no sign of the truck. The last image of Melanie's terrified face blackened her vision, her rising panic shoved the air from her lungs. Silently, she urged Jon to hurry, hurry, fighting the specters that swelled in her head. Wildly, she cast about for something else to focus on and her mind pinned on a thought. She twisted to look at Seamus, a black silhouette in the glare of Walter's headlights. "Your baby?"

Seamus grunted. As the Mercedes skidded to a stop at the junction to the highway, cricket song filled the car. Everything else was deathly still. Forgetting her question, Lil peered one way, then the other. Only wet blackness rolled in both directions. Jon slammed a fist against the wheel.

"There!" Lil pointed toward Cordelia. A flash of taillights crested a hill about a mile down the road and disappeared.

Jon stomped on the accelerator and the car squealed, then wiggled itself straight on the pavement. They shot forward. She clutched the armrest and prayed.

In the backseat, Seamus stirred. "It happened last fall. Late last fall," he started without preamble, his voice an undercurrent in the rush of the wind. "After you got married, my thinkin' turned stinkin', as they say in AA. Started going to more meetings. Some at Serenity Gardens. She was there." He blew out a breath. "Happened just like the first time. She was needy, afraid she was losing her kids. One thing led to another."

She turned to look at him. The darkness hid his expression, but she saw the shrug of his shoulders.

"Knew it wasn't right. Knew I was just trying to re-place you. So I cut it off, but I figured I owed her. And I believed her. Paddy O'Neill said you and the country star were getting tight and it scared me, think-ing what could happen. Thought what she planned to do was best. Thought whatever it took was okay. So I helped. Some help."

A few mile markers blinked by, then Jon spoke. "She's a good liar."

Tracking the twin red points of light still a good mile ahead, Jon pushed the car to the limits of safety on the curving road. The guardrails on the road's edge flashed by in long silver blades.

Walter fell back, but the Studebaker still barreled stubbornly after them. Lil wondered if Neil had col-lected enough of his mind to call the police. They were the only cars on the highway.

They crested a hill and the straightaway cutting through the farmland on the way to Cordelia unfurled ahead like a roll of black film. Empty black film. Jon slowed and fear flurried in her stomach. Where were they? Suddenly Jon cursed and slammed on the brakes, throwing her into her seat belt. "Jon?"

He didn't answer. He hooked an arm over the seat, reversed onto the shoulder in a spray of rock, and was out of the car before she could react.

She nudged her door open and it clanked against a guardrail that ended at the back bumper. She edged through the opening. Jon had already rounded the back of the car and was half-falling down the steep slope that tumbled into darkness on the passenger side. Seamus scrambled behind him.

She looked ahead of them and spotted what Jon must have seen. A flash of dull red masked by the deep underbrush at the bottom of the hill.

Taillights. Blinking in the silence.

Her mind vivid with what they could find, she fumbled in the glove box and pulled out a flashlight and a thin first aid box. She prayed it'd be all they'd need. Tires crunched on the gravel behind the car. Walter.

She pointed. "Down there! We'll need help!"

"I'll go," he called back. "Cell's out, but there's a HiPo station up ahead." He ducked back into the Studebaker.

She skidded down the hill after Jon and Seamus, the flashlight beam bouncing over the ground, the first aid kit knocking against her knee. When she reached the pickup, Jon was clambering in through the passenger door. The truck leaned drunkenly against saplings on the driver's side. A thick-barreled oak at the front had halted the truck's plunge. Seamus waded through the brush, trying to find a path to the driver's door. With each click of the flashers, the overhead light inside flickered and dimmed, flickered and dimmed.

Heart ricocheting against her ribs, she pushed up behind Jon and pointed her flashlight into the truck. Melanie sat bolt upright on the bench. Hope surged as she saw the little girl had kept her head long enough to use the seat belt, but Melanie's eyes stared straight ahead, wide and sightless.

A black void opened under Lil's feet, and her vision swam. No!

Then Melanie blinked.

Lil's breath left her in a dizzying whoosh. Jon grappled with the seat belt. Lil backed out to give him room, then climbed onto a crumpled fender and directed the flashlight beam through the windshield.

Through the spider web of glass, Belinda's head lolled back. Blood trickled from a gash on her forehead. She wasn't wearing a belt. The impact had smashed the front end and driven back the steering column. Getting Belinda out of there would take more than their hands.

A rustling sounded behind her and Walter appeared. He heaved himself up alongside and followed the track of her beam. "Goddamn. Highway patrol's on its way." He looked at the box she held. "What you got there?"

She dropped the first aid kit in his hands. He rummaged through it and grabbed a roll of gauze. "Maybe do some good. If she's still alive." He started after Seamus.

Jon had hooked an arm under Melanie's knees, another around her shoulders, and was struggling to lift her from the truck. Lil hurried to help. Between them, they managed to extract her. Jon set her on her feet and she promptly collapsed into a cross-legged heap, eyes still staring at nothing. He dropped beside her and hauled her into his lap, running hands over her limbs, her skull, murmuring her name.

Weak-kneed, Lil slid to the ground next to them, keeping the light trained on his hands. In the distance, sirens wailed. Done with his examination, Jon bundled Melanie close and rocked her.

His eyes found hers, the gold flecks in their dark depths reflecting hope. "Only shock, I think. Belinda?"

She shook her head. "I don't know."

A policeman arrived, soon joined by a crew of paramedics. Emergency lights washed in waves over the treetops. After a brief examination of Melanie confirmed Jon's suspicion that she was in shock, they turned their attention to Belinda. Hauling some evil-looking equipment, firemen scrambled down the hillside. Soon the whine of power tools rent the night.

Melanie blinked. Blinked again, then squirmed. "Daddy?" Her voice shrilled over the racket.

"It's all right, Mel baby. Everything's okay."

"Daddy?" Her arms snaked around his neck and she sobbed against his chest. "I was so—so scared. Mommy and Lil—" She pushed back, hysteria tinging her voice. "Is Lil okay?"

Lil touched her shoulder. "I'm here, sweetie. I'm fine."

"Oh, Lil." Without loosening the hand clutched on Jon's neck, she reached over and tugged Lil's sleeve.

Completely ruining her suit, and not caring, Lil scooted across the rough, wet ground. As naturally as the sun rising, Jon opened an arm and she settled herself against him, hugging them both, reveling in their warmth.

Chapter 38

At Merry-Go-Read the next afternoon, Lil picked up a Laura Ingalls Wilder book from the window display and dusted it for the third time. Behind her, tuned to a country station, the radio played softly. Lost in thought, she stared across the square. St. Andrew's glowed in the sunlight, its doors flung wide to let in the warm breeze. The square was empty.

But Jon would come soon. She knew it.

Last night, after the first ambulance had left with Belinda, he'd ridden with Melanie in the second while Lil returned home to reassure her family. After Melanie was thoroughly checked, he'd brought her back to the house. Amid Zinnia's fluttering and Mari's exclamations, they'd been unable to talk. So much lay between them, so much needed to be said, but she was still rattled by events and had avoided conversation.

Quite early this morning, she'd phoned Murphy to tell him to destroy her third-party petition. It was no longer needed. Then she'd traveled to Camden County Courthouse alone, slipping into a seat near the back just before the proceedings began. The courtroom overflowed with reporters.

Jon sat with his attorneys at the petitioner's table. Belinda wasn't there. She was in the hospital recovering from broken ribs and contusions. The baby had died. Lil cringed when she thought of the tragedy, and was glad Seamus was with Jon's ex-wife.

The proceedings were perfunctory. Belinda's lawyer approached, advising the judge the mother would not contest the petitioner. Having expected a circus, the media let out a collective sigh of disappointment. Then evidence and reports were efficiently presented, everyone eager just to get the thing done. She occasionally glanced at Jon, but didn't catch his eye.

As expected, the judge ruled in Jon's favor, but not without a fatherly admonition.

He looked at Jon over his half glasses. "While marrying a relative stranger in order to protect your children was an unorthodox action, at least your reasons are understandable. And according to Ms. Langlie's report"—here he'd sought Lil's eyes, and she'd thought she detected a twinkle—"you certainly chose the right woman."

He sobered and turned back to Jon. "The court, however, does not like the element of perjury that was almost introduced into evidence. Be glad, you rapscallion, you didn't do it. Nor is the court impressed by your patterns of absence with your children." He took off his glasses and fixed Jon with a stern gaze. "Work's the footing for life, son. Not the other way around."

Jon twisted, his gaze roaming the room. Their eyes met and held. Promise—regret?—passed between them. Then Jon turned back to the judge. "I understand that now."

Judge Dougherty had given him a long look, then nodded. Formalities were completed in short order, and the judge swept from the room.

Lil sat back, well satisfied. She'd kept her promise. And she trusted Jon to fulfill the terms of their agreement . . . at the very least. And if he didn't? She smiled wryly to herself. Once, long ago, he'd threatened her with a breach of contract suit. Well, he wasn't the only one who knew his way around a courtroom now.

While press and well-wishers surrounded Jon, she

slipped out of the courtroom, feeling like she was throwing Jon to the lions, and also feeling it might be no less than he deserved. Outside, she phoned home and told an ecstatic Melanie the news, asking her to have Roy call Zinnia. She didn't want to face her mother's questions yet. She wanted a quiet moment to think. She wanted to be sure. She wanted Jon to be sure. She'd headed to Merry-Go-Read, certain Jon would know where she'd gone.

Now she looked down at the book in her hand and gave herself a mental shake. As she did, the bells over the door jangled, although the placard on the door still read CLOSED. She glanced over her shoulder.

Jon stepped inside, eyebrows raised over his tiger eyes. For a long moment, they simply looked at each other.

Finally he spoke. "You took a risk. A big one. What would you have done if things hadn't played out like you thought they would? The judge might have thrown up his hands and awarded the kids to Belinda."

"I would have kidnapped them and run off to Tahiti, I guess."

Jon's mouth quirked, but she was quite serious. She needed to know if he understood how close to disaster he'd led them.

She put down the book and faced him calmly. "Jon, I did the only thing I could think of to buy you more time. I'm sorry I didn't tell you, but I knew you'd try to stop me. And I was angry."

"And I was acting like an asshole." All trace of a smile was gone. "You fought for us when I gave up. You fought for the kids when I might have destroyed their lives. You have more courage and compassion than anyone I've ever known."

She held still, wondering if this was a declaration of love . . . or what?

"I don't know if—" He raked a hand through his

hair. "Ah, Lil. I got so caught up in self-pity and guilt, built such a mountain out of it, I couldn't see around it. I wasn't even willing to listen to you. But you . . . you wouldn't let things be. Since the day I met you, you chipped away until last night that mountain crashed down around me."

Her heart softened, but still she said nothing.

Jon drew a deep breath. "I want you, Lil, and I love you, more than life itself. I know now I deserve you. I deserve us." His gaze held hers. "Will you still have me?"

A long sigh escaped her. He'd told her what she needed to hear. She closed the space between them.

He caught her around the waist, crushing her against him, searching her face. "Are you sure?"

She let the kiss she gave him answer for her. On the radio, a song ended and a new one began. "China Blue Eyes." For a long moment they clung to each other and let the music wash over them. Then Jon drew back.

Smiling into her face, he whispered, "Take me home, Lil."

The story of the O'Malley sisters continues. . . .

Four years after her divorce from Stan Addams, Alcea O'Malley not only has to face foreclosure on her house, but a difficult fourteen-year-old daughter, an interfering family, daily run-ins with Stan's former mistress Florida, and no job prospects except schlepping eggs at the local diner under the cantankerous eye of its owner, Peg. But all that pales beside her surprise when she encounters an old flame. Dakota Jones is back in town. He has the same disarming smile, the same chameleon eyes, a past he's hiding from . . . and a trailer for rent.

Living in a trailer has never been high on Alcea's wish list, but when Dak offers to show it to her . . .

"C'mon out." Dak held the door open.

When Alcea brushed by him, she smelled male and soap. Her brain shouted, "Escape!" but her feet moved forward. Once past him, she pinched her cheeks. Maybe if they were flaming red, it would distract him from the ghoulish circles under her eyes.

"I like the hair," Dak said, letting the screen door bang shut behind them.

She jumped and glanced back, certain he was joking. She hadn't had time for the hair straightener, and it looked pretty much like she'd slapped a shrub on her head. "Easy if you have an eggbeater."

He smiled. "It's natural. It suits you."

Natural suited her? She started to murmur a protest, but the words died on her lips as the monstrosity hunkering at the end of his property grabbed her attention.

Dak followed her gaze. "Don't mind the torn skirting. I'll take care of that." He started toward the trailer on a path of erratically spaced concrete blocks that led through two acres of yard. When she stood rooted, he paused and looked back. "Coming?"

She detected a challenge. Making an unintelligible sound, she followed.

"New paint, though. Julius painted it," he said.

Painted? It looked like someone had doused the thing with Pepto-Bismol. "Rusty's Hardware had a special on pink?"

"Undoubtedly." Now she scented amusement. "But it has a new water heater, and the window AC still works, although you might need to bang it once in a while. Nothing is rotted, but keep an eye on the corner of the back bedroom. Looks like chipmunks tried to get in last winter. If you stuff the hole with steel wool, it should keep them out." She couldn't see his smile, but she knew it was there. "I sprayed it for spiders. Snakes, though—" He motioned at piles of scrap lumber littering the yard. "Snakes might be a problem."

They reached the entrance. Dak stuck a key into an ill-fitting door of the one-room addition tacked onto the front. It opened with a squeal. "I'll oil that." He pointed toward the alley. "Dumpster's over there. Don't keep trash cans outside. Raccoons will just tip them over."

He *was* enjoying himself. She straightened her shoulders. "Any instructions for keeping out bears?"

He looked back, and his smile flashed. "Touché." He pushed the door wide, motioned her in. "There's really nothing in here a little elbow grease can't fix. If you're up to it."

Just like Peg, he thought she was afraid of work. Her spine hardened.

A step inside, though, and it wilted again. Yellowing linoleum lined the floor. A washer and dryer leaned against one cheaply paneled wall. A table, early-fifties Formica complete with cigarette burns, stood in the middle. The best thing was a ring of grimy windows. With the windows open on nice days, the place would become a screened-in porch. She eyed the rusted hardware. If they opened.

Dak pushed on an interior door to the trailer, and a ripe smell pinched her nose.

"Place does need airing out."

"I take it Julius had a cat?" she inquired politely.

"A tom named Whiskers."

"Lovely." She pivoted, intending to leave. Enough was enough.

"I showed it earlier this morning to Tansy's son," Dak said mildly. "He said he'd rip out the carpet. Of course, that's a lot of work."

Alcea hesitated. He gave her a smile. She glared, held her breath, and stepped into the living room. It was divided from the kitchen by a finger of counter. Dak stepped around it and tugged at a cord. A fluorescent bulb hissed and blinked to life. Alcea blinked back.

Pink stove. Pink refrigerator. Pink, chipped sink. Pink counters. Pink and white—or at least it used to be white—tile tripped out of sight down a short hall. She told herself to breathe.

Dak leaned an elbow on the counter. "I'd rather rent to you, though. I've heard Andy has had some troubles with the law."

"He likes to drink." She cleared her throat. "This place is certainly . . . pink."

"Julius likes pink." There was that hint of challenge again.

"I do, too." She hated pink.

Dak raised his eyebrows, but didn't comment. He stayed behind while she explored both ends of the trailer in a journey that took less than a minute. When she returned, Dak still lounged against the counter. "What do you think?"

She thought a burly man with a bulldozer might do it justice. She couldn't live here. She just couldn't. "Um, I have other places to look at before I make a decision."

"I can help you take out this carpet."

"Thank you. I'll, uh, let you know. Monday?" Mentally she prepared Monday's to-do list. Tell Peg no. Tell Dak no. Collect money from Lil. Her stomach churned. Owing Lil would be painful, but it was better than this . . . wasn't it? Her options depressed her.

After Dak locked up, they walked side by side back to the house, she picking her way, he swinging along at her side, his stride easy and unhurried. The backs of their hands brushed and her skin burned.

"How about a cup of coffee?" he asked.

"I really should—" She paused. Nothing waited for her at home, and suddenly the idea of keeping company with only her own thoughts sounded unbearable. "Okay."

When they reached the patio, Dak motioned her to a chair, then went inside. She tilted her head up to catch the sun's rays on her face. They felt . . . hopeful. She wished she felt the same.

Dak returned, handed her a mug, then settled himself beside her, locking his ankles on top of an empty planter. The sun was now well up over the horizon. For a moment, they watched the Ozark hills in the distance and the clouds scuttling across a sky as blue as the cornflowers that grew in her mother's garden. She slid a sideways look at him. He looked totally relaxed, head tipped back, eyes half-closed, hair lifting off his forehead in a light breeze.

She picked up her coffee. "So, what have you been up to for the last twenty years?"

"Traveling. Writing."

She took a sip. She couldn't get rid of the odd tension

in her body. But years at the country club had given her an ease with the social niceties, although—what a surprise—they'd never come naturally. "What do you write?" she asked.

"Stories, articles." One of his shoulders rose and fell.

"Do you—" She'd been about to ask if he made much money, but stopped to rephrase. "Do you sell many?"

A smile tickled his lips. "Enough. And I enjoy it, so what more could I ask?"

A lot more than this. Her gaze swept his "inheritance": the scraggly yard, the pink trailer, the narrow house. "Did you ever marry?" The words slipped out.

"Once. A long time ago. We were both still in college." He spoke easily. No artifice, no evasion. "It only lasted a few years. Nobody's fault."

She watched him for a moment, wondering if she'd ever be that blasé about her divorce. "And no children?"

"We never got around to thinking about it before we divorced." He turned his head to look at her. "What about you? I know you married Stan. What happened?"

She squirmed, then responded with the same directness. "Stan's a shit."

His quick smile flashed. "That says it all."

She shrugged. "He was a serial adulterer. After Kathleen was born, he had an affair because I didn't pay enough attention to him. At least that was his excuse and I forgave him that one. But not the twenty gazillion other ones that came after. He was discreet about it at first." She halted, surprised at herself. She wasn't one for the current rage of baring her soul. But, just like when she was sixteen, she was telling him things she usually kept to herself.

"At least he showed you that small courtesy." Dak's voice was dry.

She snorted and decided to forget discretion. "Oh, it wasn't for me. If she'd gotten wind of his escapades, his

mother would have killed him—or worse, changed her
will. But after she died seven years ago, he was a tomcat
in heat."

"But you stayed with him until, what, four years ago?"

That was right. He'd know when they'd divorced, because of Florida. For a moment, she'd forgotten it was
his half sister who was the final straw for a pretty rickety
camel. Somehow, instead of bothering her, the knowledge that he knew set her at ease.

"Call me a chump. Or call me a wimp. It seemed
easier to stay. I didn't leave because I didn't know how
I'd support Kathleen." She looked across at the trailer.
She still didn't.

"I wouldn't call you either of those things," he said
quietly.

She eyed him. He didn't look judgmental. She relaxed
further. "I guess one day I'd just had enough. When Lil
got married, and I saw how happy she was . . . Well.
My pride had taken all it could take and I knew if I
didn't get out, I'd . . . lose myself." She took another
sip, then thunked the mug on the table. "I don't even
know what I mean." Nor did she understand why his
presence caused an alien to take over her mouth.

"I felt the same way about my marriage. And my career. There's no shame in making changes, you know.
The shame only lies in continuing in the same rut if
you're not happy."

"Yes. Well." She looked at the trailer again. "I guess
I've dug a whole new rut."

"You never know what lies around the corner. Maybe
you'll like this rut better."

"Maybe. Kathleen won't."

She stopped, startled again at her frankness. Obviously, she'd been *way* too long without friends. She'd
had them, of course, but when she'd married Stan, she'd
taken a step up in the world and her old friends hadn't
belonged to the country club. She'd never gotten close
to the women who did.

"So Kathleen learned at school about the fore-closure."

On the verge of telling herself Dak wasn't exactly a friend, so she should shut up, instead she said, "And she's not exactly thrilled by the change in our circumstances."

"Gave you a hard time, huh?"

"Hard time doesn't begin to cover it. Screaming, throwing things, refusing to come out of her room. *That* begins to cover it. I can't blame only her, though. I spoiled her." Good God. She was clear-eyed enough to realize she'd always lavished Kathleen with too much attention, too much money, too much everything. Kathleen had provided a distraction from her marital mess. But her self-admitted failings as a mother were a secret she didn't normally blab about.

"I don't know a thing about raising kids, but I hear they're pretty adaptable."

"You don't know Kathleen."

"She'll adjust."

"She won't."

They fell silent.

Alcea picked up her mug and studied her coffee. "Do you remember that night?"

The question felt normal, natural. And she wanted to know. For a short while, he'd had a profound effect on her, and she'd always wondered if it had all been one-sided.

He locked gazes with her. "Sure, I remember." He didn't pretend not to know what she was talking about.

She looked away. "Why wouldn't you take me to the senior dance? I practically put the invitation right in your mouth." And had embarrassed herself in front of the entire school population. He'd left her sitting alone in the middle of her classmates' muffled laughter, her eyes starry from barely held tears.

She could feel his gaze resting on her. "We were young, Alcea." His voice was gentle. "And I wasn't very smooth in the way I handled everything. But you were barely sixteen, and I was about to leave for college. And . . . there were differences in what we wanted. I thought about you all the rest of that night, if that makes any difference, but there didn't seem to be a point."

"I guess not." She looked at him again. "But did you ever wonder, 'what if'?"

"No." This time *he* averted his gaze. For the first time she wondered if was being honest. "What-if isn't very useful." A blink of a smile. " 'Do, or do not. There is no try.' "

Ha. One she knew. Not like the Shakespeare he and Julius spouted at each other. "Yoda. *The Empire Strikes Back*." She reached for her mug and took another sip. "So you live by doing. No holding back. Damn the torpedoes and full speed ahead?"

"Yes, I'd say I'm a little more self-assured than I was back then." His eyes hooked hers, and she sucked in a breath. "I know what I want. And I pretty much get it." His gaze dropped to her sandals. "You have very pretty feet."

The air suddenly radiated sex.